The
Unexpected

CHRIS DAWSON

The Unexpected

CHRIS DAWSON

WORKBOOK PRESS LLC
187 E Warm Springs Rd,
Suite B285, Las Vegas, NV 89119, USA

Website: https://workbookpress.com/
Hotline: 1-888-818-4856
Email: admin@workbookpress.com

Ordering Information:
Quantity sales. Special discounts are available on quantity purchases by corporations, associations, and others. For details, contact the publisher at the address above.

ISBN-13:   978-1-953839-63-3 (Paperback Version)
                      978-1-953839-34-3 (Digital Version)

REV. DATE: 25.09.2020

Table of Contents

Epilogue

These are Stories involving wives who have sexual adventures or affairs. For 30 years I have written fiction in this theme of either the husband wanting his wife to take a lover and his reaction when she does or the previously monogamous wife being unexpectedly seduced and then getting the surprise of a husband who is not only not angry but is happy and who encouraging her to continue the adventure. Titles of stories in this book:

Table of Contents

3. **The Need to Know For Sure:** This is the story of a loving couple that really begins when the husband first suspects that his wife may be fooling around with men outside of their marriage. At first he was very angry and hurt but noticed that he was also more than a little excited and that his wife's love and affection remained and even increased. What happens when he sets up a surveillance system where he can see and hear things he least expected going on in their home and pool is the crux of this very interesting story that continues after his wife confesses to more than he already knew.

4. **The Surprise that Did Not End:** This is an adventure told by Beth that begins in a most unexpected and unusual way. Beth is a very happily married young lady who gets initially trapped by a houseguest who is her father-in-laws friend and is as old as her father. The unexpected orgasms, which are the first with any man other than her husband, are surprisingly powerful. This old friend of her husband's father who needed a place to sleep while his home was being remodeled is the surprise. Initially she tries to resist but soon finds that she, guiltily, wants more. Her almost daily mental battle is to how to keep her infidelity from her husband until her husband relates the story of how this man may have fathered his brother. Once started the adventure is impossible to stop. How she became his sex-slave is the story.

5. **Part-time Job with Unexpected Benefits:** A happily married and faithful wife takes a very part time job cleaning a nearby condo and it turns out that she is surprised the first time but came to love being fucked each and every time she goes to the job. That she likes and wants more of it becomes obvious. What happens when she, much later, in a totally unusual any very unexpected and surprising way finds out that the man who has been doing her was her husband's boss and she now feels compelled to confess her sins.

6. **My Wife's Newfound Needs:** When your wife goes out with the girls to a male review club and comes back totally taken and smitten by the size of the cocks she saw and then you tell her that, heck, our friend Joe has one like that, what would you expect to happen next. Well, you lose a golf partner and your wife gets all the big cocks she can handle and more. That it doesn't stop with Joe is the story.

7. **My Wife's Compulsions:** This is the story of a man who falls in love with a woman who he finds out is very submissive, actually compulsively submissive, to strong dominant men. He loves her and marries her knowing that she has been and will remain a true sexually active lady. When one falls in love, one accepts ones wife's weaknesses including those not expected as well as her strengths. In this story she succumbs to sexual advances of not only her bosses but also her husband's bosses and others. The hardest part of writing this story was to come to some conclusion and not make it go on forever.

8. **My Wife's First Affair:** What happens when you are trying for years to get your wife to open up and do a threesome with another man and then you see an unexpected look in her eyes when you meet a new guy in town at a networking event. Then you find out a bit later that she has been with him without your being present. When you are included you see that she is more than happy to be with him with or without you. Does, "Be careful of what you wish for" ring a bell?

9. **A Story of Entering a Cuckold Life:** What is the background, headset, and thinking of a young man in the active dating age while in college. What type of woman does he like to date? In this story he falls in love and marries a sexually active lady after his graduation expecting that she most likely will remain promiscuous. He knew she would remain sexually active as throughout the courtship and early marriage she sees other men. At first she was not open

about this until she realized that her having affairs did not, in the least, affect her husband's love. This story comes to a climax when he is finally able to watch his wife being pleasured.

Epilogue

The Many reasons Wives have Affairs: This article goes over a surprisingly number of the many reasons a wife may have an affair. Most women marry for love and may still love her husband but for a variety of reasons she may unexpectedly find herself seduced or otherwise seeks sexual gratification or stimulation from other than the man she married. The reasons a wife enters into this adventurous life and chooses or is seduced into an affair are many. The results of the affair will surprise many, as there are men who can handle it and men who love and crave these activities and these outnumber those who are destroyed by the activity of a cheating wife. It turns out that most of our societal beliefs about females are grossly distorted and many are completely erroneous.

Guide to a Cuckold Relationship: In an answer to the many questions and confusion on many sites and from the many and sometimes lengthy accounts I have read, I put together a summary of what I have seen and know from experience, and what makes sense as to what makes a husband accept the fact of his wife having sexual relations with other men making him a "Cuck". In addition how a man of this headset can get his wife willing and interested in seeing others. This is not fiction but a guide to reality written for men who would like this fantasy to become real.

CHAPTER I

The Prelude

Hi, my name is Donna. My husband and I are quite recent readers of erotica, the reason for which, I will get to but sure was surprised to see a story somewhat similar (but of course quite different) to mine and ours, which led me to write my story up to now.

My husband, Chuck, and I are both in our mid 40's and have been married for almost 18 years and have what most of our friends enviously call an ideal and loving marriage. I have been totally faithful to my husband and have had absolutely no desire to break my marriage vows. Despite two kids aged 12 and 16 we are still very much in-love and enjoy a good and occasionally great sex-life, which has definitely increased over the last couple of years. Actually, I have become almost insatiable much to my husband's pleasure, at least to date. We have both remained fit and Chuck repeatedly tells me that he is the envy of all his friends who tease him about "robbing the cradle" and how did he manage to get a "trophy wife" despite our similar ages. We have always had a good laugh over this but I do weigh only 132 pounds on a 5'6"frame. Also smooth skin and firm 36C breasts run in my family as almost no-one can believe that my mom has a 45 year old daughter, let alone a 50 year old son. My husband thinks my "butt", or as he sometimes calls it, my "ass" is my best asset but he admits to being an "Ass-man", which is a term I frown at.

I am well aware that many of our men friends are turned on by what they see in me as I have always been hit upon and occasionally fondled at picnics, dances and other group events. This had always upset and puzzled me as I have always dressed conservatively and do not dress to provoke or act in a way to invite these actions. For sure I had certainly not ever planned or even considered breaking my marriage vows. More about this in a bit as my husband,

Chuck, did not know about any of what I am going to tell you until about six months ago. We both work, with my husband in upper management in a local Midwestern manufacturing firm. I, for the last 8 or so years also work and for the last 3 years, I am a department head at a local office of a national advertising company. Despite some travel we mostly have our weekends for family or occasionally to ourselves when the kids are with one of our parents or away on school trips.

On planning a trip a couple of years ago, my boss, Mr. Frank Gerhard (who at work is, or at least was, always "Mr. Gerhard"), asked that I attend a national meeting with him as there was a competition in advertising innovation that he though I would do well at and it was his choice that I should represent the company. He added that he "needed my 'expertise' on some company matters in my area", so he said. He got first class tickets, which I thought was a nice gesture as we were going almost across the country to Los Angeles and would be gone almost 4 days.

Usually my husband tries to go with me on trips such as this type as it gives us a few days or a weekend to enjoy each other without fear of interruption from our kids. This time he was tied up so told me to be sure to bring him a T-shirt (his humor) and to be sure and get a good tan all over and (with a big smile) "To try to keep the men away". He said this last bit as we made passionate love the night before I left for L.A. At the time, I did not put two and two together to realize that he was turned on by other men being attracted to me.

CHAPTER II

The Flavor

A nyway, my boss who I now call Frank, is the VP of operations of our office and the highest-ranking company officer at our branch. He has always been very pleasant to me and seemed even more so as we prepared for this trip. On the plane, he made sure my drink was always full and talked a lot about how he saw my good work running my department. All this was flattering so I did not suspect that he was just softening me up for the real reason he got our seats together.

After a couple of hours he leaned close to me and in an almost whispering voice asked me if I would do him a very big favor this trip. When I asked him what it was he first stammered for words and then told me that he wanted to get even with, and show up, an old "friend" and colleague and put one over on him as he was what most would call a macho "jerk", who was in a similar position as he was only at the LA office. When I asked him how I could possibly help him put one over on this other person he looked me in the eye and said "I would be so very grateful for your help."

What came next surprised me. He asked if I would pretend that I was his girlfriend and mistress. I told him that I didn't think I could do that as I would not know how to "act" like I was really one as I had never been a girlfriend to anyone but my husband and certainly did not know what a mistress would do. Also, I very much loved my husband and had never even considered being unfaithful. He then told me that he was not asking me to be unfaithful at all but to just follow his lead and not deny that I was his girlfriend. The "odd innocent hug should do it" plus agreeing with what he would say. For this favor, there would be his undying gratitude and a significant raise when we returned.

For a while I was silent and after thinking it over, I reasoned that no one would know me in LA and the odd hug and smile from my boss when things were said seemed harmless and he **was** a handsome and imposing man. So after thinking and rationalizing for some time as we flew on, I leaned over to him and looking into his eyes I said, "yes, I will do this favor for you".

He was very pleased and gleefully told me just to follow his actions and try to think of a response that would convince his nemesis that he and I were lovers. I had to chuckle at that as Frank was a man in his 60's and probably more than 20 years my senior, but, like my husband he kept fit and appeared very well built and 2-3 inches taller than my husband.

Anyway, I thought that this would be harmless fun so after a bit of time when he told me things a girlfriend should know about his personal likes and dislikes in case a subject came up or I was asked, I told him that I thought it would be fun and I hoped I would not let him down. I then felt tired and took a nap while thinking what a girlfriend might say.

When I awoke, Frank was sleeping so I looked him over carefully noting that he was a handsome elderly man who appeared fit. I then watched a movie to while away the time but had to admit that my mind wandered to what a 'mistress' would think and say or what a real mistress would do with Frank. To my surprise, those thoughts led to a tingling between my legs even as I rationalized that those actions could never happen.

We finally arrived and got to the hotel. When I checked in after Frank checked in, I noted that our rooms were next to each other. He told me on the way up to our rooms that he wanted to get me something as a gift for doing this big favor and asked if, when I was ready if I would knock on our adjoining door. He hoped we could be ready to go shopping in an hour and then it would be his pleasure to take me to dinner. As it was relatively early and I had had a nap (as had he) I said "OK, see you in an hour."

I went to my room, took a shower and dressed for dinner. At the appointed time I knocked on our adjoining door and when he asked, I unlocked it and he came in praising my outfit. I thought nothing of this compliment so went with him down to the lobby and the few doors down the street to a string of a bit fancier stores than my husband and I usually shop at. Frank insisted that I get at least a couple of outfits as a small payment for making him look good and putting his protagonist in his place by making him envious of him.

He picked a couple from the models and told the saleslady to find something like those for me to wear right away. We both had a chuckle when the sales lady said, "Is this a special occasion for your daughter". Frank quickly said, that she was close but to just "Make my lady look good". I told Frank quietly that his choices were much more risqué and revealingly sexy than I usually wore to which he answered with a wink "Yes, that is the point" and added "You would look beautiful in anything in this store". I remember really blushing at that and, again, feeling a bit 'horny'.

As I was trying the choices on, I noted that they not only made me look sexy but made me feel sexy, very sexy as the material was soft and silky and a couple of them fit me like a glove thereby showing off all of my curves. They were short but not too short and had hidden zippers making it hard to tell how they were put on. I found myself wishing my husband had been able to make it as I was in the mood for some loving.

I thanked Frank profusely and gave him a peck on the cheek telling him that "They were very nice but I may not be able to wear them back home". He quickly put his arms around me giving me another hug and again thanking me for being his partner in the one-upmanship plan with his L.A. colleague and nemesis. His arms were strong and I felt enveloped and slightly turned-on. I came close to responding in kind but caught myself, as he was not my husband.

CHAPTER III

The Dinner

We dropped the packages off in my room and I quickly changed into one of the new dresses. I noticed that the door between his and my room was still partly open and remember thinking "how convenient". After I was dressed, I called Frank to tell him I was ready. He came through the adjoining door. When he came in he said "Wow, you do look even more beautiful than I imagined". My only response was to blush as I felt my cheeks becoming warm and I did feel a twinge in my pussy that almost startled me.

He then said "Lets go" and offered me his arm. Thusly, we then left my room and went to the lobby to get a cab to a place Frank said he knew was excellent. Once in the restaurant we got a table and were just starting our drinks when Frank said in a whisper. "OK, Donna, we're on, Robert just came in and I am sure he will see us." I asked him what I should do. He responded, "Nothing, just respond as if we know each other well …if you know what I mean". I recall not really knowing what he meant but smiled and whispered "OK".

Not a minute later this very good-looking man in impeccable dress came bounding over to our table and warmly shook hands with Frank. After their exchange of banter and not unexpected chauvinist barbs, Franks introduced me to his "old friend" Robert as his "special woman". The way he said it caused me to blush again.

Robert then took my hand and kissed it stating that I was "Far too young and beautiful to be going out with an old man like my pal Frank". He asked how long we have known each other and I said quickly "Over 5 years as we work in the same city." He seemed taken aback by my rapid positive response but quickly asked if he was good to me. Blushingly, I said "Of course, he is the best". To which Frank quickly added "Lover". Anyway, this shut Robert up for the moment so he just sat down and said "I'll assume it is OK to join you so let's eat."

The table was situated such that only three could sit at it so Frank moved next to me so he was between Robert and me. Robert quickly ordered a couple of bottles of wine and we were off. I really had to laugh at the conversation between these two men. It was like a bragging match between two high school classmates. Frank teased Robert about being at this meeting alone and asked if his wife or girlfriend had found something better to do. This went on all through both bottles of wine and a really delicious meal.

Frank kept moving closer to me and occasionally put his arm around me giving me hugs. At one point Robert excused himself to go to the rest room and I told Frank that, "You are going further than I want you to go or expected you would go - I did not mind doing you this favor - pretending to be yur girlfriend but …". I was cut short as Robert was back at the table. Next thing I knew, Frank put his arm around me and drew me to him for a kiss. It wasn't a short kiss and lasted until Robert made a noise that he was back. The alcohol had done something because I found myself kissing back. All Frank said to his 'friend" when the kiss ended was that, She is so good in bed that I just cannot help myself sometimes."

We all got up then and now I felt the effects of the wine as I had to, at first, lean on Frank for support. As we walked out with Robert following I felt Frank's hand feeling and fondling my bottom rather openly. I had gone this far as a favor for him so I did nothing, thinking this was for showing his friend, but inside I was very upset and more than a little angry. At the same time it not only felt good but was turning me on to the point that I felt a bit wet between my legs. I ended up putting my arm around Frank's waist to show affection that I did not really feel, but did feel something. I did feel 'naughty' as his attention was turning me on and I had never been this close to a man other than my husband since I started dating him many years ago.

CHAPTER IV
The First Time Was Special

Once Robert went his way and we were alone, I let Frank know that he had gone way too far. I almost angrily told him that I had agreed to the odd hug but not to his playing with my bottom. So, most all the way back to our rooms he was apologizing for taking advantage of the situation but at the same time thanking me over and over for making Robert green with envy.

Interspersed with his apologies, he complimented me on my great body and ass to the point I heard these comments more than his apologies and they were, somewhat surprisingly, turning me on. I didn't even notice that Frank had followed me into my room as he was begging my forgiveness. Maybe it was the alcohol or maybe I had secretly enjoyed the attention but I eventually told him that I forgave him.

With that he took me in his arms and started to kiss me. I guess I could have stopped him but he did feel good and I was a bit woozy from the alcohol so I did not stop his amorous attention until it was too late. He had started to run his hands over my body especially my sensitive bottom and soon to my breasts all the while saying how beautiful and sexy I was in his rich seductive voice. This was getting me very horny.

All this stimulation was also getting me very moist between my legs and I found myself enjoying the stimulation of his roaming hands. I became even more turned on when I felt my dress being raised in the back and his hands fondling first my bottom over my panties and then my bare bottom as he lowered my panties to my knees. I became mesmerized as his hands returned to my bottom and he started running his finger between my ass cheeks.

Once he started tickling and then probing my anus, I knew I

would not stop him whatever happened, but also felt very guilty for what was happening as I had never before broken my marriage vows. I knew that I should stop him and kept telling myself to pull away and stop this nonsense but another part of me did nothing. Talk about mixed feelings.

Then I felt the zipper at the back of my dress being slowly lowered and the next thing I knew my dress was on the floor and we were still rather passionately kissing and it was not one sided. His hands were busily exploring all of my anatomy especially my bottom, breasts and then the folds of my now very wet pussy. While this was happening my hands were around his neck and occasionally dropping to feel his back and muscular butt.

I had been feeling his hard cock pressing in my stomach but now he undid his pants and they too fell to the floor. I was lost in the passion of our deep wet kissing and was only slightly conscious of his removing his shirt, then my bra and finally my panties. As his body was the first I had felt other than my husbands, I started to explore with my own hands. When I came upon his penis I let out an audible moan, as it was much larger than my husband's and, as well, very hard.

I found myself comparing his penis to that of my husband and noting how much larger he was. Hard to put numbers on size but it was clearly longer and thicker than my husbands and I had thought all these years that my husband's was as large as they get. I could hardly get my hand around it and it was hard and ready. If I had had any doubts that I was going to be a naughty unfaithful wife they were now gone.

At this point, however, through the haze of the alcohol I thought that I had gone far enough and reasoned that if I did him by hand maybe I would be saved from breaking my marriage vows for the first time. My husband, as passionate as he was and as great as I thought our sex was, was good for usually one time a night so I thought Frank would be the same.

I manipulated our position so I could use both hands to

masturbate him to a climax, which I proceeded to do. This gave him a chance to manipulate and finger my pussy, which was certainly not helping my resolve. I thought that I had won when I started to feel him swell. I then quickly and almost automatically took the head of his cock in my mouth so the ejaculate would have someplace to go other than our bodies - or at least that was my rationale and I do love doing that for my husband. The surprise was the good taste and the large quantity of his cum.

Was I ever wrong, as after filling my mouth with his tasty cum, he did not get soft and easily picked me up and carried me to the bed and with his head between my spreading legs he feasted with his magic tongue and lips on everything between and including my clit and my anus. I was spellbound as his tongue and lips stimulated the lips of my vulva and with his tongue the inside of my vagina. Wow, a new feeling and definitely a turn on.

This continued until I had at least my third orgasm. When I was coming down from the last orgasm I felt him on top of me and his large cock at the entrance of my vagina. There was no doubt that I was about to be fucked for the first time by a man other than my husband but at that point I was so turned on that I offered absolutely no resistance and, in fact, wanted him in me.

As he was using his arms to keep his almost 200 pound weight off of my 132-pound frame, I reached between my legs and helped steer his cock to my waiting vagina. I remember him saying "That's the way, baby, help me get it in so I can fuck you like you have never been fucked before and pleasure you till you scream." Strangely, I remember his crude language turned me on very much. At that moment, I wanted him to fuck me badly.

As he entered I almost panicked, as I had never had anything in my vagina as large as he was. He was patient and slowly inserted a bit more with each stroke. He was only half way in when I had my first almost screaming vaginal orgasm.

This helped lubricate my vagina and he was able to get it all in with just a few more strokes. In answer to his question "Does if feel good, baby?" After saying, "God, yes, it feels fantastic", I pulled him down to my lips and gave him a long and passionate kiss all the while starting to grind my pelvis to feed more of his cock in my vagina. He was reaching places no other person or object had ever reached and I was in orgasmic heaven.

I could not believe the feelings I was experiencing as his cock stimulated every centimeter of my now wanton vagina. I also could not believe the number of shattering orgasms I had or how long he was able to keep up the motion of fucking and passion. I experienced a number of new feelings such as having each cheek of my buttocks fondled and squeezed as we were fucking and his inserting his finger in my anus. That alone triggered a couple of climaxes.

My new lover kept repeating "Baby, you ARE the best fuck I have ever experienced". "You are mine now". "Tell me you are mine" In the heat of passion I responded "Yes, Yes, I am yours, Please fuck me harder and don't stop". I could not believe I said that but at the moment I was that turned on and felt like I was his.

At one point he pulled out and flipped me over so he could enter me 'doggie style' which was a whole other feeling and now he was able to play with my sensitive breasts driving me crazy as I backed into him with each of his thrusts. Finally after almost an hour since we started he told me that he was cuming and asked where I wanted it. I responded with only "Don't stop, I want it all".

I felt his cock swell and then repeatedly spasm as he filled me with his sperm. What a feeling to be so taken. When he pulled out we were both so fatigued that without many words we got under the covers and fell asleep even as it was fairly early in the evening. I have always slept well after a good fuck and tonight was no exception. Not sure how long we slept before I was awakened by a ringing sound.

CHAPTER V

I Was Hooked

T he phone awoke me with a start. Knowing it was most likely my husband, I let it ring a few times to collect my thoughts before I answered. When I answered "Hi Hon" he responded by asking me how the meeting was going.

I told him that I had just gotten back from dinner with a number of other department heads from across the country where we talked about the competition. I told him that I wished he had been able to make this trip and I loved him and missed him. This was true but I was secretly glad he had not made the trip. Of course I asked about the kids and was relieved to know they were being very good. We said goodbye with his telling me that he most likely would not call the next night as he was going to our son's basketball game and then over to some friends.

When I turned around after hanging up I found myself in Frank's arms getting a hug and reassurance that I was not a bad wife but entitled to some fun and freedom. This helped a little but I still felt guilty. With that we started kissing and again he explored my body and I his until we were back in bed.

This time I turned around to get in a "69" position so I could see directly his organ of pleasure. Not sure how long I kissed, fondled and sucked Frank's cock but certainly knew it well when I could not stand another minute of his magic tongue on my very sensitive clit as well as in and around my vagina so I flopped over, spread my legs and invited him to "Frank, please fuck me again."

He smiled and said, "say please, I know you want to". "OK, damn you, <u>please</u> come and fuck me again" and I added, "If you can". With that challenge he jumped on and this time was all the way in so that his balls were rubbing my buttocks within two strokes.

His staying power was astounding and he rode me like a man possessed. His only verbal comments were "Baby, you <u>are</u> the best fuck I have ever known ... I am glad I found you". He went on to say, "If Robert knew how good you were it would drive him nuts" After several orgasms I really started to contract my vaginal muscles as best I could. Each time I contracted he moaned loudly and finally with a bellow I felt his cock contracting as he again unloaded his sperm in my vagina for the second time that night. It and he sure felt good.

We rested a bit and I got up to take a shower before going to bed. I should have suspected or known that Frank would join me and sure enough as I was soaking he came in the shower and started soaping my body. Every inch of it he applied his soapy hands to. Not to be outdone and a chance to feel his large cock while soft, I started to do the same. I must say that for a 60+ year-old man he had some body.

I did not think that after three climaxes on his part that he could get hard again but I was wrong again. I bent down to suck him thinking I could get him off as I did not know if I could handle more vaginal friction - as good as it felt. He had other ideas and lifting me up he told me to put my legs around his waist. He then set me down on his cock and that was it, I was full again. With my arms around his neck I bounced for all I was worth through a couple more orgasms until he finally came. We untangled and finished our shower quietly.

I climbed into bed expecting him to go to his room but he soon joined me and last I remembered was falling asleep in his arms with mixed feelings of guilt, passion, sexiness, and contentment.

CHAPTER VI

Day Two

I am sure I do not have to tell you that we made love again (perhaps I should say "Fucked again") in the morning. This time it was slow and deliberate and I gave as well as I got. In fact, I initiated it as when I awoke I ran my hands all over his body in wonderment as to his fitness for his age. I also started playing with his cock and had the pleasure of feeling it get hard by my ministrations. It got even harder when I crawled down to take it in my mouth as I just loved the feel of his large spongy head in my mouth.

At one point after my second or third orgasm I said, "Well, I guess I do not have to <u>pretend</u> to be your mistress or girlfriend any more". As we were laughing he said, "and I do not have to pretend that you are the best piece of ass I know". He went on to say that "I had wanted to make it with you for the last 3 or 4 years as you know that you are the best looking lady in our company", and "Now I know that you are also the sexiest of all."

I told him that I did not know that as he was the first man I had sex with outside of my marriage and my husband must never know of this indiscretion. I remember as I said this to him that I knew that as guilty as I felt that I would have to somehow tell my husband, as a marriage based on trust was how we were.

We got up and he did finally go to his room through the adjoining door to get dressed in fresh clothes. We had breakfast and took a cab to the head office. At the meeting we stayed fairly close, as he wanted me to get arranged for the competition. What they had in mind was that each of us were given a set of facts about a made-up product and had to design a 6-slide presentation to educate the sales force. I was used to this so was able to complete mine by noon. I did what I always do and was not concerned about winning the "competition".

At lunch, into which we walked holding hands, we again ran into his old buddy and nemesis Robert who complimented me on my taste in clothes and how good I looked. Frank then said, "Yes, she looks good enough to eat - again" and laughed. Robert looked at my reaction, which was a smile and hug of Franks arm and said "Well, this must be true then. Is that so, Donna". My response "Why yes, when you are with the best, one always tends to give the best."

As I said it, I realized that it was quite true. Frank beamed and changed the subject as Robert had the oddest look on his face. Frank asked Robert if he would care to join us for dinner so they could catch up on old times? Robert perked up and said, "Yes, of course, where and when". Frank then said, "I'll call you when we know."

The rest of the day was meetings sometimes with Frank and sometime with other department heads. I ran into Robert a number of times and he was very talkative and trying to get information about Frank and me. I said nothing and was able to ward off his advances as I certainly did not want any involvement with anyone else. He seemed surprised that he could not get anyplace with me.

We were back at the hotel with enough time to rest before we had to dress for the evening. I was relaxing in my panties and bra when Frank came into the room in nothing but his shorts. He came up to me and in the midst of a big hug (all of Franks hugs were big), he managed to again turn me on by playing with my bottom and rubbing my pussy through my panties.

He led me to the couch. Bent me over and lowered my panties to the floor. I stepped out of them, as I knew what was coming. He then nudged my legs apart and slowly inserted the object of my pleasure into my awaiting vagina. By the time he came I had had a stream of wild orgasms and actually did scream through a couple of them. In that position, I learned that he could even get farther in than the usual missionary position. After that interlude we showered and dressed for diner.

While dressing, you could only imagine the mixture of guilt and pleasure thoughts that coursed through my mind. I knew I really loved the sex with Frank and part of me wanted it to never end. This conflicted with the guilt over not only what I had done but how much I enjoyed it and wanted more. I was also quite anxious as to how my husband would react when I told him, as I knew I had to, that I had been unfaithful to him even, as I told myself, I did not initiate it.

Dinner was at a fabulous place LA is noted for and not much new happened except Frank was even more demonstrative of his affection and I responded as if we were actually long time lovers, much to the anxiety of Frank's old friend Robert, who had joined us again. My sensitive bottom and occasionally my breasts were discreetly touched many times for Roberts benefit. I do admit it felt good and I became lost in the pleasure of the moment.

That night as well as the last night were the same, Frank fucked me 3 or 4 times after dinner and at least twice in the morning. I was one sexually satisfied and well-fucked lady by the time I went home. I even found myself wondering if we would ever do this again and found myself hoping so.

CHAPTER VII

The Return Home

O n the last day of the meeting, I got the surprise of my life as I was awarded the first prize for my marketing skills in presenting the 6-slide talk about a fictitious product. The prize was a check to me for $1,000 and the same amount for my favorite charity. First thing I did was call my husband and tell him the news that with almost no work I had won the first prize over 26 other department heads from around the country. I also told him that I loved him dearly and that I would be home in a day.

It was on the flight back home that I had time to reflect and feel the guilt of what I had experienced in the past three days. Frank had had to stay an extra day as had all unit heads so I was by myself. I felt ashamed that I had broken my wedding vows and had sex – even great sex - with a man other than the man I loved and had children with. At times I felt so bad that I cried. Mostly it was the anxiety of what and how I would tell my husband about my infidelity. Many stories went through my mind. I slept fitfully and spent most of the trip wondering if my husband would be angry enough at my actions to leave me. I felt that I deserved whatever he did.

My homecoming was very pleasant. My husband had the kids over at my parents house and there was fresh cut flowers all over the house. We were not 5 minutes in the door when he led me upstairs to make love. It was just like times of old. I had a great orgasm and I knew that if he knew nothing our lives would stay the same. I also knew that I loved him dearly. When we were done and in each others arms I knew that I had to tell him that I had been unfaithful.

Looking him in the eyes, I started to cry. He knew something was wrong so started questioning me. So, I told him that I had done something I had never done before and if he forgave me, I would never do again. "What in the world are you talking about" he said. Not knowing how to put it gently I just came out with "Honey, I have been unfaithful to you". Then I broke down and, as 'guilt' overwhelmed me, cried again.

Of course, he had to ask what I meant and with who had I been unfaithful and why. I told him that I owed him the truth, as it was he who I loved with all my heart. I started with the "WHY". I told him that I would never know the real reason as to "why". It may have been too much alcohol or thinking I was doing a favor for my boss. It was not because I didn't love him, my husband, or that I had planned to be unfaithful. Doing what I did had never even crossing my mind at any time in our marriage or before this trip.

As to what I mean, I told him that I had sex with another man and I am ashamed of myself. I'll never forget his response as long as I live as he said, "With your beauty, charm and sexiness, I certainly cannot blame someone for trying or you for responding". With that he hugged and held me tightly and told me to start at the beginning about what happened and who it happened with. It was then that I felt his very hard cock pressing into my stomach so I knew he was forgiving me or at least was not angry.

I commented on his arousal and he said, "Yes, I feel it and for some reason thinking of you having sex with another man makes me incredibly horny". I love you and want you happy so start at the beginning and tell me everything.

So I told him that it was my boss Frank who had on the plane asked me to do him a big favor which was to pretend to be his mistress to play a trick, sort of, on an old friend who he told me was a jerk and was always on to him with his lady friends. I refused at first but he was so persuasive and told me that it would involve only the odd hug and agreeing with him when he made statements about our dating. I said that Frank was a good boss so I was weakening.

He also promised a big raise if I would help him. So I finally agreed. I told my husband that I think I was plied with alcohol at the first dinner, as it was that first night when he got to me and did more that the odd hug.

Then when I started telling him about the details of the first time and how big Frank's cock was, he got so carried away that he pounced on top of me and we made love like newlyweds as reliving the adventure turned me on also. When he climaxed he told me breathlessly to go on and that he loved me even more than he thought possible and that the thought of me being fucked by my Boss stimulated him beyond expectation.

He reminded me that he had met Frank and had seen him looking at you many times over the years and was not surprised. He reminded me that Frank was a clever man who got where he is by being smart so he thought that Frank planned the whole thing from the start. I told him that with hindsight that he may be right. I told him that I was sure dumb to be fooled like that but had to admit that overall it was pleasurable while it was happening.

So I told my husband about the first night and the next morning in detail, which got him very hard and aroused again very quickly. As I was telling him about the next morning he made love to me again and this time I also had a total body orgasm. I told him that he must really be turned on by what I was telling him as this was the first time in more that 10 years that we had made love more than once and it was already three times. I told him I loved it and him more than ever.

Anyway, we spent most of the night making love as each time I told him about a new position or circumstance he would get excited and hard and want to make love. At one point he asked me if I was going to see Frank again. I quickly said "absolutely not" as this was a slip and I am happily married to the best man in the world who very much satisfies me and I did not intend on being unfaithful again.

He then pointed out that being "unfaithful" is when one does something behind the back of ones mate. He told me that if I did have sex with someone else and your husband, I, knew of it and was OK with it, this would not be being "unfaithful". When I asked him if he really did want me to have sex with Frank again, he had to admit that this turned him on greatly even as he had no idea where that came from. He further said that as long as he always knew about it and maybe could watch sometime the answer was a resounding "Yes".

It ended up being a great homecoming as we made love more times in two days than in almost two months before. I certainly was not complaining. Yet, I had the feeling that my life was changing in that I had really enjoyed the sex with Frank in LA and had secretly hoped it could continue. I now knew it could and was both excited and scared.

I awoke the next morning with my husband's head between my legs licking and sucking my vulva and clit as never before. It was a nice way to wake-up but I also had the urge to have him in my mouth so switched around to the '69' position with me on top. Having my husbands cock in my mouth was heaven as I could actually get almost half of it in whereas I could only get the head and a couple of inches of Franks. When I told him that he erupted almost immediately. I knew then that he was truthfully accepting my extramarital tryst.

I ended up telling him about each and every time I was fucked by Frank and the more I described what happened, the hornier he got and we ended up having sex several times by noon.

I got some calls from my office congratulation me on winning the big competition at the company meeting. At the end of the third call, he gave me a big hug and said he had an idea and wondered if I was interested. He said that we should have an open house for your department and other invited friends at your company in honor of your taking home the first prize in the competition.

We would, of course, invite Frank. He then said his plan was to be called away on an emergency at the tail end of the party and then surreptitiously return to a hiding place in our closet so he could observe Frank in action. As he described his idea he held me close and was playing with my bottom. I did get turned on by this possibility and even more so now that I had my husbands blessing.

The Open House

After we had discussed the open house for members of my department and my boss, my husband then said, that he wanted to have another congratulatory open house for our neighbors and friends. I asked him if he wanted to see more action to which he replied, "Yes, of course, but who".

Then I told him of the numerous times friends of his and a couple of our neighbors had managed to briefly fondle my bottom or breasts "accidentally" and that "One time your good friend Joe followed me into the bathroom and started feeling me up and asking me to bend over so he could fuck me." I did not want to make a scene or noise and struggled to prevent that and admit I was only saved when we heard his wife calling for him. He has not tried anything since but probably only as I have kept my distance.

At this story, my husband kissed me passionately and bent me over the couch, raised my dress, lowered my panties and said, "I love you for being so unbelievably sexy" as he entered me in one thrust. He then said that these events would happen and he would get his wish to watch me have sex with another man. What a homecoming.

On reflecting about the recent events I realized that I had won a company award for a on-the-spot putting together a 6 slide promotion of a fictitious product at out national meeting. This had caught me by surprise as it took me less than 3 hours to put together what I would have done to market this particular product here. I knew that others from other offices had spent all of the first day and some part of the second day.

My husband was excited for me to win this award so he set up an open house for my department plus those in management of the company who knew about this contest and my winning. As this was acknowledgement of my whole department so everyone at work was excited to come.

Only my husband and I knew one of the main reasons he set this up was in the hopes he could observe for himself my boss Mr. Gerhard, who I came to call Frank at that national meeting, have sex with me. I asked him several times in the days leading up to the event if he was sure that he wanted to go down this slippery slope as once we start it may be quite impossible to quit. Needless to say we talked about this many times and always ended up passionately making love and avowing our love for each other.

I was anxious but also excited about this possibility as it was at that national meeting I was seduced by Frank and when I tearfully confessed this to my husband expecting him to throw me out, he surprised me by being sexually excited by what I did and wanting to see it for himself. To my question of "Are you sure?", he would always say "Yes, and I will prove it to you".

He told me that he had seen many men including some of our friends and neighbors eyeing me lustfully in the past. "heck, even the guy who cleans and checks our pool looks at you with lust in his eyes." I couldn't resist teasing him when he said that by asking him "Well, why did you not tell me this earlier?"

He told me he had often fantasized about me having sex with some of them but never had the courage to mention this to me. "And", he said, "This includes my friend Joe who has always told me how much he envies me for who I was married to". "No", he said, "I am not upset as I know we are solid and anything you do will not change my love for you." So, with the stage set, we invited my department at the agency and a number of the brass who I thought might be interested. We invited them and their other halves. My husband made a bet with me that Frank would come alone. Our sex life was at a new level with the anticipation of the evening. He, thinking about Frank fucking me and I, salivating about the same thing.

Just before anyone arrived he went over his plan. He arranged to get beeped at around 10:00 that evening and was hoping that Frank was close enough for Frank to hear him call his office and exclaim that he would be right there. He would excuse himself and go look for me to tell me not so quietly that there was an emergency and he would be gone for an hour or so. He would excuse himself from those still present and depart quietly. He would drive a block away, park where he would not be seen and come back to the house by the back way.

Once here, if most people were gone, which he expected they would he would call me and tell me that the emergency was larger than expected and he would be gone 2-3 hours. I would repeat this, tell him I love him and hang up.

The evening was perfect. I wore one of the new dresses Frank had gotten for me and everyone congratulated me about winning the competition. Frank did come alone and when he arrived he told my husband and I that his wife was called away to see her sick mother and sends her regrets. I looked at my husband to see his wink. So we knew that stage was set.

Frank was almost always nearby but was the perfect gentleman and typical boss. By 10:00 everyone had eaten most of what we had and had consumed at least enough punch or wine so I could see that the reception was dying down. Frank, my husband and I were in a conversation about nothing in particular when my husband got his beep and excused himself to call his office.

He stepped only a step away and I heard him say to no one that he would be right down but for them to call the emergency team. He stepped back and apologetically told Frank and I that he had an emergency at his office and would be back in an hour or so. On the way out he graciously said "good-bye" to those left who he passed. Within the next half hour almost everyone had said their 'good-byes' except Frank who offered to help me straighten up until my husband returned. I went around turning off extra lights and picking up a bit of the mess with Frank at my heels.

When things were in order he came up to me and gave me a big hug saying that he missed me and thought about our time together in LA a lot. My first reaction was to say that "Yes, it was enjoyable but I do not think it wise to continue what we started." He told me that I was right and said that he wanted a kiss to seal the deal. We kissed and immediately his hands were roaming over my body including my bottom and breasts. I could not believe how quickly I became horny for more.

Breathlessly, I told him that we should stop because my husband would be home shortly. Frank then said "Your husband's office is 8 miles from here and if he only stayed 30 minutes we still had a bit more than 30 minutes." With that he again enveloped me in his arms and plied his hands over my body. I started to return his kisses and with the memory of LA I soon wanted him in me NOW.

Just then the phone rang as planned and I excused myself to pick it up. I was to listen a bit, say "Hi honey, .. Yes, everyone has left … When will you be home?". Then after a bit "Oh, too bad, … well, wake me up when you get home" "Love you too". Then slowly hang up. I then told frank in a sad voice that my husband found a larger emergency than he though so he would not be home for at least two hours.

First thing out of Franks mouth was "Well, what are we waiting for" "you have no more excuses and I know you want me to fuck you again don't you." My response was a soft "yes". So he took me in his arms and started hugging and kissing me and I started returning the kisses as passionately as he gave them. As he was fondling my body and making me horny he started undressing me. When I was down to my bra and panties he stepped back and told me that I was even more beautiful than in LA and started to undress himself. It was then that I took his hand and led him to our bedroom so my husband could have the best view.

Once he was naked I took off my own bra and panties as I did not want to wait any longer. He noticed my undressing and asked what I wanted him to do. I knew what he wanted me to say but two can play that game so I said, "Well, what do you want to do with me now that I am undressed". "OK", he said, "I want you to suck my cock as you did in LA and want you to beg me to fuck you as I know you want". He added, "You do want it don't you?" At that point, he had me as I said, "Oh my god, yes" and fell to my knees and started sucking on his large and delicious cock.

It wasn't long before his Ohhing and Ahhing as I licked and mouthed his beautiful cock especially his velvety smooth and spongy head. This led to "I'm cuming, take it all". This, I did gladly as I knew from experience that the fucking I would be getting would be longer and thus more pleasurable. It was not one minute after I swallowed his cum that he bent me over our stuffed chair and was licking my whole sex area from my clit to my anus. God, it felt good. He than asked what I wanted now and I flat out said, without a seconds hesitation "Please fuck me with your gorgeous cock, now, right now." "Make me scream, I want you in me so bad."

I knew this was what he wanted to hear and I also now knew that this was what my husband wanted to hear. After what seemed an interminable time and after I had had two shaking to my core orgasms he started moving faster and faster and my final orgasm was when his cock expanded and almost exploded with another load of his cum. We then lay in my bed and almost dozed off. I became awake fully as I felt his still hard cock once again spread my pussy lips and invade my interior.

I was in heaven as we fucked slowly and deeply for what seemed an hour. I really did not know how he did it but whole body orgasms continued. His hands were all over my body from my bottom, which he squeezed and played with to my sensitive breasts, which he fondled and sucked. I knew my husband was getting quite a show as I was getting some very enjoyable and pleasurable fucking. It seems that after an orgasm, Frank would change his position and the frequency of his penetration and get me hot all over again.

Two hours later we took a shower and came back into the living room to get dressed. In that time I had been fucked in many positions and had my clitoris sucked through an uncountable series of orgasms and Frank had cum 4 times in either my mouth or vagina. On his way to the door Frank told me that he was planning a company managers social in honor of my win at his house and then said, "I cannot wait to get into you again." I then said, "It may not happen if my husband comes with me which I am sure he will."

After Frank left I went back to our bedroom and there was my husband with the biggest grin waiting in bed naked. He thanked me over and over for letting him watch and avowed his love again and again. We made love until the early morning hours until I was exhausted and literally fell asleep in his arms.

CHAPTER IX

The Party at Franks

The next week back at work was a blur, as I seemed to be in demand to present the approach that won the national prize to every department. I was asked to do the same at a Department head meeting where Frank announced that he was having an Open house at his estate the next Friday in honor of my winning the prestigious first place award thereby bringing bragging rights to "our" office.

After this meeting I told Frank when we were alone that my husband and I had plans for that afternoon and early evening so we would have to be a little late. He said with a grin that "as long as you are there, as Robert is coming". I then told him that it would be "hard to pretend that I was your lover with my husband present." To which Frank said that I would think of something like coming alone. He then gave my bottom a squeeze as I was leaving.

I told my husband about this and the event and I told him that I really wanted him to come as I certainly did not want the whole company to even think that the boss of us all had a favorite or a relationship with me. I also told him that Robert, who I had told him about, was coming from LA and I suspect that Frank has some plan or another. He said that we should play it by ear and see what the evening foretold. Perhaps Frank would try something and maybe not. The night of the company open house we arrived after things were in full swing. I was more that a little embarrassed by the attention and accolades for having done what I do routinely. I felt relieved to have my husband at my side as he helped deflect and receive the praise. At one point Frank asked me to follow him to meet some of the outside visitors from other branches in other cities.

As we moved around I did feel Frank's hand on my bottom several times but he was discreet as he did it when no one would notice it although I was sure my husband had seen it.

At one point Frank told me quietly that he was honored that I came and as soon as I met everyone the get together would be ending and he was eager to thank me in person. At one point Robert came up to us and shook my hand – holding it longer than needed. Smilingly, as if he knew something, he told me that he had heard may good things about my work and wondered if I was interested in coming back to LA to "teach" his department heads a thing tor two. He was a slick one and I had to laugh at his over the top flattery. I told him that this would be up to my boss – nodding to Frank.

Fast forward to the point where everyone had left except Frank, Robert, my husband and I. The 4 of us were standing around talking about nothing in particular and in the presence of my husband; Frank put an arm around me once and fondled my bottom a couple of times. He did both of these almost in front of my husband as if testing his reaction. His actions were turning me on and I knew they were turning my husband on.

When my husband only smiled, Frank had implicit approval to go further. I did not think he would do much as Robert was still around but he did. Frank sort of led us all over to a couch and a couple of chairs and motioned for us all to be seated. He, of course sat next to me. As we were talking he put his hand on my leg and occasionally slid it to mid thigh while watching my husband who said nothing but smiled. It seems that Frank took this as an OK to proceed. Meanwhile Robert made no comment but was also smiling.

Frank then started talking about me and came right out and asked my husband if I had told him anything about LA. When my husband said, "Yes, she has told me that the trip was very interesting and eventful". Frank then slid his hand up to my upper thigh and said, "Well, that's good, that you do not mind that Donna is special to me" as he slid his hand up under my dress to inches below my pussy. Frank now knew that my husband was seeing what he was doing and took his lack of an objection as an OK to continue, which he did.

The sexual tension in the room was high and I just sat there mesmerized by the feelings of excitement that were coming over me. I managed to look over at Robert and he was watching both Frank and my husband with a grin.

Frank then started rubbing the gusset of my ever-moistening panties and took my hand and placed it on his lap over his hardening cock. I looked over at my husband as if to say, "I can't help myself, he is turning me on too much". Frank then said to my husband, "I am very glad you are OK with this because Donna and I have a special relationship and no one gets me as horny as your wife." "And even if you were not OK, I would find it difficult, if not impossible, to stop."

Frank asked me to stand up with my back to him and next thing I knew was that he was lowering my panties and telling me to step out of them. He tossed them on the table before my husband and Robert and reached up my skirt again to play with my ass and very wet pussy. He raised my dress from behind and pulled me down to his lap and his very long and stiff cock. I very audibly gasped as it entered me. God, it felt good.

Both Robert and my husband knew what was happening but at that point I did not care, as it felt so good to have his moving cock in me. Frank then asked my husband to remove my dress. With almost no hesitation he came over and unzipped and unsnapped what he needed to pull my dress off over my head. Frank looked at my breasts; nodded, looking at my husband so he then undid my bra taking it off my shoulders all the while Frank was fucking me while I was 'sitting' on his cock. As he was taking off my bra our eyes met and we both mouthed at the same time "I love you" then we kissed sealing the arrangement.

Moments later I had my first orgasm followed by feeling Franks cock swell and pulsate as he unloaded his sperm into my vagina. Frank then lifted me off his cock said, "Clean me up for the next time." As I was bending over and taking his cock in my mouth I felt a pair of hands on my hips and a cock entering my vagina from behind. From the size, I knew it wasn't my husbands so now knew why Robert was invited to this get-together.

34

Robert was a skilled lover and holding my hips controlled his action pistoning in and out of my well-lubricated vagina. At one point he manipulated me till I was bending over the back of one of Frank's large stuffed chairs. There he brought me to two or three very large orgasms, as he really knew how to rub my G-spot with his thick cock. He kept saying to Frank that he sure knew how to pick them and that I was, "Really the best as you told me so many times".

For the next couple of hours I was passed back and forth between Frank and Robert who fucked me in many positions and brought me through multiple orgasms. I found myself being particularly active contracting my vaginal muscles when Robert was fucking me as I strangely wanted him to really know I was as good as Frank had been telling him I was and also he had an incredible body that turned me on like crazy.

When Frank was fucking me he would tell me that I was his best mistress and he enjoys fucking me again an again "With or without your husband". At one point he said to Robert, "Now you see what I mean when I told you that she has the body of a 20 year old" to which Robert responded, "I agree, you were right but you don't have to rub it in."

A couple of times I was able to glance at my husband who had his cock out and was masturbating at the sight. This actually thrilled me as I knew he was really enjoying what he was seeing as I was enjoying what I was feeling. In addition to being thrilled, I was quite relieved that my husband was OK with what was happening, as I knew that my life had changed and I would be fucking Frank and others in the future.

At one point both Frank and Robert could not get hard again despite the attentions of my mouth and tongue so I motioned my husband over who was on me and in me in a flash and told me again and again as we were making passionate love that he loved me and was really turned on by watching me with Frank and Robert. As he had masturbated a couple of times he was able to pleasure me for longer and with more orgasms than we had ever done it up to then.

When we finally finished, I gathered up my clothes, got dressed and after kissing Frank good night we went home. My husband a very satisfied man and I also was very satisfied and content. At home we relived the evening and made passionate love again until we both climaxed and fell asleep exhausted wondering what the next weeks and months had in store for us.

CHAPTER X
And Then...

O he thing that happened was that Frank would invite my husband and I two or three times a month to dinner at various places where he seemed to delight in dancing close and sexily. Right in front of my husband he would fondle my breasts and ass and seemed to delight in asking me if I was ready to take care of him.

After the meal, he would take my hand and lead me to the room he always had with my husband following behind. He often looked back at my husband while his hand was under my dress playing with my bare bottom and would tell him that "Your wife is the best piece of ass that I have had for years" and seemed to get off on whatever my husband would say.

In the room, he would direct my husband to a chair and then pleasure himself and me for what seemed like hours until I was exhausted. With his magical tongue he would bring me to my first orgasm and I would immediately take his cock as far into my mouth as I could and do my best to be sure his first climax filled my hungry mouth. He was always able to bring me to orgasm many times and enjoyed fucking me in all of my holes. Both my husband and I would marvel later at the potency and staying power of this man who was in his mid sixties.

One time he told me that he wanted me to be sort of a hostess for his card playing group and that my husband could come and would be introduced not as my husband but as his friend and fellow card player. That was some evening as whenever I brought a drink to anyone, their hands would go up my skirt and play with my bottom or my pussy. This got me extremely horny. Then Frank suggested to the group that as it appeared that they liked his lady that the winner of the next set would win this sexy lady for up to 30 minutes.

Then he said, "And Oh, there is a bedroom just down the hall". He followed this by, "you will be very pleased as she is the best lover I know". I had not expected this but soon one of the gentlemen won some set and got up and led me into the bedroom. Without a word he told me to "strip quickly" as we do not have much time. By the time I was naked, so was he and he first told me to suck him of, which I gladly did and once he filled my mouth he bent me over a chair and filled my vagina. He was good and I thanked him for the orgasms he gave me. We quickly dressed and went back as if nothing had happened.

This went on all evening as one after the other would lead me into the bedroom, fuck me as many times as they could get hard. Most of these older men did quite well and had me suck them at first and some took me anally. This seemed to excite them as much as it did me. As my husband was not able to watch he had to await our return home to hear about this unusual night. As I told him about the different individuals and what they did to please themselves he got hard again and again.

My husband seemed to never tire of these outings and would ask me if I wanted to get together with others. He kept coming back to his friend who had almost gotten in to my panties a year or so ago. His repeatedly bringing up the instance with his friend Joe, got me curious to the point that I told him to set it up somehow if he was really interested in watching me with more men than Frank and, now, his friends. Secretly, I hope he does not tire of watching me, as I am not sure I could stop.

I told him that I loved him and would stop seeing Frank, let alone fucking him if at any time he had had enough. After I said that, I realized that my hope was that he remained OK with this activity as I sure loved it and really did not want to stop. I told him that sex with him was very good indeed but there is a big difference between pure sex and making love to the man I married and love dearly. He told me that he still was turned on beyond description knowing and especially seeing me take a cock in my vagina or mouth.

When he tasted cum in my mouth or vagina it made him almost too hard and certainly very excited sexually. He kept saying that he did not know where these feelings came from but wanted them to continue and that he loved me even more than he thought possible because I had given him the pleasure of being a voyeur.

CHAPTER XI

Thinking Ahead...

I was very pleased at my husband's acceptance of my sexual activities as now that I have started, I really do not think I could stop. I certainly do not want to stop and even have been looking at the guys at the gym with new eyes. There is one guy that I have been especially attracted to. His name is Victor. He is black and very muscular as well as fit. I think he is attracted to me also because at least once each time I am there he will come over and "help" me with some apparatus or another. He has, on many occasions discretely touched many parts of my body and has yet to be rebuffed by me, often with my husband close by. He surely must now know that my husband is not the jealous type and is OK with Victor's not so discrete desires.

My husband and I have talked about Victor a few times and my husband has encouraged me to be a little more overt. He may not know it but I have been somewhat 'flirty' when no one is around and I know Victor knows that it is a matter of time until he gets into my panties. I am getting excited by this as I have never had sex with a black man or anyone with a cock as large as his appears to be.

In addition to being with my first black lover, Victor, I am now looking forward to being pleasured by our friend Joe. It will be fun to pretend that he is seducing me and not the reverse. My husband is planning on a party for our friends and neighbors and to be called away if Joe comes alone, which we both expect he will. So, my interesting life as a 'hotwife' goes on and I am enjoying it immensely.

My new life goes on.

A Return Back Home That Changed My Life

By Chris Dawson
Copyright © June 2009

An account of what could very well have been reality as when in Montréal, if you are thought to be an 'Anglophone" but speak and understand French quite well you will surely hear what you were not supposed to hear. In this almost unexpected story the wife, who grew up in Montréal, hears 'francophone's speaking lustily in French about her not knowing that she understood every word as they were planning to seduce her. What she does as she had never before strayed is the lusty story.

CHAPTER I

In The Beginning

N ot even sure where to begin but I hope it is true that confession is good for the soul. I have been and am still a very happily married 42-year-old lady. My husband, Robert, and I have been married for 18 years. We met and fell in love when I was visiting friends in Cincinnati, almost 20 years ago, on a trip from Montréal, which is where I grew up and was living and working at the time.

We have three kids from 17 to 14. Despite this, we are both in quite good shape compared to others our age and in our circle of friends. Most are quite surprised at Birthday gatherings thinking we are surely much younger than we admit. We are both fit and attend the local Gym and squash courts regularly. One secret to our happy marriage is that we do many things together. The only exception is that I am an ardent photographer and Robert is a chess aficionado. I just cannot get into chess.

Our 17 year old son, Matt, asked me one day what a "M I L F" was as he had heard one of his friends use the term and he thought it referred to me. I almost choked on the coffee I was drinking and was grateful that it wasn't hot. I quickly told him that it was a term of some disrespect and what it meant. I told him that his friend could not have meant me as I was hardly a "Madame" and "Fornication" was only between married people. I made a mental note to dress more conservatively when this or other friends of Matt were over.

Back to my story of infidelity, which even now embarrasses me a little even as I know that I would and will do it again under the same or right circumstances. In all the years of my marriage, I had never even thought about fooling around sexually. True, both Robert and I are teases and by no means prudes but to cross that line did not enter my thoughts. We were both minimally sexually active before marriage and both of us openly talk about people we meet who we would be attracted to.

We also both have a few fantasies, which we have shared but none of them involve actual sexual activity with others. All in all we have a good relationship and are definitely sexually active if even as it could / would be called "vanilla". Certainly I have been totally and happily faithful and I believe Robert has also been faithful. Stepping out had never entered my mind.

The adventure I am speaking about came about when my husbands company had an international meeting, which was held in Montréal. We were both excited to go as I grew up in Montréal and Robert had visited me while we were courting and had returned for a few family events. I was still fluent in French and Robert, who took French in school, spoke it a little but I am not sure what he understands if any.

The meeting was at a very nice downtown hotel so I really enjoyed the shopping on Rue Ste Catherine, boul. de Maissoneuve and Sherbrooke. What is very different in Montréal compared to most American cities is that the streets were always crowded with people and almost all were dressed much better than one would see on most streets back home or in many US cities. It is almost always fun to walk the streets in downtown Montréal.

It was obvious that I was seen as an American as I was casually dressed. I could tell that I was drawing stares and the comments, which were in French meaning that I understood what was said whereas the speaker must have thought I did not understand French as some were rather racy. I guess this flattered my ego as I walked a bit more erect and stopped to look at many shops soaking in the looks and comments.

I was eating lunch alone at the hotel while Robert was at one of many meetings and sitting at the table next to mine was two men who, judging by their name-tags were at some meeting in the hotel. They were obviously on the prowl as they made comments on the women they saw who passed their table. I very definitely understood what they were saying and it was clear that they did not think I understood French. Had they thought or known I was French speaking, I doubt they would have been so candid about what part of the anatomy of passing ladies struck their fancy.

In between commenting (in French) on the breasts and asses of the waitress or some women who was walking by they kept coming back to wondering where I was from. They agreed that I was very sexy looking and guessed my age "probably under 30 years old". They postulated and wondered if I was an "American". They also debated out loud (in French) as to my bra size or the color of my panties and what I did for a living or who I was here with. I just passed on these somewhat annoying comments but had to admit that they were not bad looking men and their talk was starting to turn me on.

One, whose name was "Pierre", was from Paris, France and the other, from what I heard was from Senégal, Africa. His name, from what I heard was "Nikko". They chatted away at the usual rapid cadence of French spoken in Quebec. They were certainly oblivious to my understanding what they were saying. I was certainly talked about and must have become flushed at several points in their lusty conversation. I have to admit that the talk was turning me on a bit. I remember thinking that my husband would be surprised that night.

This went on through most of my lunch when one of my husband's coworkers stopped at their table and talked (in English) as if they were old friends. It seems that they were skipping one of the meetings but, from what I heard, they were coming to the special evening being arranged later that day. My only thought was that I would possibly see these men later tonight.

As I was walking away, passing their table, their comments turned to what a nice ass I had and what they would like to do with it and me. Then I could not hear them as I was out of range. I had to admit that some of the talk was now turning me on more than just a bit. It was nice to know that at my age, I still turned heads. When I got back to the room, Robert was there so I told him about my day including some of the comments I overheard two strangers making while at lunch.

All he said was that he was not the least bit surprised as I had turned his head since the day we met. He gave me a big hug and as his usual way, his hands roamed my body especially my bottom, which he has always loved. I was getting very turned on but knew I had to wait until after the party when I could attack him.

CHAPTER II

The First Night Banquet

A s I was trying to decide what to wear he suggested that I wear my sexiest outfit, which was a purple silk wraparound, which showed more cleavage than I usually like to show, explaining that he was proud of his sexy wife and wanted to be envied to be with such a "babe". I told him he was crazy as I was definitely "middle aged" and had long since passed the "babe" age. All he said was "Wanna bet". When I asked him what he meant he told me that he had had several comments from his coworkers over the years who, he said, had all agreed that he was one "lucky son-of-a-gun". He admitted that this was not a direct quote but close. I knew what he meant.

Then he laid out on the bed a new purple (my favorite color) bra and panty set, a garter and stockings, and the soft silk wraparound elegant dress. It also had a long slit up one side. I was quite surprised. I knew he liked it when others liked what they saw but this seemed over the top.

He knew that looking sexy made me feel sexy. While dressing I was becoming more turned on by the minute. I asked him if he was sure he wanted me to dress this sexily and did he want to do it now, before the party? He thought we should wait even as I didn't want to. "Just wait till I get you back in the room", I said.

The party actually was fun. I met many people and was having a great time. After a typically great Montréal dinner the entertainment was surprisingly good. There was a pair of comedians who reminded me of "Bowser and Blue", who were the rage when I lived in Montréal. They were making fun of Canada and Quebec, singing in both English and French and "Franglais." There were also astonishing magicians, and a montage of movie snippets of Hollywood movies showing the many scenes shot in

Montréal especially Old Montréal. It was all in all a quite fantastic and entertaining evening.

As we moved into the large hall set up for dancing, I spotted my restaurant admirers, Pierre and Nikko, talking with a group, some of whom Robert and I recognized. I protested a bit but followed Robert over to this group, which turned out to be the award winners for company improvements in a variety of areas. They were the honored guests.

From there we drifted off to find a table with friends. Can you guess who was at the table next to ours, Yes, my admirers (lusty as they were) somehow were seated with a group of four including one who was apparently the wife of the third man. I managed to drag my husband to the dance floor, which is sometimes a chore as he is not into dancing. We danced a set before he pleaded to go back for a drink. We were joined by another couple and had a great time talking about everything.

I excused myself to go to the ladies room and saw Pierre and Nikko walking just ahead of me and I could not help but overhear them speaking in French about women and their possibilities for the evening. They stopped to talk to someone and as I passed them I overheard them saying that things were looking up as the "babe" who they saw at the restaurant just passed and she was at the next table. "I sure would like to get into her panties" and "Let's see what we can set up" I heard them say as I passed.

As I came out, Nikko was near the door as if he was waiting for someone. He greeted me in perfect English and asked how I was enjoying the evening. I smiled and told him that it was excellent. Then I asked him if he worked for the same company as my husband. He told me that yes, he was the head of the African office in Dakar and it was the first major job he had after his graduation from Princeton 10 years ago. He then told me that I was the best looking woman at the show.

What a flatterer but he was not so bad looking himself. He was an imposing 6+ footer and one of the most handsome black men I had seen in some time. I asked him where he was from and he told me "French West Africa" and more specifically "Senégal" or more properly "Sénégal". When he asked me if he could walk me back to my table I said yes. This was my first mistake.

Back at the table Nikko told my husband he was delivering his wife safely so she would not be accosted, as she was so attractive. A beaming Robert graciously said thanks and offered him a chair at our table. Nikko immediately accepted. Nikko promptly ordered a round of drinks, which should have sent a warning but did not. When Nikko asked Robert if he could have the honor of a dance with his wife, what could he say. So, there I was following a man who I knew was interested in me physically and sexually to the dance floor with my husband's innocent blessing.

CHAPTER III

The Seduction

A s we danced and he held me firmly but not inappropriately at least at first. By the third dance – a slow one – he was as close as anyone can be. I was almost mesmerized as his hands ran up and down my back going lower each time. I admit this was turning me on as Robert and I had not had sex for several days. Despite being turned on and becoming a bit wet I moved his hands each time I felt them near or on my bottom. He persisted and I eventually relented and he sure knew how to massage a bottom. This was my second mistake.

With the unspoken permission to fondle my bottom he then turned his attention to my breasts, which he discreetly played with, despite my moving his hands several times and telling him, "Please, No". He alternated between my buttocks and my sensitive breasts. As good as this was feeling, I was almost relieved when the set was over and he led me back to our table as I was starting to get wet between my legs.

Robert was talking with Pierre who he introduced me to. I learned (what I already knew) that Pierre was from Paris, France. It seems Pierre had brought over a round of drinks and Robert was feeling no pain. Nikko warmly thanked my husband for the opportunity to dance with the "most beautiful woman on the floor". Robert was basking in these compliments. Now Pierre said it was only fair that he also be allowed to show off Roberts "beautiful wife" so how could I refuse.

On the dance floor Pierre was most charming and funny having me laughing most of the time. As much as a gentleman as he was early, during the slowest dance I once again found my bottom the center of his attention. When I asked him not to handle me as I was a happily married woman he said "but of course" and "please forgive me" but in less than a minute my bottom was again fondled. He then told me that I was beautiful and asked me quietly in my ear the color of my panties.

As I had not planned on him seeing them, I responded that "they are purple, if you must know" to which he exclaimed "the most sexy color". I know I blushed but with this familiarity, I sort of gave up resisting as his fondling continued and expanded. This was my third mistake but it sure did feel good.

We returned to the table and there was only my husband and Nikko who it seemed to have become best of friends. The drinks had obviously been flowing as I saw signs in my husband that he was near his limit. Because of dancing and choice I had had little to drink but none-the-less enough so that I laughed at all the jokes and risqué remarks. At this point it was obvious to me where this was headed but I didn't know how to stop it. My only thought was to try, as I was not interested in where this seemed to be going.

I asked my husband to dance but for the first time I could remember he said he was too tired but to go ahead as he would dance with me back in the room. With that, Nikko held out his hand, took mine and led me, almost reluctantly, to the dance floor. As I looked back, Pierre was setting up another round of drinks. I knew then that I would be fucked by this man before the night was over and my resistance was clearly fading as he was an attractive man.

This time, Nikko held me even closer and as we danced to the other side of the floor, his hands became more and more bold. I managed to say "please, no, I am a married woman" but it hardly made a difference. He started dancing with one of his legs between mine and so close that I soon could easily feel his very large cock pressing into my stomach.

I had had just enough to drink to lower my inhibitions so thought I would enjoy the attentions as I knew I would never go further or to our room without my husband. feel his very large cock and I really did enjoy his playing with my bottom.

At one point in a slow number he leaned down and kissed me.

Much to my surprise I found myself kissing him back. This was mistake number four. From that point on I felt his strength again and again and was becoming more and more aroused. At one point I felt my dress being raised and his hand on my bare skin above my panties. I tried to pull away but he held me firmly.

I looked around and we were at the edge of the dance floor and no one could see what he was doing so I relaxed to enjoy the feelings. I felt guilty and wicked but had to admit he was turning me on so I let him play. Play he did and soon his hands were all over my bare bottom kneading and stroking. I looked up at him and managed a "please, no, we shouldn't be doing this, I am a happily married woman and I love my husband" but he silenced me with a long kiss while he exposed my nearly bare bottom to the empty section behind me.

I guess this is when I gave in to my desire and long time fantasy of wondering what sex with a black man would be like. He then turned me around when the last song of the set came on (and when the lights were dimmed) and one hand moved around to my tummy and down to my now wet sex. Ever so gently he teased my clitoris until I was very close to an orgasm. With his other hand he played with my sensitive breasts. I just leaned my head back on his chest and went with the flow and the feelings of arousal.

By now I was breathing hard and almost to the point of no return. He then took one of my hands and placed it between us and I now clearly felt what I had indirectly felt on my belly. I couldn't believe how long he was and how hard he was as I touched and squeezed his cock throughout its length. Just before the song ended he removed his hand and lowered my dress and we were back to normal – just dancing around the room.

When the set ended and we were heading back to the table I told him that, "I enjoyed our dance very much and at another time this might have gone further". I secretly wished that it was possible but regaining my composure, I reasoned that it was impossible.

Back at the table, Robert was almost passed out. I went to him and told him that it was late and we needed to get back to our room. When he could hardly stand, Pierre and Nikko quickly stepped in to help steady him and offered to help him back to our room. With a sigh, I accepted their offer. This was mistake number five.

CHAPTER IV

And Then...

S peaking to each other in French, I heard, what I had suspected, that Pierre had supplied the booze to get Robert tipsy and Nikko told Pierre that I was ready and hot and he was sure that I would be his before the night was over. He could hardly wait. I told them where our room was and followed behind wondering what was going to happen and how I could get out of it or even if I wanted to get out of it. Talk about conflict! When we arrived they helped Robert to the davenport and made him comfortable. He was very soon sound asleep and I knew he was out for the night.

I thanked Pierre and Nikko for their help and started walking to the door. Pierre was the first to thank me for the dance and give me a long kiss while running his hands all over my body. When the kiss broke, I then turned to Nikko and in the process of his kissing me we moved back into the room. As he started again fondling my bottom and breasts I managed to say, "no, we shouldn't be doing this, I am a married woman and my husband is right here".

As I said this, I knew I was his for the taking, he simple continued kissing and playing with me. I again felt my dress being raised and his hands on my bottom. This time, while kissing me fervently, he lowered my panties to my stocking tops. Then I felt him undoing the ties of my dress. When I started to protest again, he covered my mouth with kisses and told me, "Relax, everything will be OK, your husband is out for the night and you deserve some fun."

I looked over at Robert and sure enough he was out cold. The next step was that Nikko slipped my dress off my shoulders letting it fall to the floor. Still in Nikko's embrace, I felt my panties being lowered and bra strap being undone by Pierre, who I had almost forgotten. Why I did not stop him or protest more, I do not know but here I was in an embrace with a very handsome black man and was naked except for my garter belt and stockings. I knew I should not be doing this but could not, and did not want to, stop it.

His hands were all over my body and I was past the point of no return. He then put my hand on his hardening cock and told me to "Get it out". Without much hesitation I lowered his zipper and fished out what I had been curious about all night. While feeling it's warmth and considerable size, his hands were busy undoing his belt and removing his shirt and tie.

It was not long before we were both naked except for my stockings and garter belt. One last time, I said that "we really should not be doing this, I love my husband". He then said "What we are doing does not change that at all" as he led me to the bed – kissing and fondling me the whole time.

He laid me on the bed and started kissing me all over ending up at my very wet pussy. Wow, he was a master at stimulating erotic sensations in the area. In almost minutes I had my first orgasm of the night. As I was coming down, I saw that Pierre was also naked and had a nice cock at full staff. Nikko then asked me if I wanted to stop. I was hooked and he knew it. I just said, "God, no, I shouldn't be doing this but now I really want you inside me."

He then moved up straddling my chest with his cock between my breasts until his very large and long cock was before my face till I could do nothing else but try to take it in and kiss it. I like oral sex with my husband but this was totally new. First, he was large with a considerably sized bulbous velvety soft and spongy head and second the taste was very different and almost delicious. Then I felt lips kissing my legs and soon a tongue licking my very wet and sensitive pussy. This had to be Pierre but I cared not who it was as it sure felt good.

This went on until I had another large orgasm from the ministrations on my clitoris from the new tongue. After that, Nikko moved to lie next to me and rolled over on top of me and asked again what I wanted him to do. "You know what I want", I said. "Tell me", he then said. By this time I wanted him in me badly and I knew what he wanted me to say so I said "I want you to fuck me silly with that big black cock, and do it now".

He grinned from ear to ear, nodded, aimed his cock at the entrance of my vagina and slowly entered. He reached places never before touched and I was in total bliss. I could not resist "Oh, Fuck, that feels so good – Please don't stop" knowing that he had no intention of stopping.

Nikko was patient and slow but as he entered me I must have had three orgasms or maybe it was one continuous orgasm. Once in, he rode me like nothing I had ever experienced. I had to put my arm over my mouth to mute the screams as the last thing I wanted was for Robert to wake up and he was just a few feet away. Nikko's staying power was incredible as he fucked me like nothing I had experienced or dreamed of as possible. I was hooked and I think he knew that I would take everything he could give.

At one point he pulled out and got me to the position on my hands and knees where he could enter me from behind, which is one of my favorite positions. In this position it seemed he could penetrate me even further than the usual missionary position. He was also in a better position to play with my breasts and occasionally rub my hypersensitive clitoris. It sure felt good.

Soon Pierre got in position to present his cock to my gasping mouth. His was not as large as Nikko's and the head was quite a bit smaller but sure tasted good. Having a cock in two openings at one time was definitely a first but I was too far-gone to care and actually it felt very sexy. First Pierre filled or rather overfilled my mouth with his tasty cum and then, several orgasms later, I felt Nikko tense up and increase his speed and depth prior to his cuming. Nikko unloaded squirt after squirt and with each contraction I had another wave of pure pleasure flood my senses. My fantasy of having sex with a well-hung black man had been realized in spades.

Nikko, after several minutes, finally softened and pulled out only to be replaced almost immediately by a new hard cock, which had to be Pierre's. His was shorter but fatter and much to my surprise, I continued to have periodic orgasms. Of course Pierre lasted a very long time as he had just cum in my mouth. When he finally came, I was one very satisfied well-fucked lady.

We all rested a bit until I sort of came back to the present and realized that my husband was still in the room and could wake up anytime. I jumped out of bed, gathered my clothes and told them it was great but they should leave before Robert awakens. They pulled me into the bathroom, which I was OK with as I certainly needed a shower.

Once in the shower somehow I found myself being fucked again but surely was not complaining. After the shower, I knew they wanted more but I convinced them to leave as I was becoming increasingly anxious about Roberts awakening while they were still here. To get them to go, I even promised a repeat performance another day while thinking it would be impossible.

They dressed and left after kissing and fondling me one last time. I was almost ready to do it again but thought better of it as guilt became the dominant thought. To get them out, I promised to find time in the next few days to see them. As they were walking down the hall I had to chuckle as I overheard Nikko saying to Pierre "Wow, would you have believed the night would turn out so perfect?" Then they were gone. I locked the door, breathed a sigh of relief that my husband had not awakened to see me get so well-fucked, and turned my attention to Robert.

He was hard to arouse but finally I was able to get him partly up, undressed and in bed. After I was certain he was OK I got into bed. It was then that the pangs of guilt became overwhelming and I cried myself to a fitful sleep as close to my husband as possible. In my mind I kept wondering if he could forgive me as I knew I must tell him at least part of what happened.

CHAPTER V

The Confession

Robert awoke before me and had ordered room service before he tenderly and with apologies got me up. He asked me what happened and how he got to the room, as he must have drunk too much and he didn't remember anything past sometime at the dance. He asked for my forgiveness and apologized profusely for ruining my night. I hugged him and told him that it was I who had to apologize and that I hoped he did not hate me and could forgive me for what happened and what I did. I started crying in his arms.

So I told him, between tears, about what I had heard Nikko and Pierre talking about in French at lunch and at the evening party and most of what happened on the dance floor where they, despite my trying to fend them off, fondled me the best they could to turn me on and how I sensed that they purposefully saw to it that you were drunk to the point of passing out and that they knew that by helping you back to our room that they could then try to seduce me.

My dear husband stopped me at that point and asked if Nikko had, indeed, succeeded in seducing me reminding me that that had been a long time fantasy and he could hardly be angry but only wished he had been awake to watch. After I did not respond immediately he asked me how it was and if I had an enjoyable time. God, I love this man. By now my tears were one of joy as I told him about the encounter with Nikko and Pierre.

By the time I was done I noticed he had a raging hard-on and as I too was becoming increasingly horny relating the events of the previous evening we were soon in a passionate embrace and screwing like horny teenagers. We both came much quicker than usual and with a great deal of passion.

After that we again went over the seduction and my feelings.

I related that I thought Nikko and Pierre had played me like an instrument but that the sex was fantastic. Yes, it had been a fantasy but not one I ever planned on living. Would I do it again? I doubted it but he was good and we were out of town and I did say that they had asked me for more time. We ended up making love again and him telling me to do what I wanted with the proviso that I tell him every detail, or better, let him watch.

With that he got up and dressed, as he had to get to a seminar. I told him that I planned to go to the gym for a workout and to clear my head and would see him for lunch. After he left I felt a lot better about what had happened and wondered if or when the next opportunity might present itself.

CHAPTER VI

And Again...

I completed a rather strenuous workout ignoring the looks and comments by several men who were also in the gym room. As I was heading back to our room I saw Nikko get off the elevator and walk toward me. I stopped and wondered what would happen. Nikko stopped at a room, opened the door and went in. Somewhat relieved and suspecting that he had not seen me I proceeded to the elevators. When I reached the door of the room he just entered, it was open and he was just inside waving me in. Guiltily, I looked down the halls and seeing no one, I walked in and into his arms.

He asked if I had been working out which he must have guessed from my dress and that he was excited to see me. We kissed warmly and he asked me if everything was OK. I told him that Robert slept well and was pleased that he and Pierre helped him back to the room as he must have drunk more than is his usual limit. Then I said that I had to get to my room to shower and clean up as I had a rather good workout and felt sweaty.

Without more words he picked me up and carried me into the room. When he stopped he held me in his arms until I could feel is growing cock pressing into my stomach. Sensing his hardening cock, he said "Look what you do to me". He stepped back and just started to undress. I stood there unable to move as I watched his growing erection, which was getting me excited. When he was naked he came over to me and pulled down my sweatpants and lifted my top over my head with no resistance from me. I was now as naked as he was. I knew what was going to happen and I was ready and willing.

Nikko then took me in his arms and kissed me as passionately as he had the night before. All the while stroking my back, buttocks, labia, breasts and whatever else he could reach. I also was active feeling his hardening cock with the very large head and large testicles. Without his asking, I kissed my way down to his cock and kneeling on the carpet, I took it in as far as I could vowing to myself to taste his cum. A surprisingly short time later amid his Ohoos and Ahhas, I felt his cock contracting and my mouth being filled with squirt after squirt of his very delicious semen.

Next we hit the bed and wasted no time in coupling. It was as good as it had been last night but with very much less guilt for some unknown reason. I had so many orgasms that I lost track as I tried to return thrust for thrust and made an effort to contract my vaginal muscles with each stroke. Nikko kept saying that I was the best screw he had had for years. When Nikko finally came I was exhausted.

Snuggling up to him in his strong arms I actually fell asleep for an hour or so. When I awoke and looked at the clock I had less than an hour to meet my husband for lunch. Realizing this I gave Nikko a quick kiss and told him that I had to go to meet my husband for lunch and would see him later, adding, "Promise". Back in our room I took the fastest shower on record and also quickly dressed so I would not be late.

I arrived at the hotel restaurant a few minutes before my husband and as always, when he found me he greeted me with a kiss and a warm hug. Just as we sat down who do I see being led to the next table but Nikko, Pierre, and a couple of men I did not recognize. When Robert saw them he hailed them over and in thanking them, told them that I related to him that it was they who so graciously helped me get him back to our room.

He apologized for having had a bit too much to drink and not even remembering. It was all smiles around as Nikko, Pierre and I shared a knowing look. Nikko then invited Robert and I to a small party at the West African Trade Commission consulate that evening at 7 o'clock to which Robert readily agreed.

After they had gone on, Robert turned to me and said, with a wink, that I sure knew how to pick them as they both seemed young and vigorous. "Yes, they are sure vigorous," I said, "But too much for a "middle-aged" lady as a steady diet, I much prefer you." To which I added, "Also, just so you know, I did not pick them". We both had a laugh over that one. He thought it was nice of them to invite us but added he knew it was because of me. I added that going to the consulate would most likely mean that I wouldn't have any stories to tell him. With that he gave me a kiss and we parted ways with plans to meet back in the room.

I spent the afternoon going through the many antique stores and a couple of museums, which were all within walking distance of our hotel. Got back to our room and was in the midst of a long luxurious bath when Robert came back. We exchanged tales of what we did that afternoon, which certainly was interesting but not exciting.

I sensed that Robert was expecting me to have been with Nikko but I told him that as good as it had been it just may not happen but if it did I would try to set it up so he could be around. I proposed that we do a repeat of the first night except he not pass out – just pretend to. He then told me that this talk had made his cock very hard, which confirmed to me his acceptance of this idea.

CHAPTER VII

A New Adventure

I dressed more conservatively except I chose my leopard print panties and bra as we were going to a gathering of mostly French speaking people from Africa. We arrived at the 'Trade Commission Consulate', which had a sign indicating that it was the "Afrique occidentale française" trade commission and quickly saw that, as white Anglophones, we were certainly in the minority. Nikko spotted us and immediately came to greet us. He centered on Robert taking him around to meet many of those present. I followed along like the good wife.

I quickly noticed the exquisite photographs of Africa adorning the walls and commented on their beauty to no one in particular as we came upon each new one. In addition to the photos, there were large clearly African carvings of animals and people. They were also exquisite. I asked what the material was and was told that mostly they were done in Ebony. Finally we stopped before a most imposing figure as tall as Nikko and built similarly who we were introduced to (in French) as the Chief Consular General Jean-Claude Brunot. He spoke very little English so Nikko did the translating. He told Robert that any friends of Nikko were very welcome in his house. When he shook my hand he said (in French) that you (looking at Nikko) were certainly right as I was beautiful and sexy beyond description.

I know I blushed but when Nikko 'translated' he said that the Head of the Trade Commission said that it was a pleasure to welcome me also to his house. As we were starting to walk away he looked at Nikko and said, in French, that he could hardly wait. At the time, I wondered what that meant but it did cross my mind that it involved sex.

Nikko walked us around the Consular offices until we came to a room, which must have been a game room with chess sets on each of 4 tables. Even I saw the beauty of the hand carved chess pieces. Robert was in love and told Nikko that chess was his passion. Nikko brightened up and asked him if he would like a game or two with one of their chess experts. Robert asked me if I minded to which I said absolutely not. I watched the game for a while and whispered to Robert that I was going to look at the Photos and sculptures adorning the walls and hallways.

As I was walking down the hall, Nikko came up and asked if I wanted an escort / tour guide as there were photos and carvings everywhere. I thought that that would be nice but first I needed to find the ladies room. He led me to the room and I went in. When I came out I asked him what the second odd-looking toilet was for. He chuckled and asked me if I had never heard of a Bidet.

I had heard the name but did not know exactly what they were for. It was his turn to blush a bit as he told me that ladies could clean themselves out as the device cleaned the genital and anal area and could give a vaginal douch. Learn something every day.

As we stopped to look at each photograph we were joined by Jean-Claude. Nikko told him (in French of course) that I was a photo buff and was asking questions about the photos as we went. So, as I understood French, I got both what Jean-Claude was saying and what Nikko translated. There were things, however, that Jean-Claude said that Nikko did not translate. These referred to me and my body and then I heard Nikko telling Jean-Claude about how good I was in bed. When Jean-Claude said again that he could hardly wait, I knew something was up. What I felt at that moment was a bit of guilt but more excitement and anticipation.

Then Jean Claude said that my husband would be kept busy for almost an hour as he so instructed his chess expert. All this Nikko translated as banal thoughts about the consulate and the Photos. When I heard this, I decided to go along for the ride, which I knew I was going to get. I could feel myself getting very wet, as the conversation in French was very erotic.

It was a strange feeling hearing and understanding two men

talking about what they intended to do with me as they spoke to each other not knowing that I understood every word. As they spoke, I was getting wetter by the minute. We entered a larger room, which appeared to be a lounge with many photos on the wall and carvings on tables. I heard the door click when we were in the room so knew, for sure, things were about to happen. As I was looking at one photo, Nikko came up behind me and put his arms around me for a hug and to play with my breasts. I turned to him and we kissed.

Soon we were standing in the room near a large leather sofa and Nikko was turning me to face him and was rubbing whatever he could get his hands on. I had almost forgotten Jean-Claude but, in French, he was encouraging Nikko to get me hot and ready and Nikko was telling him that it wouldn't be long now.

Nikko started to pull my skirt up from behind and stroke my panty-covered butt. Behind me I heard Jean-Claude exclaim over the pattern of my panties and encourage Nikko to go further. Then Nikko undid the buttons and zipper of my skirt and let it fall to the floor. For the effect – as at that time I did not care - I said to Nikko, "But we are not alone". His lips stopped my talking as he started to undo the buttons on my blouse.

Then I felt new hands at the waistband of my panties and their slow removal down my legs. I heard Jean-Claude exclaim "Tres Belle Fesse" which I knew was what a 'gorgeous ass' I had. Now I was turned on so I reached Nikko's belt and loosened it so I could revel in the feel and warmth of his stupendous cock.

As I was doing this I felt another cock between my legs from the rear. I looked around and Jean-Claude was now naked and smiling. All this time Jean-Claude and Nikko were talking sexily about what they were seeing, doing and would soon be doing. This talk was getting me wetter by the minute. Nikko bent me over the couch and from behind, nuzzled my vulva and was soon using his tongue on everything from my clitoris down to and including my anus as only he could. God that felt good. I did not want him to ever stop.

When I finally opened my eyes, there was Jean-Claude standing with his erect cock inches from my face. And what a cock it was. The bulbous head was even much larger than Nikko's. Nikko then told me to suck him good as he told Jean-Claude, in French, that I was the best cock sucker he had ever known, which I gladly did as I was that horny and wanted to please Nikko. The head of his cock was so large that it alone filled my oral cavity but the spongy soft texture and delicious taste was something else.

Nikko brought me to at least two orgasms before he stood up and asked me what I wanted him to do next as he was pointing his hard cock at my vaginal entrance. I knew what he wanted me to say and I was too far-gone to not say "Please, Please fuck me with your big black cock, I need to feel you inside me". Then I head Nikko translate that to Jean-Claude who's cock I was now sucking and licking as best I could. He, hearing what Nikko was saying promptly came when I got his cock back in my mouth. His copious sperm tasted good.

Nikko then told Jean-Claude (in French of course) that I was the best "Piece of ass" he had gotten in a long time and it was his pleasure to share it with his good friend. Nikko had amazing staying power and drove me crazy with numerous thundering orgasms before he finally came deep in my vagina. When he pulled out I just stayed in the position bent over the plush couch back until Jean-Claude took me by the hand and led me around to the front of the couch.

Before he did what I knew he was going to do, which was to lay me on the couch, he put his big arms around me and felt every inch of my naked body. He put fingers in my vagina, played with my clitoris, put a finger in my rectum, and played with my sensitive breasts. All this fondling aroused me to the point that I wanted him in me now. He was not the only one active in that regard. I enjoyed playing with his large cock and making it hard again. He and Nikko had to be close to 10 inches long and very thick.

All the while he was doing these things he was talking to Nikko in French about how great I was and thanking him for the gift of a real women - a real sexy woman. Finally he let go and I just laid down on the large couch, spread my legs and invited him down. Nikko told him that I was ready to be screwed by a real man, which he did not need further urging to do. As large as he was, he was gentle until he was all the way in and pounding away.

I was determined to make Nikko proud of me so, in my newfound and needy sexuality, I gave as well as I got. I squeezed his cock with my vaginal muscles with each stroke and met him stroke for stroke until I was exhausted. I repeated "Fuck me good" several times which Nikko translated as "You are the best", which Jean-Claude clearly liked to hear. He could not get over this and was describing how good a screw I was to Nikko who in turn would translate some of what I had heard.

In the end, he too flooded my vagina with spasm after spasm of his cum. When he came out I took his cock in my mouth as much as I could and licked it clean. That later act he just could not get over. He praised me to Nikko as to what he had experienced and I am sure I blushed deeply as he described what had happened and what he did to me and wanted to do with me in the future. Nikko did not repeat most of what he said but I did not care as I had done Nikko proud.

CHAPTER VIII

The Afthermath is Something

At about this time reality came in and I told Nikko that we had better get dressed and get back to the chess room before I was missed. Little did he know that my husband would hear at least part of what I just experienced. When I got up I started leaking from my vagina so Nikko said this is what the bidet was made for and I could clean myself there. I slipped on my clothes without panties and made my way to the ladies room and got, for the first time a gushing douche, which actually felt good. When I came out, Nikko was waiting for me and walked me back to the game room.

We came in slowly while I kept looking at the photos. When we got to the table Robert was playing at, I noticed that he was still deep into his game and a crowd was watching ardently. Nikko asked some of the onlookers how the game was going and what he heard surprised even me. What I heard and what Nikko repeated was that Robert was very good indeed and was keeping the best they had at bay.

I was very proud of Robert and went over to let him know I was in the room but not divert his attention as it appeared that they were near the end. I put my head near his and whispered "I love you". He looked up and gave me the smile I love and said "Me too". I then told him that I would continue to look at the gorgeous photos and carvings but would not be far away.

Nikko and I walked out into the reception area and just sat down to talk. I had not realized that the sexual activity was so tiring. He told me that I was a real sport to be so nice to Jean-Claude but he wanted me again for himself. He also told me that Jean-Claude would give anything for another session. I told Nikko that I did it for him and because he made me very horny, but had to admit it was great. We talked about the time we had left and realized that in three days we would be on our way back to Cincinnati. Nikko then said that he would get to Cincinnati some how. We then heard a cheer coming from the game room and as people came out I heard that Robert had won.

When he came out of the room we got up and I greeted him with a warm hug congratulating him on his win. He was one proud and happy guy. As we were standing there, Jean-Claude appeared and also congratulated Robert in very poor broken English and in French with Nikko translating he told him that he was welcome anytime as they often had tournaments.

The prize was usually a hand carved ebony chess set. I could tell the Richard was very happy and excited with this prospect. While he was beaming I heard Jean-Claude saying to Nikko that he wanted his help to find a way to get me back as he wanted to get into my panties again and again. Nikko just smiled and told him several times, "repose", which means 'relax' in English. A tingle ran through my sex knowing that something might happen like what I experienced earlier.

We then left in a cab of which there are many anytime in Montréal. Richard was a very happy person as he spent most of the way there telling me about the game and how he would like to own one of those chess sets. He then asked me about my tour of the Photos. I told him that there were many and they were very beautiful throughout the consulate and that Nikko had been my guide.

I looked him in the eye and said that the time was not all spent looking at pictures and carvings as I had again been naughty and we needed to talk. I gave him a big kiss and said "Can you tell?" He said, "Sure as I can taste it" and then "Oh, wow, tell me about it" he said with his full attention now to me.

I started by kissing him again and saying that I hope he was sure of what he said about it being OK with him if I experienced what was once my harmless fantasy. The reason, I told him, was because, "Now that I have actually had sex with a large black man I find myself wanting to do it again with Nikko even as I love you more than you could ever know." So I told him what happened - that Nikko led me into a room with a number of pictures but after we entered I heard the door shut and a latch clicked.

I sort of knew what would follow but I just could not resist his touch and fondling. So I described a bit of what happened but as I was getting wetter by the minute and I saw that Robert was getting an erection, I stopped and said let me finish telling you in our room. Then we arrived at the hotel.

We almost ran to the room and he excitedly asked me to continue while, at the same time he started undressing me telling me that he loved me even more and was excited for me and that he really did not mind as long as I shared the experiences. So, I told him about what happened with Nikko and that another person who I did not see had also entered me from behind and that the best part was that they continuously talked about what they were feeling and what they were going to do in French not knowing that I understood every word. This talk was very erotic and sensual and turned me on even more.

While I was talking Robert was all over me and with his tongue brought me to three orgasms and we then made love for hours. I told him that as much as I like to have sex with Nikko the difference between just "having sex" and "making Love" was very real. Finally exhausted I fell soundly asleep only to be awakened the next morning by my husbands tongue stimulating my clitoris.

After making passionate love again, we called room service and enjoyed the morning wrapped in conversation mostly about what we would do the remaining time in Montréal and how he could watch me get pleasure. I said I would try but I wasn't sure I wanted my husband to see me in such rapture.

Robert left with our usual plans to meet for lunch. I told him that my plans were to walk the familiar streets in downtown Montréal and maybe take a cab to Old Montréal or the Lachine Canal, which is always beautiful this time of year. I took a leisure bath and dressed in walking slacks and a light blouse. I did wear my red bra and panty set and had to admit erotic thoughts crossed my mind.

I was just about to leave when Robert called the room telling me that he had to cancel lunch and that he had seen Nikko and he told him that Consular Brunot had heard that I was favorably impressed with the photographs and carvings and wanted to see that I received a pair of photos of my choosing as sort of a reward for my (Roberts) winning at chess.

Robert then excitedly told me that he was invited back tomorrow night, which was the last free night of the conference for a small "invite only" chess tournament. He ended by telling me that Nikko would leave some contacts at the front desk for me to look at. He said he loved me and hoped I had a good day shopping and sight seeing or whatever else I found the time to do. He ended by saying, "I love you, enjoy".

CHAPTER IX

Again a Double

I was really not too surprised that when I reached the main counter who was standing there but Nikko. I greeted him, as one would do a friend in a hotel lobby. He told me that I looked great in the tan slacks. With that I became a bit self-conscious as I did think they were a bit tight. Nikko said he had a car ready and thought I would like to run over and see pictures larger than the contact sheets he had in hand. I said that I thought that would be OK so left following the imposing Nikko.

In the cab, Nikko kissed me passionately and ran his hands over my legs. This started my juices flowing but I was too nervous in a cab. This is because in Montréal, the cabs are open without dividers so the cabbie can hear and see everything very well. We soon reached the Trade Commission and were let in. Nikko, put his arms around me and said in my ear that he apologizes in advance that everyone speaks French and that he would do the best he could to translate for me.

Jean-Claude then came out of his office and seemed very pleased that I was here. He kissed me on each cheek, as is the French custom and welcomed me in broken English. In French he thanked Nikko again and again for keeping his promise to get me back. I then knew that I was going to get fucked by Jean-Claude again and whereas I actually was looking forward to what I knew was going to happen, a myriad of emotions raced through my mind. The main one, strangely, was making Nikko proud. Nikko reminded Jean-Claude about the photos, and told me that Jean-Claude wanted to first show me more photos and carvings that I would not have seen the last time I was there.

To Jean-Claude he said "Lets proceed with the tour and get to your private room." Jean-Claude verbalized his pleasure at what I was wearing and commented about my great bottom and what he was going to do with it and me. All this was in French and quietly so none of the staff could hear. This was actually starting to turn me on as I was coming to grips as to what I was sure was going to happen.

I had to smile to myself as Nikko would 'translate' for me comments not at all what Jean-Claude was saying or what were his responses. As we viewed beautiful and large photos lining the stairway going to the second floor, I had at least one hand and occasionally two fondling my bottom. The comments passing between my escorts made it clear that they were into "her fantastic ass" and how good she would look in the gift he had for me in his room. I was curious about this but knew, in general terms that I would find out soon enough.

At the end of the main hall on the second floor, I was escorted through a door into what was obviously a master bedroom. Amid talk of what the plans were, which did excite me a bit, I was shown new photos even more beautiful. In this room, many were of African women who had, in my view, really fantastic bodies. Most were scantily clothed or were in traditional African dress, so I was told.

Nikko pulled me into his arms for his usual deep kiss and his large hands making me horny. When he came up for air he told me to take care of Jean-Claude as I would him and that he was going to leave for a while if that was OK with me. I told him, I want you to stay but will do as you ask – only for you." With that I put my arms around his neck and gave him a deep sensual kiss.

Nikko led me over to the bed where I saw that there was a full lingerie set laid out. It was a very beautiful bra, panty and short kimono in a beautiful African print. He told me that these were a gift from Jean-Claude and he knew he would want me to model these garments. He kissed me again and then turned to Jean-Claude saying, in French, that she is all yours.

Jean-Claude profusely thanked Nikko and asked if I knew what to do. Nikko told him to ring him if he did not think I knew what he wanted. I told Nikko, that I gathered Jean-Claude wanted me to model this gift to which Nikko nodded and as he was leaving he again said, in French, she knows what to do and she is all yours. I'll be back when you call. Nikko gave me a quick kiss, and a pat on my bottom and quietly slipped out.

Jean-Claude then came over to me an enveloped me in his large arms, kissed me and said in very broken English that I did him great honor to return to his arms. He then pointed to the lingerie set on the bed and said "for you". It was gorgeous so I hugged him and said "thank you" and added "merci beacoup". With that he literally beamed, giving me an even bigger hug, and then gestured to the items on the bed. I noticed that he reached for a camera, which I saw was even better than the digital SRL that I have.

I knew that he wanted me to undress and put the new items on so I did slowly and as sexily as I could think of. First I unbuttoned my slacks and took them slowly off wiggling my bottom as I would normally and then carefully folding them on a nearby chair. Then I unbuttoned my blouse slowly and added it on top of my slacks. At this point Jean-Claude looked through the view-finder of the camera so I posed in a variety of poses to his obvious pleasure. I felt oddly very sexy, as I had never done anything like this before.

I then reached behind my back and undid my red bra and slid it off my shoulders. Finally, I lowered my red panties, which I noticed were rather wet. Looking at him, it was clear that his cock was uncomfortably large in his pants. He kept adjusting it as he made comments to no one in particular about what he was seeing and experiencing and how much he was enjoying himself. I had no idea that posing this way would be a turn-on to me but it certainly was.

He again aimed his camera and took a couple of pictures of me in the nude when something happened and he cursed, as he was not getting what he wanted. He came to me and gave me a big hug and motioned for me to sit down. Then to himself he said in French, "Now I am going to have to get Leon to help, damn". He went to the phone and dialed a number and asked for "Leon". In a bit I heard him say to the party he was talking to that he was to come quickly to his room as the camera may have jammed and he wanted to get some pictures of the woman he was with.

Very shortly there was a knock on the door and a very nice looking normal sized man came in with an even better camera. They spoke briefly in French and Leon came to me and in perfect English he softly said, "Please pardon this interruption, I am Leon Merlin, from The Gambia and the official photographer for the Sénégalese office of the French West Indies". "I hope my presence does not embarrass you and I will leave when I have the photos Mr Brunot wishes". Then he added with a nice smile, "Just pretend I am not here, I am very discrete". Then he told Jean-Claude, in French, basically what he told me and asked him what pictures he wanted.

Jean-Claude told him to get several shots of me without any clothes and then several with the lingerie set that was on the bed. I was at first very embarrassed with this stranger but his pleasant manner and perfect English with a hint of a British accent made me feel at ease. When he offered me his hand I got up and followed him to the area he wanted. He asked if I would mind posing in ways that Mr. Brunot would like.

I told him that I though he wanted me to "Look sexy" and I would do my best. He took dozens of shots in different poses and from different angles. I heard Jean-Claude tell him to get some shots of, "Her beautiful ass". This made Leon blush and when I asked him what Jean-Claude had said he told me something I do not recall but certainly was not what Jean-Claude had said. In any case I moved where he placed me and did feel sexy almost naked in front of two almost strangers one of whom would soon be fucking me.

When he told me that he thought he had enough of those, I walked over to the bed and slowly put on the new panties and bra and the short almost transparent top. When I was dressed in the new bra and panty set, I did a few turns to Ooohs and Ahaas, which did not need translation. Leon, with coaching he did not need, took even more pictures of me in the new panty and bra set with and without the diaphanous kimono. Leon, told me that I was beautiful to photograph. He also said that he heard that I too was a photographer.

I went over to the full-length mirror and agreed that this set was beautiful and made me look truly sexy. Jean-Claude came to me again and could not get enough of looking and feeling my body. All of this was making me very horny. Jean-Claude then turned to Leon and thanked him for this big favor and he would get the photos later. Leon then left saying goodbye to me and he hoped he would see me again.

I then saw Jean-Claude starting to undress himself and he was soon as naked as I had been a few moments before. Knowing what was going to happen I started to undress again as I did not want this new gift to be soiled. Once naked I first attended to his monstrous growing cock with the very large soft and velvety head, I kneeled on the plush carpet and tried my best to again take his organ in my mouth and even tried to get it down my throat.

As good as he tasted, at best I could only get two or three inches in and still had room for both my hands and could not get them completely around his burgeoning organ. I did use my tongue to his great pleasure. While I was doing that he played with my breasts including lightly pinching my sensitive nipples. What also was turning me on was feeling his very muscular buns and back and very large testicles.

He then picked me up as if I were a doll and carried me to the large bed. He bent me over the edge and from behind he poised to enter me. Both of us were well lubricated so it wasn't long before I felt him inch his way in. Almost immediately I had the first of many orgasms. I reached back to spread my bottom cheeks to facilitate his entry. Soon I was almost screaming with pleasure and, as well, Jean-Claude was more vocal than the last time and repeated over and over, in French, what a good fuck I was and how he loved to fuck white women and especially those with great asses.

I do not know how long he pounded into me from behind but it seemed very long. I sensed that he was quickening his stroke and becoming more verbal so knew his climax was close. When it came his cock swelled and pulsed almost violently, which brought me to another thundering orgasm. He collapsed on top of me exhausted.

A few minutes later he pulled out of my vagina and I turned to lick him clean. That accomplished he lifted me to the bed where we lay in each others arms for a period of time long enough to settle both of us a bit. I reached over and found him almost hard again so went down to lick and suck it back to life, as I knew he wanted to do it again. As if I were a feather he lifted me so we were in the 69 position. Wow could he ever use his large tongue. He paid attention to every erotic area from my clitoris to my anal opening. In no time I was more than ready so I turned around and lay on my back next to him thinking I did not need to tell him what to do next. It was then that I saw that above the bed in the canopy was a large full-length mirror.

Jean-Claude rolled over taking care not to put all of his weight on me and with my help we were soon screwing like the first time. I gave as good as I got contracting my vaginal muscles with each stroke and physically meeting him on each stroke to drive his cock further and further. It was interesting and a great turn on to see in the mirror his buttock muscles contracting with each stroke. We did it in this position for what seemed like a long time and then he rolled over so I was on top and rode him until I was exhausted.

I think we both rested a bit but urgency again took over and we went back at it. I was having a climax every few minutes and with my last one I felt Jean-Claude lift his buttocks at an increasing rate. Then he came, triggering a final one from me. Wow that was a sexual marathon, the likes of which I had never before experienced with a cock like I had never seen before.

We were both exhausted so it was not surprising that I, and I guess we, fell asleep. When I awoke, I looked at the clock on the wall and was surprised to see that I had had sex and had been in bed with this very large black man for almost 4 hours. I certainly felt satisfied sexually and more than glad that the lunch with Robert had been cancelled.

Shortly Jean-Claude got up and showed me to the bathroom where I saw and again used the bidet. Then we showered with Jean-Claude washing and soaping every inch of my body. I collected my sexy gift, dressed and went on with the tour as if nothing had happened. We were met by Nikko on the way down the stairs.

As we walked around 'looking' at more photos and carvings, Jean-Claude and Nikko jabbered away in French. J-C thanked Nikko again and again for the opportunity to take me to bed again as he had a fantastic time and a great screw. When we got down stairs, Jean-Claude laid out a number of framed African Scenery and animal photos and three very nice ebony carvings for me to choose those I would like to have. I chose two photos and one carving of an elephant but asked Nikko to ask Jean-Claude to hold them until I came back with my husband as he would not have know that I was here. Guess, I gave him another opening and what he told Nikko even I blushed at.

CHAPTER X

Cell Phone Usefulness

N ikko returned to the hotel with me and when the elevator reached his floor he just put his arm around me and led me out of the elevator. I knew what he had in mind but said that I really should get back to the room as I expected my husband to call. After I said this, I realized it was a weak reason so I did not resist as he just continued to his room with his hand on my bottom. I really hope no one would see this from behind us.

Once in his room Nikko wasted no time hugging and kissing me while telling me that he really wanted me. I had to admit that he didn't have to convince me that much as his kisses and fondling of my bottom and breasts and cupping my sex with his knowing hands. He then started to undress me saying that he wanted to see if Jean-Claude was accurate in the color of my panties. I asked him what he heard and he said "red". "Well', I said, "I guess you are just going to have to see to know if this is correct". When I was down to my panties and bra he stepped back to admire what he saw and started to undress. As he was undressing I heard my cell phone ring.

I sort of panicked and telling Nikko to be very quiet I went to my purse to get and answer it. I saw that it was my husband so told Nikko who it was and to shhhh. I answered it cheerfully with "Hi hon, miss you". Robert asked how was my day and if I had enjoyed shopping and did I get to Old Montréal. "So many questions", I said, "will have to tell you about my day when I see you but the walk along the Lachine canal was stupendous". "How is it going? When are you done?" I queried. He told me that it should be a couple of hours and he then asked if I got the contact prints and had I chosen the ones I wanted. I said "Yes, and I saw Nikko who told me that a car had been arranged this evening when we were ready."

"Did you see Nikko?", he asked. "Yes, at the hotel", I said.

"Are you with him now?" he asked. "Yes", I answered. "Are you in his room?", he asked". "Yes", I answered. "Are you thinking of fooling around?", he asked. "Maybe", was my reply. I could tell he was excited when he then asked me a series of questions that only needed a yes or no answer. When he said, "Will you leave the phone on and let me hear you?, I said "Yes, of course" but admitted to myself some anxiety about that.

He then told me to not press the end-call button and put the phone on the bedside table and enjoy. He ended by saying I love you" to which I replied "I love you too, honey, see you later. Bye now". I did as he said and turned to Nikko who was very naked. I told him that I had better keep the phone close in case my husband called again which he said he would when he was on the way to the room.

I knew that for Robert to know what was going on without seeing that I would have to be more verbal that usual. So, when Nikko came to me and enveloped me in his arms, I exclaimed how good he felt. When Nikko stroked and fondled by breasts and bottom I squealed in delight. I even commented about how big and hard he was and that I could hardly wait to taste him and feel his large head in my mouth, which I did as noisily as I could. It was not long before Nikko came in my mouth with equally loud comments as to how good my mouth felt on his cock.

After that we lay on the bed and I directed the conversation to our first time and how good he made me feel and how surprised I was at what happened as I had never before stepped out of my marriage. Nikko exclaimed that it was his honor to be the first and as I was stroking his cock back to life he told me what he was going to do with me in the next hour or so. He asked me how I wanted him and I said "Every which way but let's start with my favorite position".

As I got on my hands and knees on the bed I made sure I commented on how hard he had become and, of course, I moaned extra loud as he entered me causing at least two orgasms before he was all the way in. Once in I said what may not have been needed if we had been alone. It was "Oh, you are so big and fill me up so much, I do not know if I can handle it".

Of course I knew that I could and would. As he started to fuck me as only he could, I moaned to frequent orgasms and said repeatedly "Fuck me with that big cock – please don't stop". In my mind, I pictured my husband going wild with excitement.

After some time and many orgasms he somehow rotated our bodies without removing his cock until I was on my back trying to keep up with him stroke for stroke. God, it felt good and I let him know that. I knew I would miss him but did not want to say that with the phone so close. In this position his cock more often rubbed my clitoris so I continued to have loud orgasms. I soon felt his cock expanding as he quickened his pace until he told me that he was coming which brought me to a final large one. "Wow, that was something else", I said, "you are the best and I no longer have the fantasy of making it with a black cock."

We laughed at that as we rolled over with me on top. In this position he stroked and squeezed my bottom while telling me how great it felt and how lucky my husband was. I then moved down and took his partially flaccid cock in my mouth and with my tongue, cleaned our juices. While I was doing this Nikko kept up a running comment about how good it felt to have me sucking and tonguing his cock. Finally, we got up and I told him I needed a quick shower so I would not smell like sex to my husband when he got home. I grabbed the phone saying that I had to keep it close in case my husband called.

In the bathroom it was obvious from Nikko's and my comments that we were fooling around and I was being washed all over. I too made sure Nikko's cock was clean as a whistle. I am sure my husband got an earful. We dressed and I collected my phone and before I hit the end button, I told Nikko that I hoped we would be able to get together again sometime. He said that he was counting on it. I closed the phone and went straight to our room.

When I entered, I got the surprise of my life as my husband was on the bed naked with a very stiff cock. When he saw me he got up, removed the Blackberry earpiece and swept me off my feet. He told me that he loved me as much as one could and while undressing me thanked me over and over for the show. Once we were in bed and came up for air from kissing I asked him if he was sure. He then told me that as much as he loved me he had always wanted to see me make love to someone better endowed than he was but had never had the nerve to bring this up to me.

I told him that what I did with Nikko was "fucking – pure sex and not making love in any way as much as, however, I had thoroughly enjoyed it". I also told him that he is as well endowed as anyone and certainly enough for me. I reminded him that not only have I not complained, I have been a very satisfied woman throughout our marriage. As I was saying this, whereas it was true in the past, I knew that in the future I would do this again and again. What followed was that I was again filled and more in love than I could imagine.

We napped after this romp until it was time to get ready to go to the French Africa Trade Commission for a chess match. I wore my new panty and bra set under my favorite silk dress. Robert told me that I looked good enough to eat. I laughed at this and gave him a large hug saying wait till I get you home tonight.

CHAPTER XI

My Love of Photography

O n the way to the consulate I asked him again if he really wanted to be present if I were to be with Nikko again. He said of course he still wanted to watch me get pleasured and asked me when this might happen. I reminded him that on the final night of the meeting there was a second dinner dance and I was sure that Nikko and maybe Pierre would try what they did the first night and that if he faked being drunk and dead asleep once we were all in the room that I would give him his wish. I reminded him that just like I did when he was listening, I would say things that I felt at the moment but anything I would say would not, in any way, change my love for him and our life together.

I told him that I was excited to be the wife of a respected chess player and hoped he won the, or a, chess set. I told him that Nikko had told me that many of the superb photos adorning the walls of the consulate were, in fact, taken by a Leon Merlin but that many were taken by Jean-Claude himself and that he was going to give me a couple because he heard that I was also a photographer and that I was complimentary of his photos. Luckily we arrived at the consulate as I had expected that Robert might ask if Jean-Claude had come on to me.

Once in, we spotted Nikko who came to greet us and tell Robert that he was pleased to have him back as it is not often that real chess masters graced our game room. He also told Robert that Jean-Claude had gotten word that I was favorably impressed with many of the photos and because he had taken some of them, he wanted to give me a gift of at least two framed enlargements. "Wow", I said to my husband, "if they are among those I chose from the contact sheet, you will just love them".

Jean-Claude in all his splendor entered the room and warmly

welcomed my husband (translated by Nikko) and presented to me a package of framed photos and a large box which I assumed was the carved elephant. I noted that Nikko did not translate accurately and had to chuckle. As what Jean-Claude said was that he was pleased to present these photos to the most sexy lady he had the pleasure to fuck and he hoped I would get to see some of those he took the last visit.

I blushed as I recalled Leon and he took many shots of a nude me as well as in two bra and panty sets. I quietly told my husband that he had complimented me for my good taste in Art photography. Robert whispered to me that Jean-Claude had eyes for me and to "have fun". "What ever do you mean" I said as I smiled and winked. I told him "You have an overactive imagination", even as I knew he was right.

Nikko herded the group into the game room where several ladies and gentleman were sipping wine and eating snacks. They all came around Richard and were complimenting him on beating the group champ. Everyone was complimentary and most were able to speak English so Richard was in his element. I followed Richard as he was led to one of the tables and watched as the game started. After a bit I needed to use the restroom so told Robert that I would be right back.

As I was leaving the ladies restroom, Nikko came up and quietly told me that he wanted to make love to me again. I told him that the next night was the final night dinner and dance and that that was a possibility and to just do what he did the first night. He persisted but I told him that I would have to at least go back in the room as my husband was expecting my return.

On the way to the game room we passed several ladies in various dress heading to another area of the house and when we were about to pass Leon, Nikko stopped and introduced him to me saying (what I already knew) that he was another real photographer. We exchanged pleasantries and made eye contact. This man I liked so I said that, "I am only an amateur photographer" followed by "the photos you and Jean-Claude have done of Sénégal and the other parts of the African French Community are truly superb." "Wish I had your expertise". This is what I said, but I found myself getting excited sexually as he had seen me nude and posing in very un-ladylike ways.

Back in the game room, Nikko said to me quietly with a wink and a smile that he would see me later or possibly tomorrow night. When we reached Robert he said basically the same thing at which point Robert invited him to our table for the dinner-dance. Nikko graciously accepted and bid us goodbye until later. After he left, I spotted Leon taking pictures of some of the guests. I pointed him out to Robert telling him that he was the main photographer who took most of the very beautiful pictures adorning the walls of the Trade Commission. I excused myself telling Robert that I would like to follow him to learn a few techniques.

Leon was easy to talk to. I asked him how a person from The Gambia, admittedly surrounded by Sénégal, would get involved with the AOF (as it is known). He laughed and was surprised that I knew even where The Gambia was but that he had long been interested in photography and had photographed most of West and Central Africa. He grew up in Banjul, the capitol, and like everyone in Gambia, he spoke both French and English. As we talked he effortlessly stopped and photographed each person including Robert.

He than asked me if I wanted to go with him to another function taking place a few rooms away. I said yes and followed him to a room with mostly women. These were the ones I saw earlier as some were in western dress, and some were in wraps typical of West Africa. Leon told me that this was an important meeting about women helping women in many ways but especially getting jobs with equitable pay and that West Africa was very chauvinistic often relegating women to second-class status. Heavy stuff, I thought to myself.

When we were done He asked me if I would like to see more of his photos and for him to identify the ones he personally took. I, of course, said I would be honored to see what he has taken. As we walked around, I was becoming highly aroused as I had been before him when he was a stranger about to be fucked by his boss. As we walked around he told me that I had been more than a good sport to let a stranger come in and take pictures of you mostly undressed.

I know I blushed, but what surprised me the most was my growing desire to strip for him again. He said he thought I was beautiful and very sexy and had to admit he had gotten hard seeing me in a bra and panty set. I had to laugh when he said, "That session was far more interesting than most I do". Without thinking I said "Any time any place" and once said, I realized that I meant it as Leon was very sexy, charming, and nice. He gave me a look that I hoped meant that he understood my meaning. I was becoming very aroused.

As we walked and talked he became closer and occasionally put his arm around me to lead me to one photo or another. He at one point asked if I had seen any of the photos he took of me last night. When I said no and that I really would like to see them he looked around and said, "Lets go". Holding his hand, I followed his lead. We were soon in what appeared to be a library at the back of which was his office. I noticed that he checked the corridor and locked the door. When he did that, I started feeling even more sexy and noticed that I was starting to get wet between my legs.

He showed me some files with photos of Senégal and The Gambia and not only the countryside but also some modern construction. We were close together and the contact was getting me warm also. After a bit, I asked him about the photos he took of me. He hesitated and said that he would show them to me but they really did make him amorous. I liked his manner and said, that they may also affect me the same way but nevertheless I am very curious to see them.

CHAPTER XII

The List Expands

He then told me that they were not in the library and to follow him. We went down the hall and up a back stairs and into a room, which he told me was his for the time being. He got out a folder and we started going through what he had taken and I also saw that he had those taken by Jean-Claude. They were actually very well done and, as I thought they would, they made me horny. At one point I just came out and asked him if he wanted to take more of me.

He then took me in his arms and said that nothing would make him happier. When I asked where he would like to take them he said, "Right here". He got out his camera and said, "OK, it is your show". I looked at him and I am not sure why but I just started to slowly undress. When I was down to just my panties and bra he said that I was even sexier than he remembered from the last time.

He then asked if he could hug me. I answered by coming as close as I could and into his arms. He held me tightly until I could feel his hardness on my abdomen. His hands were gently touching and rubbing me all over. I looked up into his eyes and we started kissing. I felt as wanton and needy as I ever had in my life. I felt as if I was starting to get wet between my legs and I knew I wanted him inside me.

When the kiss was over I stepped back and said, "How do you want me to pose?". He took a number of shots and then I asked him if he wanted me to take off more. He just nodded so I slowly removed my bra and panties while he took photos of the process. When I was naked and he had taken several photos he came over to me and while hugging me he said that he wanted to make love to me. I wanted it too so followed him to the bed and watched him undress. His body was magnificently sculpted which told me that he did more than just take photos. He was also fully erect and I noted he was the size of my husband and had a normal sized crown that was almost a bluish color.

I immediately went down on him taking as much as I could in my mouth and down my throat. He just kept repeating, " you are unbelievable, you are even more sexy than I remembered". He soon came in my mouth and I swallowed it all and noting that all cum tasted differently and his was the best yet. We stood and hugged a bit and I found that he got hard almost immediately.

He lay me down on the bed and got between my legs and did magic with his tongue and fingers. After three of four orgasms I pulled him up and he entered me with one stroke. He had marvelous staying power as he screwed me through three of four thunderous more orgasms before he came. I was in orgasmic heaven and knew then that, for sure, I would be seeing men outside of my marriage and only hoped that my husband would accept my new needs and wants and would not love me less.

We lay on the bed but not quietly as his hands were all over especially my bottom. He went down on me again and with his tongue spent a lot of time stimulating my anus. Then he used my and his lubrication to insert one then two and then three fingers in my rectum. This was a new feeling but strangely stimulating. He got me on my hands and knees and from behind I was expecting his again hard cock to enter my vagina but instead he slowly entered my rectum. This was a first for me but I knew that it would not be the last as the feeling was not only very different but took intercourse to a new level. He pumped in and out and much to my surprise when I felt him swelling and ejaculating, I had a last large orgasm.

We slowly got up and talked about when we could get together again. I told him the hotel we were staying at and that my husband was gone all morning. He took me in his strong arms and said he would call and we could at least get breakfast. I looked at the clock and told Leon that we really must go downstairs as I didn't want my husband to miss me. I paused and then told Leon that my husband loved to hear about my adventures and this is one I would tell him for sure. He looked at me strangely for a second and nodded as we quickly got dressed stopping to kiss several times and then made our way back to the game room stopping to look at photos as if that was what we had been going all evening.

CHAPTER XIII

Was I turned on...

When we got to the game room everyone was milling about and talking. Our timing was perfect as we were about to enter the room, Robert came out with a very large smile and a sizable box. He grabbed me and with a big hug he excitedly told me that he had won a beautiful hand carved ebony chess set. He then gave me a big kiss and then looked me in the eyes and winked. I knew he had tasted Leon's cum so I kissed him again saying, quietly, "I love you so very much."

I then introduced Leon to my husband telling Robert that he was the main photographer who had taken most of the photos I had raved about and that I learned a lot about my hobby that I did not know and that Leon had guided me regarding the African Art. A quick wink and Robert warmly greeted Leon. After shaking hands, Leon told Robert that I, his wife, was very modest as she knew the answer to any camera question he asked and she spotted the good from the just OK immediately.

Leon added that it was he who was honored as he had just escorted a most beautiful lady to view his Photographs. Robert just beamed and gave me a wink so I knew that he understood that I had been doing more than just looking at pictures with Leon.

I retrieved my packages and Robert his and we thanked everyone and had a cab called for us. Once we were in the cab, I leaned close to my husband and told him that I had been a naughty girl again as I kissed him so he could taste Leon's cum residue still in my mouth to know what I had done. I told him that I loved every minute of it and would tell him all about it when we got home as it was for his ears only. We snuggled and in whispers affirmed our love for each other. While this close I felt that Roberts cock was very hard.

Back in our room we literally torn our clothes off and headed to the bed and made love again and again for at least a couple of hours. While coupling, I asked him if he was really sure about my being with other men as I had never done this in the 18 years we had been married. I told him quite clearly that I really liked the sexual tension and multiple orgasms and the feeling of being naughty but would stop in a second if he were uncomfortable. I further told him all about Leon and his incredible muscles as if he were a body builder and that we had had sex in multiple positions.

Then I told him that there was more. That Leon asked to photograph me in stages of undress and how this had made me feel even more sexy and horny. I told him that I was so turned on when he took pictures of me in my bra and panties as well as in the nude that we did it again. He was particularly interested in seeing those photos.

I told him that I would call Leon and see if he would bring a set to the hotel tomorrow and that I knew I would have another story to tell him. As we were in the act, that brought Robert off immediately. He told me that he was in some meetings but if he was able to call, could he listen. I told him "of course" and we drifted off to sleep.

The next morning we slept a bit later and Robert had to leave for his meetings before we had breakfast. He hugged me as he was leaving telling me "I love you – the new you – have fun."

So, I got up slowly, showered and was having a room service breakfast lost in thought. I knew that I would be making love – well, actually fucking – more than once this day as I knew Leon would want to come and I certainly would want him in me again and again. Then tonight, I was sure that Nikko and Pierre would do what they did a few nights ago and get Robert drunk only they did not know that he would be pretending and that I would again be fucking both of these men. I wondered aloud how Robert would really take it actually seeing me in the throes of multiple orgasms. I vowed to not hold back to find out.

Then, I thought about returning to the quiet Midwest and home and if Nikko meant it when he said he could or would come for a visit. How I, and Robert would handle that, was a big question. I thought about the surprising array of cock sizes and shapes that I had experienced and especially the differences in the heads and even the taste. I sure learned a lot of unexpected things on the "trip back home."

I also thought about all the guys at our gym who have come on to me in the past. How would I handle that in my present frame of mind, as some were really hunks and I saw myself viewing them through new eyes and wondering what their cocks looked like and tasted like?

CHAPTER XIV

...Stay tuned, as this unexpected story has not ended.

© June 2009 - Chris Dawson

The Need to know For Sure

By **Chris Dawson**

This is the story of a loving couple that really begins when the husband first and unexpectedly suspects that his wife may be having sex or fooling around with men outside of their marriage. At first he was very angry and hurt but noticed that he was also more than a little excited and that his wife's love and affection remained and even increased. What happens when he sets up a surveillance system where he can see and hear anything going on in their home and pool is the crux of this story.

CHAPTER I

Falling in Love

I am not even sure where to begin. This is a story I never ever expected to write but documenting what I am living is, I believe, some solace for the calamity I have lived – at least in the earlier days. I use the word 'calamity' for lack of a better term to describe the "Roller Coaster" or 'Yo-Yo' feelings and emotions I have experienced over the past few years in my marriage to the love of my life. Presently all is well but there are waves rocking the boat. How I got to this point is the essence of this story.

Let me set the stage; I married some 11 years ago the most beautiful, sexy, and intelligent woman any man could wish for. Lorraine and I met at the marriage of her cousin and a man who I had been a friend with since high school. Lorraine was 5' 5" and about 125 pounds with the warmest personality as well as the sexiest body I had seen in years. To say that I was attracted to her would be an understatement.

I was not known as a "ladies man" but clearly she attracted me. I admit that between her perfect breasts, which I came to know as 34C as I often bought her sexy underclothes and in addition her most attractive and alluring "Bubble Butt", I could not choose a favorite, When I was introduced to her at the wedding of my friend she was 25 and I was surprised that she was not spoken for let alone married. I had been busy building my business and was also not actively dating at that time.

My name is Charles. My close friends and teammates called me Chuck. I was 32 years old and fit from being active in a number of sports through the years. Was starting to learn how to play the game of golf but regularly played squash and city league basketball. In college I swam and ran the 220 and 440 in track and of course played squash. I knew from showers after sports that I was only of average endowment.

I was envious of the studs with 8-9 inches soft and always felt my 5 inches soft was lacking but I never had complaints as a lover. The opposite was, in fact, the rule. There are more ways to please a woman than just a large cock, I rationalized.

Lorraine and I hit it off at the wedding and before the festivities were over both my long-time friend and her cousin were teasing us about being the next to get hitched. We both laughed this off but I admit that I was starting to have feelings as she was a great conversationalist and we were both surprised at the number of things we were both more than casually interested in. We were both avid classical music lovers and symphony goers and seemed to like the same other music. Recreationally we were both water skiers, downhill skiers, and both loved scuba diving. It seemed that whatever subject either of us brought up, the other was either interested in or participated in. We had many a laugh at these similarities.

After the wedding we started dating and spending a lot of our non-work time together. I felt very comfortable with her and was in no hurry to start having sex as I sensed that she was not a very sexually active person. When our hugging and kissing got to the point that we both wanted more, I suggested that we take it slow as I was becoming more interested in a long time relationship than a short time sexual romp.

At this suggestion she gave me an exceptionally big hug and confessed that she had broken up with several guys who just did not understand this same point. She admitted to having sex with a few guys but when she found out that they were interested in their pleasure alone she dumped them. Yes we petted, and yes we both used our hands to bring pleasure to the other but I was so in-love that whatever she wanted I would gladly do or not do.

As time went by I became more in love than I ever thought possible. We talked a lot about our life goals and plans and simultaneously believed that we were meant for each other. She told me that she was very much in love with me and had been thinking long term for some time. We laughed at this as I told her I was feeling the same thing. So, we set a date and got married about 6 months after we met. Both of our parents liked very much our choice so we started life together with both of us very pleased with our choice of mate.

For our honeymoon, we went to Hawaii and had the most romantic and loving week of my life up to that point. I felt as if I was the luckiest man on the planet. In addition I felt really loved for the first time in my life. Yes, I had dated and had several relationships but always something was missing.

With Lorraine, I felt complete and was in heaven when she told me that she had the same feelings. That we could talk about anything was a pleasure. We told each other about our past loves and modest sex lives and seemed to have no secrets. For sure, I was totally honest with her and felt that she was the same with me.

Our sex life was far more than I expected in that Lorraine was very open to anything I had in mind and, in fact, she often initiated acts. I was able to bring her to orgasms most of the time and when I came early I was always able to get her over-the-hill and a thundering orgasm orally. She was sheepish at first but her oral skills soon surprised both of us.

She often said that she loved to please me this way and had no trouble swallowing my loads. The reverse was certainly true as she was the most vocal when I pleasured her with my lips and tongue. She has the tastiest secretions I had ever experienced and this became almost a nightly activity.

Sex with Lorraine was always stimulating. There was little that we did not do or would not do for each other's pleasure. We spent a lot of time pleasing each other orally and she liked my cock in any of her openings. Yes, she even liked anal sex claiming that it was the most intimate of sex acts and that I was the first and last to do her that way. I loved her bottom especially when I was playing with it or kissing it. Both of us seemed to derive great pleasure when I was playfully spanking it. Actually playful spanking was a frequent prelude to great sex. She told me that the stimulation made her hot. All in all, there was never a dull moment in our lovemaking.

Together we decided to start a family and she easily became pregnant. This brought us even closer together our sexual activity changed very little until the last month. Our son who we named Andrew after my dad, was born 9 months later so began another chapter in our life. My business had grown and prospered so we were able to join a country club. I picked one with a 4 courts for singles squash plus a doubles court and a really nice gym and a great restaurant. We looked for and got a larger house and thinking ahead we got a 4-bedroom house and one with a very private and almost hidden swimming pool.

I was amazed at how soon after the birth of our son, Lorraine was back to her pre-birth weight and was back to the gym exercising and even learning the game of squash so she could play with me when convenient. I had asked one of the squash Pro's, whose name was Shawn, and who I had come to know and like to show her the ropes. She was also amazed that she had not one wrinkle on her abdomen, which her doctor told her was very rare indeed.

Three months after the birth of Andrew she excitedly told me that we had gotten pregnant again. It was she that used the word "we", which made me love her all the more. Nine months later our year-and-a-half old son had a sister, who we named Robin as she was born in the spring. Again within three months of this second child she and I were back playing squash and exercising at the gym as they had a babysitting section for parents like us who had kids but were still active. Everyone at the gym was quite surprised to see her in such shape for a 28 year old (although not everyone knew her age) after two kids. I was one proud husband.

CHAPTER II

Seeds of Suspicion

To get on with my story, I will skip some years ahead to the time when both our son, Andrew or Andy as we called him, our daughter, Robin were now going to grade school letting Lorraine have her mornings and at least early afternoons for herself. I started sensing a little restlessness in her but other than that everything seemed as it always was.

Some nights after the kids were in bed, Lorraine was aggressively horny and would almost attack me. I was slow to pick up on this but looking back she was very wet and lubricated at these times. I though nothing of it at the time and just thought I was a very lucky man indeed.

About then or at one point in our workouts, I began noticing the squash Pro, Shawn, who was also one of the trainers spending some extra time with her and one time I saw him enter a changing room a few minutes after I thought she had entered it. I said nothing because, at the time, I did not put two and two together.

I guess I did not see any wrongdoing as he was a very muscular black man and Lorraine had indicated through the years that she was not turned on by muscle types and had not told me about any curiosity regarding black men. He was also very nice looking but this still did not register with me. Anyway, that night she was exceptionally horny and very lubricated and I still did not put these events together.

Looking back, I should have seen a number of times when he was close to her and helping with her workouts but it was only when I came out of a squash game once and came across the two of them unexpectedly that I saw anything suspicious. It never occurred to me what may have been going on the days the kids were at school and she went to the gym for a workout. Thinking that she might be playing around got me not only a bit angry but also very jealous but also surprisingly somewhat excited.

One day, I was having coffee in the lounge with Shawn, who I had come to respect, know, and liked a lot. We talked briefly about how Lorraine was doing in squash. He told me she was ready to give me a game. After a bit I asked him how he resisted the sexy bodies he worked with. He admitted that his job was great to meet women who wanted to explore sex with a black man with a big cock.

Once I saw his cock when we were in the shower, I realized that he was almost twice as large as I was. Soft, I was 5 inches and a bit but without a measurement his was almost 8 inches soft. I was very envious but still did not think that Lorraine was fooling around. I was the jealous type and would have been very upset and angry if this had crossed my mind.

I was sure slow to put what I saw together but he was not the only man I saw in proximity with my wife and began to suspect that something may be going on but as our lovemaking and affection was not changed, I put these thoughts out of my mind.

As we had a pool, I had contracted with a group for service and when the service guy, who introduced himself as Ronald, first came over to bid on the job, I almost did not hire him as I saw him eyeing Lorraine with a big grin on his face. For the most part he was all business and I did hire him for a bimonthly check to see that all things were maintained and working.

A third instance and the one that really got me thinking that something was going on behind my back was when we went to the yearly symphony support ball where, as usual, we danced with each other as well as friends. I was coming back from the restroom and spotted Lorraine and a man we had come to know who's name was Greg. He was always at symphony functions like fundraisers. He was one of the musicians who played the base string instrument. He was tall and filled out his tux as if he were very well built, unlike most of the other musicians.

They were dancing a slow dance and I spotted one of his hands fondling Lorraine's bottom. I was very surprised when she did not make any moves to prevent him from continuing. Then much to my surprise and shock I thought I saw her arm between their swaying bodies. Anger and hurt only partly describes the feelings this brought out. I made my way back to our table trying to decide how to ask or confront my wife and Greg about what I saw. As I sat down I noticed that my cock was twitching.

I was not there 3 minutes when Lorraine comes bouncing back and gives me a big hug saying that she missed me and loved me more than I will ever know. With what she said and how she said it I assumed that I did not see what my eyes thought I saw. We went out to the dance floor and she was her lovable affectionate self through the next set and up till the evening was over.

After a bit I was sort of ashamed of myself for suspecting infidelity when I was experiencing such affection and love. That night, I was practically attacked when we got to bed and she had a tremendous climax quite soon after my head was between her legs. When I playfully and lovingly spanked her sexy bottom she squealed and told me not to stop. When we made love she was as wet and lubricated as she had ever been.

What really got me to thinking that my loving wife was seeing others for some reason was one day when I was a bit ill with a cold and stayed home in bed. I awoke mid-morning to voices I heard outside so I got up and went to the window, which was partly open. What I saw startled me to say the least. Lorraine was in her smallest swimsuit and talking to the pool maintenance guy.

What I heard her say shocked me. She told him that he had to go because her husband was home and upstairs sleeping. She got up off the lounge and seemed to walk him to the gate in just her abbreviated swimsuit. I was surprised that she did not even put a towel around herself.

Excitedly, I ran to the guest room with a view to the gate and what I saw gave me a shock. He was kissing her and his hand was inside her bikini bottom playing with her ass. I had to blink, as I did not believe what I saw. As angry as I was, I felt my cock get hard so I held my temper as I asked myself if the love of my life needed what other men could give her or that this man was somehow too aggressive for her to say 'no', or that she was falling out of love with me.

I thought that I could live with the former but would be crushed and a broken man if she no longer loved me. As I thought this I noticed, with some surprise, that my cock was telling me that seeing her with another man was a sexual turn-on.

I ran back into our bedroom and pretended to be asleep. Lorraine came into the room with a tray of cookies and a hot cup of tea. She asked how I was feeling and told me that she wanted me better as soon as possible as she loved me. When I told her that I was feeling much better and held open the sheets she got a smile on her face, quickly stripped out of her clothes and jumped into bed.

As we were making love with her on top I played with her bottom and gave her a few spanks. She told me again and again that she loved me. I was struck by not only what she was saying as I brought her to a climax but the enthusiasm of her lovemaking. She climaxed even before I did and asked me to bring her to another with my tongue. She was one horny lady and I loved it. It was clear to me that the brief contact with the pool guy had no effect on her love for me but seemed to markedly increase her libido.

We spent the rest of the afternoon until the kids were due home in bed. I explored her body with my hands and tongue and came to the conclusion that whatever she was doing or had done, it had not only not affected my love for her or from what I sensed her love for me and she sure had a fantastic body.

She was also active giving me a couple of fantastic blowjobs. It is no wonder that she attracted men and as long as I did not lose her love, I would find a way to benefit from her activities and maybe in the end she would share her lust or need for larger men if this was the issue.

CHAPTER III

The Next Step

It occurred to me that this might be the best time to get a modified security system. We had been talking about this, as we wanted to be sure the kids were safe and while I was at work she was also safe. We discussed this at length as I told her my thoughts. She agreed completely so I called a company I knew did the best work.

I did not tell my wife or anyone what my actual plans were. In addition to the usual door and window security I wanted a second system of external and internal surveillance so I could not only see but hear what went on in the pool area as well as throughout the house. I wanted to be able to control and observe each room.

With the system I put in, I wanted to control the volume and the camera angle at least in a limited way. My wife had to visit her parents as her mother was briefly in the hospital so when she was away I got the job done. One part of the regular security system was that through an app I would get notified if the system was "Armed" or "Disarmed".

It was neat to be able to see most of the rooms of the house from more than one angle. Thus I had the whole house and outside covered by rather well hidden high-resolution cameras and microphones so from my personal computer I could see and hear anything that went on.

I was not sure why I did this but at one level I was hoping that I would find nothing. At another level, I knew that I was opening up a new part of my life and wondered how I would handle my wife, Lorraine's, infidelity if this is what I discovered.

I did know from what I had seen that something was going on with a member of our symphony who was one of the Base players, and two well-built black guys. One was Shawn, who was one of the squash coaches, and who had become a friend, and the other was the technician who came to service our pool. I couldn't see if anything happened at our gym but with her being free all morning, the possibilities were open for them to see her in our home if this is what she wanted to do.

Now that the surveillance system was set up, all I had to do was live as we had been and check the cameras occasionally, as I had no idea who else she may be playing with. I figured that I would find out the reasons in due course.

I had some pangs of guilt with regard to putting in this surveillance system but rationalized that if she did need more sex than I could give her, I wanted to see for myself that this was the case and that one day I would tell her that I knew but loved her so much that she should continue to see who she wanted as long as her love was for me was as true and deep as mine was for her.

In addition, I had come to see that Lorraine's affairs made me very sexually excited even as I had no idea where this came from and it was certainly unexpected.

It was interesting that all along I had no intention of seeing any other women for sex even as I would have had no problem getting any of the women from my work life who rather outwardly hinted of their availability even as I knew that they were also married.

I am not sure that I can adequately describe the emotions I felt as I went from room to room of our home from my computer on my desk. There were times I felt like I was betraying the one I love and would contemplate entirely removing the rather costly surveillance system.

Then, my curiosity and the possible excitement of watching Lorraine receiving what I cannot give her would again surface. In the end the voyeur part of me won out. I was sure that the hardest part would be to see my wife having sex with another man and not say anything when I returned home. Yes I lived a real rollercoaster of of emotions.

Lorraine returned home in a week as her mother recovered and was now home. Her homecoming was wild, as she just could not get enough sex. As we had not had sex in more than a week, she seemed tighter and was almost insatiable. At one point I jokingly said, "I think I need some help taking care of you." The look in her eyes was priceless but she quickly told me that I was all she needed and ever wanted was me as she said "You have no idea how much I love you and our life so why would you want me to be with another man."

I quickly told her, "I was just teasing but I have to admit that there are times when I do not think I satisfy you as I wish to." This got no response but a warm hug and many kisses as she assured me that I was all she needed and wanted. I now knew differently and thought to myself that 'time will tell'.

The next week was almost a honeymoon as almost daily we made love in our bed, in the shower, and even in the lounge by the pool when the kids were in bed or away. I just could not get enough of her delicious succulent pussy and shapely bottom. That weekend was the same as the kids were visiting my parents, which was what they liked to do every 2 to 3 months. I guess, our kids liked to be spoiled as all kids do and I knew my parents did that in spades.

They spoiled them royally, but we both thought that knowing both of their grandparents was important. Anyway, these weekend vacations were our parent's gift to us both. We would go to movies and always to the club and squash courts for a few games of squash and exercises.

While at the club, I got to know Shawn better and found him interesting and bright. Once when I made the comment that I bet he had the ideal job with the pick of the crop to dally with. He gave me a strange look before he answered that he was lucky as a lot of the ladies at the gym were curious about being with a black man and he was only too willing to comply. He told me that I would be surprised at who he had been with.

He told me that I would be surprised as some were in their 50's and 60's yet still sexually very active at least with him. Obviously he did not suspect that I thought for a second that my wife was included as he added that, "Sadly, some of the best, like your wife, are unavailable."

CHAPTER IV
Talk About an Eye Opener

I had almost forgotten the surveillance system I had installed and when it popped into my mind during a break in meetings at work. I logged in with my computer and curiously went from room to room. The living room was empty, our bed was made and then I realized that it was a warm sunny day so I checked the pool.

There was the love on my life laid out on the sunning bed in her sexy bikini reading a book. I mentally threw her a kiss and was about to close the screen when I heard a man's voice say, "Hi sexy, nice day for a swim." This seemed to startle her as she reached for her towel to cover herself.

As he came into view, I saw that it was Ronald and he had on a speedo type swimsuit. The first thing I noticed was the large bulge in the front of his suit. He then said, "Hey it's me, no need to get all modest – is there now", as he pulled the towel from my wife's body and sat down on the edge of the tanning bed.

Almost immediately he started rubbing her legs. She moved his hands a couple of times but then sort of gave up. I did hear her say, "we shouldn't be doing this, it is not right, I love my husband and what we did a couple of weeks ago was wrong." To this he quickly replied, "The pleasure I gave you was too good to be wrong. I know you loved it and I know you want it again and I am going to give it to you again." He added, "Just do as I say and you will be just fine." He then started kissing her. She started to resist but then I saw her melt in his arms.

I quickly called my secretary and told her to absolutely hold all calls until I called again. As I watched the action unfold before my eyes multiple emotions raged through my head. Certainly, I was angry, jealous, and also hurt but, at the same time, undeniable excited. When I was again able to concentrate on the screen, I put on headphones so I would not miss any of the conversation as I watched in anticipation as he seduced my wife.

After the long kiss with his hands roaming everywhere on my wife's body, he stood up and removed his swimsuit exposing a very impressive circumcised cock that was not yet fully hard but was the largest I recall seeing to that point except Shawn who was about the same size except Ronald's head was quite a bit larger.

He was certainly dominant as he next said, "suck it girl, you know you want to." I watched with fascination as my wife sat up on the tanning bed and after looking at his eyes said, "please go slow" just as she opened her mouth to take the very large head in as far as she could. Once she started she seemed to really enjoy it as I heard her moaning as she sucked and periodically would run her tongue up and down the shaft.

I was mesmerized watching the woman I am married to, and love, give what I knew was great pleasure to Ronald's lengthening cock. At one point he started literally fucking her face and I was amazed at how much she could take in her mouth and throat. It was not long before he said, "Girl, I'm about to cum, take it all down this time."

With that I became painfully hard. I saw his body stiffen and could see my wife trying to swallow what he was spurting into her mouth. After several minutes he patted her on the head and as he slowly removed his cock from her mouth he stated, "Good girl, now get naked for some real lovin."

She looked up at him and said rather faintly, "Please, no, I don't think we should do this again, I really love my husband and this is cheating – please." He quickly countered with, "Girl, you loved it last time and you are mine now. Get naked or do I have to undress you myself?" "If I do, you get another spanking."

I guess she knew that she was his as she rather quickly undid her top and slide out of her bikini bottoms. She got up off the tanning bed and into his very muscular arms. I was getting very hard and was leaking far too much pre-cum as his hands explored and played with the body of my kids mother. He fondled and played with her bottom saying, "This ass is mine, isn't that right?" When she was slow to answer he gave her bottom a resounding spank much harder than any of mine.

With that she said, "Please Ronald, you know it is but don't make me say it." With that he gave her bottom another resounding spank leading her to say pleadingly, "Oh god, yes, my ass is yours but please treat it with care." He then said,

"That's better Girl", as he started to finger her pussy.

While he was inserting first one and then two fingers in my wife's vagina he guided her down on the tanning bed and lying next to her fingering her vagina and sucking on her breast he asked her, "Girl, what do you want me to do next?"

Her response brought me to orgasm and I had not been playing with my cock. She said in an almost pleading voice, "Please, I want you in me again." He then said, "What do you want in you and where do you want it? Speak up, Girl, or I will turn you over my lap until you show me and tell me what you want and where." She then said, "Oh, please you know I want you to fuck me with your big black cock in my vagina till I cannot take it any more." With that her hands went down to play with his cock and they started kissing passionately.

At one point, he gently pushed her head down to his cock until she started sucking it to get it to full hardness quicker. Once he was hard he rolled her over and got between her legs with his very large cock poised at her vaginal entrance. I saw him smile and say, "Good girl put it in your pussy like I told you last time" when she helped guide his cock into her vagina. As I watched his cock go slowly in stroke by stroke, I knew that this was her new life as I could never satisfy her like this man could.

Even his crudeness and aggressiveness seemed to turn her on. As I watched them fuck and her moan and scream with pleasure. I knew that hers and my life had changed forever. I only prayed that she would still love me even as I could not satisfy her sexually as this man could. I know that I still loved her totally.

It was amazing to watch her take all of his gigantic cock into her vagina and flex her hips to meet each of his muscular thrusts while saying again and again, "Oh God, yes, fuck me forever with your big black cock. " "Oh, Yes, Fuck me" all the while moaning and Ohh-ing and Ahh-ing with each of his thrusts in sheer pleasure.

In addition she had what appeared to be orgasm after orgasm something I could only hope for once a night'. They fucked for what seemed to be an hour but looking at my watch it was only 25 minutes. Heck I have never lasted half that long. When he came he came in her, which brought forth in my mind a whole new set of anxiety type emotions.

After he was done, he just got up and jumped into the pool and swam at least three laps before coming out and getting dressed. All the while Lorraine lay on the tanning couch as he left her as if in a daze. As he was leaving he leaned down and gave my wife a big kiss and said, "Girl that was good. The next time I come I want you stripped and naked when I get here before I ask, Got that?" My wife nodded as he left.

After about 10 minutes she got up and slowly walked naked into the house holding her swimsuit and towel. Out of curiosity and by switching cameras I was able to watch her go through the kitchen and then come into our bedroom. She went into the bathroom and I could see her take a shower and after a half hour she flopped on the bed and I heard her crying. God, I wanted to be there for her but knew I could not until I came home. I closed my computer to give her absolute emotional privacy knowing that she loved me still.

CHAPTER V

The First Visual

I called home before I left the office as I usually do to see if she wanted me to pick up anything for the store. She thanked me for calling but told me to come right home as she missed me and was horny. When I asked her what brought that on she said that she had been too long in the sun and dreamed about being in my arms. I told her that I loved her and literally raced home. I was lucky to not get a speeding ticket.

It was special and neat being met at the door, by your kids and the love of your life, with a glass of wine. After hugging we all went to the dining room for our now usual family dinner. Knowing what had happened earlier in the day by our pool had me almost uncomfortably hard but it was not that difficult to hide, as I am not large in that area.

I was aware that Lorraine was especially attentive to me. Her arm was around me when ever this was possible. Andy and Robin were, as usual, a handful and this was especially true when we were in the mood for some quiet / romantic time. Tonight was definitely no exception. Seemed like forever before they were both in bed and asleep.

When we finally got to our bedroom and the kids were found to be soundly asleep we shared a long hug and kiss. While kissing her I became almost instantly hard, as I knew where the different taste in her mouth came from. She, of course, noticed my excited state and hugging me closely she said in rapid succession, "Yes, I love you too and want you tonight in the worst way." "I have been horny for you all day." "Guess reading in the sun does this to me." "I love you very much." "God, I really do love you, honey." "Please make love to me and hold me close to you."

In a record time we were both undressed and in bed hugging and kissing. I knew that I would cum almost instantly so went down on her licking her nether lips and clitoris. I almost came on the spot when I tongued her vagina as I swear I tasted what I thought was her lovers cum. I think she was horny also as I was able to bring her to a climax rather more rapidly than usual.

After she calmed down I made the comment, "Wow we sure are horny tonight and I mean both of us as my love for you is over the top." After playing with her bouncy bottom and showering it with my usual love pats I did just that. God, I loved her. As we made love, I was secretly glad that her vagina was very loose as this prolonged my eminent orgasm. Knowing why it was loose was difficult to not think about but had I dwelled on that fact, I know I would have cum immediately.

While making love, which would describe what we did, she kept repeating how much she loved me and seemed to have a climax at the same time I came. I was not sure if hers was real but loved her even more when thinking that she maybe faked one to please me. As we were basking in the afterglow of 'making love' I had a moment which may have been best described as a "Gulp" when she said in my ear that she wanted to tell me something in confidence. With my heart in my throat I told her that of course she could tell me anything and it would stay between us.

She then told me that her cousin confessed to her recently that she was having an affair and told her about it excitedly. You cannot imagine how relieved I was that this was what she wanted to talk about and it was not a confession about what she had done. She asked me what I though about this information and what should she tell her cousin when they next meet.

Once I got my head around what she asked, I told her that we should not judge her on this information as there are a lot of reasons why either one or the other of a couple might have a relationship outside of a marriage.

I went on to tell her that her husband who was and had been a very good friend was known to me as a bit of a ladies man and maybe she went outside of their marriage because she found out or suspected that he had done the same or maybe she just did it because she always has had lovers and just does not want to stop. Lorraine looked me in the eye and said, "Honey, I think it was the later as she was always the wild one in our family." She then said, "You are unbelievably perceptive."

I went on to say that I did not know this for sure as my friend had never even hinted to me that he was other than faithful to his wife – your cousin. I then told her that I certainly would not ask him as this matter was between them and in my view would rarely be a reason for a divorce.

I saw a funny look in her eyes before she gave me a big hug and said, "Wow, another reason to love you more than I have ever loved anyone before." "You are a kind and thoughtful soul." With that we snuggled and at least I was very soon asleep. Most likely, I was dreaming about my wife being pleasured and wondering when she would feel comfortable sharing her pleasure with me.

I awoke during the night and felt compelled to run my hands over her marvelous body and felt her amazing and still almost firm breasts and her almost flat and well-muscled tummy. As if she was reading my mind she turned on her stomach so I was able to fondle and play with her bottom. Of course, this woke her up and rather than be a bit irritated she immediately come into my arms and said, "Oh honey, I love you so much, make love to me again."

I told her that I loved her more than anything and her pleasure makes my day. Of course, I got rapidly hard as I said that thinking of her being pleasured by Ronald and Shawn. With that I got between her legs and gave her pleasure as long as I could.excited. When I was again able to concentrate on the screen, I put

CHAPTER VI

The Challenge...

T he next morning after our usual breakfast with typical wide awake and active pre-teens and they were off to school, I gave my wife a very big hug telling her that I loved her and hoped that she would always be happy with her choice as a husband even if I could not always satisfy her as would be my want and desire. Her look, I recall was priceless as she told me, "Love is not always about sex and you do please me very much." I left saying that I would see her at the gym for our usual squash game after work.

Going to work I reflected on what I knew, which was that she was getting fucked by the pool guy, Ronald, and would most likely be doing this again giving me the great pleasure of watching from my computer screen. On the other hand, I was sure she had played around with Shawn from the gym and most likely with Greg from the symphony but how would I get to watch meaning how could I get their activity to be at the house. This situation dogged my mind all the way to work and some of the morning.

I hatched a plan so I called Lorraine mid morning and asked her if she wanted to meet me at the club's gym for a workout. She jumped at the suggestion saying she would see me there at noon. I arrived a bit before and looking in the exercise room I saw Shawn standing at Lorraine's head to be sure the weights she was lifting would not cause her any problem.

My view initially was from the side and I swear his groin was inches from her head and I swear her gaze was on his bulge. I went to get dressed and came in the usual way. By the time I came she was on another device so we went to adjacent treadmills and chatted away while exercising. God, I love her.

Later, I ran into Shawn and we had our usually friendly

conversation where I usually ask him who he had nailed recently. We always talk light-heartedly about this as it is rather personal but we have developed a friendship to the level that we talk openly about this matter. It always turns me on to hear about a new conquest of his.

He never mentions Lorraine but up to now I have been shy to ask him about my wife. We had become friendly enough that he felt comfortable actually telling me about some new lady he had nailed. He sure got to several, even some who I would never have expected to cheat on their husbands like the wife of one of the elderly Board members.

He was very confident about his ability to attract and fuck almost anyone. This day I was emboldened enough to challenge him. I said, "You say that you can get any woman, married or not to sleep with you, right?" His response was, "Yes, it is my experience that almost any woman can be seduced and I have the added advantage of being black and you would be astounded at how many otherwise faithful wives have a hidden fantasy to fuck a black man." Looking directly into his eyes, I said, "bet you could not seduce Lorraine, my wife".

The look he gave me was priceless telling me that he had already had some luck with my wife but he said, "Are you sure you mean this, we are friends and I would not want to change that." I then said, "I am dead serious as I do not think you would be able to seduce my wife."

Shawn then said that he had no doubt that he would succeed but if he did, he wanted my assurance that this would not affect our friendship. I assured him that I was confident that he would not be successful but that it would be our secret should he succeed and I promised him that we would remain friends no matter what.

I added that I would have to have proof and would additionally want to see them together, at one point, with my own eyes. Thinking ahead I told him I additionally challenged him to do it at our home in our bed telling him that it is one thing to have a 'quickie' but to get the woman to do it in her marital bed was 'true seduction'.

His almost immediate response was that he was confident that this was possible but how would I know that he had succeeded. I told him that whereas I wanted to eventually see the end result with my own eyes, that this was possibly not in the cards at this time but if he left a squash ball in the drawer of my nightstand, I would know he was there and that he had successfully seduced Lorraine and won the challenge. In any case, I assured him that there would be no repercussions should he get lucky.

I told him that the important thing was that I wanted him to be completely honest with me. I asked as an additional favor that he call me on my cell phone with how it went in the event he got lucky, which, I added, was unlikely. In my mind, I knew he would get to fuck my wife and the best part of it was that I would be able to watch. I did feel a bit guilty putting one over on my friend but knew that I would eventually tell him that I knew all along.

I knew he had been working on her and probably succeeded as in the next couple of weeks there was a few times a week that she would almost attack me when we were in bed and not only was she very well lubricated but felt very loose. On three occasions while kissing her I tasted what must have been his cum.

Needless to say, I came in just a few strokes and had to finish her orally tasting not only mine but his cum. She was not only especially horny but also very warm and loving on the nights of suspected activity. We continued to play squash a couple of evenings a week and exercise with the same frequency. I checked the cameras frequently and saw nothing until last Thursday.

It was noon and she knew that I had a meeting with staff on Thursdays. She did not know that these were not weekly meetings and that there was not one this day. Around noon, I checked the system and was surprised to see Lorraine walk into the kitchen with Shawn. I quickly called my secretary and told he to hold all calls telling them that I was in a meeting. I put on my headphones to better hear and glued my eyes to the computer screen.

The first thing I heard was my wife saying, "So, has your curiosity been satisfied as to what our house looks like." He responded that it was a beautiful home fitting for a beautiful lady and, "Your husband is a lucky man indeed." He thanked her for the invite over and said that one day when I come over again, we will have to go for a swim. Her answer to this was, "Why yes, that would be nice, I love the pool".

As they were talking my wife was making some coffee and a couple of small sandwiches. As they sat at the kitchen table I sensed some anxiety on her part as the banter was about nothing. Occasionally he would hold her hand and tell her that she was special and once he kissed her hand.

After that they got up from the table he asked her to show him the pool from the house. They walked over to the window and she pointed saying, "There it is, looking forward to a swim one day." I saw him put his arm around her as they looked and his hand went down to her bottom. A moment later they were kissing and he was fondling her bottom with both of his large hands.

I knew at that moment that he would be fucking my wife shortly. After the lengthy kiss, she said, "You know we shouldn't be doing this as I love my husband very much but in your arms I am putty." His response was to kiss her again and say, "Show me the one room we have not seen yet and I will show you the real pleasure you like and need." She responded with an audible sigh and led him upstairs to our bedroom.

I quickly changed cameras and was able to watch them enter our bedroom. His arm was around her and I saw a smile on her face. Yes, a myriad of thoughts passed through my mind. One was that he had won the challenge as I knew he would but I was also jealous as to what I knew would soon fill my screen.

The first thing my wife said was, "Well, is this what you wanted when you asked to see our house?" He responded with, "I have enjoyed our quick get-togethers at the gym but I am looking forward to pleasuring you till you scream for as long as you have time for." "You are a beautiful and sexy lady and I am so looking forward to the next hour."

With that he started to undress my wife. When she was down to her bra and panties I noted she was wearing the new set I had just gotten her. He then started to undress and did not stop till he was quite naked. His cock was larger than I recall seeing it at the gym but I had to remind myself that I had not seen him hard.

He took her in his arm and almost romantically moved over to the bed as they kissed. I had to admit that he was one smooth and romantic lover making quite a contrast with the pool maintenance guy, Ronald. I was sure looking forward to what I knew would follow.

I did not have to wait too long as he gently pushed down on her shoulders until she was kneeling at his feet looking right at his hardening cock. He then said, "Go ahead, Lorraine, take my first load as you are really the best lady at sucking my cock that I have ever had the pleasure to be with."

With that she started to literally make love to his cock with her mouth as she bobbed her head up and down. I was amazed at how far she could take him in and now knew why she was easily able to deep throat my much smaller cock.

While she was giving Shawn head he was continuously giving her praises and compliments making her moan as she worked on his cock, which I knew was not the first time. A little longer than 5 minutes of this and he said, "I am about to cum, where do you want it?" Her response was to grip his buttock and take him even deeper in her mouth. I watched in utter fascination as his strokes became faster and then stopped and her swallowing indicating that he had cum in her throat. When he slowly pulled out of her throat he said, "Yes, my little one, you are the best. I love to cum this way the first time with you."

He then laid my wife down on the bed and slowly removed her bra followed by her panties, which I could see were already quite wet in the crotch. He commented about the color and pattern of her bra and panties and said, "You husband has great taste." At that they both had a chuckle.

He then pulled back the covers and placed her in the center of our bed and with his head between her legs he brought her to two rather rapid orgasms. This was much quicker than I could ever have done and made me almost grateful to him for bringing that much pleasure to the woman I love more than anything in the world.

After her second orgasm he crawled up and lay next to Lorraine with this hands rubbing and fondling what ever he wanted on her body. He was not in a hurry and they lay there hugging, kissing and playing for almost a half hour.

He was some lover and I sure saw why he was so confident that he could have any woman. After this interval of snuggling and petting he asked her what she wanted next. Her response I will never forget was, "I want you inside of me" then after a very short pause, "No, I want you to fuck me with your big cock till I scream – God, I am so ready for you, please fuck me now." Then, "I feel so naughty for doing it in the bed I share with my loving husband, but I cannot help myself with you - maybe I need a spanking." Then they both laughed and he said, OK, you got it."

With that he sat on the edge of the bed, pulled my wife over his knees and actually did spank her. The spanking he was giving her was quite a bit harder than my 'love pats'. He continued until she pleaded with him to stop saying, "Enough, enough, I was only half serious – but thanks, I feel better already." He gave her almost a real spanking as her bottom was a nice red and his handprints were obvious. She then jumped back in the bed and, invitingly, opened her legs.

He did not need to be told what to do as he quickly poised his cock at the entrance of her vagina. I noticed that she was using her hands to guide his organ into the seat of her pleasure. I was a bit surprised at the short time it took for him to get his entire cock in her vagina. With each slow stroke she would give a low moan of absolute pleasure and had her first orgasm in less than a minute. Wow, I could never do that.

I have never been a porn addict but this was different. Here I was watching the love of my life, who was my wife and mother of our kids, fucking a very muscular black man who I knew as a friend. As little as a year ago I would have been angry, furious, and very jealous to the point I would have considered violence on the intruder. Now, here I was not only OK'ing what she was doing but encouraging her, unknown to her, to fuck others to gain what she cannot get from me. Now I watched in rapt excitement with a continuous hardon as another man was fucking my wife.

While being fucked by Shawn, she was in a special space as she kept very vocally moaning and almost screaming with each stroke and every few minutes the volume went up as she had another orgasm. I marveled at his staying power, as he was able to keep going in and out always changing his speed and pace for her pleasure.

I had to take a break to go to the John and when I returned they were still fucking. With Shawn, she kept saying, "Oh God, please don't stop, you are so good. Please fuck me any time you want." With that I erupted in climax into my shorts.

When they were finally done and I noted that she told him, I really 'love' what he was doing to me" and to "Cum deep in my Pussy." When he was done they lay there for a bit and then they got out of bed and went into the bathroom for a shower. While showering I heard him tell her that he had to get back to work but would love to come back again and give her the pleasure she deserves. My wife's response was, "Yes, I hope you do come back as you are the best – I love what we do, really love it."

He came out of the bathroom first and quickly he went to his pants and I saw him put a couple of squash balls in my bedside table. One day I would tell him that I had seen him in action but in the meantime this system would have to do.

About 30 minutes later my cell phone rang and I saw by the number that is was Shawn. I answered, "Hi my friend, how did it go?" His response was, "I sure hope you were honest and will not be angry at me but check your bedside table drawer when you get home." "Your wife is the best and with your permission, I want to see her again."

Then, he added, "Are you OK with that". After a pause, I said, "Congratulations, it seems that you were right and I do agree that she is the best" "If she wants you, and needs what you give her, I love her enough to say OK". I told him that I respected his honesty and that our friendship was, for sure, intact but we had to find some way for me to actually watch one day. This was some lunch hour.

Needless to say, I was again the beneficiary of her afternoon tryst as once the kids were in bed I was all but attacked. I loved the sex but even more was how she told me again and again how much she loved me. I even spanked her a little harder than usual but it still seemed to make her want me even more.

While kissing and licking, what was most intriguing was the smell and taste of his sperm in her mouth and vagina. Even though she showered, I could still taste cum. This was a big turn-on for me as it was real proof that my wife had been fucked and had sucked a cock.

CHAPTER VII

A Home Delivery...

I got into the habit of checking my computer more than a couple of times a day. If she was out, I would invariable hear about the shopping trip or the trip to the gym when I came home. Many times I would see her cleaning the house or one of the rooms or reading a book or lying out by the pool. I kept waiting for the next adventure. I did not have to wait too long and this one was unexpected.

Mid morning a few days after Shawn had been there I was watching her reading a book in the living room when the doorbell rang. She got up and went to check who it was and I heard her say, "Just a minute, I'll unlock the door." She opened the door and invited the person, who she seemed to know, in with a, "Hi, have been expecting you as I ordered this several days ago."

I quickly saw that he was a young white UPS delivery guy who was very good looking and well built. He had a package that needed to be signed for and from what I heard there was a small amount to be paid. I saw him eyeing my wife's chest and when she turned away to get her checkbook, his eyes were clearly on her bottom. As she was walking away he said, "I love to deliver here as you have one of the sexiest asses on my route."

Looking over her shoulder she said, "I'll bet you say that to all women and as for my being sexy, that may have been in the past, but I am a mother of two kids and almost old enough to be your mother so knock it off." She appeared feisty with this "kid" but he shot back, "You look far too young and hot to have kids and besides, I have dated older women and, in fact, prefer older women as they know what they want and need like a good fucking, whereas younger women play games."

She shot back, "What did you say, young man, be careful how you talk." He too was quick as he said, "You know full well what

I said and I have fucked a lot of you 'cougars' and they are usually grateful – so there."

She came back with her checkbook and standing next to him she started to write out the check. As she was writing, his hands softly touched her bottom. When she did not immediately move away he became more bold and played a bit more forcefully. Lorraine stopped what she was doing and looked at his tented shorts and said, "Boy, you must not get as much as you are telling me as with one touch of forbidden territory you get a hardon."

Not one to be put down he shot back, "Yes, with what I've got, there are plenty who order just so I can service them." My wife countered, "So how much does my little man have that you brag about." In a flash he had his cock out and grabbed my wife's hand to hold it. Once his cock was in her hand she did not let go and as it got harder she just looked back and forth from his cock to his eyes.

As she held his cock, she asked, "By the way, what is your name?" His response was, "Lucas, and your name is Lorraine from what I see on you packages." "Now that we are introduced, I want to show you pleasure like you may not have had before."

With that he encircled her waist and gave her an open mouthed kiss. Her response was, "Wow, you are some bold young man" but she still held his cock. Guess this gave him permission to start fondling her breasts saying, "Wow, these are very nice for an old lady." She countered, "The way you are playing with them tells me that you are all talk and have less experience that you profess."

I could not hear everything but I saw him undo his belt and his pants fell to the ground. He also slipped off his shorts and started raising my wife's blouse saying, "Guess you like that cock, wanna try it or are you all talk." Well one thing led to another as he more or less maneuvered her into our living room and it was not long before he had my wife bent over our couch with her skirt above her waist and her panties off and was feeding his good sized cock into her pussy from behind. I guess she wanted to show him that an 'old lady' was a good fuck because she was far from passive.

I heard her keep saying "harder, deeper, is that all you got." This got him really going as he poured his energy into fucking her as hard as he could. He was holding on to her hips as he fucked her. When he came he pulled out shooting all over her bottom and upper legs. He then helped her lie down on the couch, as he did not get soft. Ah, the plus of youth.

He then offered his cock to her mouth and she took it in sucking him until he pulled out, got between her legs and fed his cock into her vagina. He then fucked her like a madman. I sensed that she liked what he was doing as I heard three climaxes before he came the last time.

When he climaxed the last time he just laid there between her legs and after a few minutes he said, "Wow, you are some hot cougar – I hope you order something again so I can deliver it and satisfy your need for a large cock." My wife then said to this delivery guy, "You were lucky this time as I do not know what came over me except maybe to show you that us 'older ladies' can fuck with the best of them and besides I do not cheat on my husband." His response was to laugh and say, "Lady, you just did and it was great. If you want more at any time, just let me know and I certainly will keep our secret." Before she could say anything else he was dressed and out the door. I turned off my computer as she picked up her clothes and walked out of the room naked, most likely to shower and dress.

I was not surprised that when I came home and after the kids were in bed that she was very horny and well lubricated. I now knew that when she is this well lubricated it is because she had been with a male having sex of one kind or another. Our sex was like always, stimulating, fill of passion and love. As long as she loves only me, I can live with this and besides. I get free porno.

CHAPTER VIII

A Changed Ronald

Well I knew that in two days it was Ronald's time as the pool is serviced every two weeks. I was very curious as to what would happen next now that Shawn was in the picture. The next day I guess I got lucky as I tuned in she was fixing a snack in the kitchen and the phone rang. She put it on speaker for some reason and when she said "hello" a males voice said, "Hi, Lorraine, this is your poolside lover. Just wanted to tell you that I will see you tomorrow." "Looking forward to seeing you by the pool. Will be there at 11:30."

Before she could answer, he said, "Have missed your great body. Gotta go now so will see you tomorrow" and then he hung up. I saw her look at the phone and say, "Oh god how do I get myself into these things." Then she added to no one in particular, "I guess I could not be home, but…" and then she said nothing.

Well you can believe I was on the computer at 11:00 the next day. When I saw my wife in the house in her housecoat and at one point through the window I saw that it was raining so figured the visit by Ronald would be postponed. She went about her business seemingly nervously watching the clock.

It then struck me that she was facing a dilemma, which was the last order by Ronald to be naked when he arrived or face a spanking. At one point she went upstairs and I saw her take off her bra and panties and slip on her robe before going back downstairs. She was thus naked under her robe so I knew she intended to comply with his order. This got me very hard.

I saw her pick up the phone and a minute later my secretary through the intercom informed me that my wife was on the phone. I picked it up saying, "Hi babe, to what do I owe the honor of a midday call" "Are the kids OK." I heard a chuckle and saw her smile. She then said, "No, love, I just missed you and wanted to hear your voice." Then, "No, the kids are OK – Long ago off to school. - I love you and you are in my mind as I have finished my morning cleaning." I responded, " Well you know that the feeling is quite mutual. I love you too and you are in my mind all day every day." She then said, " I won't keep you as I know you are busy but just wanted you to hear me tell you that I love you dearly – before you go to lunch." "Bye now, Love you", and she hung up. Wow, deep love is some feeling and I was sure feeling it as I went back to the computer.

From 11:15 to 11:30 she did nothing but pace the floor of the kitchen by the back door. At almost exactly 11:30, there was a knock at the back door. I saw her freeze and then slip off the robe and go to the door very naked to open it. Yes, in came Ronald with a big smile on his face saying, "I just knew that you would do as I said." He then took her in his arms and while hugging and kissing her, his hands explored her body. I noticed that her breathing was getting faster the more he squeezed and fondled her breasts, pussy and ass.

Once he had his fill, he stepped back and asked her, "Where do you want it, I have actually missed you." She just pointed to the living room and followed him in the room she indicated. Once by the couch she said in a soft voice, "Please be gentle, I am not happy cheating on my husband but know you will not stop and I do love your cock and what it does to me." God I loved her.

He seemed to almost ignore her as he undressed. Once naked he asked her if she knew what she wanted now. I saw her shake her head yes and kneel on the floor to more easily take his large cock in her mouth. Once she started she seemed to enjoy the feel and taste of his cock as I heard moaning and saw her very actively bob her head up and down.

After some time I could see him fucking her mouth faster and faster until he said, "OK, Girl, here it comes." When he erupted she swallowed it all to his pleasure. She continued to lick and suck his somewhat soft cock until it came back to a full erection. I remember thinking that I wished I could get hard that fast after an orgasm.

After he pulled his slightly softer cock from her mouth he pulled her up into his arms and while hugging her warmly he said, "You are special and not at all like many of the other bored housewives that I fuck." "I am impressed that you came to the door naked as I asked - I will not ask you to do that again unless you want to." Then he said, "You have been in my mind a lot and whereas I would like to fuck you, I will stop here if that is your wish."

This change in his demeanor caught me and, obviously my wife, by surprise. Her response was to give him a hug and a big kiss and say, "I really appreciate your respecting my feelings but we have gone this far and we are both naked, which makes me feel almost wicked, and you do make me very horny so I do want you to fuck me with your gorgeous big black cock till I scream." With that she laid down on the couch and spread her legs inviting him to her sex.

He then caught her by surprise as he lowered his head to her pussy and said, "First, I want to pleasure you with my tongue as your pussy has the best scent and I want to taste it." He went on to say, "I do not usually do this but you are irresistible". With that he proceeded to bring my very sexy wife to orgasm after orgasm with his tongue, which must have made his cock spring back to life as when he kissed his way back up to her lips I saw he was ready.

Once he was in place I saw my eager wife guide his cock into her vagina saying over and over as he worked his way in to the hilt, "Oh Lord, please fuck me and don't stop, I love it so much that you are so big." This was followed by, "I need you fucking me, I need your large cock, I hope and pray that my husband can forgive me, but I very much need you to fuck me." If I did not know this before, I knew now, for sure, that this was my new life and if I really loved my wife then I would not interfere with her need for a larger cock.

Fuck her he did as I almost stopped watching as it went on and on. I would snap to attention each time my beautiful wife would scream out at another orgasm. When he finally erupted and filled my wife's vagina he rolled off and after a short rest he gave her a big hug and an equally big kiss and said, "Wow, you are the best… I hope you were pleased and will want to do this again.. I am not sure I can get enough of you… Your husband is a very lucky man." With that he got up, dressed and bid my wife goodbye telling her that he would let himself out and to stay where she is and rest. She did just that and when I got back from a short meeting she was still resting on the couch.

CHAPTER IX

Shawn at our Home

I knew for sure at this point that I wanted her to know that her pleasure with others was OK with me as long as our love was first. If this was possible, I knew, now that I had actually watched her with three men that I would be able to live very happily with her as a "Hotwife". What I wanted more than anything in life was for her to accept what I am feeling and either tell me everything or want me to be present when she is in the mood to take on a lover. I wanted her to be comfortable knowing I accepted her having lovers. I knew that my cock was just not enough for her yet felt that her and our love was secure. I now knew my love for her had only increased if that was possible.

My first step I thought should be with Shawn as it is he who fucked her openly in a way. True, they very likely had done it before the time I watched but I was sure that Shawn would be honest with me at this time. So, the next time we were at the gym and finished our squash game, I went to his office. He seemed a bit nervous when I came in and sat down but I quickly put him at ease by thanking him for the squash balls while shaking his hand and then confessing that I knew as I made the 'challenge' that she would be receptive.

He asked me how I knew that and I said, "When you are married to a good woman and you have honest conversations you learn her wants and needs even if the other person cannot speak of all their feelings." I told him furthermore, he was not the first she has dallied with but I have learned to live with her needs that I cannot fulfill and still love her as much as the day we were married.

He than said, "Well she is someone very special and I am very pleased that sleeping with your wife has not changed our friendship or your marriage." He added a moment later, "What's next, my friend. I would sure like to do it again." I told him that I not only expected him to fuck her again but reminded him that my ultimate desire was to watch first hand if he would accept that. Shawn looked me in the eye and said, "If seeing and fucking Lorraine comes with the only condition of your watching, you're on."

I then looked him in the eye and asked if he would be honest with me and tell me how many times he had had sex with Lorraine prior to last week when I made the challenge. I went on to say that I will not be angry or upset with the truth as I have suspected some sexual activity for some time. After a reflective pause, Shawn said, "Chuck, I owe you honesty." "We have had some sex two or three times a month for almost a year." "At first it was only her sucking my cock as one day I caught her staring at it so intently that I started to get hard." " She made some mundane comment and I said 'follow me' – when I got to my office and she was right behind me I knew I had her." "That was the first time maybe a year or so ago.

After the first time we had intercourse, she almost cried. When I asked her why she told me that she felt very guilty going outside her marriage, as she said that she loved you dearly. We talked about the reasons and she finally admitted that as much as she loved and cared for you, your size was not giving her orgasms since the birth of your second child, Robin.

I then told her that my door was open and her secret was safe and left it at that. He then said, "last week at your house was the first time there but I hope it is not the last." I assured him that it would not be the last time but my problem now was how to get her to understand that her pleasure brings me pleasure and that I can be trusted to not stop loving her just because she likes sex with well hung guys like you.

I then asked Shawn to do what ever is possible but to please have any sexual activity at our house as here at the club, even in the gym, it is far to public and someone at sometime will see you and her go into a room together or nearly together. I want her reputation to be and remain sterling and there are some nosey members.

Then I told him that I had spotted that very thing several months ago so actually knew something was going on. I was not angry then but very curious. I told him that, as he knows, she comes to exercise a couple of mornings a week and either those mornings or ones when she does not come would be the best. I asked him to be open with me so I would not call or come home and embarrass her and added that this was not to ask permission but to add to her comfort and protect her reputation.

We left it that he would try to make it Tuesday mornings as this was his light day. I thanked him and assured him that I would not be there even hidden unless he knew about it in advance and I would not want to shock Lorraine so it may have to await her knowing that I know, which is up in the air. I told him also that that was my busy morning for meetings anyway. OK, I told a friend a small lie but the purpose was for my wife's pleasure. So, now I had cleared one hurdle and communicated with one lover. Who would I approach next? For the moment, I ruled out Ronald but it occurred to me that Greg, from the symphony might be approachable and as we had a ticket for this Friday's concert and there was a fundraiser coming up. Now to think up a plan about how to set it up.

CHAPTER X

Music has Many Beats

W ell, in the intermission of that Friday evening's concert at a time when many of the members of the orchestra mingle with the crowd, we did see Greg roaming around talking to those he knew. When Lorraine went to the ladies room I waved to Greg and he came right over. I told him that Lorraine was momentarily indisposed. He asked if we were planning to come to the fundraiser the next week. At first I said, "Of course, we almost always come if only for the entertainment as your string quartet is second to none." I asked him for the date again and when he told me, I said, "Darn, I have to go out of town but I am sure Lorraine will come.

At this point a thought came to me and I asked if he would do me a big favor. He said, "Of course, what is it." I told him that as we are almost always together, I do not have to worry about her safety but coming downtown to the concert hall alone and going back home alone is a different matter. The favor is that, "I would like to find someone to keep an eye out for her and maybe take her there and bring her home or at least be sure she got home as these event usually last till late evenings."

I then said, "I have been thinking about who to ask and it occurred to me that we know you better than many others who we know will be there and actually, none of our neighbors are adamant concert goers like we are." "Would this be possible for you as I know you are married also.

Just as he said "Of course, my wife and I will be honored to pick Lorraine up and see that she gets home." Just then Lorraine returned to my side and greeted Greg as usual with a small peck on the cheek. The first warning bell announcing the end of the intermission rang giving me only enough time to tell Lorraine in

Greg's presence that, "I have arranged for Greg and his wife to pick you up and take you home next week for the fundraiser as I must be out of town that day and will not get home till the next day. My wife smiled her usual warm smile and said, "That would be nice as I was thinking of not coming alone – I hope this will not be too much trouble for you and your wife."

Greg assured her that it would be their pleasure and as he parted he said, "See you at 5:30 next Saturday." As we were making our way back to our seats I chuckled to myself thinking there was no way his wife would be with him so he would have full control of whatever happened when he brought her back home. I was also pleased that this was the weekend Lorraine's parents had asked to take the kids to the Zoo. Lorraine's only comment was, "That was very sweet of Greg and his wife to go out of their way so I will not miss the event." "Honey, you are so thoughtful – One more reason I love you so much even after these years of marriage."

After we got home and I took the sitter home three blocks away, I again found a horny receptive wife who initiated sex by giving me a blowjob to the point that I could not take it any more so I pulled out saying we had better make love before I cannot. She quickly laid on her back and opened her legs and said, "Come to me baby, I need you to fill me up with your love potion." Then, "I am the luckiest woman in the world to have you – come make love to me."

As always, at times like these I do count my blessings as she was and still is the sexiest woman I have ever known and making love to her is a heady experience. It was I that was the luckiest person in the world.

To get on with my story, the night of the event I was in the hotel and on my computer at 5:30 to see if I was right. Lorraine was dressed and had set out three glasses next to a few snacks and a bottle of wine. This was her usual thoughtfulness on display. She looked elegant in her blue form fitting dress. The doorbell rang and I moved to the living room to see her open the door for Greg.

She gave him the usual innocent peck on the cheek and looking past him said, "Greg, where is your wife – invite her in as we have time for a little wine to start the evening." As Greg came into the living room he said, "Dorothy came down with a cold and will not be joining us but it will be my pleasure to be your escort." He then added, "Your home is beautiful fitting for a very beautiful lady – and, Yes, a glass of wine would be nice."

As Lorraine led the way into the kitchen it was not lost on me that he was checking out her curvy bottom as he followed her. So concentrated was he that when she stopped he almost ran into her. Both of them seemed relaxed, however, as Lorraine poured the glasses of wine and offered Greg a snack. They talked about what to expect at the fundraiser and who was going to be the entertainment. Greg told her that in addition to the String Quartet there was gong to be a special treat as they had arranged for the chorus to sing a series of opera vignettes.

With that news my wife became visibly excited, as I knew she would, as the pieces mentioned were her favorites. Greg then added that there would be dancing after and he was looking forward to that for sure. Twenty minutes later I saw Greg help Lorraine on with her coat pausing to give her a small hug before they left.

Fast forward to 10:00 when I got back from dinner and got the computer on and the front door camera ready. While waiting for them to return, I undressed and slipped on the hotel bathrobe and turned on the TV. My timing was good as about 10:15 or so I saw the front door open and first Lorraine came in followed by Greg. He helped her off with her coat and then took his own coat off. Before Lorraine could say anything Greg took her in his arms and gave her a big hug and I saw her hug back so I knew I would again get to witness my wife in the arms of another man. While doing this he said, "Do we have enough time for a second glass of wine?" She told him that it would have to be just one as she had enough at the event.

I followed them into the kitchen and saw that Greg had his arm around my wife in a very familiar manner. Once the wine was poured they raised their glasses to toast the evening. Greg stated, "Here is to a great evening where I give you pleasure like we have wanted to do for some time." They then put their glasses down and went in to a very warm embrace with Greg kissing her neck and then her lips. She returned his kisses for sure. After this introductory kiss my wife said, "You know, Greg, we really should not be doing this – we are both married and I love my husband very much." She seemed about to say more when Greg kissed her again and I could see their tongues probing each others mouth.

During the kiss Greg started feeling and playing with my wife's bottom and raised her dress exposing her panties. At the same time I saw him pull his zipper down and almost immediately his almost hard cock became exposed. I was impressed as it was very thick and certainly longer than mine. My wife reached for it and started running her hands up and down his length. At one point she took his hand and led him out of the room. I moved to a different camera and saw her leading him upstairs. I went to look into our bedroom and when they did not come in I went for a search.

Found them in the guest room undressing each other. Heard him say, "Lorraine, I have looked forward to this moment since we first met and I am going to love giving you orgasm after orgasm." Her response was, "I feel very guilty as we start this because I do love my husband more that anything in this world. I am also looking forward to finally feeling and tasting your very large cock."

Among the emotions that flooded my mind, I was so very pleased that she did not share our marital bed with Greg. Yes, she was about to suck his cock and fuck him but not in our bedroom. This little thing made me love her all the more even as I recalled that she had fucked Shawn in our bed. Somehow, the fact that he was a friend, my squash coach and exercise trainer made him special and I was OK with Lorraine and he fucking in our bed.

Anyway, I could see that she was very into sucking Greg's cock and even his balls. She started going up and down faster and faster and deeper and deeper until he shouted, "Here I cum." He must have had a big load, as he seemed to ejaculate for more than a few minutes. When he finished he gave my wife a very passionate kiss and started playing with her body.

He then laid her on the bed and pulled off her remaining clothes before he stripped. Once he lay next to my wife he started kissing and running his tongue all over her body. I mean all over. For almost a half hour he licked and sucked her sensitive breasts then went down and brought her to two loud orgasms sucking on her labia and clitoris. Just when I thought he would soon be fucking my wife he turned her over and started licking her bottom. Lorraine became very vocal as he tongued her vagina and then her anus. I do this for her and I know she gets very hot from this stimulation. Tonight was no exception. After several minutes of moaning and telling him to go deeper she finally totally relaxed as if in a slumber.

With that he turned her over and in the missionary position with her legs over his shoulders he entered her. She had her first orgasm when he was only half way in. Once he was all the way in and stroking in and out, I swear I could hear his balls slapping my wife's anus. She kept saying between shuddering orgasms "Oh my God, you are so good, so big, you are stretching my vagina like no other – please do not stop fucking me." I knew that she was being pleasured by a new cock and a new person, which I thought must have been the reason for her extra horniness. Or maybe it was because she had been drinking a bit. In any case when he finally came he sort of rolled over and seemed to go to sleep or at least he wasn't moving except to feel my wife's breasts.

During this fucking I had a shuddering orgasm myself and now I had to go to the bathroom. When I came back, they were still in each other's arms. I dosed off and an hour later I was awakened by my wife's screaming orgasm. Wow, they were still at it and he was still able to bring her to orgasms.

As they fucked I dosed off again and when I awoke, the bed was empty. I quickly went to the cameras in our bedroom and there was my beautiful wife, asleep alone in our bed. God I loved her. I knew that I just had to find a way to convince her that what she does is OK as long as she loves me as she has for the last 9 years.

The Conversation

I came back Sunday morning to a very loving and horny wife. Kissing her got me almost rock hard in a minute as I would swear that I could still taste Greg's cum in her mouth. I knew that one day soon I would tell her how much that turned me on. She met me at the door in only her robe. She quickly made us some breakfast and telling me that she missed me far too much, and a bit about the entertainment of the evening. When I asked if Greg and his wife treated her well, she hesitated a bit and said, "Gosh yes, I was picked up and brought home and it was very pleasant." It was not lost on me that she made no reference to Greg's absent wife.

She then almost dragged me upstairs to our yet unmade bed. When I commented on it she said that she purposefully did not make it until we had made up for my absence. I had the overwhelming feeling of love and also wonderment at how or why she is so extra horny after she has been fucked to exhaustion the night before. I wonder for a minute if guilt played a role but decided that was unlikely as she gets so into sex with whoever, as her need is first.

Anyway we did what we usually do except the vision of the night before had me hard and when sucking me she commented saying, "Wow what happened on the trip that made you so hard today." I told her that it was her and that I missed sleeping with her that much. Also I got her into a 69 position and found her quite vocal when I tongued her vagina and anal opening – especially the later. I had Greg to thank for showing me a new place to stimulate the woman I love. We stayed in bed playing, which included my playfully spanking her bottom till she cried 'enough' and after making love again we talked about our love for each other till almost noon. Then we got up and showered.

Once downstairs and getting a light lunch, I started the life changing conversation by asking a question the answer to which I knew. At a good time in our conversation I asked her if she had spoken again to her cousin about her affairs. Lorraine looked at me with an indescribable and priceless look and said, "Why yes, we have spoken almost weekly and she has told me a lot about the other men in her life." I then asked her if she thought the reason for the affairs were because she was not happy with her husband who was a long time friend of mine. I also said that, anything we say stays here in confidence."

She then said (what I have known from the almost monthly lunches with my old friend), "No, she claims that she loves her husband dearly but that she was very sexually active before marriage having many lovers and found it almost impossible to stop this sexual activity just because she was married despite her strong feelings for her husband." "She claims that she has kept her activities a secret from her husband but believes that one day she will have to tell him." I agreed with Lorraine that one day it is bound to come out but I did not think their marriage would suffer, as I know my friend cares for her a lot.

I went on to tell her that there are many reasons why one part of a couple fools around and it would take psychotherapy to uncover the reasons.

I told her that she would be surprised about how many women flirted and went as far as possible with men not their husbands. I told her that I saw it at company functions, at the club, and probably in our own neighborhood. Then I told her that I suspected that more wives fooled around with extramarital affairs than men despite the general sense that it is men who have affairs. Lorraine seemed surprised at that and asked me how I knew. I told her that I did not know for sure but that over the years this is what I have read and heard from 'guy talk' even starting in college. In fact, I told her that I was quite surprised at how often I heard guy friends talk about their girlfriends cheating on them. I then inwardly gulped as I went on to say, "In my humble opinion it is all about need. If a woman cannot fully satisfy her man in some way, he might seek to fill the void elsewhere."

I went on to say, "Unlike you, some women, I have heard, are up tight when it comes to sex in that some women do not like oral sex, some do not want to experiment or are very limited in what they will do in the sexual area to please their husband or themselves." I added, "So, you see, you will never have to worry as you are the complete woman – so much so that I can hardly keep up with you and I have no unanswered needs."

With that she jumped up and flew into my arms giving me a very big hug saying, "Chuck, I love you so much and hope you know this to be true. I guess I had a wise mother who hinted at just what you said and that is 'to keep your man be everything for him both in and out of bed'." She went on to say, "Besides I love sex with you." Then she got quiet as if pondering something and said, "Honey, you talked about the male needs, what about what the woman needs." I asked her then if she remembers any of my comments over the years about my concern that since the birth of our second child that I did not think I was enough for you in size?" The love of my life got serious and said, "Of course I remember but would you not hate me if I had a lover?"

Well, that opened the door and now I had to enter carefully. I looked at her and said, "I could never hate you and what is important is that deep down, even if you had been with other men, you would always be there for me. A lover might fulfill a need for a larger cock or a need for a personality that I do not have but would it be more than good sex." "If in the end your love for me remained intact and as I feel it now, what you did or do with other men would have no consequences." "If in outside sex, your love for me suffered, then, yes, I would be crushed. But even then I would still love you." "Does this answer the question I think you are asking?"

When I looked up I saw my love crying. I went to her and lifted her so that I could cuddle and hug her to find out what she was thinking even as I thought I knew. I guessed that I had just lifted the weight of the world from her shoulders. Through her tears she said, "Oh honey, I have done something that I hope you can forgive me for and that is that I doubted your love and integrity. I now know that you would forgive me and still love me if I had sex with another man and I have to tell you that yes, I have had sex outside of our marriage and I am so ashamed." Then she started almost uncontrollably bawling. I too almost started crying but my tears were those of joy.

I told her that I loved her and only her and that whatever she feels guilty about and whomever she has been with that it is very OK if it is me who she really loves. Well now the tears really flowed as we hugged. After several minutes during which her sobbing gradually diminished, she said, "Since before we were married and all through our marriage, I have known that my love for you was complete and I have been so embarrassed that in a moment of weakness, I wandered off the path and have not kept my marriage vows." "I now feel that you understand me and still love me and that makes me happier than you can ever know."

Before she went further as it appeared that she might say that she would not do it again, I said, "Yes, I now know that our love – mine and yours – has not been changed just because you have had sex with others." 'I also know that they have been able to give you what I cannot and your need for a larger cock and a stronger more aggressive personality is deep seated." "Please for my sake and your sake, do not stop fulfilling these needs but as you do, please continue loving me." "I mean this from the bottom of my heart."

After I said that she came into my arms and said, "Yes, I do love you more than I though possible but..." I cut her off by saying, "No 'buts', I do not want our life to change including your taking lovers as long as you love me in the end and are honest in all ways." She then told me that she knew from the start that the day would come when I would have to know everything but that as long as I did not ask she thought she was OK. She went on to say, "Now that you know that I have been a naughty wife, what else do you want to know." "I owe you honesty."

"Honey", I said, "Let's not confess everything at this time. Tell me what you want me to know in short bits and let me forewarn you that when I first suspected that you were having your needs met by others, I was hurt and angry but with time I am not only comfortable with the mental picture but knowing your love for me continues has me very turned on so I really do want to hear from you all of the details of your affairs." Then with a big grin I said, "Besides, I am sure I know about a couple of the men you have been with." "Start with the best, the rest can follow in due time." Boy, did I get a warm hug with that statement.

She asked in a low almost shy voice who I suspected she had been with. So I told her that I really suspected that my friend and her squash coach, Shawn had taken care of her several times. With an almost shocked look she said, "Yes, he was one but how in the world did you know?" She then said, "I and we have been so careful about being discreet and hidden."

I told her about the times I had come across her and him too close to be strictly professional and the one time I saw him go into a changing room that you had just gone in." When I saw the surprise on her face I said, "Please do not worry, I am not at all upset or angry with my friend Shawn. In fact, for taking care of your needs, He is still a good friend, if not a better friend as well as one of my squash partners." I added, "Incidentally, I do hope no one else saw anything so I do recommend you see him here, at our house, OK?" The look in the eyes of my wife as she nodded yes was priceless.

After that I though we should not extend this so I told her that she could tell me anything and at anytime when we are alone but suggested we go to the Club and I would beat her at a game of Squash. With that she jumped up and when I got up she gave me a big hug. During that she felt my hardon and said, "Wow, you really are turned on my cheating." I quickly said, "Honey, it is not 'cheating' if I, your husband, knows and approves of the activity but please do not tell anyone ever that I know of and approve of your fulfilling deep needs from others or that it makes you husband horny to think about it – Please." We laughed over this and after a big kiss we got our stuff and went to the Club.

CHAPTER XII

One down three to go

Well, we had a lot of fun at the club and she actually almost beat me in the set of games we played. Lorraine was very happy and bubbly before, during and after our workout. When we got home and went to bed, she stared telling me about the first times with Shawn. Of course that got me instantly hard so we made love. It was that way all weekend to the point she remarked that now that she knew how to get me instantly hard that maybe she would not need anyone else. I teased her back saying, "Not a chance that you will stop as once a person tastes the excitement of a affair it is almost impossible for them to go back and I love you too much to want you to forego the pleasure you have lived." Her response was, "God, I love you Honey, I really really do."

Monday night in bed she asked me if I was sure that I was really OK about Shawn coming over. When I assured her that I was not only OK but I wondered what took her so long, she then told me that she had invited him to come over Tuesday morning and would tell me all about what ever happened. After I told her that we both knew what would happen, she found my hard cock under the covers and just before she sucked my cock into her mouth she said, "Yes, you do want me to fuck Shawn as whenever it comes up you get hard as a rock – and very tasty too." I will love you forever. After I came she told me about another time with him and when I got rapidly hard she climbed over me and from the top and made me cum again. Amazing life we were living.

Can you guess where I was most of Tuesday morning. Yes, on my computer. I checked periodically between calls and at 11:00 Shawn dropped by. After a quick cup of coffee, they stared kissing and at one point he literally picked Lorraine up and carried her up to our bedroom. Once there I heard him ask her if this was the place to be. I heard her say that Yes, Yes I want you here and now. Please fuck me till I scream. Well, he undressed her as before and as he slid her panties off, he sat down and pulled her over his knees and gave her a mild bottom warming causing her to say, "Oh you sadist, this is making me so hot, please fuck me now." Well he was out of the rest of his clothes in a second.

Before she scooted into the bed she took his cock in her mouth and sucked him to full hardness and flopped back on her back and said, "Come fuck me, I need your big hard cock in me as I really do love what you do for me." Well, he did as I had seen a week or so ago. She had multiple orgasms and when he came she sucked him to hardness telling him to do her again. She seemed insatiable and she loved his cock. When they were in the post coital rest phase Shawn asked her if she was OK fucking here rather than the Club as he wanted to protect her reputation.

Then he asked her, "Do you think Chuck knows what we have been doing?" With that she gave him a very big kiss and said, "Yes, the love of my life knows and seems very happy that I am being pleasured by you, his friend. One day I think he would like to be present when we do this – what do you think? Shawn then said, "Any time my friend wants to see me get the best piece of ass in this city he is more than welcome." With that they both had a good laugh.

That night my loving wife gave me a quite accurate accounting of what happened further cementing my confidence in our long-term love and trust. Of course, while she was telling me I was giving her orgasms with my tongue and after a great blowjob got me hard again. At one point she told me that now she really knew that I was honest and sincere about my desire to see her satisfied by his very large cock and not be upset or jealous. Then we fell asleep in each other's arms after the last mutual orgasm.

Then a week later on a Thursday, Ronald called just as I happened to be looking at my love doing housework. She put the phone on speaker and when he told her that he would be there in an hour she said nothing but, "See you." I saw my wife then strip and walk around the kitchen very naked. I knew that she had stripped to please him. An hour later he knocked on the door and she invited him in without a stitch on. He looked surprised and told her she was a good girl to be ready for him. I was then able to see her again succumb to Ronald's dominant personality as he stripped and fucked her to several orgasms.

After Andy and Robin had finished their homework and were in bed and we were getting ready for bed she said, "Honey, I have a confession, The guy you hired to check our pool has been in my pussy at least 5 times and was here again this morning – are you mad? I said, "God, no, I love to hear about you getting made love to." She then told me that she got 'fucked' and it was definitely not 'making love.' The she told me about the morning and it was exactly as I saw it. I now knew my wife trusted me enough to share her experiences as she knew for sure that I loved to hear every detail and that during and maybe afterwards our passions and love making was the best.

As the alarm sent my computer a message whenever that system was 'armed' as well as when it was 'disarmed' and whereas she armed the system when she was alone for general safety measures I did not have to spend all day at my computer and also, she got into the habit of telling me in advance when Shawn was coming. I never tired of him fucking her as he was a very good lover giving her several total body orgasms and always a mouth full of his cum.

I told her, that night when we were in bed, that I could taste his cum in her mouth. Hearing this, she blushed and said, "So that's how you knew all along when I had been with him or Ronald or…" she paused and said, "You know honey I have been with more than just those two. I hope you are not angry." I told her that of course I was not angry and just loved her more each day and with each demonstration of her trust in me and that I had suspected there were more but knew she would tell me about them with time. So that night she told be about the Delivery guy leading to my giving her a couple of orgasms with my tongue and the first one with her pussy.

As we rested in each other's arms she said, "Honey, do you remember the Symphony fundraiser I went to alone when you were out of town?" When I told her that I did remember and thought of her all evening she then said, "Well Greg's wife did not come with him and when he brought me home, I just couldn't help myself. He was so big and so masterful we did it more than once. As I had seen it her telling me got me hard again and after playfully spanking her for being so naughty, I came in very few strokes meaning I had to bring her off by my tongue.

CHAPTER XIII

Mr. Robins' Visit

It was a week or so later, I think on a Wednesday night after the kids were in bed and we were cuddling that Lorraine told me of a new and surprising happening. She started by saying that she thinks her times with Shawn at the club may have caused her and us a problem and she was very embarrassed about it. In addition she hoped I would not be angry with her.

She cuddled up to me and told me that after working out and as she was walking out, that the busy body, Mr. Robins, who was in his 60's and on the Board of the Club, stopped her and said, "Mrs. Roberts, may I have a word with you." She said, to him, "Of course, what is it you wish to know." When they were in a more private area he said, "May I call you Lorraine." To which she immediately said, "Yes, of course". He then looked at her rather sternly and said that he knew that she was acting inappropriately with one of the staff and I think you know what and who I mean."

She then, almost in tears, told me that he said, "Yes, you have been a naughty lady and I wish to speak with you privately at your home as I do not think you want your husband to know what you have been doing. "Honey," she said looking at me imploringly, "I guessed what he was referring to and despite recalling your asking me not to tell anyone that you knew anything", I snapped back, "I have done nothing but if you must spread rumors by all means tell my husband." She told me that she said that to him as more-or-less a bluff thinking he would back down but he didn't.

He then responded to her saying sternly but quietly, "Young lady, I know you are bluffing as I am sure you would not want your husband to know what I know but it is not only your husband who I would tell." "Our Board may want to know this and possibly your lover could lose his job." Lorraine then told me she was quite anxious about this matter and wondered how best to handle this situation. At that point, I thought about becoming involved but Lorraine told me that this was her doing and she must see what he has to say and take it from there.

She then told me that she told him that he could come over tomorrow to discuss this in private but she has not been with any of the staff inappropriately as she is a very happily married woman. When he said, "We'll see if this is true – see you at 10:00 tomorrow." I had not seen my wife as agitated as she was as she asked me what should she do. I told her that I did not really know but perhaps after her discussion and talk with Cecil we would know more. I maybe should have but did not tell her that I doubted that the Board would care as I knew for a fact from Shawn's own mouth that he had seduced Cecil's wife and another of a Board member's wife among others but told her, "Let's see what develops and what he says first."

I could tell that night and the next morning that Lorraine was very nervous about her reputation and she did not relish being talked to by a man as old as her father. You can bet that I was on the computer shortly after the message of our system being 'disarmed' came knowing that Cecil had arrived. I called my secretary and asked that all calls be held and that I was not to be disturbed for an hour or so. I put on the headphones and opened the computer. First thing I saw was Lorraine taking his coat and hanging it up and inviting him for a cup of coffee.

After the usual pleasantries he said that he would like to get on with the reason he came this morning and asked her where she wanted to go to talk. I saw Lorraine get a bit anxious but said, "Lets go to either the living room or even better, our Den as this is smaller and even more private." He responded by saying, "Lead the way." On the way out of the kitchen, through the living room and then into the den I saw his eyes almost glued to my wife's sexy bottom. In the den she offered him a seat in one of the chairs we have there but he said rather sternly that he would rather remain standing for the present.

He then folded his arms and asked her if she knew why he was there. Her response was, "Well you told me you wanted to talk with me about what you thought was going on at the Club." As she was about to go on he interrupted her and asked her if she understood the seriousness of what he saw. When she said that she did not know what he saw but, "I do not fool around as I am very happily married and am not in the habit of cheating on my husband."

His response was, "That's enough, young lady. I know that you are having an affair with at least the Squash Pro, Shawn, and if you do not do exactly as I say, I will not only tell your husband but go to the Board with the recommendation that Shawn be let go." "Is that clear, Lorraine."

Then I heard my wife change her tone and say, "Please Mr. Robins how can I convince you that what ever I did, I will never do again and I admit that you are right in that I do not want my husband to know or be responsible for Shawn losing his job, Please, Mr. Robins how can we resolve this? His response was, "Young lady, you will do everything I tell you to do without question or I will leave and start the process of what I just said." "Is that clear, Lorraine?" Meekly she replied, "Yes, it is clear."

The love of my life then looked down and said, "Well, OK if this will solve the issue – what is it that you want me to do other than stop seeing Shawn?" He then tilted her chin up so she had to look into his eyes and he said, "Young lady, what you have done was vey naughty and I intend to give you a spanking that you will not forget right now, right here." Lorraine jumped back a step with a startled look and I saw her hands go to her bottom before she said, "You cannot spank me, you are not my father, and you have no right to spank me."

When he asked her if she wanted him to leave right now as she must have known that he was very serious. I guess she knew she was trapped as she said, "Oh please Mr. Robins, I'll do what you want, but please not hard." He immediately said, "Young lady, you have no choice in how long or how hard now take off your skirt unless you want to get it wrinkled as your spanking will be on your bare bottom, not above clothes." He then added is a forceful and stern tone, "Now!" as he picked up a ruler form our desk and sat down on the small couch we have in our office. I noticed that he placed the ruler on the nearby table. I became very hard at the prospect of what I was about to witness.

I saw my wife slowly unzip and take off her skirt, folding it and placing it on the small table. She walked over to where he was sitting in her half-slip to which he promptly said, "Take the slip off too." Her look was priceless as she lowered and stepped out of her half-slip and stood in front of him in her panties plus her blouse. Before he pulled her over his lap he looked her up and down and said, "I hope you know why you are going to be spanked." Then, "Do you?" Her response was a soft, "Yes, I do but please, this isn't necessary as I am so sorry about what I did and will not do it again."

He then pulled her down in a position of over his knees with her bottom in the middle. He then smoothed for some minutes her panties covering her bottom as he asked her, "Tell me Lorraine, why are you being punished?" When she did not answer right away he gave her a couple of what seemed to me to be very hard spanks. My love quickly responded with, "Ouch, please not so hard – You are punishing me because you believe that I was a naughty girl and have had sex with Shawn."

With that response he rained down 15 or 20 hard spanks causing her to say, "Ouch – OH – Please – Ohh – Ouch – please stop - with each spank and when he stopped she said, "OK, I did have some sex with him but only oral sex." At that response he again spanked her with a similar flurry of seemingly hard swats, saying with each spank, "You – will – not – lie – to – me – ever – and – when – I – ask – a – question – I - expect – an - honest – answer – now – tell – me – the - truth". She responded to each spank with squeals and ouches and pleading but to deaf ears. When he stopped he said, "Lorraine, Pull down your panties this instant."

When she hesitated he again spanked her with several spanks quite hard until her hands reached behind her and she lowered her panties to her mid thigh saying in an almost crying voice, "please,

I'll do anything but not so hard. I saw him then reach down and pull her panties completely off and placed them on the floor below her head as if to make sure she knew she was bare bottomed over his lap.

The next spanks were softer and when he would stop he would feel and stroke her bottom for a minute or so. He asked her again, "Tell me what you did with your lover?" When she hesitated he again rained a flurry of very hard spanks. When he stopped, she said, "OK, yes we did have real sex but only a couple of times. With that he started spanking her hard again saying, "I – told - you – to – be – truthful – to – me – at – all - times – and – I – will – continue – to spank - this – bottom – until – you – are – honest – is – that – clear - Lorraine."

Now, in an almost tearful voice she said, " Oh please stop, I will tell you everything – Yes, I had real sex and oral sex with Shawn many times over the last year but I promise to never do it again." I noticed that while she was talking he was stroking and fondling her bottom and this alone got me very hard.

He then said in an obvious question, "Never do it again?" and started to spank her harder again. He did not seem to care what she said, like "ouch – please – Ohh - please stop." When he did stop she said in a tearful almost sobbing voice, "What do you want me to do, I will gladly do it." He then said that he just wanted her to be honest and tell him what she did with Shawn and any other lover you have."

As he was saying this he was lightly spanking her now red bottom interspersed with fondling and squeezing to the point she actually said, "Oh don't stop what you are doing, it feels so good as my bottom stings from the spanking you have given me." He did keep fondling and now I saw his fingers slide between the cheeks of her ass and her squirming told me that he was touching her sensitive vagina or clitoris. Many moans, Ohhs, and Ahhs confirmed this to me. At that point I came and I was not masturbating.

At this, he helped her to a standing position and while she was rubbing her bottom and almost dancing around I saw him take off his pants and shirt and start taking off my wife's blouse and then her bra. When they were both naked he led her to our desk. At this point she did not resist anything he did even when he put her hand on his cock, which was surprisingly thick and long for a man of his age.

When she felt his cock growing was when I suspect she knew what was going to happen so she sat in our desk chair and took his very thick cock in her mouth. He kept saying, "That's a good girl, take it all. I am going to enjoy fucking you so much. You are one sexy lady and now, I cannot blame Shawn or any other man for wanting to seduce and fuck you." He then obviously came in her mouth as I saw her swallowing vigorously.

After he came out he pulled her to him and gave her a very big hug. For a man of 60+ he had a reasonable fit body. A bit of an early paunch but what was very noticeable was the diameter of his cock. It was not much longer than mine to be sure but it was the thickest I had ever seen and in showers through the years I saw a lot of them.

At this point he helped her to the position of sitting on our desk while he stood between her legs. He then had her lie back and placed her legs on his shoulders. As he was doing this, her hands were working on his cock. When, after maybe 15 minutes he was hard enough I heard her say, "Please go slow as I have never had a cock this big so please go slow but I really do want you in me."

Well, for the next half hour, my loving wife had several tumultuous and loud orgasms and she kept saying, "Oh wow, don't stop, you fill me so good, Oh, another one, Oh fuck, you are so good." Her rapture got me hard again and I knew that we would have a hot time reliving this tonight. Anyway when he was about to cum he asked if she was in a fertile time. Her response was, "I don't care, please fill me with your cum." Well, he did and after several minutes he pulled out and helped her off the desk. He gave my wife a big hug and thanked her for, "The best sex I have had for years and the best bottom I have ever spanked."

I then heard her tell him that she also enjoyed the sex very much but the spanking was the worst she had received since she was a pre-teen aged child. She told him that she would do anything to prevent a hard spanking again. She added that, "I sure hope that my husband never finds out about what we just did or what I have done with Shawn."

He assured her that his mouth was sealed and that he will definitely find a time to return to, "Guarantee my silence." He then added, "If that is what you want." I had to laugh at her answer as she said, "Oh yes, I would like to have you in me again to assure that Shawn will not lose his job, but please don't spank me, at least not as hard as you did today."

His reply was, "Now you know, Lorraine, how hard and how long I spank you for your naughtiness is my decision but if you welcome me back when I wish to see you, you will be very happy with the results. She then put her arms around him and gave him a big sensuous kiss saying, "I will welcome you back in these arms as long as my husband, who I love dearly, does not know about this and that Shawn is not in danger of losing his job." She then kissed him again.

While kissing, his hands were fondling and stroking her very red bottom and after a bit he said, "Yes, Lorraine, I will return and because what you did was so very naughty I will again turn you over my knees and spank you so that you learn your lesson and will remain faithful to your husband – except for me." Her response was a quiet, "I will do what you want as I never want my husband to know that I have been with Shawn or you but please be more gentle the next time."

With that he got dressed and I noticed Lorraine winching when she put her panties back on and then she walked him to the door and after a long goodbye kiss and his saying, "I will call you when I wish to come back."

CHAPTER XIV

Mr. Robins' Visit

That night, after we were in bed cuddling Lorraine said, "Honey have I got a story to tell you about this morning but before I begin I want to tell you that I love only you from the bottom of my heart, however, even as I have the strong desire for what we are living, which is a loving, emotionally monogamous relationship, I still find that I want and need what you have given me, which is the freedom to openly explore my sexuality beyond the confines of our relationship.

I love and cherish you more than you will ever know for giving me this freedom and I admit now that a larger cock experience started it all. I do promise to never hide anything I do from you in the future." Lorraine then told me all that I had observed, which made me not only very horny but even more in love that I thought possible. She said, "The morning went not at all what I expected and I was certainly wasn't expecting anything like what happened. I found that at first he was cross and made me believe that I either did exactly what he told me to do or he would not only tell you but he implied that as a Board member he could get Shawn fired." Then, "Honey, I wasn't worried about your knowing as I hide nothing from you but the Board of the Club and my being responsible for Shawn losing his job – that was too much for me to handle so I succumbed to his demands."

She went on to say, "Well he told me that I was going to get a spanking and to strip." "Honey, after I was over his lap he gave me the hardest spanking of my life." "It hurt so much that I was crying but tried very hard to not let him know I was in such pain." She then in a guilty voice inflection said, "He kept spanking me until I told him the truth about what I had done and all of the times I had sex with Shawn."

"Then he let up and after a bit the spanking actually felt good like the playful ones you give me and he would often stop and rub my butt and after a bit he went between my legs and rubbed my sex area, especially my clitoris." "I knew then that this would be more than just a punishment spanking."

She then told me all about his quite large cock, at least in thickness and how good it tasted and felt as he fucked her to several orgasms. She told me what I knew that they had gone to our Den and that he fucked her on our desk in a new position for her. She then told me, "Honey, he is not much longer than you but oh my god is he ever thick." "With him the orgasms seemed continuous." She then mused that it may have been because the spanking and the confession really cleared the air and her mind. My loving wife then said, "I did really deserve the spanking for my deception to you of what I had been doing but it was far harder than I needed or wanted."

Giving me a super warm hug she went on to say, "I did not expect the morning to go as it did but he sure fucked me nice – I hope you won't get angry if I do it again with him." "At least now he will not be able to tell anyone because he too has been between my legs." "Is that OK, Honey?"

Well, of course, I told her that her pleasure and happiness always gives me great pleasure and as long as she really loves me and kept no secrets, that I would love and care for her forever. With that we made love as we so often do and I lasted longer because she was dilated from his cock. Thinking about that did make me cum faster the first time but she now knew that by relating more about her morning that I would get hard again.

Before I fell asleep my mind very actively reviewed the feelings I have experienced since this all began and I came to the conclusion that although, in my heart, I am now convinced that my wife loves me, I am just unable to keep up with her sexual appetite. She seems to have insatiable sexual needs that must be met to relieve the tension her needs bring on.

I do not know where this came from or how long it will last but do know that as long as I know that our love and affection for each other is first and she is willing to share her pleasures, I can and will live what I am now living.

What I have come to accept is that Lorraine is a very sexual being and just loves sex in all forms. Yes, the need for a larger organ of pleasure may have been a factor in her starting to have affairs but once she started it became more than his size. Can I live with this was what floated through my mind just before I fell asleep.

The next day, while I was at work it occurred to me that Lorraine had been very honest with me about all that had happened and now I had to find a way to trust her in return. I realized that because I had the need to know for sure, I had set up a surveillance system that she did not know about. I admitted that I very much not only enjoyed what I saw but also enjoyed her telling me about it the next day but I had to find a way to tell her about at least part of the system I set up.

So, Monday after we had had another round of sex and when she again asked me if I was sure that it was OK that Shawn told her that he would see her Tuesday morning. I told her that I was absolutely positively OK and that one day I wanted to watch in person and was she OK with that.

When she assured me that nothing would make her happier than to have me present I then said that one way would be to set up a camera so I could watch from my computer either at the office or from wherever I had my computer. What she said next caught me by surprise, "Oh you mean the camera you have in the bedroom as part of our security system?" How do you say "Caught"?

We both started laughing and hugging as she said, "Honey, I just found the bedroom camera and it really is OK as knowing that you can now share in my pleasure is special." I then told her that I had felt quite guilty putting in the camera without her knowing but I was compelled to know for sure what I had suspected.

I went on to tell her that now that I knew that our love and our marriage was secure and that whatever she did with whoever was

OK and that even with a camera I would most likely not be able to see her every time she was with Shawn or anyone else but I found that I enjoyed her telling me about it far more than watching as the time I have watched was as she told me. I knew our love was intact and that was enough for me.

Falling asleep in the arms of the woman you love and feeling her body is a most pleasurable experience especially thinking of the pleasure her body has received from a variety of lovers. I am sure I got hard often as each time I would run my hands over her breasts or bottom or pussy I would envisage this same action being done by one of the men now in her life. Along with the pleasure there is also an admitted anxiety about losing my wife's love. Right now, this is on the back burner and I am comfortable on our love remaining.

After a weekend with activities at the club and spending time with our kids, I was almost looking forward to a week building my company. What was special about the weekend was that I think we got both Andy and Robin hooked on the game of squash. I had been teaching them both how to serve and why the game is so stimulating and I noticed that they both wanted to beat the other and I was impressed with their competitive spirit, which was the same as their mother's. They almost wore me out. Robin had become very proficient and often beat her brother and others older then she was. Was I a proud father or what.

The next week was busy for both of us as Lorraine had been volunteering at the kid's school and I had been in talks about buying a competitor thereby expanding my company. Lorraine was again with Shawn Tuesday morning but I only caught a bit of the action amid my busy schedule. Of course she told me about it Tuesday night. She was sure hot and once in bed I was almost attacked as she told me how he pleasured her again and again and how much she loved fucking him.

At one point she told me that if her weeks went like this one she couldn't be happier and that whereas she occasionally like the variety of a different lover she would be happy with just me and

Shawn. She told me that she wanted to make love with me for the "Love" and to be fucked by Shawn for the pure lustful filling sex and his big cock. She then said that she was coming to have feelings for Shawn akin to "love" but it was not at the level she loved me. Then she added, "Honey, I am sure I will have sex with others but I really do love to "Make Love" with you."

CHAPTER XV

A Week to Remember

T hen she told me that the assistant Principal at the kids school was sort of aggressively coming on to her with flattery subtle touching's and that she has put him off for several weeks now but he has insisted that he needed her help to plan a student retreat and sort of invited himself over for this coming Monday. Lorraine then said, "Honey, I don't think anything will happen but he is a bit of a hunk and as the football and track coach he certainly is in shape." "Are you OK with this?" I, of course assured her to go with the flow and whatever happened, I would still love her.

Well, when I kissed her goodbye Monday morning I said, "Have fun – I love you." My loving wife's response was a questioning look at first and then, "Oh, I had almost forgotten that Mr. Davis was coming over this morning." She then added, "I am sure nothing will happen as he really does not turn me on besides, my need is you."

When my phone beeped and I saw that the alarm system was disarmed I did turn on the computer. What I saw was that a very tall and rather imposing man in his 50's entered and after he removed his coat he gave Lorraine and very large and long hug indeed. As I saw this, I knew that I would have to see the recording later or, better, hear from my wife what followed as I had some important meeting to attend.

By the time I got back to my office I saw that a bit more than two hours had passed but thought I would look at what the cameras showed anyway. The kitchen, living room, and den were empty so with anxiety I went to our bedroom, which was also empty and with the bed made. At the last second I thought I would check the guest room, which got me hard instantly.

There was Lorraine on the bed stark naked and on her hands and knees and her visitor had apparently just gotten off the bed and

I saw him lie next to my wife and pull her into his arms. I assumed he had just fucked her doggie style, which I know she loves.

They were hugging and kissing and I heard him say, "Lorraine, you are something, I enjoyed being in you very much and hope we can do this again." The love of my life responded, "Well, Mark, I certainly had not expected our meeting to go the way it went." "You know, that until I gave in to you, I experienced what a lady being raped would feel but once I gave in to your persistence and strength, You certainly gave it to me good and I admit that I am no longer as upset as I was at first."

She went on to say as he continuously hugged and fondled her, "We really should not have had sex especially your taking me in my ass as I am very uncomfortable due to your position at the school my kids go to and what we did and you did to me must never be known by anyone especially my husband as he would not be pleased at all." "I hope that this is OK with you?" "You are getting me hot again but we must stop as my husband comes home after lunch often and we cannot take a chance."

So he got out of bed and started dressing and in a few minutes Lorraine did the same. Next they were at the front door and he again kissed and hugged her saying between kisses, "Lorraine, I am very discreet so you do not have to worry about anyone at the school knowing we are other than co-committee members on whatever we do, but I do want to see you again as you are the best fuck I have had in ages."

Lorraine looked at him and said, "Mark, I don't know what came over me but we should not have done what we did as I do not cheat on my husband … but … if we do meet again, please do not ever tell anyone." With that he kissed her again while patting her bottom until she said, "Please go, as my husband may come home any time." I saw him then leave and Lorraine set the alarm and went into the kitchen.

That night, when we were in bed Lorraine gave me a very big hug and told me that she had quite a tale to tell me about the assistant principal's visit. She began with, "Oh honey, I had not expected or wanted what happened." "From the first moment when he walked in the door he was hugging and fondling me despite my telling him 'No' many times." "He was so strong that whatever I did to try to get out of his arms he prevented."

She went one to tell me, "It was not 5 minutes after he arrived that he had his hands up my dress and into my panties." "I kept telling him to "Please stop" and that I didn't cheat on my husband but he just kept going." As my wife was relating this story I was very hard and excited and with only soft touches she brought me off more than once. "He carried me over to our couch and no matter how I tried to move his hands away, he persisted in playing with my bottom and pussy."

"At one point he had both of my hands in one of his hands and he held them firmly above my head. He was so strong that I was unable to move at that point. All the while, despite my protests he was kissing me. It was when he started undressing me that I realized that no matter what I did or said that he was going to have his way with me and would soon be fucking me. At this time I was starting to get very turned on even as I knew what a woman about to be raped could be feeling."

"I did keep saying "No" and "Please no" and "not that" but admitted to myself that I wanted him to continue." He sure knew how to undress a lady as he had my skirt and panties off and had undone the buttons on my blouse in a very short period of time. As I saw that to undress me further he would have to rip my blouse and bra, I said, "OK, you win, please let me take off my blouse and bra before they tear. He let go of my hands and as I was taking off the rest of what I had on I saw that he was undressing."

"Honey, he then pulled me to him and with his very muscular arm hugged me to his naked body and a very erect cock and gave me another long kiss." Yes. I was starting to get very turned on but I sensed that my protests made him even more aggressive so when the kiss ended I said "Please, we shouldn't be doing this, I am a happily married lady and do not cheat on my husband" I had to inwardly laugh at his response which was, "Well now, there is always a first time and today is your day" at which he told me rather forcefully, "lead the way to your bedroom unless you want it right here on the floor."

"So there I was walking toward our guest room as there was no way I would take him to our bedroom and it wasn't because of the camera. As he was following behind me he commented on my ass, as he put it, saying, "God, what a gorgeous sexy ass, I can hardly wait." I did not realize the implication of that statement but later found out what he meant.

"When we got to the room, I quickly took down the bedspread and sheet and turned to say to what I knew was to deaf ears, "Please, no, I have not done anything like this before with anyone else but my husband." His response was to almost push me down on the bed and get into a position with his head between my legs and his cock staring me in the face." Honey, it was different from any I had seen. It was only a bit longer than yours and only a bit larger around but the head was huge, like a large plumb." As I was staring at his organ he brought me to two orgasms." "Finally, I could not take it anymore so I took ahold of his cock to more carefully see it and feel it."

He stopped to say, "Lorraine, put my cock in your mouth, as I need to cum badly." Love, I couldn't resist saying, "Please, no, I have never done this before, not even with my husband." His quick response was, "Just do it and you will see what you have been missing." I did as he said, as I wanted to do it and was very curious as to what he would feel like. In addition, the head was quite large and spongy soft. On top of that his pre-cum secretions were quite good. I licked and sucked on the head as he kept pushing it further and further in my mouth. As he was starting to tense up and was about to cum, he reached down to hold my head so I would take his cum in my throat.

After several spurting contractions and a lot of cum to swallow he pulled to slowly and asked, "Well, how did you like that experience?" I told him that it was very different but enjoyable. He then changed his orientation and poised himself over me with his cock between my legs. I knew that I was about to be fucked by him and I was actually a bit excited and turned on but said, "Please, no, I have never done this with any man other than my husband and I am afraid." "Honey, I had to stifle my chuckle at this lie."

All he said was, "I am too heavy to lie on you so I can put my cock in your pussy, so put it in for me." "Well, of course I 'had' to obey him so I moved around and with some rubbing to get my juices flowing, I helped him enter me." "And enter me he did, it took him only a few strokes to be all the way in and the feeling was different from any I had ever experienced probably because to the large size of his crown. Guess the head was what stimulated my G-spot because I had my first orgasm within the first minute of his fucking me."

Oh honey, he had amazing staying power and strength as he pounded me for what seemed like an eternity. After my third to fourth orgasm he said, "well, my little one, I guess you like this don't you" I responded with, "Yes I do love what you are doing to me and you can keep doing it." "Honey, at the time, I really meant it even as I had not wanted him at the start and was not planning on having sex as Shawn was coming the next day and on top of that Mr. Robins called and invited himself over Wednesday morning.

"Anyway he finally came giving me an total body orgasm." He then lay on the bed and held me in his arms for several minutes when he finally said that he was glad he came over as I was the best. He then asked me to get him hard again with my mouth. By then I was curious and turned on so I did as he asked. This time around we switched positions several times and we must have fucked for almost an hour. At one point he got me up on my knees and was fucking me from behind.

This felt wonderful and even better when he started sticking his fingers in my ass. I was in total bliss until I felt him come out and put his cock to my ass. I told him, "Please no as I do not do anal sex." I tried to get way but he was too strong and once he was in my ass, it actually felt quite good but I did not want him to know that as I repeatedly moaned and told him "No, I cannot take this" but in reality it did feel quite good. I want you to take me that way soon. When he finally came he pulled out and I stayed in the position he left me in for some time before I was able to convince him to leave. I told him that you might come home. "Honey, as good as it felt, he plum wore me out."

All the while Lorraine was telling me what happened she was playing with my cock and amazingly brought me off two times. Just before we turned out the lights she said, " Honey, I love you more than ever and I would be happy maybe having outside sex once a week maybe twice but it looks like this may be a full week. Today was interesting but tomorrow Shawn comes and now Wednesday Mr. Robins is coming over and I just remembered that this is the Thursday that Ronald comes to service the pool and (she said with a big grin) me." "I hope you are OK and I want you to know that I would not plan for a week this active." I gave her a big kiss and said, "enjoy and tell me all about it." And then I fell asleep in almost seconds.

As I left in the morning, I gave my wife a special hug and told her to enjoy her day. She gave me a big kiss and said, "I sure will as usual with Shawn." He did come over and I was able to watch a couple of orgasms but I could tell that she really liked his long and large cock and he seemed to be able to go on forever slowly pumping all the way in her vagina and then almost all the way out.

It seemed to almost drive her crazy with lust as she would say over and over, "Oh God, I love what you do to me, you are the best", as she would meet each of his thrusts with her own. Then in the throes of passion she said, "Oh Shawn, I love you, I really do, please do not ever stop making love to me." I saw Shawn look at her differently as he said, "hey, Lorraine, only love one of us, not both." She then became very silent except for some orgasms.

That night between our own 'love making' she told me all about the morning. She added that after they finished she went to the club and played a game of squash with him so when she came home she was so exhausted that she slept till the kids came home from school. Before we fell asleep she shared a bit of anxiety about Mr. Robins visit the next day.

I looked in on the house between meetings and calls and I could tell that Lorraine was anxious as her activities seemed all hurried so I gave her a call to reassure her of my love. She responded, "Oh, Honey, you are so thoughtful to call and yes, I am anxious as I sure did not enjoy the spanking last time but if I have to put up with a sore fanny to get his pleasure, I think that I will." "Mostly, I am anxious about what room he will take me to." "I do not want him to know our bedroom but knowing you could possibly be watching has my mind in a whirl and it is more sexy in our bed than in the guest room." "Does this make me a bad wife, honey?"

I told her I though that is was also sexy to know that you have been fucked in the bed we make love in but that whatever she chose would be OK with me as I know where her heart is. I did tell her that I had a busy day as there were meetings planned with the owners of the company we have made an offer on. I closed by telling her that I would see her tonight and was looking forward to hearing what happened. Got a nervous laugh when I said that I would sooth her bottom if needed.

I happened to be free when the signal came that the alarm system was disarmed so got to see Cecil's entry and more. When he entered the first thing he said was, "So how has my naughty little girl been behaving the last couple of weeks?" followed by a big hug. Lorraine responded with, "Why I was very good, what did you expect after the spanking you gave me a couple of weeks ago?" She hung up his coat and he followed her into the kitchen where she had made a fresh pot of coffee and had some of her super buns laid out. Before he sat down he went up to my wife and gave her a big kiss and a hug, which I saw her return.

Before he let go of her he said, "We can discuss whether or not you have been a good girl but tell me something." "Did your confessions make you feel better on my last visit?" I was a bit surprised but excited when she put her arm around his neck and said, "Oh my goodness yes as I had been keeping these activities a secret and I must say I felt better after I owned up to my infidelity." She went on to add, "but the spanking sure hurt."

"Well now", Cecil said with a more stern voice, "lead the way so we can talk further about how you have lived since our last talk and maybe there are other things you need to confess that we did not discuss." Lorraine was quick to say, "Ok Mr. Robins, I will tell you everything but please don't spank me as hard as you did the last time you were here." He then said, "Do you have a better place for us to talk than your den?" With a little hesitation she said, "Well, we could go to our spare room."

As they walked out of camera range, I switched to the guest room and when they didn't come to the room in a reasonable time I went searching and when I got to our bedroom, there they were much to my surprise. Cecil was sitting on the bed and Lorraine was standing in front of him. I heard her say, "I wish you had not taken me to the bedroom I share with my husband as being here with you makes me feel even more guilty."

His response was, "Lorraine that is the point, now come closer." When she got next to him, I did not hear what he was saying as he was speaking softly but could see him saying something and her nodding as if she understood or agreed as he started undressing my wife. I became very turned on as he undid the buttons on her blouse, took it off and then he unzipped her skirt and held it as she stepped out of it and then he reached around her back and undid her bra and took it from her shoulders and tossed it on top of her other clothes leaving her in just her panties.

He then stood up and took her in his arms and I did hear him say, "That was a good girl and I am looking forward to what you will tell me when you are over my knees." He then rather quickly undid his belt and stepped out of his pants, took off his shirt, and sat down on the bed. He reached for my wife's hand and pulled her over his knees. When she was in position and his hands were busy stroking her bottom over her panties he said, "Lorraine, I am going to ask you a number of questions and you know what will happen if I do not get a truthful answer?" "Do you understand what I am saying?"

Lorraine then spoke in a somewhat fearful voice, "Oh please don't spank me hard, I could hardly sit for a few days the last time. I will answer you truthfully, I promise." She told me that night that at this point she was quite anxious and almost afraid, as she did not know what he knew and if she could admit to him her being with other men beside Shawn.

He then asked her what she was feeling and thinking because she seemed very nervous to him. Her response made me love her all the more as she said, "Oh Mr. Robins, I feel like a little girl about to be spanked by her daddy for telling a lie." " I promise that I will be honest but part of my anxiety is that if I tell you everything, would you not tell anyone ever especially my husband." I heard him reassure her that she did not have a worry. Then he said, "Lorraine, when I ask you a question, I will count to three slowly and if I do not get an answer, I will start spanking for real, OK?"

He then started spanking her almost softly but hard enough that I heard the odd 'ouch' and 'Please, I'll be a good girl'. He stopped and asked her if she had been with Shawn since his last visit. I am sure her pause before her answer was what his reaction would be if she told the truth. She was about to speak, I thought, when he said "Three" and his hand came down hard on her pantied bottom. Her response was, "Oh please no, I was about to answer." "Yes, I have been with Shawn since you were here – please no more spanks." He then asked her how many times she had been with him and she responded quickly, "Twice". He then started lightly spanking her bottom alternating with pats and rubs as he asked her, "where did you meet him." Again she hesitated a bit but answered rather gingerly, "Here in my home in the guest room." He then asked as he pealed her panties down and off, "Tell me Lorraine, what does he do that you need so badly."

Her response made me very proud as she said, "Well, he is very large but most of all he treats me with kindness like my husband does." Cecil then startled me when he said, " You know that you are not the only one he sleeps with as I recently found out that he has even taken my own wife to bed." When he said that he started spanking a bit harder as he went on, "I think they have been together several times and I do not want to lose her." This led to, "Ouch, Oh please, why are you punishing me for what your wife did?"

With that he started again the pat and fondling saying, "yes, I am sorry. Lets get back to your activities." "I want you to tell me if you have been with any other men behind your husbands back." After a short delay, she said, "OK, if you promise to not spank me hard, I will tell you who I have had sex with, OK?" So as he played with Lorraine's bottom she told him, I have had sex a couple of times with one of the teachers at my kids school and several times with the technician who comes to service the pool a couple of times a month." and she then said, "Please never tell my husband that I had been this naughty." He then said, "As long as you include me in your infidelity, you are forever safe."

I heard him promise to keep her secret as his fondling went between her legs and she started to moan in pleasure. He then told her that she had nothing to worry about, as he would never betray her trust and disclose her activities. With that he helped her to stand and gave her a large hug while he lowered his boxers. The next thing that happened was that he said, "Well, Lorraine where do you want it, here or elsewhere." She gave him a kiss and pulled him down on our bed and without any or much foreplay she was screaming in her first orgasm and he stimulated her vaginal walls with his very thick cock.

I got called away and when I returned almost an hour later he was still pleasing her with frequent orgasms but now they were from behind. Lorraine kept saying, "Oh please, don't stop you are so good until he came what must have been a final time and they seemed to collapse in the bed and fall asleep as they were still there after I got back from the restroom. I sure got a good story and great lovemaking that night.

The next day I knew that I would not be able to watch her with Ronald but that night she told me what happened. She had taken off her bikini and was getting some sun with only a towel covering her. She told me that when she heard the gate open she flung off the towel as it excited her to be nude when he came. She said that she had no idea where that came from but it did turn her on.

Lorraine then shared his aggressiveness and that after he came in her mouth he was able to have two more orgasms over a period of almost an hour and he brought her to more climaxes than she could count. She went on to say, "As great as it was when he was fucking me I was glad when he finished." "He then told me that he was promoted to a manager position and that he would not be coming back every two weeks but that he hoped he could still see me on the occasion of his having some time." She then said, "Honey, as much as I like it when he is fucking me, the excitement was getting less so I told him that he should call several days prior to an opportunity and if I could that I would love to be with him, knowing I would see him less and less."

A Lover Each Day

J st before we had our goodnight kiss she said, "this was some week, honey, I have had sex with four different men, one each day and as sexy as it was and they were I really do love making love with you knowing that you love me as much as I love you." "I thank you with all of my heart for allowing and encouraging me to satisfy my sexual urges, yet your love remains as does mine - I love you, honey, I really do." We then fell asleep in each other's arms.

The next morning after the kids were off to school, Lorraine again told me that the week almost wore her out four straight days of being taken – or giving herself to men who have come into her life. She thought that this was a record and was enough and that she was going to get a good workout and maybe a squash game this morning. I told her to have fun and left telling her that maybe she would get lucky this morning to make it a full week. We laughed at that.

Well, guess what, she did get lucky and I was able to watch. Around 10:00 I heard the 'beep', meaning the alarm 'disarmed' and I tuned in to see her in her gym clothes, open the front door to the same delivery guy. First thing she said was, "Hi Lucas, what are you delivering today?" He responded, "Well, Lorraine, just a small package in my hand but I have a larger package also for your pleasure."

Lorraine was quick to reply, "Hey, back off young man, I do not play around on my husband." "You were lucky a few weeks ago but not likely today." I saw him look at her and say clearly, "Lorraine, why are you saying what I know is not true." "Do you not know that this area of town in my route and every day this week, there was a new and different car in your driveway." "I would see it when I was going in and the same car was there when I left the area."

"I even did not deliver this box to you yesterday as there was a pool maintenance truck in your drive for far longer than they usually stay." Then he went up to her and as he tilted her head so she had to look him in the eyes he said, "Well, what do you say to that?" I heard her say in a softer voice, "So, what is it you want me to say young man, what I do in my private life is private."

"Look Lorraine, you do not have to say anything as what you do in your home is your business and just so as you know, I will not and would not ever tell anyone but you what I saw or, for that matter, what we did a couple of weeks back." "I am telling you as I get a real chuckle out of your telling me you are innocent but I strongly suspect otherwise." "This said, your secret is quite safe with me whatever we did or might do in the future."

With that she put her arms around his neck and said, "Lucas, I have misjudged you and I sincerely thank you for your discretion." With that she gave him a kiss, which quickly became passionate as his hands roved over her body including fondling her bottom. As she was kissing him, I saw him quickly undo his pants buckle and slide his pants down his legs. He then slid down his shorts and resumed his hugging and fondling her body.

Quite shortly after that he placed her hand on his cock. She stopped her kissing to say, "Oh, Lucas, you have the hardest cock I know and I have a feeling that we will be naughty again." His response was to start kissing her again but while doing this he started peeling down her gym shorts and then slowly but continuously raised her top till she raised her arms to make it easier to remove.

Once he had my wife quite naked he asked "Am I right that you do not want me to stop what we are doing?" Her response brought me to an orgasm as she said, "Oh, Lucas, I do want you to take me and give me pleasure as much as I want to show you how much I need your exceptionally hard cock." "When you first came, I did not want you but when you showed your true colors and now have undressed me, I want nothing better than to make you glad that you persisted."

With that he led her to the couch and bent her over the back similar to what he did the first time. He then got on his knees and nuzzled his face in her crotch. I could only imagine that he was tonguing her vaginal area, clitoris and anus by Lorraine's moaning and vocally encouraging him to continue. After some time he got up and soon had his cock in her pussy from behind and very shortly she had her first orgasm of the day.

I was not able to watch it all as I had some calls coming in but it seemed that he never really got soft and I counted four times that he came as he would pull out and shot his cum on her bottom or belly and one time in her throat. Each time he came he would get my very willing wife in a new position. They must have been at it for almost an hour with her riding him like a cowgirl to his fucking her from behind both over the back of the couch and in the 'doggie' position.

Lorraine must have been in orgasmic heaven as she kept encouraging him by complimenting him on his staying power and continued hardness. The last coupling I saw was them on the couch with her legs over his shoulders and he was going in and out in a tantalizing slow motion to the point that I heard her plead with him to go faster and bring her to another climax saying, "Please Lucas, faster, you are driving me crazy." When she said that he asked her, "OK, Lorraine, if I do as you wish, will you open your legs for me without argument, and do this again the next time I come to deliver a package?"

My wife's response put me over the top and I luckily grabbed some Kleenex to catch my load as she said, "Oh, God, yes, Lucas, you can have my pussy anytime you want. Never have I cum so many times and had a man stay as hard as you do for as long as you can. I really do love fucking you and only hope my husband doesn't find out what a naughty and horny wife he has married."

His response I am sure floored her as after he said, "Lorraine, never sell your husband short as he may not only not be angry but also be turned on my your sexual antics. I know that I would only hope I marry a woman as sexually active as you are", she threw herself at him and gave him quite a hug saying, "You are some young man and I hope when you marry you will still be around to give me a little on the side even when I am older." He then told her that, "You have a deal as I would always be there to give you a little or a lot as you are by far the sexiest lady and best piece-of-ass I have been with".

CHAPTER XVII

And In Conclusion

Shortly after the UPS delivery guy left, I called my love and told her that I will be able to get home early and told her to be ready with the kids for a trip to the Gym and a game of squash or two. I asked her how her day was and chuckled as after a bit of a hesitation he said, "It was interesting and I will tell you all about it when you get home."

Well she did tell me what I had seen, which got me very horny, as always, but as the kids were about to come home, I promised that she would get it again tonight. A few minutes later the 'wild bunch' arrived home and were excited about going to the gym. Robin was most excited as she was eager to get ready for the 12 year old Squash tournament, which she "planned" to win. Also, Andy, was excelling himself in Squash and they were both looking forward to their lessons with Shawn.

I learned from Shawn that evening that he had finally found a young lady who he wanted to marry and wanted to invite both Loraine and me to the wedding. His question to me was how I thought Lorraine would take this news. My answer was that I really thought she would be happy for you but if he wanted, I would break the news first. I did and she was or seemed genuinely happy for him.

At the wedding, Shawn's buddy and Best Man, Randy, danced with many of the ladies but more often and more warmly with my wife. When I asked her about this and his attraction she told me that he was quite forward and came right out, while serendipitously feeling her bottom to ask about her "availability". She admitted right there on the dance floor in my arms that she found him interesting and was turned on by his aggressiveness and hoped that I was not angry at the rapidness of this response.

The first question I asked her while we were dancing was what her response to Randy was. The love of my life looked me in the eyes and with her heart-melting smile said, "Honey, I told him that "availability" could be arranged as long as he was totally discreet so that my husband or anyone else does not find out what we may do." "His big grin and squeeze of my bottom told me his intentions." "Yes, he did turn me on." So a new chapter is in the future.

I had to almost laugh at her question as I told her that I was looking forward to this new adventure and hope in the end, her love was still with me. Lorraine gave me a very large hug as she told me that she was the luckiest woman alive to have such a loving and trusting husband where she can think and say what she wants and still knows that her love for and from me is safe.

Looking ahead, I could see an interesting life that has been and will be highlighted by my wife's sexual appetite. At this point I felt comfortable with her love and honesty, as in the last years I have sensed and believed and witnessed almost total honesty from my wife in an area most wives are quite secretive about.

Because of my wife's needs, I have enjoyed an absolutely fantastic as active sex life that appears to be far beyond that of other males in my age range. What will happen in the future as our son, Andrew, becomes a man and our daughter, Robin, becomes an adult woman remains to be seen. It is my hope that their mothers adventures remain private between Lorraine and me.

Stay tuned as Lorraine's adventures do not end.

The Surprise That Does Not End

By **Chris Dawson**

This is a story, told by Beth, about an adventure that begins in a most unusual and unexpected way. Beth is a very happily married young lady who gets initially trapped by a houseguest who is her father-in-laws friend and is as old as her father. The unexpected orgasms, which are the first with any man other than her husband, are surprisingly powerful. Initially she tries to resist but soon finds that she, guiltily, wants more. Her almost daily battle is to how to keep her infidelity from her husband but once started the adventure is impossible to stop.

CHAPTER I
The First Time Orgasm

My name is Elizabeth, my friends and husband call me Beth. I am 26 years old and have been married to a wonderful man for 6 years. I know it is odd these days but I was a virgin when I married. I guess it was the strict upbringing and I do know that my mom told me in no uncertain terms that I must be pure when I married so my husband will love me more that anyone else and will always love me.

My husband, Reginald, is two years older than me and is a wonderful and thoughtful man in addition to being a superb lover – or at least I thought that there could be no one better. Greg, as he is called, was slow and gentle with me at first but now we make love at least 2 to 3 times a week and occasionally more. He almost, but not always, brings me to what I thought was a large orgasm.

Greg is almost 6 feet tall and is in superb physical shape from playing sports and continuously going to the gym. He is an imposing figure at 190 pounds. I am 5 foot 5 inches and weigh about 125 pounds. My husband and others tell me that I have a very sexy figure even as I do not know what that means. My husband says that he was first attracted to me because of my "nice butt" as he calls it but fell in love with me when he learned that I was not a 'dumb blond.'

What I feel I must confess began a couple of years ago and has changed my life in so many ways. I still love my husband with all my heart and am more that a little embarrassed at what I have been experiencing but did not think originally that I could ever tell him what I am doing and with whom.

It all started when one of my husband's father's long time best friend and hunting and fishing partner, Karl, needed a place to stay while work was being done on his house. Karl is retired and must be in his mid to late 60's and both my husband and I knew him fairly well. He had been at our wedding and I do remember dancing with him more than a couple of dances. He did surprise me out on the dance floor as he held me closer than most of the male family members who I danced with and I felt my bottom fondled a number of times.

Karl did not fondle or touch me long enough for me to move his hand or say anything as just before I would say or do anything to avoid his contact he would stop and go about innocently and talk to me as if nothing unusual had happened. He seemed otherwise very sweet and I knew my husband liked him very much as he and his dad were very close friends. For this reason I said nothing but at the time and in my innocence this made me blush furiously.

No one other than my new husband had felt my bottom but I had to admit that it made me a bit excited as his hand felt different from my husbands. I did not know where theses feelings came from and was very ashamed to have these lusty thoughts.

When the possibility of our having a houseguest came up, Greg asked me if this would be OK. Before I could say anything, he told me that he would stay in our guest room and that he thought he would be gone a good bit of the time, He also told me that Karl was a superb hobby gardener and he was sure that Karl would help me make our back yard to the garden I wanted it. At that point, I could hardly argue, as it seems this was decided.

For the first couple of weeks the visit was very pleasant. He had dinner with us a few times but mostly he was out dong his thing in the evening and helping me plan our landscaping and flower beds. He seemed the perfect older gentleman so I relaxed maybe more than I should have.

My husband was building his business so got up quite early. I would put on my robe and panties and fix his breakfast and we would have a very pleasant time before he left for work. Then I would go back to bed and sleep an hour or so before I got up for my day. This became our routine broken by our occasionally making love when we woke up. Our 'love making' was warm, tender, and almost quiet.

One morning I had gotten back in bed and was almost dozing off when I heard my bedroom door open. Before I could turn around to see who I thought would be my husband, Karl had climbed into bed without a stitch of clothes on and held me down with his arms. I tried to struggle free to get out of bed but I was no match for Karl's strength. I first said in an angry voice, "Karl, please leave this bed at once." Then, "Please, Karl, you must leave immediately, I am a married woman." Then, "Stop doing that this instant", when his arm tightened around me and he held me pressed against his body.

As my struggles had been futile and I was almost breathless from the work expended to move away, I sort of relaxed. I guess this was his clue to start feeling my breasts which at first startled me leading to my saying, "For Gods sake Karl, stop this this instant, please stop." Well, he did not stop and I had to admit that it did feel good so I rationalized that it would be harmless to let this old man feel my breasts. I did add, "Greg will be quite angry when I tell him what you are doing."

His first words were, "Relax, Beth, I am not going anyplace and you know you like what I am doing." I shot back to him, "Karl. Please stop, it is just not right for you to play with my breasts." I again tried for several minutes to struggle free from his grasp. For all my struggles nothing was accomplished but that our bodies were closer together so when I relaxed again, he slid his hand down my tummy and back up this time under my nightgown to feel and play with my bare breasts. As good as this felt I was most mortified.

Even as I knew it was fruitless to resist, I said, "Please, Karl, what you are doing is not right. Please stop." My problem was that it was starting to feel far too good and I was almost mesmerized by his stroking my breasts and tweaking and lightly pinching my nipples. So, resigned to what I did not think I could control, I relaxed again.

The next thing I knew was that his left arm was around my neck fondling my breasts while his right arm was stroking my tummy and occasionally my pussy. I started struggling anew exclaiming, "Karl, don't you dare touch me down there, you have no right." As I said that I knew I could do nothing as he now had two hands and arms to hold my in the position he wanted.

At one point I just laid there feeling my breasts being played with and now my pussy being stroked through my panties. All I could say weakly was, "Please, no, not there, this is wrong." This of course fell on deaf ears so I relaxed again rationalizing that I would just have to let him have his fun for now. After all he was an old man of the age of my father.

The next thing I felt was his hand slipping beneath my panties and softly rubbing the lips of my pussy. I panicked as I realized that only my husband had touched me there but it did feel wonderful and made me feel delightfully wicked. Then I felt his finger lightly rubbing my wet clitoris. At that I moved my bottom away from his finger but then I felt his hard cock thrusting between my buttocks. I was thus caught with the increasingly delicious feelings of his stroking my clitoris and as I moved my hips I could feel his cock between my legs rubbing my pussy lips from behind. What a dilemma I was in.

I tried again to get Karl to stop by saying, "Please Karl, we shouldn't be doing this." His response was, "Beth, you know you want me to continue so just relax." He said that in such a soothing warm voice that I actually did relax. Next I found that his finger was actually in my vagina and did that ever feel good. As I felt trapped and knew that struggling was useless (or so I told myself) I did relax and actually moved my pelvis in time with his in and out moving finger so it could go deeper into my vagina. This continued for several minutes feeling better and better by the second.

All of a sudden I almost screamed as my body was consumed by the largest orgasm of my young life, which seemed to go on and on. When it finally stopped I just laid there in Karl's arms feeling totally content while he continued gently stroking my body to my guilty delight. When he turned me around and kissed me I found myself kissing him back and when he moved his body up and asked me in a soft voice to suck his cock I felt strangely compelled to do as he said, so without further argument or hesitation, I reached for the hard object I had felt between my butt cheeks and put it in my mouth and sucked him as good as I could. I found myself surprised by his hardness and size noticing that he was not only quite a bit longer and thicker than my husbands but the head was huge as well as soft and spongy. An even bigger bonus was the new taste that somehow turned me on even more.

While sucking Karl's cock I fielded a wide range of emotions. The strongest was guilt at having betrayed my marriage vows and had had a form of sex with a man other than the man I loved and who I married. When these feelings were in my mind I have no idea why I did not stop. I suspect that in part I wanted to please him as he had done me, as the orgasm he gave me was better than I had ever experienced and I guess that I was grateful. I recall rationalizing that at least we had not had real sex where he could have forced himself by penetration of my vagina. The emotion at the other end of the spectrum was lust.

I was just getting into and enjoying his cock in my mouth when I felt him contracting. At that moment, Karl put his hand behind my head so any thoughts of my pulling away were now gone. I had no choice but to swallow pulse after pulse of his rather tasty cum. For some reason the act of sucking Karl to the end filled me with passion so I crawled up and gave him a big hug. I would have kissed him but he got up and giving my bottom a squeeze he said, "That was nice, see you again tomorrow." Then he left the room and me to my privacy.

I laid in bed for some time reliving what I had experienced while going through a wide spectrum of emotions including wondering what I had done to give Karl the unsaid and unwritten permission to do what he did to me. On reflection about what I had just done, I started crying out of guilt. I finally got up, showered and dressed and went downstairs not knowing what to expect. Karl was in the kitchen and acted as if nothing had happened. The conversation was like it had been in the past and all about our landscaping progress and plans.

When my husband came home, again it was all like it had been before this morning. We had dinner together and it was as if I was not there as the conversation was all about "man stuff". Later, I think my husband, Greg, was surprised at my horniness but we made love twice and I told him how much I loved him. It was clear that this morning's events with Karl had not made a ripple in my relationship with my husband even as the events played in my guilt ridden mind as I drifted off to sleep in the arms of the man I loved dearly.

CHAPTER II
The Second Time

The next morning, after I saw my husband off with a kiss and a big hug I cautiously went back to bed but for some reason this time I took my panties off and lay there wondering if Karl would try something today. I had almost dosed off when I felt someone get in bed. Yes, it was a very naked Karl. I rolled over and said, "Karl we really should not be doing this, I am very happily married." Karl didn't say anything but got under the covers and gave me a big hug and a deep kiss using his tongue to play with my tongue.

After this he turned me around to the same spooning position we were in yesterday and he pulled up and off my nightgown. Thus, here I was almost instantly naked in bed and in close body contact with a man older than my father and who a short time ago was almost a stranger. Yes, I certainly knew him better than I had expected. I did struggle a bit making what, in retrospect, was a half-hearted effort to escape his clutches. I did manage to say, "Please, no, Karl, this is not right." As I was saying that his left arm was around my neck fondling my breasts and pinching my nipples while his right arm was already stroking my clitoris.

What he was doing was starting to feel quite good and I found myself rolling a bit toward him and opening my legs to make it easier for him to do what I knew and sort of wanted him to do, which was to make me cum with his fingers. He must have noticed my actions as he said, "That's a nice girl, Beth, I am pleased that you want me to make you cum again." "And Oh, you will let me know when you want more, won't you?" My only response was a loud moan as he already had his index finger in my vagina and was rubbing my clitoris with his thumb.

As I was now almost on my back he freed his hand from my

breasts and leaned over to lick and suck my nipples and breasts. This sure felt good and he was now better able to use his right hand literally fucking my vagina with his finger and rubbing the most sensitive area in my vagina and he was also able to use his left hand to stimulate my clitoris. Wow, it sure felt good. I admit that I had pangs of guilt when I would think about where I was and who was lying next to me stimulating me sexually in the bed I shared with my loving husband. Yes, I would feel guilty but the good feelings won out and I would pump my pelvis making his fingers go further and further.

As I lay in my bed being stimulated with increasing intensity I wondered how this was going to end, as he sure knew how to bring me over the top. As I was thinking these thoughts my orgasm enveloped my being and I almost screamed with pleasure. This time the feeling so permeated my body that I almost passed out. When I came to, my first thought was to return the pleasure, so I sought and found his cock and vowed to give him the best blowjob I could.

It was only after I had swallowed his load that it occurred to me that now that I have done this twice to Karl, how can I refuse him in the future and this gave me real pangs of guilt as I really do love my husband and having sexual contact with a man not my husband was, at least in the past, a big no no. There is just something about this older dominant man that I found hard or impossible to resist.

As he did yesterday, Karl just got up out of bed and said only, "will see you next time", as he gave me a kiss and my breasts a pinch. When he closed the door my feelings surfaced as they had done before and I promised my self that maybe in the future that I just would not go back to bed and maybe go outside early so this does not have to happen again. As this thought played in my mind I reminded myself just how good he made me feel and that if my husband did not know, what would be the harm. Certainly my deep love was his and not Karl's.

The rest of the day and weekend went by as if nothing untoward was happening. Karl was the grandfatherly gentleman and my husband said many times that he was honored to have him as a houseguest. Actually, the weekend was like a honeymoon with my husband as I was sure horny. Greg even commented that he was one happy dude.

Actually, Karl paid not the slightest attention to me as long as my husband was anywhere or even potentially around. It was like I wasn't there. He acted and talked around Greg as if women were the furthest from his mind. Greg, even said to me in the quiet of our bedroom that he wondered at what age he would be like Karl and not be interested in women. He told me that Karl had told him that the last lady he dated was 7 or 8 years ago. To me, it was clear what Karl was doing but I certainly could not say anything to my husband that might suggest that I thought or knew anything different.

CHAPTER III

The Change of Venue

The weekend ended and as usual I got up with my husband and we had our usual breakfast and conversation about the plans of the day. He told me that Karl had told him that it was time to make the first of many trips to the nursery to get a start on our landscaping project. He asked me to go with Karl to keep 'The old man company'. When he said that I almost choked on my coffee.

After my husband left, my first thought was to get up and dressed and start working in the yard. This way, I reasoned, I would not be tempted to be naughty again and certainly what I had done with Karl was not what a proper wife would do behind the back of her husband. Back upstairs in my bedroom, thoughts of the pleasure I had received became overwhelming so on a whim, I removed my robe and panties and slipped under the covers as I had done in the past but now there was 'expectation' of pleasure.

I dozed off and when I came back to an 'awake' state and Karl was not there I admitted to myself some disappointment. I reasoned that he would come in soon so with those thoughts I felt my sex getting wet. I even reached down and played a bit with my labia and clitoris but it was not the same as when Karl was doing it. For one thing my doing it was not as exciting and certainly was not 'naughty' or guilt provoking. I found myself anxious and wanting Karl to be there as wrong as it was. Not sure how long I awaited anxiously but at one point I got up and went down the hall to see if Karl was OK – at least this was the reason I gave myself.

I walked quietly down the hall scolding myself for making this decision but at that point I literally could not help myself. When I got to the door of his room – our guest room - I almost turned back but curiosity got the best of me and as the door was open a crack

I opened it further and looked in at the bed. There was Karl lying naked on the bed holding the covers up and open in an obvious welcoming gesture. He was emphasizing the point by waving me in. With a feeling of my heart in my throat, I opened the door further and walked in slowly. As I approached the bed I could not help but stare at his large hard cock.

When I reached the bed, Karl sweetly said, "good morning little one, I have been expecting you" and then before I could say anything he said, " take off your nightie." When I hesitated a bit he said a bit more forcefully, "Now." Well, I knew it was wrong but I pulled my nightie over my head and quickly got into bed next to Karl. He pulled me to him and while kissing me (to which I was kissing him back) and feeling my body all over I became very turned on.

Once in bed with Karl and in his bed, I had a moment of guilt and shame knowing I should not be there but with his hands fondling my breasts and bottom plus everything in between, I just could not help myself, as the feelings were overwhelming. At that, I faintly said, "We really should not be doing this, but damn you, I do not want it to stop."

He easily positioned me where he could suck and tongue my breasts and at the same time use one hand to rub and stimulate my clitoris and the other to literally finger fuck my vagina. I was in heaven, as he sure knew how to rub my vaginal hot spot.

He would rub my clit and G-spot till I started 'climbing the mountain' of pleasure and then he would almost stop or at least the stimulation was less than I needed to get to an orgasm. After the third or so time I found myself asking and almost begging him to not stop. I remember him saying, "Tell me, Beth, what is it that you want me to do." I would say something like, "Please don't stop." He would say, "Tell me what you want me to do." All the while he was bringing me close to an orgasm and then backing off. It was driving me crazy.

Finally after more than a few times I said, "Please, Karl, bring me to a climax, please." He then said, "And tell me, Beth, what will you do for me in return." I knew then that he had me and wanted me to admit that I would do anything to please him so I said softly after giving him a hug and a kiss, "Oh, you know that I will suck you till you cum when you want it." As he started building the pleasure up again he said, "And you will do this any time I ask you?" As I was getting close I blurted out, "Oh yes, I will suck you any time you wish, any time" and then I erupted in an almost shattering climax from which I was very vocal and almost passed out.

When I came back to reality, he had changed his position in the bed so when I opened my eyes his beautiful cock was right there in front of my mouth. I put one of my arms around him and pulled his cock into my mouth to give him the pleasure I thought he wanted for what he had given me. In the position we were in he was able to literally pump in and out of my mouth and seemed to go further and further even causing me to gag at first. I felt pride when I was finally able to take him deep in my throat and not gag.

After a bit I felt his tongue flicking my clitoris and the feelings of pleasure seemed to start all over again. He pulled me so that his head was between my legs and he was able to use his tongue on all of my pussy from my clit to my vaginal opening. The pleasure he was giving me with his tongue going in and out of my vagina was so great that I am sure I made love to his cock as he soon came with spurt after spurt of his tasty cum.

After his climax he turned to me and gave me a warm hug saying, "That was good, Beth, I am looking forward to seeing you tomorrow same time, same place, OK." I remember thinking at first that I would definitely be back but as I reflected on what we had just done I did feel guilty about what we had done and had been doing the last week or so but I reasoned that I still had not had sex – real sex anyway- with Karl so had not really been unfaithful to my husband.

After a bit of hugging and his fondling my bottom he got up out of the bed and helped me do the same. Once we were upright he pulled me into his arms and gave me an open mouthed kiss, which

I returned with glee. After that he gave my bare bottom a playful spank and said, "That was nice but we will have to go the next step tomorrow." In the meantime I will see you in an hour so we can choose the shrubbery we want for your yard. With that he picked up my nightie and helped me get it on. I felt like a child being sent out of the room but said nothing as I went back down the hall to my husbands and my bedroom.

CHAPTER IV

The Aftermath

It was when I got back to our room and was in the shower that it hit me what I had done and been doing and what I might be doing tomorrow. My thinking was that it was one thing for Karl to come to my bedroom and sort of force himself on me sexually but now I have gone down to his room and in addition to what we had done last week he had kissed and tongued my pussy like my husband does but far better. I was really in a dilemma about what to do and whereas I really loved what he was doing to me, I was hoping that his house would be finished soon so he would not be around to tempt me. As I was thinking those thoughts, I knew I would be seeing him and enjoy his special way of making me cum so very hard.

I guess I do not need to tell you that the rest of the day went by almost normally as we went out to the nursery to pick out some trees and shrubbery. I had to chuckle as the gardener commented to Karl that he sure had an attractive granddaughter. Karl's comment back was, "yes, she sure is special." I know I blushed deeply as I thought about the morning in his bed. I used the term 'almost" normal as on the way home he pulled into a wooded area and after giving me a hug and his usual kiss, he unzipped his pants and said, "Beth, do what you do best." My first response was, "Please, Karl, we can't do this in public, what if someone sees us."

As he lowered my head to his slightly hard cock he said, "I was sure I heard you promise to suck me any time I wanted, is that not so?" Just before I took his cock in my mouth I said, "Oh, Karl, you know I said that but did not think you meant outside of our house or your bedroom." Then I got into what I was doing and it was a thrill to feel his cock go from a bit turgid to his usual hardness. I had to admit that the naughtiness and the risk of been caught by someone had me giving him the best deep-throat suck I knew how to and was thrilled when he came with a moan.

After I cleaned him up well and he softened he put himself together and we drove home. He did get me going a bit as his hand was under my shirt and he was rubbing my pussy through my panties but not enough to make me cum so I remained horny.

The rest of the afternoon and evening went on as if nothing unusual had happened. Around my husband, Karl was a typical grandfather showing no interest in me except as his friend's granddaughter. Greg and he got on great joking about anything and everything except about anything suggestive or sexual.

That evening, I was certainly horny and receptive to my husband's romantic advances and told him again and again how much I loved him. That night while sucking him back to hardness for a second round I actually compared his cock to Karl's and noted quite a difference not only in size but taste. While we were making love, I even wondered what a larger cock would feel like. On thinking that I angrily scolded myself for even thinking such naughty thoughts and reminded myself that I was a married lady and my husband, Greg, was my first and must be my last sex partner.

While thinking these thoughts I felt very guilty, as I really do love my husband. I felt so guilty that I silently cried myself to sleep knowing what I would be doing the next morning when my husband went to work leaving his innocent wife behind. Then when the thoughts of what I would most likely be doing the next morning flooded my mind I felt myself becoming very wet between my vaginal lips.

When we awoke the next morning and we were having breakfast Greg told me that he had to go out of town for a couple of days tomorrow after work through Friday. The trip was for business and whereas he would have loved me to come with him, he would be busy all day and most of the evenings. He added that at least I would not be alone and Karl would be there and he would be good company.

He saw my sadness and giving me a big hug he told me that he would make it up to me when he returned. We kissed and he left telling me that he loved me and would see me tonight. He added that he was impressed with what Karl and me had accomplished in the yard and again said how glad he was to have a good friend like Karl helping him with this project.

CHAPTER V

The Next Step as hinted..

A s my husband drove away to his work and I was walking upstairs to our bedroom, the roller coaster of emotions returned. On the one hand I felt guilty and ashamed about the fact that I would soon be going down to Karl's room and he would be pleasuring me with his hands till I climaxed and then I would be obliged to suck his cock.

On the other hand I was already getting excited and wet between my legs for the same reasons. Another emotion that came in and out of my consciousness was what was the "Next step" Karl mentioned yesterday. He has kept me on the edge, as I never knew what he was going to do. All I knew was that at one point I would have a total body orgasm and I have come to want this much more than I ever thought I would. I just never knew that I could or would get to be so excited being so naughty as to do things behind my husbands back.

By the time I reached my bedroom, I had decided to seek the pleasure route so I shed my robe and panties and walked down the hall to Karl's room in only my nightie. When I opened the door and was walking in it appeared that Karl was still sleeping but he was in the nude and sporting a stiff cock. I stopped and looked at his pulsating cock while I removed my nightie and then just crawled in to the bed and snuggled up to the man who would be giving me unbridled pleasure.

Karl woke up then or he had been awake and the first thing he said was, "Ahh, good girl, you do as you are told." He then rolled over and pressed his body to mine, which I have come to like very much as for a man of his age he has a very lean and muscular body.

He wasted little time positioning me so we were in a 'spooning' position where I could feel his cock between my legs going slowly back and forth. He did as he usually did at first by fondling my breasts and lightly pinching my nipples. This was at first a new sensation, as my husband did not do that at all. He then fondled his way down to my pussy and started the expected and anticipated soft rubbing of my clit.

As I was so wet with my juices and also his pre-cum was increasing it was not long before I could feel his cock rubbing and sliding between my labia and up to and including my clit. Wow, this was a new feeling and it was sure nice. I never occurred to me that his cock was stimulating my vaginal opening as the feeling was close to what I had felt in the previous days and I could feel my orgasm building.

However, just like yesterday, Karl seemed to want to tease and excite me as he would slide back and forth till I was about to burst and he would stop. When he would stop, he would kiss my neck and play with my breasts. As before, after the third build-up and his backing off I started to beg him to bring me to a climax. I would say softly, "please" and he would say, "please what?, tell me what you want me to do." All the while he was stimulating my vaginal area and clit to the point of 'almost' no return and then he would slow down.

Finally I said, "Please, Karl, fuck me with your finger and bring me to a climax, I really need to cum." As I was saying that his stimulation of my whole sex area with his cock continued and I found that if I pushed my butt way back that his cock was long enough to rub my clitoris and that was the feeling I wanted and needed. As the feeling was building up he moved his finger to my clit and when I reach the point where the whole of my sex craved an orgasm I felt the head of his cock slide into my vagina.

At that point the need for a climax trumped my shock at this new invasion. At that exact moment of his first penetration I felt the feelings of my impending orgasm ascend so almost as a reflex I pushed back, impaling me even more on his cock. The feeling was so good that all I could say was, "Oh Karl, fuck me - that feels so good." He then grabbed my hips and pushed his cock further and further in until he could go no further. No more that 6 or 8 strokes later, I had the most stupendous orgasm of my life after which I could feel his cock pulsing and could also feel his cum flooding my vagina.

As I was coming down I was compelled to say, "Oh my God, Karl, that was the absolute greatest feeling I have ever had." His response was, "Well Beth, you deserve to be fucked by an expert and I will please you this way from now on." Then, "Is that what you want?" My headset at the time was full of endorphins as I said, "Oh, yes, I want you to do this again many times."

With the sex act done he pulled out of my vagina and turned me around to face him as he hugged me close and played with my bottom he said, "I really love a wet and tight vagina and you will feel me again." As I came back to reality, I realized what we had just done and hugging Karl closely, I started to cry. Karl knew exactly what to say when he said, "Please do not feel guilty, my little one, what we did was natural for two people together and your secret is totally safe with me forever." He followed up with, "You should be allowed pleasure and what is the harm if your husband never knows." He added what I had suspected from what I had observed, "Your Greg thinks I am done with women so you are very safe with me."

CHAPTER VI

The Real Thing

W hen I responded, "Karl, you are very reassuring and I know we will do this again but I still do feel guilty and very naughty." "I know that I will get over it, give me time." "That was some experience." "You are some lover." As I said that he asked in his grandfatherly soft voice if I would get him hard again.

I immediately positioned myself and took his somewhat soft cock in my mouth. The taste was a surprise, as I had never tasted myself before. I guess I must have really made love to his cock because it was not long before he was hard. I was expecting to suck him to an orgasm but once he was hard he laid me down and looking me in my eyes he positioned himself on top of me.

Even as I knew what was about to happen, I was almost afraid. What if I liked it more than my husbands and thoughts like that coursed through my mind. I did not have long to think about it as from on top he slowly fed his very large cock into my vagina. The feeling was incredible.

This was different from the first time as then he caught me by surprise when his cock entered my vagina. This time, he was on top and I knew exactly what he was about to do. I now wanted him in me but said, "Please go slow as you are larger than I have ever known but I do want you in me."

He did go slowly but I had my second orgasm of the morning when he reached bottom and he really had not started fucking me yet. When he did start moving his cock in and out the contact on my sensitive area was overwhelming and I must have had several orgasms during what seemed like almost an hour of pleasure that I experienced as he fucked me.

I was in total bliss and did not want the feelings to ever stop. He was touching and stimulating me in places never before touched.

At one point I knew my life had irreversibly changed, as I knew that as guilty as I felt at times I would be doing this with Karl again and most likely again.

When he finally came and I could feel him spurting in my Vagina, the prevailing feeling in my core was almost overwhelming pleasure but also exhaustion from the expenditure of the energy by my trying to be as active as he was. When he pulled out we lay next to each other and I actually fell asleep in his arms.

I am not sure how long I dozed off but when I was awake the main thought coursing through my mind was that I had just been made love to or better, fucked, by a master and the experience I knew I would never forget. I remember hoping that we would do this again but at the same time I realized that I had been unfaithful to my husband and I hoped more than life itself that he never found out that he had a cheating wife but one who loved him more than ever.

I saw that Karl was still asleep so I carefully got out of bed, picked up my nightie from the floor and walked back to my husbands and my bedroom. Talk about a spectrum of emotions. On the one hand I was still on a 'high' from the multi-orgasmic sex and mixed in with this feeling was the guilt and fear that I had been unfaithful to my husband, which I was sure, when I married, that I would never ever do but now that I had done it I knew that I would do it again at least with Karl as the feeling was addictive and I knew it.

CHAPTER VII

The Day After my First...

I showered and dressed for our outdoor activities of the day and went to the kitchen to fix breakfast for Karl and myself. While there, I got a call from my husband who told me he loved me and just was wondering how my day was going. I told him that I loved him and missed him as usual but I had been lazy and had just come downstairs to make some breakfast and that either Karl was still asleep or had gone out. I laughingly said that if he is still in the house, I will make him some pancakes as the smell might wake him up.

We laughed about that and Greg thanked me for being nice to his fathers old friend, Karl. We ended the call extolling our love for one another. The thought crossed my mind that he had no idea what I had been doing the last several mornings and what Karl and I had been doing.

After hanging up you can just bet I had feelings of guilt at 'being nice' to my husbands 'old' friend Karl. I had to chuckle over that one, as he had no idea how nice I had been to him and how very super nice he had been to me. After I calmed down from the emotions of Greg's call amid my morning of sexual depravity, I stared making fresh coffee and pancakes.

The smell must have done it as Karl came down in a very good mood. He gave me a big hug and a few pats of my bottom as he said, "My little one is making my favorite breakfast – that is so very nice." "What is on the schedule for today?"

As we were eating I had to ask him how he is able to have more than one climax in a short period of time. I explained that the reason I asked was that my husband, who is much younger than he was, has rarely gotten hard twice in a night.

I apologized for the question but I was very curious, as I know he had two orgasms while giving me many. He laughed at what I was asking and told me that it was just the luck of the draw as when he was younger he has had as many as 5 or more climaxes in one evening of sex and then he said this was usually with more than one woman and not with his wife at the time. Thus, with one question I learned the Karl was a bit of a ladies man and a stud in his younger days.

When he told me that, I guess I had a funny look in my eyes because he came over to me and took me in his arms and while giving me a big hug and his usual rubbing of whatever he could reach he said, "Beth, I want to tell you that you are one of the best I have had. Yes, I was a ladies man but any partner I had never regretted the pleasure I gave them.

We talked a bit about this and he told me how he came to want me in this way and how, after some thought he put his plan in action and was rewarded by my wanting him in return.

I felt comfortable enough to tell Karl that there were times that I felt very guilty and naughty with what I was doing with him. When I confessed these feelings, Karl looked at me and rather sternly said, "OK, that's enough young lady – you have no reason to feel guilt, shame or any of those feelings but I know how to assuage these feelings so you will not feel any guilt or shame.

CHAPTER VIII
My Guild is Absolved

When I looked at him with a questioning look he said, "Beth I am going to give you a spanking as punishment for your naughtiness and will continue to do it again and again until you absolve yourself of the guilt, is that clear. I said to him, "Karl, you can't spank me, you are not my father." As I said that I realized that that was not the thing to say, as he was certainly old enough and powerful enough.

Karl then got out from the kitchen table, picked up a chair and brought it out to the living room and called to me to come to him right now. I did not know what to do as I thought he was kidding – sort of – but I got up and went to him. When I got to where he was he told me to stand in front of him, which I slowly did.

He then said, "Young lady, I do not want to hear any more talk of your being guilty for being naughty as this punishment will absolve you of your naughtiness." "Now, take down your jeans." I admit to being scared as I stood before him but I said, "Please Karl, isn't there a better way. I promise I will not feel guilty any more."

"Elizabeth, do as I tell you right now or I will take them off for you and you will not like what follows." Thinking quickly I thought that I had better do as he said so I undid my jeans and lowered them to my knees. He then pulled me between his legs and first lowered my jeans to my ankles and then lowered my panties. I was very embarrassed even as he had seen me naked before as here we were in our living room and not in bed. He then told me to step out of the jeans which I did saying, "Please, not a spanking on the bare."

Even as I said it, I knew that I had no choice so thought that I would bear the punishment as I knew he was determined to complete what he started as this was his style as evidence the events since he came to my bed a week ago. So as embarrassed as I was I removed my jeans. When they were off he pulled me down over his knees exposing my bare bottom to his gaze. He then pulled my panties all the way off removing the last vestige of my modesty and started patting and fondling my bottom. At first, this felt good letting me relax a bit and get used to this position.

He then told me that I was not to put my hands back to protect my bottom and If I thought I might do that I should give him my hands behind my back. In the position I was in, I was holding on to one of the chair legs and one of his legs as I seemed to be almost upside down. I tried once more saying, "Please, Karl, I will be a good girl and not feel guilty as I do everything you ask - please."

His response as he started spanking lightly was, "You should have though of that before my little one. Now get ready to be spanked hard for your perceived naughtiness."

He then started spanking rather smartly alternating cheeks. As he was spanking me he kept talking, saying a word or two with each spank, "Beth, I am going to fuck you any time and in any place from now on and you are not to feel guilty in any way, as you have no choice in the matter – is that clear." "You had no choice from day one and now you will do as I ask." The spanks were quite painful and amid the 'ouches' 'oh's' 'please stop' and 'I'll be good' I heard what he said but did not answer immediately.

He then started spanking harder as he said, "answer me when I speak to you, young lady." As the pain was almost unbearable, I said in a pleading voice, "Yes, Karl, what you say I clearly understand, I will do what you say when you say it with out question and as I have no choice, I no longer will feel guilty."

During my talking the spanks became almost tolerable. He then said as he continued spanking sharply, "Yes, young lady, you are mine to do with what I please – is that not correct?" This time I quickly responded saying, "yes, yes, I am yours to do your will when you want it." I added, "You fuck me so good, I want it again and again."

As I said that last bit it came to me that it was true, that his strength and dominance led to my seduction and I really did not have a choice but to do as he asked. I had really tried to prevent what happened the first two times and once under his dominance I really had little to say. Besides what he did felt wonderful and as I had not had screaming orgasms before in my life, I really love what he did to me. All the while I was thinking this he continued spanking one cheek and then the other and they all hurt in a stinging way as he varied the force and frequency. My bottom was burning.

As I started concentrating on the stinging pain in my bottom I suddenly erupted in sobs. It was when I started crying that he started spanking less hard and then stared rubbing and soothing my inflamed bottom. When he stopped spanking I just lay there reflecting on how good his soothing hand felt and how much at that moment I loved him. Several minutes of his fondling he said, "OK, Beth you can get up now, you have taken your punishment well.

I slid off of his lap and standing up I gave him a very big hug and a warm kiss saying, "Thank you, Karl, for the spanking I needed. I really love you for helping me see that I am not naughty to be having sex with you –Thank you, thank you" as I kissed him again. I then asked him if I could do anything for him. Of course I was thinking that maybe he would want me to suck his cock or the spanking might have gotten him as horny as it did me.

It seems as if it did as he got up off the chair and led me to our davenport and had me bend over it. He came behind me and using his tongue he made sure I was wet and then he slowly fed his cock into my vagina. This was a new position and feeling for me and I soon felt that it was giving my G-spot area maximum stimulation. While he was fucking me from behind I just had to say, "Oh God, Karl, This feels so good – I love what you do to me, please do not stop." Then I had my first orgasm of this session and it was a barnburner.

As I was having one orgasm after another I came to realize that I would do anything Karl asked as I had come to love him as a father-like figure who could and would fuck me often and that this relationship would not and did not change my love for the man I married. When Karl finally came I thrilled at the feeling of his cum pumping into my vagina. After he finished he helped me up and said, "lets get going on the yard." So I gathered my clothes and got dressed as if nothing unusual had happened.

We did our errands and at the nursery we arranged for them to deliver the plants and trees and to start the process according to the plans Karl, with their input, put together. We were introduced to the person who would be doing the work and I realized that he was the young man who had been eyeing me each time we came out. I admitted to myself the he was a very nice looking black man and left it at that.

When we got home, Karl told me that he would be out for the evening but would see me in the morning. As he said that a tingle went through my sex, as I knew for sure what he meant. As he left he gave me a big hug and patted my bottom which still tingled and was a bit sore from the spanking he had given me that morning.

CHAPTER IX

My Husband's Suprise

When Greg came home, he seemed even more amorous and loving than usual but I certainly was not complaining, as I loved him in return. I told him that Karl would be out for the evening and I filled him in on the landscaping progress. He was pleased that the work was going to start this weekend. We had dinner and after all was cleaned up he took my hand and led me to the bedroom.

As we were hugging and kissing I asked him what had happened today that got him into this 'lovin' mood. He said that he would tell me everything after we were in bed and had made love. Well, we did and he was certainly horny and I remember feeling his love and loving him in return.

He easily brought me to an orgasm as thoughts of earlier in the day made me exceptionally horny and of course my climax triggered his. I said, "Wow, whatever happened today can happen again – I love you so much in any case."

My husband then told me that he had a long lunch with his Dad and one of the things his Dad asked him was, "How is my friend Karl behaving?" I told him the visit was quite OK as I liked Karl very much and he seemed to get on with Beth but he paid her little attention except he was helping get out landscaping organized. Then I asked him, "Why the question".

Greg went on to say, "Honey, my dad told me that Karl was the consummate ladies man and had made it with more women than he could count". "Dad said at one point, Son, he even had a long sexual affair with your mother, god rest her soul, and to this day I am not sure all of your brothers and sisters are mine even as I love them all." He went on to say, "I am sure you are mine as you are hung normally like me but think about the size of your brother's cock." "He very well could be Karl's biological son".

My Dad said, "Karl's affair with my wife - your mom was for many years and she told me it started soon after our honeymoon". When she finally confessed this in her last days she told me that she did not know how it started but he was so persistent that she did not think she had a choice. She told me, Once started the pleasure outshone her guilt and she never lost her deep love of me."

My Dad went on to say, "Greg, I am telling you this because I think it is time you knew and I really needed to warn you about Karl and his proclivity for seducing women." "Yes, Karl is and has remained a good friend and I was not only not angry but never confronted him with my suspicions which were only confirmed by your mother who confessed this long time affair to me in the weeks before she passed away."

"When your mother confessed her long time affair with Karl she was crying". "I had to tell her repeatedly that I knew she was seeing Karl, even as I didn't, and that as long as she loved me that I was OK with it as I told her that I knew that he had a much larger cock than I did and that I was happy that she was being satisfied by a friend even if it was behind my back". "Actually, I said this to comfort her as I was not aware of the affair". "In fact, I was not only not upset but very turned on."

Then Greg told me that after a few minutes he told his Dad that, "I certainly am not worried about Beth as she has known only me and was for sure a virgin when we married." He then turned to me and said, "Honey, I do not know where this comes from but as much as I love you, I would really love for you to know a bigger and better lover." Then, "Well how's that for a confession."

I then asked him, "Why would you want me to have sex with another man when you are all I want and need." As I said that I felt more than a twinge of guilt but recalling the spanking I put this out of my mind. I did, however, want to find out what my husband was thinking.

His response left me loving him more that ever as he said, "Well, you know, honey, I do not give you climaxes every time we make love and there have been times when I feel and almost know you would like more but I cannot get it up. You never say anything, which makes me love you all the more. Gosh, I think twice is my maximum and I love you so much that I know you deserve more." My response was, "God, I love you, you are a wonderful and thoughtful man."

I then said, "Wow, that was some emotional conversation with your Dad and you are right that I was a virgin and have certainly not been interested in initiating sex with anyone besides you." "Would you still love me if I did have sex with anyone else, even Karl?" "Besides, Karl is in his Sixties and may not be as he was in his Forties how would we know if he was interested."

The love of my life surprised me by saying, "Well, Honey, you could surely get his interest if he saw more of you or if you became physical closer. You know, seeing you in your sexy nightie or somehow only in your panties." I then asked him, "How would I do that?"

"Well, leave our bedroom door open as you dress and maybe wear a bit more sexy and tighter clothes around the house. Find a way for him to see you in partial undress by "accident". That way, if he is at all human, he would want to see more and touching is a natural next step." I asked him then, "Would you really want me to expose myself to Karl so that he might initiate sex?"

My husband then said, "Yes, Honey, I would really love to know about and maybe in the future see you having sex with Karl or some other man with a larger cock than I have. I have no idea where this comes from as I have thought about this well before my Dad informed me of Karl's sexual predator nature."

I then said what had been flashing in my mind, "Well, If I did what you wish and I do have sex with Karl or someone else, can you be sure that you will still love me. Keep in mind that if he does make love to me this cannot be undone. This was the point my mother made so often that once a man has had you sexually there is no return to virginity meaning once he has been where only you have been, there is no turning back. And I would not want to lose you because you changed your mind. What do you say to that?"

Greg rolled me over and said, "Here let my hard cock answer your question as it is reacting to the thoughts of your possibly having sex with Karl." As he proceeded to put his cock in my vagina I did note that it was as hard as I had ever felt it. When he made love to me I had, for one of the rare times, two orgasms before he came. When he pulled out and I had sucked him clean we lay in each others arms for what seemed like several minutes.

At that moment I was more in love with my husband that I though possible so I said, "Well, OK, if this is what you really want, I will flaunt myself a bit and tell you everything as it goes and if you change your mind at any time you have to let me know because once it is done it cannot be undone, OK." I went on to say that thinking about this potential even did make me a bit horny.

The love of my life, Greg assured me that this is what he wants and has wanted since almost before we were married. He reminded me of his questioning me while we were dating, and his reaction to my telling him that I had slept with no one. I did recall his telling me that it would have made no difference and that he would have loved me no matter how many I had slept with.

We were just about to fall asleep when he told me that the trip was postponed and he would be leaving the next day and get home on Sunday but that he would call each evening to get news.

CHAPTER X

Decisions, Decisions

When we awoke the next morning we were both horny as we made love for longer than usual. We showered together and while soaping me down feeling my body he said, "Karl is in for the treat of his life as I know you will be successful. I told him that I would try but he should not count his chickens before they were hatched.

We went down and I fixed him his usual breakfast and we went over the plans for the landscaping. As we kissed goodbye for the day he said, "Good hunting, I will look forward to lusty tales this evening. Remember, I love you and want you to succeed." My response was, "I make no promises but I will try some of the things you suggested you dirty old man." We kissed again and he was off to work.

I went back upstairs and got into bed to collect my thoughts. I knew that I would soon be going down the hall to Karl's room and that I knew I would be fucked at least once. I dozed off and when I though it the right time, I got up took off my panties and started done the hall.

When I walked into his bedroom he was on the bed naked as usual and with a big smile. Before he asked, I removed my nightie and walked to the bed naked already feeling tingles and wetness in my sex area. When I got to the bed Karl asked, "What is it you want this fine morning, Beth?" Whereas his question caught me by surprise I said, "I want you to make love to me."

Karl's response was, "You are not here for me to 'make love' to you young lady, you are here for me to fuck you till you cum many times, is that not right?" I answered quietly, "Yes, you are right, I need you to fuck me." As I get into bed with my now familiar lover he positioned me as he usually does so he could first play with my breasts, then my still tingly bottom and then with his head between my legs and his cock in my mouth we started.

Once he had brought me to within a second or two of an orgasm he moved between my legs and before he entered me he put his arms under my legs and put my legs over his shoulders. This was a new position for me and I felt very exposed. This feeling was not for long as he sank his cock slowly in my vagina. I had my first orgasm before he was all the way in. I really love the feeling of being stretched by his large cock and his even larger spongy head and his stimulating sections of my vagina that had never before felt a cock before he laid claim to the area.

He then started slowly and tantalizingly stroking in and out of my now wanton vagina stimulating me like nothing I have felt before knowing Karl. Once I was used to his size and had lubricated he started fucking faster and faster. This drove me crazy and I seemed to have one orgasm after another. Karl's staying power was amazing and whereas my husband would have cum some time ago, Karl kept on almost till I was exhausted, revving only when I felt his cock contract and fill me with his cum.

When he pulled out I went down to clean him off, as I knew he liked. When I finished I lay in his arms and told him that I loved what he does to me. Then, I actually went to sleep for a bit. I awoke by his stimulating my clit till I was close to cuming. When he stopped, I asked him what he wanted me to do next.

He said then, "Well, you really do like a good fucking and I am pleased to oblige you whenever you want as I know you are happy to oblige me when I want your pussy." My response was, "Yes, I do love it when you fuck me as I cum many more times than I do with my husband. I do love him but I also love you for the pleasure you bring to me."

He then asked me if I wanted to try to get him hard again. I said, "Of course I do" as I took his partially hard cock into my mouth and throat. He moaned his pleasure at the blowjob I was giving him and commented that I was the best at deep throating since a lady some years back. Once he was hard he told me to get on my hands and knees.

In that position be got behind me and fed his cock into my vagina in this, another new position. I chuckled to myself, as I would have some stories to tell my husband once I got past the seduction I knew he wanted to hear about. In this position Karl held my hips and fucked me through at least three more orgasms and for maybe 20 to 30 minutes before he climaxed again. I was in orgasmic heaven.

When he was done he asked me if I felt guilty. I was quick to say, "Absolutely not, I do not feel guilt but do feel pleasure, warmth and love." His response with a big smile was, "Good girl or is it maybe that you just do not want another spanking." I said, "No, I actually do not feel at all guilty and I have already thanked you for the punishment spanking helping me see the light."

I did not tell him that the main reason was that now I knew my husband wanted me to do this. The question now was what do I tell Greg what happened today so I can be sure he is really OK with my having sex with Karl.

Karl then said, "Beth you may need a spanking, as I keep hearing you tell me that you love me. You may love and need the pleasure I bring you as I love the pleasure of fucking your sweet lithe young body but "Love" is not in the equation, is that clear?" As He said this I knew he was right as the one I really loved was my husband so I said softly with my head looking down, "I'm sorry, Karl, it was the passing emotion as I really do "Love" my husband and it is the pleasure you bring me that I guess I have been interpreting as a feeling of love. Maybe I do need a spanking but not a hard one, as I, laughingly gave him a big hug.

Anyway, he shooed me away to get dressed, as we had to get to the nursery to finalize the first stage of the job we started. I quickly showered and dressed and went downstairs to fix Karl a nice breakfast. When he came in the kitchen the first thing he did was take me in his arms and fondle and play with everything that felt good. I asked him, "Are you trying to turn me on again because if you are you are doing it." He laughed and patted my bottom saying, "keep that thought for later."

Later at the nursery Karl had his hand on my ass most of the time and especially in the presence of Brian who was the one assigned to oversee our project. It seemed like Karl was doing what he was doing on purpose to show Brian that I allowed it. At one point I even said, "Karl are you turning Brian on, on purpose?" He said in my ear, "Yes, my little one maybe he will give you the thrill of a black cock." "I see by your blush that this is of interest to you."

I admit that the thought did get me horny but I said, "Karl, why would you want me to be with another man?" His response told me that I could expect surprises in the future as he said, "Beth, nothing pleases me more than fucking you than watching you get fucked by a new man and I intend to make this happen. I became a bit anxious at this thought as I realized that Karl lived on my anxiety.

On the way home we again stopped in the same wooded area and this time I went right down, pulled out his almost soft cock and gave him what I hoped was a good blowjob. I admit that I really got into what I was doing and admitted to myself that I really like the feeling of a cock in my mouth – the act itself along with the tangy taste and the ability I had to give a man such pleasure. After he climaxed he said, "Well, Beth, you have learned very well what I want you to do and you do it splendidly. I am looking forward to seeing how many times I can fuck you when Greg is away this weekend." I had no response but I did feel a tingling and burst of wetness in my sex area.

The rest of the day was uneventful and filled with thoughts of what I would tell my husband when he came home and asked how my day went and was I successful it attracting Karl to any activity. I didn't like the idea of lying to Greg but I had to be sure that he really meant what he said about wanting to hear of my having sex with another man.

CHAPTER XI
My Very Horny Husband

Greg came home a bit earlier as he said he had to pack for his short trip but he sure was amorous. My love for him certainly was at a high plateau as we sat and had dinner. He told me that we would talk about my day when we were upstairs. He did ask if I had had any luck. He got visibly excited when I said, "Yes, I did and it was more than I expected. I will tell you everything upstairs."

The evening shot by like a rocket as he packed a small bag and we got undressed for bed. I saw that he was excited as his cock was as hard as ever. When I commented on his state of excitement he said, "Honey, I have been like this most of the day thinking of a number of scenarios that might have happened." "I called my Dad to ask a bit more about his Dad's friend and his, Karl and how he found out that Karl had fooled around with 'Mom' and other women he knew." "That call alone had me hard."

As we got in bed he asked, "well, how did it go?" Did he bite or take your bait and what did you do?" So this is what I told my husband that had happened to test his real feelings, "Well, as you suggested I was in our room in only my panties and bra sorting and resorting clothes on our bed with the bedroom door open."

At one point I sensed that I was not alone and looked over my shoulder and guess who was standing just outside of our door. He must have seen everything as he had a big smile on his face. I actually felt embarrassed and grabbed my robe to cover myself and said to him, "Oh, I though you were gone, please excuse my near nakedness." Karl then said, "Beth you have a fantastic body that I would like, no, intend to come to know it better."

Well you can imagine how I felt when he said that. What I did say was, "I will be down in a minute to fix breakfast." Then I turned and walked into the bathroom to collect my thoughts. "Honey, You had been so right as the look in his eyes and the gleeful smile said everything. I felt like he was undressing me further than I was."

At that point Greg pounced on top of me and after three to four strokes came with gusto. As he pulled out he said, "Oh, my love, I am so sorry but that beginning was such a big turn on, I could not help myself. I want you to continue the story. I am so excited and more in love than ever."

What had happened felt good but certainly I had not had an orgasm so I though I would add a few things to todays story to see if he got hard again. I was beginning to believe that Greg was not only OK with what he thought was going to happen but very pleased.

So, I told him that I did not dress but went downstairs to the kitchen in my robe and while fixing breakfast Karl would repeatedly come close to me with one question or another and cop a feel of my bottom. When I said, "Karl, you should not be doing that as I am a happily married woman and Greg is your friend."

His response floored me as he said, "Young lady, an open door is an open invitation and I hope to see your door open tomorrow morning and every day." With that I saw that my husbands cock was again hard. This was very soon after his last climax leading me to say, "Oh, I guess what he said turned you on. Would you like me to leave the bedroom door open tomorrow morning?"

That thought did it as he was on and in me to the hilt in almost seconds. This time he lasted till I had a couple of orgasms. As we were making love I said, "Oh honey, you really do want me to have sex with Karl. I really do think it will happen as what he was doing to me and saying turned me on also. At first, I was ashamed of my feelings but knowing I have your permission, I will let it happen and tell you everything but will not tell Karl that you will know everything." Saying that led to my second orgasm and my contractions led to his.

When he was done and sort of rolled off me I said, "Honey, there is more to today that I want to tell you if you want to hear it." His response was, "Oh, please, I love you so much and you are making me a very happy man – and yes, I do want the hear everything as I am so excited about what my mind thinks will happen." I then said, "I sure hope this works out positively as I love you very much and, again, once done it cannot be undone."

"OK", I said, "I answered his query about my open door with saying that 'I might, but I have to think about this." "Honey, he then said that he expects to find my door open tomorrow." "He certainly is forceful." "Anyway, I went upstairs to change for the trip to the Landscaping place and without thinking, left the bedroom door open. After I removed my robe and before I could put on my jeans I looked up and there he was looking through the door. Thus, he had seen me again in just my panties and bra.

His comment was, "Very nice ass – I expect to see this door open any time I am around." My response was not really to what he said as I was blushing but I did smile at him and said I'll be ready in a minute so we can go on our errands.

I then told my husband what actually had happened today at the nursery where Karl had his hands on my ass as much as he could and often in front of Brian, the technician who was assigned to our house as if he were demonstrating to him that I was a loose woman. I also told him sort of what Karl had said implying that I should see more than him sexually.

I then asked my husband while looking him in the eyes, Honey, do you really want me to go down this path as it seemed to be happening". I then told him, this process is getting me horny and if you are OK with my being with Karl, then I was also." His response was to give me a super bear hug and tell me that he had never loved me more and so very much wanted me to receive the pleasure of his friend Karl's Large cock. With that we lay in each other's arms whispering our love until we fell asleep.

My husband stimulating my clit awakened me and we were soon having a slow and deliberate love making that I knew so well from My Greg. We got up, showered and he left for the next few days after we had breakfast. I then went back up to our bed and dozed of for what may have been an hour as the night's activity was tiring.

CHAPTER XII

A Weekend of Pleasure

When I finally awoke I knew what I was going to do or what I had to do, which was to walk down to Karl's room, get in bed with him and as the expression goes, I was going to get it good. I had to admit to myself as this excited me most likely because I never knew what was in store for me.

Thinking back, every day and every experience opened a new door. From the first morning when he all but forced himself on me followed by my sort of wanting it followed by my going to him and then no two times he has made love, or should I say 'fucked' me have been in the same position. As I go down the hall to his room I have no idea what he plans to do or have me do – and with whom, except make me want him more.

Before I opened his door, I slipped off my nightgown so I entered his room naked, which made me feel very sexy. When I walked in, he is lying on his bed as usual without a stitch of bedclothes and a big smile. First thing he says is, "Well, little one, what is it you want today?" This caught me by surprise and I said nothing while thinking what to reply, as I got in bed under the covers with him as I had come to love doing.

As I was giving him a big hug he asked again, "Beth, what is it that you want this morning?" This time I answered, "I want you to make love to me." His response was, "Beth, unless you want another spanking you will not use that term again. You are not here for me to make 'love' to you, you are here for me to fuck you because you need and want to be fucked – is that not right?"

My response was a soft embarrassed, "Yes, yes I do." "Do what?", he persisted. I seemed to have no choice and it was true so I said, "Yes, I want you to fuck me till I scream." "That's better", he said and then pointing to his almost soft cock he said, "Well, get down there and make me want you as much as you want me."

As I took him in my mouth and throat I realized how things had changed from what I thought was, Karl wanting me to now the reverse where he has made me want him. I just never knew what to expect and came to the realization that he was keeping me on the edge on purpose. Thinking about this as I sucked him to hardness, I realized that he had changed me from an innocent monagaminous housewife to almost a whore for his pleasure.

Once I got him hard he pulled me over on top of his body and with his cock between my legs and his hands feeling and fondling my bottom, he soon got me to flexing my pelvis repeatedly so his cock would stimulate my clitoris. At one point he lifted me up and said, "Use your hands to put my cock where it belongs."

Soon I was on top riding his cock making sure my clit was stimulated. This was another new feeling as I was sort of in control of how deep or how often he stimulated my vaginal walls and clit. I loved the feeling and soon was bouncing up and down and occasionally riding him like I was in a saddle.

My first climax was so strong I almost fainted. When I came back to reality Karl had a big smile so I went down to him and kissed him as sexily as I could. I then said, "God, Karl. I do love you and if saying that I love you gets me a spanking it is worth it. You have no idea how much you give me pleasure with your cock and also the fact that you are the only man other than my husband who I have had sex with. Please understand my feelings."

"I hear you and will take care of your bottom later but now see how soon you can bring me off." So I sat up and started going faster and faster while at the same time concentrating on contracting my pelvic and vaginal muscles with each up stoke. I know he felt that as he moaned a bit each time and it was not long before he started flexing his pelvis.

As he was cuming, I felt his contractions and this brought me another thundering climax. In the midst of his cuming he said, "Oh, wow, Beth you are the best I have had for years. Your contractions have milked me dry. You are the best." I responded, "Thanks and I can say the same for you as no one has ever made me cum so much."

After he was done we lay together and when in his arms 'contentment' is what I felt. I knew that this weekend I would feel him in me many times and actually was looking forward to whatever was going to happen. When we awoke from the short post-coital nap he reminded me that we had to eat and get to the Landscaping place in less than two hours. I got up and made my way down to my marital bedroom and jumped in the shower after brushing my teeth. I had just stepped under the stream of water when I felt Karl feeling my naked body. Yes, it felt great so I did the same for him. After a fairly long and stimulating shower we got out and while drying I saw that he was hard again so knew what would follow.

This time we hopped into my husband's and my bed and he was in my wanton vagina to the hilt in a matter of moments. It was sometime later that we both climaxed. I reveled in the feeling of his large cock going in and out and worked to contract my vaginal muscles in time with his pulling out. When we were done screwing I was totally exhausted from the work I had done but Karl was as active as ever. In any case, we rested as I was now finally satiated and cuddled up in his arms.

I awoke first and started dressing so I could fix Karl breakfast and I would be ready for the planned arrival of Brian and his crew from the Nursery. As I came out of our closet dressed, Karl said, "Hey, Beth, for me will you put on your short shorts – I just love to see more of you." Without thinking that he would not be the only one seeing more of me, I went back in our closet and chose the skimpy shorts that I never have worn outside even as my husband has asked me to. Actually, the very short shorts made me even feel sexy and several times while I was fixing some breakfast Karl would fondle and lightly spank my bottom. Once he slid his hand down the back and squeezed my bare bottom. This turned me on more than I would have expected. We had just finished eating when the landscaping truck pulled into our garage area.

We went out and went over with Brian the plans and they started to unload and place the bushes and trees and stones where they were planned. Karl asked me to go to the kitchen and fix a pot of coffee for Brian, visibly patting my bottom as I left. It was not lost on me that Brian had witnessed this and I saw his smile.

Just as I was entering the house I overheard Karl saying to Brian, "Now there is a nice 'piece of ass'." The was followed by, "Wait at least 10 minutes and… , then I was out of range. This was all I heard as I closed the door amid a spectrum of emotions especially anxiety as I had not thought Karl was serious when he made the comment about my seeing and being with more than him a day or so ago.

CHAPTER XIII

A New Twist

You can imagine the whirlwind of thoughts that filled my mind and imagination. Part of me was very angry, as I had always thought the term "Piece of Ass" was derogatory and showed no respect. On the other hand I inwardly found it humorous and 'sexy' and wondered what was crossing Brian's mind and if this was an invitation to him. Once again, I was confronted with an emotional dilemma. I had been having quite stimulating sex with Karl who was almost my father's age and this activity started as a complete and total surprise which at this point I hope does not end. Now a young good looking well built black man may be entering the picture.

My first thought was to run to my room and shut the door but for reasons I cannot describe I stayed in the kitchen setting about to fix Karl and Brian a snack. Shortly, Karl came in and came up behind me and gave me a big hug and said, "you sure can make a man horny" as he fondled my breasts.

Karl then took my hand and led me to the davenport and sitting down he said, "you know what to do so get busy as I want to see you pleasured." Knowing what he wanted, I bent over and helped him free his already enlarging cock. I had to chuckle to myself as I knew what he wanted and I also knew what I wanted. Having Karl's large head of his cock was not only pleasurable but knowing I was giving him this pleasure, I knew that he would be giving me multiple orgasms in short order.

I had literally forgotten about Brian until I heard the back door open. I instinctively tried to straighten up but Karl held my head in place over his cock and in a commanding voice said, "Elizabeth, do not stop until I tell you!" I had no choice but to continue, as embarrassed as I was, to know that another man was watching me suck Karl's cock.

Karl then told me that Brian was in the room, which I knew, and then he said in a soft voice, "Elizabeth, I want you to lower your shorts and then take down your panties to give Brian a thrill." "Do it now or I will take them down and spank your bare fanny in front of Brian." What a dilemma, as this was not what I expected.

I was in no position to argue as my mouth was full of Karl's cock and my head was being held, so slowly I reached back and unbuttoned my shorts and lowered them to my knees and wiggled my bottom till they fell to he ground. I then stepped out of them hoping that Brian did not see my face, which must have been beet red.

I then hesitantly and slowly reached back to lower my panties with a myriad of anxiety and embarrassment only to feel Brian's hands already there in position to lower my panties. What a twirl of emotions from surprise to embarrassment to anxiety to some fear of the unknown. Then I heard Brian's soothing voice saying, "Elizabeth, If you want me to leave just push my hands away and I will go outside." He continued in his quiet voice, "I would be honored to pleasure you but will understand if this is not your desire at this time."

I have no idea what went through my mind but at this point, the garden company employee took on a new persona and I squeezed his fingers and dropped my hands back to Karl's cock, which was starting to contract.

At this point I wanted this man to give me pleasure and I knew I was ready as I felt moisture running down my legs. At this point Karl erupted filling my mouth with his cum. He then got up from the davenport and moved me so that I was over the back of the davenport. I heard him walk into the kitchen saying, apparently to Brian, "Enjoy". He must have gone outside as I heard the door close.

I now felt Brian very slowly lowering my panties and helping me step out of them. The next thing I felt was his hands fondling my bottom. His gentle but firm action were having quite an effect on me as among other feelings, there was a tingling in my vaginal and clitoral areas. In his quiet voice he then asked me, "Should I continue." It took me but a brief bit of time to tell him, "Yes, please continue. Right now I want you inside me." As this came out of my lips, I knew I meant it as for some reason his gentle actions turned me on tremendously.

I got even more excited as I heard him unzip his pants followed by the rustling of clothes. At this point I really wanted him to fuck me till I screamed, which I was sure was about to happen. I did not have to wait long as I felt his quite stiff organ nestling between my legs. At about then I wanted him in me so badly that I reached back and assisted his cock's entrance into my vagina. He was slow but I was so lubricated that it was not long before I felt the pleasure of his large organ deep inside my vagina as his pubic bone jarred my bottom. Never before had I felt so 'full'.

As his hard and slippery cock was going in and out the thought that was raging through my mind, In addition to the raw pleasure, was wonderment in how I had progressed from a very happy one-man woman with the first man I was ever with sexually and whom I loved dearly to now having almost regular sex with an older man and now wanting this new sexual adventure.

This thought did not last too long as the pleasure mounted to the point of first one and then followed in moments by a second total body orgasm. After the second orgasm I lay limply over the davenport when Brian said, "Elizabeth, that was super but lets get you in a more comfortable position". After he slowly pulled out of my vagina he pulled me to his body and gave me a warm hug. He then led me to the other side of the couch and in a short time he was deep in my vagina fucking me in the usual missionary position.

He had amazing staying power as I think we were at it for what seemed like an hour. I really loved his gentle firmness and staying power. His mannerisms and gentleness was unexpected as he was a large very muscular man. His physique reminded me of the athletic well muscled men I dated who were almost all crude and dropped me when I did not accept their advances. They sure all tried to get into my panties and the thought crossed my mind at what I had been missing these last years.

I started getting a little worn out so I tried to flex my hips and contract my vaginal muscles with each stroke. I kept it up till I became exhausted and then I felt him start to contract. With the first contraction he pulled out and came all over my stomach. At that point, I knew he was a gentleman so I gave him a big hug and said, "Thanks." His response cemented my feeling toward him as he said, Now you know that I will not cause you any anxiety so you will be open to do this again.

My response surprised me as I said, "Oh yes, Brian, we will do this again as you were so good to me," and 'never ending pleasure' is hard to say no to. Guess our garden will have to be worked on all summer. With that I gave him a big hug. We each got up and dressed and went outside to do what Brian had originally come for.

As we were dong the work of setting up the garden landscape, Karl came over to me and, placing his arms around me with his hands playing with my bottom, asked if I enjoyed Brian. I looked up at him with must have been a shy smile and softly said, "Yes, it was wonderful but unexpected" and then I added a less than truthful, "I prefer you." That got me a big hug and his promise to take care of that later.

Well, when the work was done and we said goodbye to Brian and we were back in the house, Karl smacked me on my bottom and said, "Go get cleaned up and meet me in the guest room". With Karl what he said was like an 'order' but I had been programmed to want the ensuing pleasure so I did as I was told.

When I got to the guest room, Karl was already in bed naked as always so I crawled in with him and beat him to the punch by saying, "Please fuck me till I cannot take more." We both laughed at that but more than an hour later I was totally bushed. My being with Brian must have made him extra horny.

At one point he even asked me If I was going to see Brian again. I told Karl that I didn't expect so but I inwardly sure hoped so.

CHAPTER XIV

The Beginning

That weekend was the beginning of a very new life for me. I did spend a lot of time in bed with Karl and at one point he told me that his house was close to ready and that he planned to see me as often as he could whenever his friend, Greg, who was my husband, was away or out of town. I had to chuckle when he asked me if this was OK. Of course, I told him that our door was always open.

Greg returned Sunday evening and his homecoming was special. First, we were alone in the house and I could scream through the many orgasms he gave me as I told him, hesitatingly, about how Karl 'seduced' me. My hesitancy was that I really needed to be sure that the man I really loved and who I was married to was comfortable with and wanted me to experience sex with another man.

He assured me again and again reminding me that Karl had an affair with his mother for many years and that he was sure that his younger brother was fathered by Karl. He repeated that this somehow made him more than curious about and less worried about Karl having an affair with his wife. He did not understand why this made him over the top horny but it did.

Anyway as I was describing the seduction, I used mostly the third and fourth times, which were the first times Karl penetrated my vagina. My husband could not get enough of me as he came more times that night than he would in a week in the past. He kept telling me how much he loved me and how pleased that he was for trusting in his love when having sex with Karl became a reality. Yes, I felt a bit guilty as I had not been totally honest but reasoned that this would or could come out later.

The relationship with Karl continued as it had been for the remaining two weeks he lived with us prior to his moving back to his house. Each morning, if Karl was there and after my husband was away at his office, I would go to Karl and get my fill of thundering orgasms to be followed by a repeat in the arms of the man I loved who literally could not wait to hear my story of the day.

The hardest time for me to keep a straight face was when Karl and my husband would talk or at dinner where Karl paid literally no attention to me and seemed to act as if sex was in the past or I was not there. Later Greg and I would laugh at that antic of Karl's but kept it to ourselves, as neither of us wanted it to stop.

When Karl was away on business and especially when both Karl and my husband were away for a weekend or a few days, I would stop by the Nursery to pick up a plant and to let Brian know that the coast was clear. He would come over and I came to love the sex with Brian more than anything. He had the longest cock and longest staying power of any of my other lovers. I would feel a little guilty, as I had not yet told Greg about my affair with Brian. I did mention that I had wondered what it would be like with a black man and my husband's only comment was to "Go for It". So, this is open for the future.

Since my sexual awakening with Karl, I have been a lot more observant of the actions of men who I would meet at events, the gym or even when out shopping. I would tell Greg about each encounter and he would always tell me to have an open mind and if the opportunity presents itself to 'go for it'. So far I have not been with any other sexually as Karl and Brian are all I can handle. I do enjoy the unbridled sex with both of these men coupled with the reward sex I have with my husband.

My sense is that I am at the beginning of a new life, which is miles apart from the virgin monagaminous relationship I had with my true love to the present frequent almost 'whore-like' sex I am experiencing today. I fervently hope that this new me does not change my relationship with my husband. So far, everything he has said and his actions tell me that he is more than OK with my extra sex. I am counting on this to be the case.

Stay tuned as this totally unexpected story develops.

A Part-time job with Unexpected Benefits

By **Chris Dawson**

This story is told by a happily and monogamously married woman who just could not help herself and who found unexpected extramarital pleasure while still in love with her husband. She took a part-time job cleaning a condo and ended up getting quite a surprise the first time. What happened when she got fucked each and every time she came to the condo was that she came to want it. Several 'mistakes' later, a new me develops. One can only imagine the feelings when she finds out her lover is her husbands boss and this all comes out and the husband's reaction to his wife's newfound sexuality.

CHAPTER I

A New Job

Y ou cannot believe the anguish that has led to this letter, but I just must tell someone what I have been doing and right now. As I write this, I cannot, yet, tell this story to my husband. Later in an Addendum to this story I will tell you what happened when I finally confessed to my husband what I had been doing with another man.

I am a 37 year-old married stay-at-home housewife with two young grade school children and a good husband, Charles, who is 41 years old and a middle executive in a large growing corporation. We are monogamous or at least I was and had had no interest in exploring. I am in good shape and both my husband and I have kept our fitness fairly well for our age. We have a very good relationship and a fairly good sex life. My husband comments often about my sensitive breasts and well shaped bottom.

With the kids both in school during the day, I admit that I have been restless so when I saw in the paper an ad for a part-time housekeeper in a townhouse, which to my pleasant surprise was not far from our neighborhood, I was almost excited. The ad asked for flexibility and the extra money would really help so I sent in my contact information. My husband was OK with this as I explained that this money could be really mine to get things for him and the kids on my own.

A few days later I received a call from a gentleman to come for an interview. The owner of the townhouse was an imposingly good looking fit man who introduced himself as Vic and my guess was that he was in his late fifties as he had some greying of his temples. He was very pleasant and I found myself eyeing him approaching flirting but I passed this off as not even a possibility as I was happily married and had never even thought about stepping out of my marriage. He too was very friendly as he explained that he was a bit of a workaholic but just did not have time to clean his townhouse as he thought it should be.

As we talked I saw that his eyes were all over my body especially my breasts. I had not dressed to provoke this and was mildly amused that he seemed to like what he saw as I viewed myself a matronly type and certainly did not fool around or have any affairs behind my husbands back. I admit that I felt a twinge of attraction but mentally scolded myself and dropped the thoughts. I kept thinking to myself, that if I were much younger and unmarried, I would like to see more of this man as he was very handsome and obviously successful.

When I asked him what he expected me to do he got up and showed me around the townhouse that was on two floors and things like where the vacuum was and how to use the dishwasher. I had to chuckle to myself as it seemed that he did not think I should know these things. He said that he expected 4 or so hours twice a week would be enough but when he had gatherings such as friends in for card playing he might ask if I was available to clean up before or after. This seemed like an ideal job as it was not many hours and somewhat flexible and he seemed to be a nice man. After he had answered my questions and I answered his, he offered me the job. As I left, he handed me a key and told me I could begin this coming Friday, which was a few days later.

CHAPTER II

The First Time

When I arrived, the townhouse was quiet and I assumed he was at work. I cleaned the downstairs in short order and was going upstairs to clean the bathroom and make the bed. When I walked into Vic's bedroom I got quite a shock and I am sure that I audibly gasped. Vic was sleeping but was totally uncovered revealing his naked body. The gasp was when I saw that he had an erection and wow, was it ever large. Certainly his organ was much larger than my husband's. To me it was a huge erection.

I'm sure I was beet red and my first reaction was to run home. What I did was to hurry out of the room and go to the bathroom and catch my breath. I finally thought I would just go ahead as if nothing out of the ordinary happened and clean, which was my first mistake.

The sound I made must have awakened him because he called out to ask me if it was I. I told him that it was indeed I and that I would start with the bathroom unless he wanted me to return the next day. From his bedroom across the hall he told me to continue and not to worry about him.

My heart was racing and I know I was blushing, as I had not seen a penis that size except in pictures. Try as I might, I could not put what I saw out of my mind as I tried to concentrate on cleaning the tub. I was bent over the tub when I heard him come padding across the floor behind me. I was too embarrassed to do more than continue to clean so as not to have eye contact.

Suddenly I felt his hand stroking my bottom. As startled as I was, I did not move. I knew I should protest and move away but something kept me glued to where I was. As he now had at least unspoken permission to continue with what he must have had on his mind, I felt him raise my skirt over my back and I became even more embarrassed as I knew he could now see my bottom covered by only my scanty silk panties.

He then started running his hands over my ass and a combination of soft caresses and mild pats had me mesmerized. Without a word from either of us I now felt him pulling my panties down to my ankles. I knew what was coming next and I also knew that this was not the proper behavior for a married women who had never cheated on her husband but, as embarrassed as I was, I was unable to move as he resumed fondling and playing with my ass.

The next surprise, though I should not have been surprised, was that I felt his hard cock rubbing my labia from behind between my legs. I could not believe what was happening but was becoming so turned on that I knew I could not stop even if I had wanted to. I held my breath as he proceeded to use my lubrication to ease the entry of his cock into my very wet pussy. It felt huge as he entered me getting deeper stroke by stroke. My first climax occurred as he reached bottom. I could not believe the pleasure of feeling so full.

Then he started a steady rhythm of fucking me that got me so excited that I moaned loudly in an almost continuous orgasm. I was wrong as these were not the real climax I felt coming which flooded my sensation at the same time I heard and felt him shoot load after load of sperm into my vagina and unprotected womb. This felt so good that I did not even think to ask him to pull out, which I should have as I was not on the pill. The sensation of feeling his warm sperm entering me with each pulse of his cock was out of this world. He then slowly pulled out, patted my ass and walked out of the bathroom without saying a word.

I stood up very slowly and pulled back up my very wet panties and wondered if what I though just happened did indeed happen. The feelings that were coursing through my veins were at once guilt at allowing a man other than my husband to be intimate with me, but also great satisfaction and pleasure over what I had just experienced. I was not sure what to do now but to resume the work I started seemed the best course.

A bit later, I heard Vic downstairs and then I heard him leave, presumably to go to work. I finished cleaning as expected and went home. Many thoughts raced through my mind as I walked home. I thought briefly about confessing to my husband about what happened but couldn't think of a spin to put on it that would be acceptable so I decided that I would not tell him as, I reasoned, it was a one time thing. I was able to clean up before he got home and he did not suspect anything.

I thought about little else over the weekend but reasoned that it was just one of those things and that it would not happen again, but deep inside I knew better and a small part of me almost hoped that I would again feel his big cock in my vagina. I felt guilty and naughty for having these thoughts.

CHAPTER III

Again and Again

T hus it was with some anticipation and underlying excitement that I turned the key in the lock the next Tuesday morning. All seemed quiet so I just went to work cleaning up the kitchen. That done I quietly went upstairs and started on the bathroom. I was cleaning the mirror when I saw him come up behind me. My heart was racing as I felt myself starting to get wet between my legs and he had not touched me. Without a word he came up behind me and pulling up my dress stood as close as he could – his hard cock between my legs tickling my labia.

Again, without a word, he bent me over the sink, pulled my panties down and off and slowly inserted his large cock in my already well-lubricated vagina. Unbelievably, a man I hardly knew with a large cock and great stamina was fucking me. I was in orgasmic bliss but conflicted by the naughtiness of what I was doing. I do not know why but I also did not say a word but moaned through several orgasms until he again erupted and filled my vagina with his sperm. He very slowly pulled out, patted my ass and left for his bedroom without a word.

I remained in the position he left me for several minutes reveling in the feeling I had just experienced. Yet feeling guilty, as I had now cheated on my husband a second time knowing that it would not be the last. I slowly retrieved and put back on my panties and went back to work. As last week, Vic dressed and went to the kitchen probably for something to eat and left without a word. As before, I finished cleaning the bathroom and his bedroom and left for home.

On Friday I was sure he would do me as the last time so I put my panties in my purse, which gave me a naughty almost wicked feeling. This time, when I opened the door, I saw Victor in the kitchen in his bathrobe. I assumed that he was about to go to work so put sex out of my mind as I greeted him and started doing the kitchen dishes. His presence in the kitchen caused me to get wet between my legs and a feeling of desire that I put off as silly.

Unexpectedly he appeared behind me and led me to the breakfast-nook table over which he bent me forward. I heard the rustling of clothes and then he deposited his robe in front of me on the kitchen table. Knowing he was naked behind me caused me to gush lubricant, which I felt running down my legs. Despite how I was turned on, I was able to weakly say "Please, we shouldn't be doing this, I am a happily married woman and I love my husband". As I did not move away, he must have known that I would not stop him from what he was about to do.

Again he raised my skirt to my back and immediately started to squeeze and play with my panty-less ass including putting his fingers between the cheeks and tickling my anal opening. This was a new sensation and I could not help but gasp in pleasure. He seemed to take great delight in my naked bottom until, as before, I felt his now hardened cock work its way into my awaiting and by now very well lubricated vagina.

Vic had almost amazing stamina as he fucked me for what seemed like many minutes of uninterrupted pleasure. We both climaxed simultaneously as he again poured spurt after spurt of semen into my receptive yet unprotected vagina. Without a word he pulled out, patted my bare bottom several times and left for upstairs presumably to dress.

I completed the kitchen work and in the revelry of what I experienced climbed the stairs to tend to the bathroom. As I neared the top of the stairs and started toward the bathroom he appeared from his bedroom door stark naked heading to the bathroom. We met in the hall and I avoided his eyes by looking down only to see his large cock at half-mast. He must have noticed my gaze because the next thing I knew was that his hand was on my head pushing it downward until I was kneeling with my face opposite his cock.

I knew what he wanted and admit I was curious so I took hold of his member and put it to my lips. His circumcised cock felt and tasted very different to that of my husband. The soft velvety head and slightly salty lubricant was intoxicating. He tasted delicious and I was soon licking and sucking him with gusto even as this was not what I had done often with my husband as I usually begged off that act. Here I was enjoying the feeling of his large cock getting larger and harder. While sucking him he started playing with my breasts, which turned me on greatly.

The more he tweaked my nipples, the more and deeper I mouthed his cock. It should have come as no surprise but did when he started pulsing and erupting into my mouth. My first reaction was to pull away but he held my head so I had no alternative but to swallow his load. That was a first for me but I knew it would not be the last. When he had finished he slowly pulled his cock out of my mouth, patted me on the head and headed to the bathroom without a word.

While he was in the bathroom I went to make up his bed and tidy up the room. When I pulled back the covers, I saw a pair of panties and felt a jealous twinge. I picked them up, folded them and placed them on his nightstand. Now he would know that I knew that I was not the only one he was fucking. Oh yes, I did have a feeling of jealousy. I finished before he came back and busied myself with other cleanups as I waited for him to dress and leave.

This days experience had me in an emotional whirlpool. On the one hand, I basked in the sexual aftermath of powerful orgasms and on the other hand the feeling of naughtiness at performing intimate acts, especially sucking a cock, with a stranger albeit less of a stranger each day I cleaned his house. Anyway, I finished my morning's work and left for home about an hour after he left for work.

CHAPTER IV

My Husband Benefits

My husband did not know what came over me as I almost attacked him when he came home. We had sex over the weekend but I had to admit that it was not near as exciting and delicious as what I had guiltily experienced with Vic in the last two weeks.

Tuesday came and I found myself putting both my panties and bra in my purse, which made me start to get wet almost immediately. Of course, each time I came to work, I got soundly fucked. Mostly from behind bent over what ever was convenient. He did me over the tub, the sink, the kitchen table, a chair, his bed, and one of his davenports. I came to love being taken this way meaning I did not see but only felt the object of my pleasure.

He really seemed to like my bottom as he always played with it and onetime when I was a bit late he spanked me. This hurt but at the same time felt terrific and heightened the subsequent orgasm while we were fucking. He caught on to this and many times I was spanked before sex sometimes very hard.

On a couple of occasions he led me to his bedroom and with a wave of his hand I knew that he wanted me to strip fully which I did. Then we fucked like teenagers in his bed in both the missionary position and from behind with me on hands and knees. At no time did he use a condom, which added to the 'excitement' in an almost perverse way.

Frequently, he fed me his cock and made me swallow his cum which I came to like very much. Of course, I also found that I liked very much being under his control as well as being fucked by him. I was one satisfied lady kept in a state of anticipation as I never knew what he was going to do to me and he never spoke before, during or after. I felt at times like a whore partly because there was always a generous bonus in my envelope but had to admit that he was satisfying a deep need.

Several times over the weeks, I would find different panties either in his bed or the bathroom and each time a curious wave of jealousy would creep over me. Once I left my own panties in an obvious place. The next time I came to clean the spanking I received suggested to me that I would not do that again as it stung almost to the point of my starting to cry. After that I was led to the bedroom and fucked through three orgasms.

One week he told me that he was having a gathering and could I clean both Friday and Saturday morning. My husband knew that I was working the few hours a week and he was OK with this so it was not hard to ask him to entertain the kids that Saturday. He knew I worked close by but did not know for whom I was working and I only knew his first name at that.

CHAPTER V

My First Anal Sex and More

When I arrived on the Friday, I found the house particularly messy so went right away to cleaning and making the place presentable. I had both my panties and bra in my handbag but thought that there was too much to do to play. How wrong I was.

When I was finished in the downstairs, I went up to see what needed to be done. It was quiet so I thought he had already left. When I opened the bedroom door, there he was naked in bed but not sleeping. He motioned me over and pulled me down to his already erect cock, which I started sucking and making love to as I liked to and as I knew he liked and wanted. At one point he pulled me off and pulled me over his lap. I knew what was to follow and I was therefore not surprised when he started spanking me but this time the spanks alternated with squeezing and playing with my bottom. I was squirming with desire and delight. I just love the feel of the head of his cock running over my lips and trying to take him in further in my mouth each thrust as he fucks my mouth.

As he was playing in my crack, I opened my legs and soon his fingers were in my vagina, which was already well lubricated. Then he stared fingering my anus first with one finger, then two and finally three. This was a new sensation as anal play had never been part of my married life. I anxiously awaited what I sensed was to follow.

I was almost disappointed when he stopped this play and got up out of bed. He then undressed me himself for the first time and helped me to the bed on my knees. He then positioned himself behind me, and it then dawned on me that he wanted to fuck me in the ass, which he had never done and I had never done. Suddenly his well-lubricated fingers were probing my anal passage followed by his cock. He was patient and slowly worked his very large cock in to the hilt.

What a feeling to have your anus plugged and being fucked while your partner plays with your clitoris and breasts. I was surprised to feel a climax coming and more surprised at the magnitude of not only the climax but the feeling of intimacy the act of anal intercourse portends. I was hooked and 'in love' with how I felt being taken as I was.

After his climax he pulled out, went to the bathroom, got dressed and left. I stayed on the bed basking in the afterglow of this new experience and even fell asleep for an hour or so.

Saturday morning when I opened the door I was surprised not by the mess of an obvious party but that there were two men asleep on the couches. Seeing them I was very quiet to not awaken them and decided to clean upstairs and if they were still asleep I would leave and come back later. I quietly went upstairs and was cleaning in the bathroom when I felt his hands fondling my breasts and pulling me close to his hard cock. As turned on as I was, I did not think this would go further as he had 'sleeping' guests downstairs.

He had other ideas and without a word, led me into the bedroom. First he bent me over his easy chair and had his way fucking me from behind. I had to hold my mouth so my orgasm was quiet. After we both came, he laid down in the bed, which I knew was when he wanted me to suck his cock. He turned me around so that while I had his cock in my mouth he was able to suck and play with my clitoris with his tongue. This seemed even more exciting as there was the element of possibly being caught by his sleeping guests.

While I mouthed his beautiful cock, I felt him playing with my clit and anus. I was lost in revelry when I was startled to feel another pair of hands on my hips and could feel a cock probing my genital area and then entering my vagina. At first I was puzzled but soon it became clear that one of his friends had come upon us and was taking advantage of the situation. Not a word was spoken as I found myself with two openings filled with a cock.

The harder this new cock fucked me, the harder and faster I

sucked Vic's cock. Suddenly there were three climaxes nearly at the same time. The cock in my vagina became soft and when he withdrew there was an almost immediate replacement with an even larger cock. A second stranger was now fucking me and Vic was moving out from under me.

Next, I saw that I was at eye level with what I thought was the cock that must have been in my vagina. He fed it into my open mouth and I discovered that all cocks are not alike. This one was even sweeter but not circumcised. For the first time I could taste my own juices. I still hadn't seen the faces of Vic's guests but knew their cocks well.

For the next couple of hours I was fucked by each man at least twice and had swallowed cum from each in turn. All the while there was not a word spoken. This was certainly a new experience and very exciting until I saw for the first time, and recognized, one of the men with the largest cock whom I had just sucked off as a neighbor of my husband and I whose name was Rod. He must have seen my startled and worried look as he whispered in my ear that the secret was safe with him. I was relieved sort of but wondered if I could trust him.

Well, I had been away from home long enough so while Vic and his friends dozed I cleaned up and made my way home a very well fucked but anxious woman.

CHAPTER VI

A not so Surprising follow-up

I was really not surprised on Monday morning fairly shortly after my husband and kids had left, when Rod (our neighbor) came by and wasted no time coming on to me by telling me what a great time he had Saturday how he was going to enjoy being with me on occasion. I protested of course, but what could I say as he had been a witness to what might be called a 'gang bang'. I knew my fate was in his hands when he said he knew that I wanted to keep this secret life from my husband and 'not to worry' he would not tell anyone.

With that he put his arms around me and started kissing me and fondling my bottom and pussy. I felt that I had no choice but to succumb to his wishes so when he raised my skirt to play with my panty covered bottom all I could do was submit and pretend to enjoy it. Actually, in a perverted way, I was enjoying his touch, which was very different for that of both my husband and Vic.

Rod led me into our living room and as he had been to our house he knew to put on the sound system. He selected a piece and told me to slowly strip for him. What choice did I have so as I started to move with the music. I wished I had told my husband of my sexual indiscretions and begged forgiveness. Well, I thought, might as well try to enjoy the inevitable so I did the best striptease I could think of. I could tell that he was getting hard as the bulge in his pants was getting larger and he was almost salivating.

When I was down to my panties and bra he motioned me over to where he was sitting and said, "you know what to do now!" Yes, I knew he wanted me to get his very large penis out and suck it so, realizing that I did not have a choice, I did unzip his pants and get his growing member out. While I was mouthing it, I undid his pants and got him to stand up while I lowered both his pants and underpants. I continued sucking hoping that one orgasm would be enough but after he came in my mouth he said, "Wow, that was great, I have wanted to have you ever since we moved into this neighborhood. You are some sexy lady."

He then started to dance with me feeling my bottom and breasts as we went around the room. His hands were all over my body and it was not long before I really did want him to fuck me but still did not like it that I had to, to keep him quiet. He undid my bra letting if fall to the floor and slowly worked my panties down my hips until I was able to kick them away.

"You are a beautiful lady". With that he laid me down on our couch, got between my legs and brought his head down to my pussy and did magic with his tongue. He quickly brought me off to a thundering orgasm with his mouth that left me panting.

Moving up my body stopping to play with and suck my breasts and give me soul kisses, which I found myself returning. The kissing and fondling left me wanting him in me right now. I moved under him and placed his good-sized cock at the entrance to my vagina and gave the push needed to feel him firmly planted in my 'love pocket'.

We fucked with me meeting thrust with thrust in this position until my strength was ebbing and then we switched to the doggie position where he could more easily play with my breasts as we fucked.

He had great staying power so it was some time before he finally pulled out and came all over my bottom. He had been here for almost two hours so I told him that Charles (my husband) might be coming home early so it would be best if he left soon. He got dressed and gave me a big hug and kiss stating that he would see me again. As he was leaving after I dressed, I added that he must call first and it would be best if the kids were away visiting grandparents and Charles was away on business. That I would be seeing him again was not in doubt and actually, I really had enjoyed being naughty in my own house.

CHAPTER VII

The Aftermath

Well, it finally happened, as I feared. I had been having unprotected intercourse with Vic for more than two months and now I was late for my period. I still do not think I can tell my husband that the child may not be his. Well, time will tell and in the meantime I get all the sex anyone could want.

Now, each week, I can expect to get laid any day I wish and certainly every Tuesday and Friday when I go to clean Vic's place. These visits are always explosive and I never know what to expect. He has caught on to my submissive side and need to be punished for my naughtiness and regularly includes a sound spanking in addition to explosive sex plugging any of my holes. I think he likes me but I know I love what he does to me. I may never know as not a word is exchanged – just great sex – and now possibly a child.

My neighbor, Rod, comes over and on to me at least a couple of times a week. When he is over, I do enjoy the sex and he has the greatest tongue I know of and the tastiest pre-cum and cum. I really enjoy the feel of his cock in my mouth as big as he is. He is over for at least an hour and I get fucked to at least one great orgasm at least a couple of times.

Originally, I thought I had to have sex with him to keep him quiet but, I now know this was a bluff as his wife (who is the money in that family) would leave him in a second if she thought he had sex with anyone when he was at a gathering with friends. I do not tell him that I know that, as the illicit sex is great.

Not only is my extramarital sex great, my sex life with my soul mate and husband, Charles, is definitely on the upturn. I have slowly introduced many of the techniques I have learned at the hands of my (now) many lovers and realize that I love my husband more than ever and will one day share my pleasures with him.

What I am about to relate was what led me to confide in a close friend who suggested this rather long letter. My husband recently received a large promotion to Senior Vice President of the company he has been working for. There was a reception at one of our luxury hotels in honor of this promotion. As there would be drinking, my husband got us a room for after the reception and the kids were at my parent's.

I proudly stood beside him in the greeting line. The attendees included many of my husband's colleagues and those he supervised. It was a gala affair and I was basking is my husbands success and he was obviously pleased with the comments his colleagues were making about me like "where have you been hiding this lovely lady?" and "I hope we will be seeing more of you both."

I had been greeting and briefly talking to one person in the line but got the shock of my life when I turned back to my husband and he was shaking hands with none other than Vic. I'm sure my mouth was open and the gasp was audible, but for sure my heart was in my stomach. I managed to smile as my husband introduced me to "Victor Worthington the third" who, he went on to say, "Victor is the Chairman of the Board of our company and one of the smartest persons I have had the pleasure to work with."

To say that I was nervous would be a gross understatement. I smiled, shook his hand and said the usual greeting but my heart was thumping wildly in my chest. Victor was charming as he spoke without a hint that he knew me intimately and we had been fucking regularly for more than three months. His comment that, "You are even more attractive than the picture Charles has on his desk" told me that he had known who I was from the start. Thus I knew that he had seduced the wife of one of his colleagues and now one of his Vice Presidents.

As Victor passed on, my husband put his arms around me and said that the man I just met was responsible for his promotion and to be especially nice to him. He then gave me a kiss while discretely patting my bottom. He had no idea how 'nice' I had been to him and also how "nice" he had been to me. Now I knew that I had to tell my husband what I had been doing. He had to know whatever the consequences. I looked him in the eyes and said "We have to talk". I just could not, at the time, tell him that it is for Mr. Worthington that I work a couple of days a week".

After the reception line was done, I told my husband that I had to find the ladies room as I was bursting. I excused myself and went looking to where I could relieve myself. When I came out very much relieved, who did I see but Victor who immediately came over to me and taking my arm led me away from the crowd. In a private alcove he gave me a big hug followed by a bigger kiss, which I found myself returning as his roving hands started turning me on. He then told me that our secret was safe with him and, yes, he did know who I was but that no matter who my husband was, he would have done the same thing.

I was about to say something about his deception when he whisked me into a vacant small meeting room, kissed me again and bent me over the conference table. My confused mind was flooded by what usually followed when I was in this position plus the fear of being caught but I did not resist or say anything as he raised my skirt from behind. When he had my dress up to my waist he stopped and asked if he should continue. Damn him, he knew I had never stopped him before but even I was surprised at what I said next, "No, please don't stop, You know very well that I want you to fuck me but please hurry so we will not be missed."

Well, he then pulled down and off my panties, spread my legs and fed his fabulous cock into my vagina. God, it felt good and as naughty as I felt, I urged him to continue. It may have been the situation, the surprise, or a combination of events but as he slid in and out I had an almost continuous orgasm, which was one of the best in my memory. I had to put my fist in my mouth to mute my screams of pleasure.

The situation of this event and the revelation of who he was must have affected him also as his orgasm was far quicker than usual. After he climaxed he stayed in me for a few minutes while telling me that he was looking forward to my continuing to see him and clean up his flat. After the pleasure I had just received my response was, "of course I will, what did you expect?" We both laughed as we cleaned ourselves with some napkins and got dressed.

As we exited the small conference room we made sure we were not seen and walked back to the reception area. As we got closer Victor came close to me and said that he would see that I got back to my husband safely. We both laughed at that but when we found my husband, Victor shook his hand and told him that he, "Ran into your lovely wife down the hall and wanted to be sure she got back to you safely". He then said, "Charles, congratulations on your well deserved promotion and I hope we will see more of your beautiful wife than a picture on your desk." Then, "I will bid you both good night and see you, Charles, at work Monday."

CHAPTER VIII

And then

O nce upstairs in our room, I was in such need to be close to and intimate with my husband than I quite literally dragged him to the bed. After we made love and basking in the post-sex bliss, he asked me what had gotten into me that made me so horny. My first response was to say that it was because I was so proud of him at being promoted and then I paused and started with, "Honey what did you mean by telling me to be 'especially nice' to your boss, Mr. Worthington". His response was that he was embarrassed to tell me but that he knew that Victor was a ladies man and he was occasionally fantasizing about him coming on to me and being with me.

He went on to say that he was not sure wher e this came from but he had the feeling that I was almost more than he could handle and had always, since before we were married wanted to see me in action because I was so sexy but was too chicken to suggest anything that might upset me. With that admission I gave him the biggest hug of my life and said, "Well, honey I love you more than anything in this world but have I got a story to tell you."

I then told him, "You are aware that I have a small part-time cleaning job a couple of times a week at a fairly nearby house, do you not?" I continued, "Well I did not even know the name of the person who lived there but guess who he is". When he only looked quizzically at me and shook his head, I said, "The house I am at twice a week and the person for whom I work is your boss Victor" "I have known him only as "Vic", and yes, he is a ladies man". Charles then got an odd look in his eyes and asked "Have you had sex with him?"

Well, the floodgate was open and I made the decision to be totally honest and be willing to suffer the consequences so I looked my husband in the eyes and said, "Yes, he has taken me several times, almost every time I have been at his place" "It all started the first time I came by to clean." "that, unbeknownst to me, he was still in the house." I had cleaned downstairs and went up to make the bed and when I opened the door there he was asleep in his bed, naked and with a large hard-on." I went on saying, "I had retreated to the bathroom but visions of his large cock followed me."

"I was quite embarrassed and even thought about leaving but in the end went to clean the bathroom." "In a few minutes, I heard him crossing the hall but was too embarrassed to look up from my position cleaning the tub." "The next thing I knew he had my dress pulled up and was lowering my panties." "I should have stopped him and I will never know why I didn't, but I did nothing and he was soon doing me from behind." "Honey, as much as I loved you and as guilty as I felt, the pleasurable sensations won out". "Please forgive me as I had never ever been with any man other than you in all our married life and here I was being fucked by a man I really did not know."

I looked over at my husband, Charles, perhaps expecting to see hurt or anger yet there he was smiling and sporting a hard and dripping penis. He gave me a big hug, rolled me over on my back and entered me in one stroke. The passion I experienced was a first time for me with my husband. When he asked me, How many times has he made love to you", I responded, "Not sure of a number but he has fucked me many times". When I said that, he immediately came.

When we came down from the high of our love-making, the first thing he said to me was, "Wow, You have no idea how much more I love you now that I know you are being satisfied by a lover". He went on to say, "I have no idea where this is coming from but I am very turned-on knowing you have made love to Victor - I want to hear about everything".

I assured him that I would hold nothing back as I loved him also but told him that I was ecstatic that he felt this way as I did not know if I could actually stop enjoying sex with others, now that

I had started. I clearly told my husband that, "The sex was very pleasurable 'fucking' and that it, was quite different from the love-making I do with you."

I then went on to tell my continuously horny and hard husband about the best times and best experiences even the Saturday when two of his friends had their way with me. When I told him that one of the men at Victor's party was our neighbor Rod he became instantly hard again and as we were making passionate love he had me relate this experience.

He then told me that he was not at all surprised, as he had seen Rod eyeing me at neighborhood parties for years. He got hard again when I told him how Rod had come over to our house the next week and I had thought that to keep him silent that I had to screw him and that he has been over several times when you and the kids were gone.

He asked if Rod was a good lover and looking him in the eyes, I said, "God yes, but I will stop allowing him to come over in a minute if you wish." The love of my life then said, "Gosh no, continue seeing him as long as I know about it and maybe we can set it up so I may observe first hand you being pleasured by another man." He went on to say, "Nothing would give me greater pleasure than watching Rod or anyone make you scream with pleasure.

Oh, and some good news is that I had a recent miscarriage so I will not have to contend with a pregnancy with an unknown father. It may well have been my husbands but I was certainly filled by more loads for Victor and Rod than by my husband.

Thus, my life goes on where I have become far more confident in my sexuality and now, do not hesitate to share with my husband everything I do in bed with anyone. I still go to Victors at least twice a week and it is now even more pleasurable as the feeling of guilt is absent. I think he suspects that my husband knows about what we do but I never fail to tell him what Victor does to me when he gets home and it never fails to make him horny and hard so on those days I get it several times.

© March 2009 - Chris Dawson

My Wife's Newfound Needs

By **Chris Dawson**

Forward

When your wife goes out with the girls to a male review club and comes back totally taken and smitten by the size of the cocks she saw and then you tell her that, heck, our friend Joe has one like that, what would you expect to happen next. Well, you lose a golf partner and your wife gets all the big cocks she can handle and more. That it doesn't stop with Joe is the story.

CHAPTER I

The Start

I should have been more careful what I wished for. More about this matter in a bit. My wife, Barbara, and I have been married for 21 years and have had a moderately good but somewhat waning sex life typical of a couple married having three kids. Business and raising kids has a way of taking the passion out of long-term relationships and I was worried that this may have happened but recently it is as when we were courting and first married. Initially the clues of a possible infidelity were manifest by what I perceived as an fairly recent increase in my wife's interest in sex and occasionally she has worn me out.

I am a 52 year old business executive who has kept active and fit for who knows the reason but do play squash weekly and do golf about twice a month usually with my wife but occasionally with the guys. We have been what I thought was happily married but now know that I am not enough for my wife at least in the sex department. Rather than making me angry, this possibility has made me almost constantly horny.

My wife, Barbara, is 49 years old and up to a couple of years ago was slightly overweight. Through diet and three times a week exercise at the close-by gym, she is now in the range of 130 pounds and has a strikingly curvy body that I have always loved. She still turns me on when she dons a swimsuit or dresses for rare parties.

She is almost back to the weight she had before our first child. Our three kids are 16, 18 and 20 years old respectively and will all be in various colleges by next year. Up until a few years ago we went on family vacations and we all enjoyed these immensely. As kids develop new interests these have almost stopped.

Anyway, with the freedom of two kids away at college she had more time for herself and started spending 3-4 days a week at our local gym and a night a week or so with her girlfriends. All the ladies we have met over the years live in our block. These were usually on weeknights but then they started doing these the odd Friday or Saturday. The weekends were when I was out of town so it did not interfere with our time together.

One time she told me that they were going into the city to take in an all male show. She laughed at this saying she wondered why they decided to go to a male "review" and asked me what she should expect if she went. I told her what I had heard that these were usually exotic dancers and women would act silly seeing nude of near nude young men parading around. We had a good laugh at this turn of events and I told her to enjoy and if they made her horny, I would take care of her. She looked at me and said that I sounded like a "dirty old man" and she would go to show me I was wrong.

Well, they did go and when she came back she was as horny and hot as I had seen her for a long time – literally attacking me with kisses and amorous strokes. After her second climax, I asked her to tell me about the show and why it had affected her so much. Her response was: "hon, it was a strip show and some of these men took off everything and wow, did they all had gigantic penises". She went on to say: "I have never seen a penis so large, certainly much larger than yours and I couldn't take my eyes off what they were showing."

As we were still coupling she instantly had another orgasm. When I asked her how much larger she took a hold of my cock and said that she did not think she could have touched her fingers together like she could with mine as it was so thick and guessed that is was at least 2 inches longer.

I realized later that I may have made a mistake by telling her that yes, this was large but heck, even our friend Joe has a cock like you describe. I had seen him many times in the locker room and he is as you describe very thick and about 9 or 10 inches long – quite a stud. Then I laughed and said that he uses it also. When she asked me what I meant I said that he seemed to be always meeting someone and tells me that most of them are married. I then said that I didn't want to appear nosy but I had seen him with other than his wife. She then asked me if there were any that we know. I looked at her through new eyes and told her that yes, there were some surprises as he sure loved women and they him.

As I looked at my wife her expression led me to ask if he had ever come on to her. She then totally surprised me by saying: "Yes, in fact, he has come on to me at several parties but I have always put him in his place. At last years holiday party at the Meyer's he caught me in the bathroom and told me that he wanted to make love to me. I did not want to make any noise to call attention to what was happening but had to really struggle as he was feeling me all over.

I think I was saved only when we heard his wife calling for him but I had no idea he was so big. Nothing since that time as I keep my distance. I hugged her and told her that I loved her but said that "maybe the next time you would get lucky."

With that she took my cock in her mouth and played with it until I got hard and she moaned asking me to make love to her again. She had three orgasms, which was very unusual for her, before I shot my load. She was the horniest I had seen her in years. Also, I had the strange feeling as she was sucking and playing with my cock that she was comparing it to the large one she saw at the male strip place.

Putting two and two together, it was clear that my wife had been taken by what she had seen and was more than a little curious about large cocks. I teased her a bit about wanting to see a big cock again when she told me that the girls wanted to go back to that club the next week. The frequency of her being horny and giving me the signals that she wanted more sex so I became the beneficiary of her fixation. In addition her attention to my cock increased dramatically.

I found that her preoccupation with cock size a real turn-on and would get hard and excited thinking about her playing with and even being fucked by a large cock. When I would mention this to her she would tell me I was crazy as she could never do anything like being with another man and that I was quite big enough for her. Little did I know that her curiosity would get the best of her and she would actually experience that which she was fantasizing about.

CHAPTER II
The Confession Plus

When she returned from the male strip club that next time she was as horny and receptive to my advances as she had been when we were first married. When I asked her about what happened she blushed noticeably as she said "Nothing really". When I asked her if the evening "turned her on" she said, "No, why should it" but her color and the expression on her face told me otherwise.

Finally one night after we made love she told me that she had a confession to make and hoped I would not be upset. She then admitted that she found the large cocks of these young men exciting to look at and she actually touched one and it excited her beyond belief. Then she noticed my arousal and asked if her telling me about touching the dancers cock excited me. I admitted to her that it did and also admitted my long time fantasy of watching her being intimate with another man.

She then told me that she really doubted that she could do anything with another man as I was quite satisfying to her and had been for many years. I told her then to keep an open mind and keep me in the loop. At this point, deep down, I knew that my loving wife would at some point succumb to this desire of hers and it excited and embarrassed me at the same time. Yes, I felt pangs of jealousy but the overwhelming feeling was one of sexual excitement.

Nothing was said again and things seemed back to normal when we were at a neighborhood party and Joe was there without his wife as she had to tend to her ailing mother. Of course he socialized with everyone but I noticed he paid particular attention to my wife and I caught her watching him on more than one occasion. There was some dancing music and I was not surprised when Joe came up to us and asked me if he could have the honor of dancing with the prettiest lady at the party.

One point in their dancing I noticed that his hand kept lowering to her shapely bottom. She would always move his hand away but he persisted. When I came back from refreshing my drink a roundabout way they were playing a slow dance song and now his hand was fondling her bottom without her moving his hand away. This excited me and I became uncomfortably hard. I wonder what would follow and hoping I would get to see her getting fucked by my 'friend'.

When they came back to where I had been standing and I was not there, he took her by the hand and led her back to the dance floor. It was getting late and our hosts had turned the lights down so it was more difficult to see them dancing so I asked the hostess for the pleasure of a dance to thank her for the excellent gathering.

I swung as innocently as possible close to where Joe and my wife were dancing making sure I did not make eye contact. What I saw made me instantly hard. Had to keep a distance between whom I was dancing with as my excitement would have been far too obvious. Not only was Joe playing with my wife's bottom but one of her arms was not around his neck but between their bodies. I knew that she had to be feeling his cock. The next time I circled around they were not on the dance area. I feigned exhaustion and brought our hostess back to her husband so I could look for my wife.

She was nowhere to be found and I started to be worried as to where she had gone and what she was doing. A bit over a half hour later I saw Joe come back in the room alone and start to mingle as he always does. A few minutes later Betsy came in from another direction. I knew they had been together and wondered why they did not come back together. I may have wondered but did not have any doubt that Joe's big cock had made some headway.

Barbara came over to me and told me that she had gone to the bathroom after the last dance. I told her I missed her and gave her a kiss. With the kiss, there was no doubt that she had been exploring his cock as she had the unmistakable odor and taste of semen in her mouth. I asked her how her dance with Joe was and she told me, " Oh, it was OK but he was still trying to come on to me."

When I asked her what had he done this time she said "Nothing really but filled the air with flattery and tried to fondle my butt". After a moment she added with a look of guilt in her eyes, "Actually he did fondle my butt and it did feel good – I hope you are not angry with me for allowing him to play with my bottom". I quickly told her that it did not bother me and, in fact, turned me on and I loved her even more as she was comfortable with telling me about this bawdy adventure.

I left it at that but then she commented about my hardness and teased me for being turned on by Joe's trying to play with her bottom. She then said that she would take care of that when we got home. When we got home an hour or so later she was as hot and horny as I had ever seen her. She was also far more wet and slippery than usual and we made love well into the night. I even commented that, "Dancing with Joe must have been a real turn-on for you" I was hoping that she would tell me about what else they did and what it was like to suck a large cock.

With that she looked at me with wide eyes – almost fear but said nothing. What she did was reach for my cock and put it in her mouth. While she was sucking my cock I could tell that she was feeling the size difference but she remained silent on that subject.

CHAPTER III
My Friend Joe

The next Saturday when I arrived at the golf course the others told me that Joe had called in ill and sent a replacement. I could hardly concentrate on my game as I was sure he was up to mischief with my wife. I begged off our usual after golf drinking and bullshit session and went straight home. When I arrived, Barbara was nowhere around but on going upstairs I heard the shower going. As she almost never takes showers this time of day I quickly undressed and surprised her by joining her. Of course I had a hard-on that would not quit as I fantasized what she had been doing and with whom.

I told her that I missed her and I was needing her in the worst way. She asked me what had made me so horny. I do not remember what I told her as it was a made up tale. When I gave her a kiss, my tongue again tasted the unmistakable taste of semen. Then I cupped her pussy and slid a finger along the lips and they were very wet and slippery. I lifted her up and told her to hang on as I lowered her wet vagina on to my throbbing cock. When it slid in much more easily than it had in the past I knew that she and Joe had fucked. I came very shortly after which she had an orgasm. Boy, was I ever horny.

The next Saturday was almost the same except she was out of the shower and literally attacked me when I came into the bedroom. She was dilated and slippery and must not have realized that his cum was still in her vagina. When I kissed her she again had the taste of semen in her mouth. I asked her what had made her so horny and she said it was because our son was away for the day fishing with his buddies, which he usually did on Saturdays.

It was driving me crazy to wonder what actually was happening and if my once faithful wife was fucking my friend. I was not angry but was sort of jealous and very excited, wanting to see her fucking Joe somehow. The thought of her with Joe made me exceptionally horny and my cock very hard. I wanted to see her fucking him in the worst way.

The next Saturday when we arrived at the golf course, the manager told us that a storm was coming according to the Doppler weather channel they have on despite what appeared to be a nice day. He told us that he did not recommend us starting a round as the rain would be upon us soon.

This was my opportunity and I am sure I broke many speed records heading back home hoping that I would catch Barbara and Joe making out or even fucking. Sure enough Joe's car was in our driveway so I went around the block, parked, and walked back between nearby houses. I quietly went in the back garage door and stealthily made my way to our living room as I thought I heard voices.

There was Joe and my wife hugging and kissing and undressing each other. Joe was telling her how he had missed her this week and was happy that she wanted him again. My wife then said, that she just could not get enough of his big cock. When she said "I just have to have it in me as it is so big", I almost came even without touching myself.

Once they were both naked, my wife got on her knees and started licking, kissing and sucking his cock all the while moaning "I love it, I love it". She really got into sucking and I was amazed at how much she was able to get down her throat. After a surprisingly long time with her head bobbing up and down he said "OK, Baby, get ready, I am about to cum". I was very proud of my wife as she swallowed it all and licked him clean.

My next surprise was that she took his hand in hers and led him upstairs to our bedroom. I waited a bit and quietly went into our bathroom and then into our walk-in closet to get the thrill of my life. Sure enough when I quietly opened the door a crack, they were fucking like crazy. Joe was repeating over and over how much he loved fucking her as it was always a pleasure to fuck a married woman who wanted it so much. My wife was constantly moaning and almost screaming when she would have an orgasm, which seemed to come every few minutes. She said may things but what I remember the most was "God, I want you in me, I need you in me, you are so big that I must have you in me". With that I came all over the closet floor.

I then quietly left and made my way back to the car. It had started raining so once I was close to home, I called my wife who sounded almost breathless, to tell her that I would be home in a half hour because golf had to be cancelled due to the rain. I asked if she wanted me to pick anything up from the grocery store. She told me that we needed milk and she would see me soon but her voice sounded anxious. I asked if she had showered yet and when she told me "no", I asked her to wait for me as I needed one also.

I was in the store as I knew she would want more time. Picked up milk and went home. Came bouncing in and ran upstairs. Barbara was in her robe and told me to hurry and undress as she wanted to get her shower. When she saw my raging hard-on she asked "What made you horny this time."

As I took her in my arms, I realized how much I loved her and that I had the opening I was looking for. I told her that "I am horny not only thinking of you making love to a large cock but watching you....." The look on her face as her eyes opened was priceless. She could not find the words as she said "What? How?, What do you mean?, When...?" Her expression was priceless.

Then she said "You know" followed by a tearful and pleading voice "Can you ever forgive me". Then she put two and two together and looking at my tenting erection, smiled and said that she would take care of that. We were both naked and in bed in seconds. As I was kissing her, I said, "I love the taste of semen in your mouth" and seconds later when tonguing her wet vagina I told her that she tasted like she had been recently fucked and when I sank my cock in her very slippery vagina I said, "I also love to have sloppy seconds". We then had probably the best sex of our lives. Barbara literally had tears of relief and joy as her secret was out.

After I came and as we were cuddling I asked her to tell me how many times she had been with him. My wife of more than 20 years said in a tentative voice that I was owed the truth as she had been with him maybe 10 times since the neighborhood party a couple of months ago. That she has become literally addicted to his large cock and knowing he was a bit of a player she had the notion of wanting him all to herself. That surprised me as I had only suspected a couple of Saturdays. As I was sexually excited again, I added another load to her already filled pussy and in her renewed excitement she also had big climaxes.

I told her that I had seen her feeling his cock while they danced at that party and had tasted semen in her mouth and asked her if she had had sex with him that night. She said "No, but close to it" and then she told me that it started out with her compelling fascination with the size of his cock so when he put her hand on his cock she could not stop. As the dance ended, he asked her to meet him by the back door she knew she would and was looking forward to feeling his cock again. She told me that they went outside and kissed and he again put her hand on his cock, which he had now taken out of his pants.

Next she said to me, "Honey, it was so large and warm that I just had to see it up close." "I sat in one of their lawn chairs and with both hands explored his increasingly hard cock". "When he asked me to kiss it I hardly hesitated as wrong as it was". "Once I kissed and used my tongue on his cock it was not long before I wanted to taste it and the next thing I knew I was giving him a blow-job and could not stop even as he filled my mouth with his cream". "God, was I excited" was what she said next as we again made passionate love.

She went on saying, "I then panicked and told him that we must stop and get back into the house before we were missed". I was very excited and horny for you and did not even think about the taste in my mouth and when you did not seem to notice or ask me I thought that this slip of infidelity had gone without your notice or upsetting you.

I then asked her to tell me about the first time as I thought that this would be the most exciting. My wife then told me that she loved only me but what she was about to tell me has led to an almost "uncontrollable compulsion for your friends very large cock." She went on saying, "Anyway, the next morning after you had gone to work he came to the door and said that he had something for me". She told me that she let him in and as they were talking she noticed he was getting hard and he did not make it any better by saying "Look at what you do to me as he saw that my eyes were on his crotch".

Barbara told me that she told him, although not convinced herself, that what she did last night was the first time she had been unfaithful to me and that she just could not risk being caught as much as she might want this to go further. He put her alarm at ease by agreeing with her and saying that he would never do what she did not want to do. She went on, "So I made him a cup of coffee and we talked about many things but eventually came back to how I liked his cock". "When I did not answer, he got up and came to me and pulled me to him saying that he had better go before he couldn't."

"He took me into his arms and again telling me thanks and gave me a kiss". It was not a friendly kiss but a long a passionate one that literally took my breath away". "When he stopped and I did not say anything he kissed me again". "This time his strong hands found my bottom and he started squeezing and fondling it". "When the kiss finally ended I was almost out of breath but told him that we should not be doing this as we were both married."

"He then asked me if I wanted him to stop". "My hesitation was the answer he hoped for so he kissed me again but this time not only did he play with my bottom but also my breasts". "When he put his hand between us to feel my pussy, I reached to pull his hand away and felt with the back of my hand his very large and hard cock". "I knew I was weakening when I turned my hand to feel it for real I was quite surprised at what I felt and let out an audible gasp."

"This was all he needed as he unzipped his pants and brought out what his clothes partially hid". "Wow, was he large and hard".

"As I held it to get a measure of what he had as I remembered it from the night before, I almost did not notice that he was undressing me until I realized that I had on only my bra and panties". "I was still mesmerized by his size and was still holding his cock in my hands while he dropped his pants to the floor and took off his shirt and tie."

"I once again said in an even less convincing voice that we really should not be doing this as we were both married and what if my husband would come home". All he said before we kissed again was "I won't tell if you don't tell" followed by "I have wanted you for years and I think you want me also". I then told him that I have never done this before and … as he was smothering my mouth with kisses he picked be up like nothing and carried me into our bedroom.

"His strength was obvious and actually exciting and I did not resist him as he unhooked my bra and lowered my panties to the floor". "There I was naked and sexually excited knowing you were at work". I sat on the bed and pulled his briefs down and off telling him "OK, but this can never get to our spouses". I then took what I could of his monstrous cock in my mouth and licked and sucked him until he started moaning and saying that he was cumming. Cum he did as I almost could not swallow fast enough.

He said then, "wow, I have dreamed about this but your cock sucking far surpasses anyone I have ever been with. Now, let me return the favor." He proceeded to apply his tongue to every square inch of my vulva from my very sensitive clitoris down to and including my anus. She went on by saying, "Wow was he good and my moans and sighs let him know that I was being pleasured." After the fourth and most massive orgasm he stopped and said with a glint. "Should I stop now or do you want to get fucked?"

"I told him that I wanted him, no, had to have him in me but to go slow as I have never had a cock as large as his". "He loved that as he smiled from ear to ear as we made our way to the center of the bed". "He was large and he only had the glans and maybe another inch in me when I had my first large orgasm". "This lubricated me so the next few inches went in easier". "He was slow – almost too slow – but soon I was stuffed beyond what I had ever known". "When I felt his balls on my anus, I knew he had made it all the way in and I could not believe the feeling. "I wanted it to never end".

My wife went on telling me "As he was going in and out I was in orgasmic bliss very similar to our first times making love before we were married and, later, before we had kids". "The feelings of being stuffed to the core of my being was beyond description and I knew then that I would be doing this again with him". When he said "How do you like it babe" "Am I big enough for you", I could not help myself as I almost screamed, "Please fuck me with your big cock forever" "don't stop, God, don't stop, I cannot get enough of your big cock". My loving wife then told me that they fucked several times in many positions until nearly noon when Joe told her that he had to go as he had some business appointments. She told me that at that point she knew she had to have his cock in her again.

This story led to my getting hard a record 4th time in one morning so as were making love more slowly this time I asked her when the next time was. She hesitated a bit and then told me in a soft voice that it was the next day and the day after that. That when he came back he barely said hello and was kissing her and undressing her and himself. He told her that she was his and that he would fuck her anytime he wanted. As he would say these things she told me that she would audibly sigh as she knew it to be true. Then knowing I would be out most of Saturday morning golfing he told my wife that he would see her Saturday and to be naked when he arrived.

CHAPTER IV

The Joy of Watching

I then told her that I had suspected the last two Saturdays as Joe had arranged a substitute for our foursome and that when I came home I tasted semen in your mouth and a slippery very easy to enter vagina. When she asked me why I did not say something or confront her I told her that I loved her and her happiness and pleasure was what I wanted most in life. I knew that she would tell me sooner or later. I also told her, "This was my fantasy to actually watch you get fucked by another man with a large cock and now it has come true." I added, "I love you so much, you'll never know how much and how happy I am that you have been pleasured by your own fantasy – a large cock."

I told her that if she really loved me she could be with him or anyone else with me knowing about it and, better, observing. That would be sharing your pleasure and would make me very pleased as well as super turned-on and horny. She then said that what if the person did not want to have anyone around as she was thinking of Joe who she suspected would not want you, his friend, knowing he was doing your wife.

Well, I told her how about doing him with me hiding so I could see, first hand, your pleasure like what I saw today. I asked her if she would be inhibited with me watching knowing that she was sharing this intimacy and that seeing her in the throes of passion made me love her even more. We talked about this and she told me that it was OK but she could not promise that I would be able to see every time as now that she was hooked on his big penis she knew there would be times when I was just not available. I told her that as long as she loved me as I did her and did what she did in the open I was OK. With what she said I had my first pangs of concern about my wife's fixation on large cocks.

Anyway we decided to try to set it up at Joe and Betsy's annual holiday party. She told me that I could be called away and that she could ask Joe to take her home. She told me that I could do my part and get Joe's wife Betsy so tipsy or drunk that she would not come with Joe. We agreed that I would be home and out of sight and she agreed to be as she felt with him in her.

The night of their party worked out as my wife and I had planned. I saw to it that Betsy (Joe's wife) never had an empty drink and at 11:00 I got the call telling me that there was an emergency. Over the phone, and in earshot of my friend Joe, I told the party what to do and to call back if this did not fix it. Fifteen minutes later I was again beeped and I told the phone I would be right there and who else to call as "this might be larger that you expect". I quietly told Joe that I had to go and should be back to take Barbara home in about an hour.

We both knew this was a ruse and that I would be calling back telling her that I was home waiting to have fun but tell Joe that I might not get home for a few hours but would let me know – and could you get a ride home with someone. Of course, Joe immediately volunteered. The party was winding down anyway so she said that she would help him clean up a bit and then they could take me home. Saying this we both knew Betsy would be asleep or passed out by then.

Sure enough when Joe found her she was so tipsy that Barbara had to help Betsy to her room and to get her undressed. She was asleep almost immediately so my wife came down and gave this news to Joe who, of course, could hardly hide his glee and said he would be delighted to run her home. He went to check on his wife and came back to give my wife a big hug and her bottom an even bigger squeeze saying that his wife was out cold and thanked her for tending to Betsy and helping clean up. The hug was longer than necessary and included his usual fondling of her bottom as they kissed. Barbara told me later that she was so turned on that she could hardly wait to get home.

Barbara told me that Joe was every bit the gentleman as he drove her to the house. He insisted that he come in to be sure all was safe. Once inside, he again thanked her for taking care of his wife and asked if we had some Baileys to top off the evening. She poured two on the rocks and sat down on our couch in our living room. He told her that she was the best looking lady at the party and he looked forward to fucking her tonight as he does every time he is with her.

By now, I was upstairs and was able to clearly see Joe and my wife kissing in the living room. At one point he asked her what she wanted. When she didn't say it loud enough for him he told her to speak up and tell him what she wanted. What she said caused me to get instantly hard and horny. She told him "I want to feel and play with and suck and be fucked by your big cock". Joe stood up before her and told her to, "Get over here and get what you want."

I watched my wife lower his zipper then undo his belt and pull his pants down and hold them while he stepped out of them. Then she lowered his undershorts and took hold of his cock and rubbed it over her face as she kissed it and licked it. She literally made love to his cock with her face and mouth like she was possessed.

Soon she was giving him a good sucking and she must have been doing it as he wanted as he kept telling her what a good cocksucker she was and after a bit he held her head and pumped his load down her throat. He then sat down in my chair and told my wife to "strip". It was starting to get to me that my fiend was ordering my wife and she was doing as he asked without question, which is not how our life together had gone.

When she was completely naked he asked her what she would do if David (that's me) came home at this time. What she said was that he had better hope that I didn't come home as it would be the end of her marriage and maybe his end also.

With that he got up and said "lead the way so I can give you what you crave". Hearing that I then knew that Joe had figured out that she was hooked on his big cock. I snuck quietly into our closet and soon they were on the bed and my wife was begging Joe to fuck her with his big cock and he did just that. His staying power amazed me and I was also not only surprised but very excited to hear the number of total body orgasms that my wife was having and how she could not seem to get enough of him.

Finally, when she could not get him hard anymore they went back downstairs and he slowly got dressed. Well, Barbara just put on her panties and walked Joe to the door. I heard Joe tell her, "I will see you in a few days and I will be bringing a friend who is even larger than me" then, "I have been telling him about your need for large cocks" "His is so large he has trouble finding ladies who can take him" "He is excited to meet you."

When my wife said that she didn't think she could see anyone else he said, "Yes, you do want to see him as his cock is even larger than mine" and then, "You will want him as you want me so find the time". He kissed her passionately then and when she came up for air I heard her say… "Well, OK, just this once". Joe then responded, "We'll see about that, Roger is like me in that he loves cock loving sluts like you. Will call you in a few days."

At the door Joe gave her one of his big bear hugs with his hands feeling most of her erotic areas. It was some turn-on to watch his hands feeling and playing with her breasts and sliding beneath her panties to fondle her bottom. It must have turned her on also as she was moaning and telling him to hurry back.

CHAPTER V

Joe and More

It was a pensive Barbara who came up the stairs and into my arms. She seemed to be holding back tears as she looked into my eyes and said, "God, I really do hope that his was OK with you and now that you have seen me with another man that you will still love me". As I enveloped her in my arms I reassured her that I loved her even more now that I knew she trusted me enough to share her pleasure.

She then said that, "Joe has become more demanding and dominant and whereas this excites me it also scares me" then she softly said, "Did you hear him tell me that he had a friend who wants to see me" "I am afraid of what his may lead to but at the same time I am very curious". Then with a look in her eyes that I love she asked, "Is it OK if I see him at least one time?" I had to chuckle a bit but reassured her that I still loved her and hoped above everything else that what ever she did and whoever she saw and played with that she would still love me. I said this because I too was a bit anxious about this turn of events.

With that she literally attacked me with hugs and kisses and assured me that the pleasure of our "love making" was far greater and more important that the pleasure and curiosity of a big cock. She was quick to add, "Well at least far more important." We had a good laugh over that admission. With that we were soon in bed making love. Slipping into her vagina was nothing like I had been used to. Wow, was she ever loose but the good thing about that was that I lasted a far longer time than I had in the past and was able to give my wife more than one orgasm.

Joe did call her in a couple of days and she told him she would only see Roger at her home and when I was guaranteed to be away. She told me that she said this so if possible I could watch and she did feel safer in our house.

It got arranged and I was safely hidden when Joe and Roger came over. It turned out that Roger was a very handsome older man and when he arrived both men took turns hugging and removing clothes from my wife. When she was down to her panties and they were mostly undressed she led them upstairs to our bedroom. I was quite hard from what I had observed from our balcony and got even harder as they both undressed and let her play with and suck them both off.

Joe was right as Rogers cock was larger and with the largest head I had ever seen. Barbara told me later that she really loved sucking him as the head was smooth and spongy and his cum tasted better than Joe's. She related that his head alone filled her mouth.

Joe went first to loosen her up a bit or so he said but at that point I did not think she cared who was first. Joe brought her to two screaming orgasms before he filled her vagina with his cum. Almost the minute Joe pulled out, Roger was between he legs and feeding his monster into her vagina. I could tell that she was in orgasmic heaven as once he was in she kept saying, "Oh, please fuck me with your big cock and don't stop – ever". His staying power was almost unbelievable so when he finally released his sperm she was exhausted.

They each fucked her one more time but when they were finished, she asked Joe to show Roger out as she was too exhausted to get out of bed. So the two men dressed and left leaving my exhausted wife in bed. When I saw them leave, I went down to lock the door and returned to our bedroom to my well-fucked and satiated wife. I crawled in bed with her and we reassured our love for each other before I rolled over and literally slipped in.

Over the next few weeks she saw Joe only on a couple of occasions, which I expected as I knew he was seeing a new lady he had met. I was not able to watch but Barbara's descriptions were something else. She held nothing back. She saw Roger three times in that same time interval and really liked him as he was a gentleman. As big as he was he seemed more about her pleasure than his. She even arranged for us to meet him socially but telling him that I knew nothing about their affair. We met at a concert with Barbara introducing me to him as an old acquaintance. I liked him a lot so her seeing him when I was not able to be there was OK.

CHAPTER VI

Roger

We had Roger over for dinner a couple of times and it was fun for me because initially, he did not know that I knew that he had fucked my wife several times and that I knew he had a very large and potent cock. After these evenings my wife would almost attack me wanting sex and asking why I was teasing her this way as she was craving his big cock. I then said that I really did like Roger and the next time he came over I would see to it that you and he got together.

Well, the next time we had him over for dinner we were all sitting in the living room talking and I asked him how long had he known my wife and where did they meet. I saw him quickly look over at my wife so I though I should come clean. "Roger', I said, "I hope you will forgive me but I know of my wife's desire and need for large cocks and I know that she has been with you and wants to be with you again and again". I quickly added as the look on his face was priceless, "Not to worry, from now on you can have her whenever you are over and with my blessing. Then looking at my wife I added, "Is that not right my love."

Well she jumped up and came over to me and plopped herself on my lap hugging me and kissing me and thanking me. Looking at Roger I saw surprise. She then got up off me and went to Roger and gave him an even larger hug and kiss. She then said, "Lets go eat the dinner I have prepared first before we get to the main course."

As we walked to the dining room I followed my wife and Roger who were walking with their arms around the other. Roger almost immediately lowered his hand to my wife's bottom and began patting and fondling it. He turned to look at me, I guess to see my reaction. I smiled and nodded slightly so he knew he had my blessing.

I told them to, "Sit down and I will be the server tonight." They did and my horny wife almost immediately had her hand under the tablecloth. I knew what she was doing and this got me hard even uncomfortably hard almost immediately. As we were eating I asked Roger what was special about Barbara. He then said that being large is not all a plus. Growing up many girls were afraid of his size. Later married women were also reticent to fuck him as they were worried that their husband would notice the loose vagina.

Then he told me that my wife was one of the very few ladies who not only could take all of his cock in her vagina but who was also multi-orgasmic. He then said, looking directly at me but hugging my wife, "Your wife almost cannot get enough and I really do love fucking her. I am so glad you are OK with this and my relationship with Barbara will not change our new friendship.

Needless to say that dinner went fast. When we were finished I said I would clear the table and put things away and will join them in a bit. My wife got up and came to me saying how much she loved me and gave me a big kiss while feeling my erection.

She then turned to Roger and said, "follow me for a good time." They left the dining room and ascended the stairs arm in arm so I knew that I was going to get a good show. By the time I finished cleaning up and went up to our bedroom the site I saw got me, again, instantly hard. My wife was sitting on the bed in only her panties and Roger was naked standing next to her and she had the head and a couple of inches of his cock in her mouth audibly moaning.

I stayed in the closet so I was not, in any way, a factor in inhibiting their actions. Sort of 'out of sight, out of mind'. After swallowing his first load, he helped her lie down and nuzzled his head in her pubic area and I knew she was receiving pleasure via his tongue as she was moaning and almost screaming in pleasure.

After she calmed down they laid together kissing and fondling each others body. Once he was erect again, I heard him ask her if she was ready for the 'main course'. I had to chuckle and she said, "Main course and desert all in one. Please fuck me until I cannot take it anymore". Well, I had a first row seat and watching a very large cock go all the way in and then out of my wife's vagina was a treat.

At one point I undressed and came out of the closet and sat in the chair next to our bed. Our eyes met and despite being in the throes of passion she said, "God, honey this is so special and I love you for allowing….." at that point she could not speak as another orgasm racked her body. I was amazed at Rogers staying power and it was certainly more than a half hour of continuous fucking including a change to the 'doggie' style before he came and it was some cum.

When he was done climaxing he rolled over and hugging my wife, sort of drifted off to sleep. I leaned over to my wife and told her that I would join them and to let him snooze. It was a good thing that we have a king sized bed. I got in bed and from behind (as we were spooning) I entered her and lasted only a few minutes before I spurted my load into her juicy vagina.

And hour or so later, I felt movement and saw Roger up on his elbows looking at my sleeping wife and me. I whispered to him where the bathroom was and told him that he was welcome to stay the night. He thanked me, got up and was back in bed in a few minutes. Last I knew, until I was awakened by them fucking beside me, we were all sleeping.

Roger has spent several nights with us servicing / fucking my wife, Barbara. She has not gotten tired of his monster cock and shows her love for me in many ways not only in his presence but when we are alone.

CHAPTER VII

Two Male Strippers

S he still goes out the odd weekend night with her girl friends and told me excitedly when she came home late one night that after she had felt and played with one of the show guys that he had whispered to her to meet him in the lobby after this show. When she told me about it when she came home her voice was a mixture of guilt and excitement.

She told me that she gave the excuse to her girlfriends of needing to go to the ladies room and out of curiosity and a feeling of naughtiness she went out to the lobby and sure enough there he was looking as handsome a virile as he had earlier when she had played with and kissed his cock to the Ohhs and Ahhs of the other ladies in the crowd.

He put his arm around her waist and said "Lets go someplace more private". She told me that it was the recollection of his large cock and knowing that she might see it again that threw all caution to the wind and she followed him. As she followed him she noticed one of the other young men following. When she mentioned this to the one she was with he only said, "Relax and enjoy. I sense that you want me to fuck you and I do want to fuck you."

She then told me that before she could say anything the three of them were in a small dressing room that had a bed. She heard the door being locked and when she turned around he was already undressed. She then said, "Honey, I knew what was going to happen but I was so excited that these young well muscled Adonis's would be interested in a middle age woman that I said nothing as he undressed me. He then led me over to a table and bent me over and with his tongue on my vulva and clitoris got me very stimulated. The other young man came around to the other side and when I saw his very large cock in front of my face, I looked up at him, smiled and opened my mouth to receive his cock.

As one cock entered my mouth, the second was working it's way up my vagina. My wife then said, "God, this was exciting as two young muscled and handsome men had picked me." She then told me what followed which got me rock hard again. It seems that after they each came they switched places and each fucked her vagina and mouth again.

After this they led her to the bed and got into a 69 position so she got to see and feel and suck both off of them. As they were fucking her in the missionary position the third time each they both told her that she was far better than any young chick they had been with. All in all, she told me that is was a very exciting evening as she had the ego building sex with two young men with very large cocks who were younger than our oldest son.

Life goes on…

© July 2010 – Chris Dawson

My Wife's Compulsion & Submissiveness

By **Chris Dawson**

Forward

This is the story of a man who falls in love with a woman who he finds out is very submissive, actually compulsively submissive, to strong dominant men. He loves her and marries her knowing that she has been and will remain a true sexually active lady. When one falls in love, one accepts ones wife's weaknesses as well as her strengths. In this story, she succumbs to sexual advances of not only her bosses but also her husband's bosses and others. The hardest part of writing this story was to come to some conclusion and not make it go on forever.

CHAPTER I

Love Comes in Many Forms

I have been married to a most loving and still sexy woman for more than 9 years. I think that I am very lucky as she is very attractive and wherever we are or whatever she has on, she draws second looks. The looks probably are because she has a fantastic body with all the right curves and good-sized breasts plus a bottom I just cannot get enough of. She is 5 ft 9 in and about 135 pounds.

Marie, who has the appearance of an innocent young lady in her 20's is actually 42 years old. She is also a very bright as she has a Masters degree in Business Administration and manages a large personnel department at one of the cities larger Companies. Our life together is all that I could ask and I certainly am not wanting in anything including all the love, affection and all the great sex I can handle.

My name is Charles and I am 48 years old. I am also quite fit from, a lifelong addiction to squash and good workouts. I am 5 ft 10 in and weigh 170 pounds. I am average looking but also well educated and in upper management in a fairly large heavy equipment manufacturing company in town. So why am I writing this story you may ask. Well, I just recently saw an erotic book casually mentioning several scenarios much like that which I have lived. Through this, I found out that I am not alone in what has happened in my life and thought I would share our story.

My wife, Marie and I met almost accidentally about 12 years ago and I was very taken with her from day one. Marie first told me that she did not date often as her work was too demanding. We began seeing each first weekly and then gradually up to several times a week and got along so well that I was thinking long term within a month of our meeting and at that time it wasn't because of the sex as I had not pushed this and we both seemed reticent to start for some reason.

I did not want to rush things as she was the most caring and best person I had ever met. She was a hard worker and almost weekly she told me that she worked until late at night for her boss, who was the CEO of the company she was now working for. Only much later would I learn the truth about these nights? Once we started to have sex I was blown away by how open-minded and active she was especially the night after she worked late. She seemed to have no limits and we explored every thing to my total delight. Her breasts and bottom were as sensitive as anyone I had known. I was floating on cloud nine.

When I first started talking about the future she seemed to change the subject yet she always told me that I was the most kind and considerate man she had ever dated and that she loved me and that also I was a great lover. I was not sure where this came from as I was only a bit larger than normal but who was I to complain. She was, for sure, the best in bed I had ever experienced. She was multi-orgasmic and very vocal actually making me feel that maybe I was a good lover.

One night after a great dinner at one of our best restaurants, I asked her to marry me. Her response caught me by surprise as she started crying. When I asked her why, she looked me in the eyes and said that I really did not know her and she did not think she could ever marry as she had a compulsion, passion and weakness for older dominant men that would, for sure, at some point compromise the fidelity in any marriage.

I told her with my naiveté on display, "So, what does that have to do with us". She then told me that I must not have heard her or didn't understand what she was saying. I admitted that I did not fully understand but told her I really was falling in love with her and asked her to please help me understand.

She looked me in the eyes and said that it was a long story but she loved me also and more than that she trusted me so if I really wanted to know, she would tell me but that she would not hold it against me if this was our last date. She said that we should not talk about this in a restaurant so we left for my townhouse.

On the way, I held her close and again asked her why she did not think she could marry me if she loved me as she said. Then she started to tell me what I did not know about her at the time.

"To start out, I could not promise that I would be faithful to you and I do love you much more that I ever thought I could love anyone" she said. She went on to say "The reason is that I have a totally uncontrollable weakness and a passion for older dominant men". "It all started right after college when I get my first job working for a medium sized head office of a chain of stores." "I was first given the job as the assistant buyer". Shortly after I started, I was introduced to Ronald who I was told was the President. He was in his late 50's making him more than twice my age and very handsome. He must have seen through me from day one because he arranged to personally train me to his taste."

"He called me into his office at the end of one day and started telling me what he expected his employees to do in a variety of ways. Then he asked me if I dated, which I responded that yes I did. He told me how he thought I should dress and what to do if any man, other than him, should approach me or get fresh. Then he caught me by surprise and asked me if I was having sex with the person I was dating. I blushed a deep crimson as I was having the occasional sex with my boyfriend but to tell anyone was out of the question. Nice girls do not talk about sex, he told me. I was very embarrassed by this question but strangely turned on."

"He saw this and came closer to me and said that he now knew the answer to that question and that if I were his father I would get a good spanking and on my bare bottom. When he said that I felt a rush and tingling in my sex and felt for a minute like a little girl about to get punished yet I was not afraid, only excited. This caused me to blush even more and to not be able to look him in the eyes. I was both ashamed and more than a bit aroused by this talk."

"Next he told me to come close to him and when I did as he

said, he removed my suit jacket saying that he wanted to see if I was as built to be a model as he suspected. I blushed again but did not resist. He told be to turn around and as I did this he commented on how he liked my body and especially my "..nice and very shapely ass and long legs". Once again I blushed but made no protests. He then took me by the shoulders with both of his hands and turned me back to face him saying that he would like me to be one of his models."

"With that he went into the closet and brought out a dress and told me he wanted to see me in this to help him decide what line I should wear. When I looked around to find a place to change he took my hand, look me in the eyes, and told me to change "right here, right now" and that "modesty was not allowed in my models". When I hesitated he said "strip, right now!" in a more stern voice."

"Well, I did as he said slowly as I was totally embarrassed but did not want him to get angry. I wanted him to think I was in charge but deep down I knew I was the one being controlled. I slowly unbuttoned my blouse and placed it on the nearby chair. "now your skirt" he said which brought me back to looking at him as he eyed me up and down. Blushingly, I started to undo my skirt but not as fast as Ron wanted so he came to me and moved my hands away and completed the process of unbuttoning and lowering the zipper and pulling my skirt down so I could step out of it. For some reason I just let him do what he wished."

"He then turned me around and commented on my legs, my ass, my breasts as if he knew them well. I had to admit that as embarrassed as I was in by bra and panties in front of an almost a stranger but who was my boss, but certainly felt more than very sexy. He then held up the new dress and helped me get into it using his hands to feel me all over under the guise of checking the fit of the dress. When I winced he would look at me sternly and tell me to hold still so I did."

"He then told me I looked and felt fantastic and took me in his arms and gave me a big kiss while running his hands over my body especially my breasts and bottom. He also brushed and then cupped my mons and vulvar area, which really sent a shiver through my body. This was really turning me on as I realized that I was at his mercy and would do anything he asked of me. I remember being ashamed of my feelings and did not understand them."

"He started to undress me placing the new dress on the near chair and then turning me around he unhooked my bra and removed it. He then told me to turn around so he could see my breasts. Looking down averting his eyes, I did as he told me and did not wince as he held both breasts and lightly, then with more force pinched my very sensitive nipples."

"By now, I knew where this going so when he told me to remove my panties, I did so without hesitation knowing I was under his control. He then put my hand on his large and very hard cock, which caused all resistance to what was happening to disappear. This time when he kissed me, I kissed him back enthusiastically while his hands explored every inch of my now naked body."

"Then he said, "undress me". I undid his belt, unzipped his pants and lowered them. Then I held them while he stepped out. "Shirt next", which I did as fast as I could. "You know what to do now, don't you" to which I responded almost whispering "yes". I got on my knees and lowered his jockey shorts and was startled as his very large cock almost hit me in the face. Once his underwear was off I was face to face with his large and hard cock."

"He moved forward putting his turgid organ to my mouth. I had never sucked a cock at that point but when he said "My cock needs attention, open up" I did and for the first time I tasted the pre-cum liquid lubrication. He was almost delicious. He started to move it in and out of my mouth. When he stopped moving I just took over as I knew he wanted me to do. He then told me that I was to 'suck his cock' whenever he asked."

"It didn't take long before I felt him swell and stiffen in my mouth. His contracting told me he was about to cum. My first reaction was to pull away but he held my head and told me to never move away as to swallow his cum was what he wanted. So I stayed with his cock in my mouth until he was done. He picked me up and led me to the couch against the wall and pushed me down." "He started kissing and licking my upper legs and in a few minutes another first happened as I felt his tongue stimulating my vaginal opening and clitoris. I could not believe how good this felt and had my first climax in only a couple of minutes. He brought me to two orgasms with his tongue."

"He then told me to get on my hands and knees and rest my head on the cushion. I did as he said feeling very vulnerable with my ass in the air and open to his eyes. He got on the couch behind me and started rubbing his cock on my vulva. "Tell me what you want me to do next" he then said. When I said "make love to me" he pulled away and slapped my bottom a couple of times. He then said as I recall, "Oh no, not making love, Fucking" "Tell me you want me to fuck you."

"I'm not sure I ever had used that word but managed to get it out to say "Please fuck me", which made me feel very naughty. "Fuck you with what" he said. "Fuck me with your big cock" I said and a thrill went through me. I knew that I was hooked. Fuck me he did and for almost an hour. He brought me to so many orgasms that I lost count and I knew I would be doing this again and that I was hooked on his cock as well as his almost total dominance over me."

She went on to say: "It didn't end there and before the night was out he had taken my anal cherry." and "Anal intercourse became a regular event and I came to love the intimacy and ultimate submissiveness of this act".

While Marie had been relating this story, she was too embarrassed to look at me but when she did, she could not help but see that I had a huge erection. I kissed and hugged her and told her that I loved her even more as I knew she had been honest and her story had turned me on more that she could know. At this time we reached my apartment and I told her that we would finish this in the quiet of a familiar place and that I loved her even more than she could imagine.

Once upstairs I took her into my arms not only to console her but to let her feel how turned on I was. She then asked me how I could love someone who acted like a slut with her boss. She told me that she felt naughty and needed a spanking, which I was glad to do. I turned her over my knees, hiked up her dress, lowered her panties and reddened her fabulous bottom. Afterwards she literally attacked me and had a thundering orgasm minutes after I penetrated her vagina. God I loved her and still do.

She went on to say that he called her in to model selected clothes for special clients once every week or two and sometime more often. The sessions always ended up with the clients wanting to touch her all over. This turned her on and led often to a sexual marathon. This went on for almost two years before he left for the head office in another state.

She told me that she became quite turned on to being sometimes almost nude modeling in front of strangers. She told me, "He would occasionally have me model swim suits and panty and bra sets clothes for buyers and invite them to have their way with me after modeling, which always got him and them and certainly me very horny". She went on to say that there were times when she "had cocks in all my holes" and this always made her feel very naughty as well as sexy. I remember her blushing deeply when she told me that.

To this new revelation I then hugged her tightly and told her that I loved her even more, I put her hand on my hard cock. This started her crying. Between sobs she professed her deep love for me and told me that if I really meant it and would put up with her compulsive infidelity she would surely love me back and marry me and try to not end up in these positions once we were married. I remember very well that she next said "Please still love me if I slip."

With that I started undressing her and we both literally ran into the bedroom and made love well into the night. At one of the points just after our 3rd or 4th orgasmic time she became very quiet. When I asked her what she was thinking she said that whereas she told me about her first boss she had not told me anything about her present boss and she felt that I should know everything. I remember her saying "Please don't hate me when I tell you about my present boss."

279

CHAPTER II

Present Boss

She then related that: "about two years ago I took my present job as personnel director at the company you know about. The President, whose name is Carl, is an imposing man in his mid sixties who is at least 6'2". I saw him first in the office cafeteria a month or so after I started. He came up to me, introduced himself and asked me – no, told me – to come to his office before I went home. I told him that I had a date right after work to which he said "break it" and "see you at 5:00 o'clock" as he turned and left the hall."

"The familiar feeling of submission had me starting to get wet between my legs and he had not even touched me. The rest of the day I got little done as I nervously waited for 5:00 o'clock except to break the date of the man I was seeing. At 5:00 sharp I sat down in the waiting area of his office suite. I was not there long when he came to his door and without a word waved me to follow him into the office."

Marie started relating the start of her current situation and her boss, a guy named Carl. She said, "Carl then told me that he had been hearing very good things about me as to the running of my department and he wanted to meet me to see for himself if I was as pretty as he had been told. He then told me that he was looking for someone who would help his staff serve his card playing guests at private parties he was having at his home." and "now that he had seen me, I had the job". The following is my recollection of what my Marie told me one evening more than 10 years ago:

"Carl (as I now call him) then told me that on this job I would be wearing a uniform and that his friends and guests were not associated with the company. He then told me in a forceful voice while looking intently at me that he wanted to get the correct size so "please remove your clothes" so "you can try on this uniform". He then snapped at me, when I hesitated "do it now, quickly" Then he added "Strip!!" so I just started to undress feeling very conspicuous and embarrassed but at the same time excited as he certainly was an imposing man and almost a stranger." She then told me that shades of her first boss, Ron came back to her in a flash."

My love then told me: "Once down to my bra and panties and feeling very vulnerable he beckoned me to come to where he was and told me that I had a beautiful body and he would enjoy "making it sing". As I had not protested he now had unspoken permission to do as he wished. Once I was close he turned me around and first patted and then fondled my ass telling me to stay put and not move away from his hands. He reached round and felt, then played with my breasts while saying that "these would do just fine, in fact, they were perfect."

"As this was going fast, I was relieved when he handed me the maids uniform which I quickly put on under his gaze. The outfit was a bit tight and the skirt we very short but he seemed pleased. He had me walk around and bend over which further embarrassed me as I was sure that my panties could be seen. This was confirmed when he said that he would have to get me some panties that matched the outfit. He then said, that sometimes wearing no panties would be required. I remember blushing deeply but also being quite turned on."

"It was then that I noticed that he must have been hard as the bulge beneath his zipper was prominent. He caught my gaze and told me to get undressed and to come to him. I took off the uniform and slowly walked over to where he was standing. Carl put my hand on his cock and told me to take care of it as it needed to be sucked. When I hesitated he said, "right now girl, before I lose my patience."

"Well, I knew I was hooked and compelled to do his bidding so I undid his zipper and pulled out his very large – largest I had seen- cock and slowly brought it to and into my mouth. I knew what he wanted and at that point I knew I wanted it too so I gave it my best and when I felt him coming I did not move away but swallowed it all and kept it in my mouth gently mouthing it until it started to get hard again."

"Get yourself out of what's left and get over to the couch" was my marching orders and I did as I was told. He put his head between my legs and it was magic. I came in less than a minute and several times before he quit. He then slid up my body and with his cock just touching my pussy he said "what do you want now". My answer of "Put it in" got "not good enough, what do I put where". My meek answer was "please put your cock in my pussy". Well, we went back and forth until I told him to "Fuck me with your big cock." This too brought shades of my first boss back into my memory.

"Did I ever get it good. He felt and made me feel unbelievably good. I could not stop having orgasms. I started repeating over and over "Fuck me, fuck me, harder, harder, fuck me harder". He pulled out at one point and told me to get up and bend over the back of the couch. He then fucked me from behind until I was nearly delirious from pleasure. Finally he climaxed and I felt every pulse of his cumming. At that point he was the best I had ever had and I did not want to stop but he had other ideas."

She went on to say that: "The card parties he was taking about were regular occurrences and at the first one I attended as the server, he told me to take off my panties before the guests arrived. For some reason, this excited me greatly and had me acting sexier than even I could imagine. It has been that way since and most times the men who remain to the end do me one after the other after I have sucked them all at least once. Again, at least some of them got off fucking me in my ass."

Marie then took my face in her hands and looked me in the eye and asked where I thought she was the evenings she told me that she was working late? She answered her own question saying that she was either in Carl's office or at his home or at an affair at a downtown hotel being ravished and not only unable to control it but loving it. Then she said, "Honey, do you really think you could love me and put up with all that? Then, "I feel that I have been naughty and need you to spank me, which I did as her bottom was the greatest.

CHAPTER III

The Engagement Party

Her story had my cock hard as a rock again. I placed her hand on it and kissed her before saying "what do you think". With that we made it again and she repeated that yes, she would be happy to be my wife as she trusted what I said that not only did her compulsive submissiveness not concern me but turned me on. That I was not angry or upset at her that she reveled in sex with her boss, Carl, and his friends was a pleasant surprise.

Marie told Carl, her boss, the next day that she was engaged to me and his reaction was to call in his secretary and tell her to arrange an engagement party and invite the heads of all departments and to find out from Marie who else she wanted to come to the affair. She thought that very sweet of him and came to tell me about the party very excited. Little did I know that I would be in for a surprise and to see, for the first time my future wife's submissiveness.

The party was exquisite with wine, liquor, great food and music fit for a princess, which fit my fiancée. At one point when we were all at tables our host Carl, asked Marie to come up to the microphone as he had an announcement to make. Beaming she went up and when he motioned her over next to him he started telling everyone that Marie had found love and she was now engaged. He then sung her praises. At one point Maries eyes suddenly opened and I caught a nervous glance at me. I then knew and Marie later confirmed that with his free hand he was fondling her bottom.

Anyway, he gave her the microphone to bring me up and introduce me to those who did not know me. As I approached her it was obvious to me from Maries facial expressions and movements that her boss was continuing to play with her bottom. Anyway, she got through introducing me to her boss and to the gathering and the next thing we knew there was a reception line with Marie between her boss and me with him on her right.

As we were shaking hands, I had a small break and stepped back a half step and sure enough his left had was fondling and squeezing Maries bottom. When I came back I looked over at him - he smiled and winked which told me that he still was going to do as he pleased with my fiancée and without regard to my feelings. Without realizing it, my inaction or lack of anger gave him permission to continue.

Fast forward to the end of the evening when Marie, I, and Carl were the last ones remaining as everyone else had left. She went to him to thank him for the very nice party. I told her quietly that I had to take a bathroom break and would be right back to take her home. As I left the room they were hugging and I saw her give him a kiss on the cheek.

When I returned, she was still in his arms but now he was fondling her bare bottom as his hands were under her dress. I stepped back in the shadows a bit so as not to intrude and embarrass my love. As I stood not 6 feet from where they were embracing, her boss undid her skirt letting it fall to the floor telling her to behave and not resist him – that everything was OK. I heard you say, "But Charles will be back in a minute". To that Carl replied, "Just do as I say."

He looked over to where I was and smiled, which signaled to me that he knew I was watching but was not deterred in what he was going to do with and to my wife to be. My future wife started to moan as Carl's hands fondled her erotic bottom and equally erotically sensitive breasts.

Carl then motioned to me to come out of the shadows and over to where they were making out. My emotions, as I approached them, went from being upset and jealous to being embarrassed as well as excited. I certainly knew what I was seeing was turning me on as I became uncomfortably hard, which I am sure Carl noticed. When I got close, Carl asked me to go make sure the door to the room is locked and then come back to remove Marie's dress. Marie turned quickly and her eyes told me she was resigned to what was going to happen. When she saw my smile and nod she turned back to Carl and became lost in her pleasurable feelings.

I did as he asked without saying a word and I unzipped, unsnapped and unbuttoned what I needed to remove my fiancée's outer clothes and watched with growing sexual excitement and horniness as Carl had his way fondling her near naked body especially her bottom which had her moaning in pleasure. He then told me to remove her bra and panties, which I did after some hesitation and with even more anticipation and embarrassment.

Here I was being also submissive to her boss and doing whatever he commanded. Once Marie was naked Carl's fondling escalated and as he was sucking on my fiancée's sensitive nipples he inserted his finger into her vagina and brought her to her first orgasm of the night.

He then led her over to a couch and had her bend over the back following which he entered her with one stroke giving her a second immediate orgasm. Carl had amazing staying power, as it must have been a half hour and several orgasms before he pulled out and told her to "get on your back on the couch". When she did that, he got between her legs and drove her wild with pleasure.

This went on for some time until finally he pulled out and moved his cock to her mouth, which she sucked until he came. He then pulled his soft cock out of Marie's mouth got dressed and said, "Charles, very nice meeting you. Your Fiancée is something else". Then to Marie he said, "You are a fantastic fuck as usual. See you next week". Then he left.

When he was gone, I removed my clothes and kneeled beside the couch so I could hug and kiss my future wife. I told her I loved her more than ever and kissed her passionately. The taste of Carl's semen turned me on even more and I moved to enter her vagina. I had never seen Marie so receptive and horny and she literally screamed through two orgasms in the short time it took me to cum.

We lay together on the couch for some time talking about what had happened. I had to reassure her that as long as she loved me and did not do anything behind my back that I was OK with what happened knowing that it would happen again with Carl. She had tears of joy as she repeated over and over that she loved me more that she ever though possible and hoped that one day she could get over this submissive passion to be dominated as with me she does not have that feeling.

This talk got us both excited and aroused again so we went at it making love again and this time I brought her to at least three big orgasms before I came a final time. She said that despite my love she felt like she needed punishment for being so bad so I took her over my knee and spanked the butt I love to a nice rosy hue.

We got dressed and went home arm in arm like the lovers we were. I asked her if she believed in a long engagement to which she said "not with you I don't." So we thought about getting married a month later. During that month Marie attended to two of Carl's card parties and events and when she would get home to the apartment would drive me wild with the story of what happened and I would turn her bottom and nice shade of red until she thought she and been punished enough and her 'guilt' was assuaged.

CHAPTER IV
Marriage Changes Nothing

The common denominator was that she was royally screwed by at least Carl and whoever else it was his fancy to have enjoy her luscious body. The sex we shared with these confessions lasted most of the night so we both went to work very late the day after one of her nights in. One of us had a tingly bottom.

We had wanted a quiet small wedding for a number of reasons but mostly because what family we had lived throughout the US and some lived and worked abroad. Plan as we may, the word got out and so we elected to elope and just tell every one we had tied the knot. So, by mid September we were happily married.

A month or so later she came home telling me that her old boss, Ron, had contacted her and told her he was coming into town with a clothing and style convention and wanted to see her. She told me that she sent an email back telling him that she was married thinking that this would give him pause. She showed me his return email telling her that "your husband was welcome but I expect to see you" and then "will send you the time and place once I have made arrangements."

That night both of our passion was greater than normal and Marie came multiple times. After I came a second time I asked her if she had been thinking of Ron. She nodded yes but told me that she wanted me to go with her as he was a long time ago and that he would now be in his mid 60's. I reminded her that Carl was in his mid 60's and it sure did not stop him from wanting you. We made love again.

A week later she got an email and call from Ron telling her that entrance passes for her and me were in the mail and she was to meet with him at 3:30 at the convention center at his companies booth and he gave her the number and location of the exhibit. She told me that some old feelings returned, as he was as domineering as ever. I reassured her that everything was OK and we would play it easy. That night she was especially passionate, which told me that I may again see or hear a new story of adventure.

Well, we were at the exhibit a few minutes early and it was impressive. They had an actual runway with models coming out every few minutes with some outfit on or another. I looked up and there was actually some very large pictures of Marie among other models in different styles and dress. When I pointed out these to Marie she turned bright red and I could see that she was excited. She said that they had to be old but admitted they did not seem out of place. I told her that she was the best looking of the models.

At 3:30 She spotted Ron who came up to her and gave her a big hug and rather long kiss. The hug included squeezing her bottom in plain sight of where I was standing. When that was over, Marie smilingly brought Ron over and introduced me as her husband of almost two months. He seemed personable as he shook my hand and then he grabbed Marie by her waist and told her he wanted her to meet some people who knew her only from her pictures. I might as well have not been there.

I followed behind wishing it was me stroking my wife's great bottom but knew my time would come. Ron introduced or rather reintroduced my wife to several people who all made gushing comments about how she had been their best model. Most of the men seemed to know Marie and seemed genuinely pleased to see her. At one point Ron said to the group as if it had been arranged that Marie looked as good as the younger models and she has agreed to show her stuff.

Marie looked very surprised but followed Ron into the exhibit. Even I was impressed and so was the crowd when she started coming out in this companies top of the line dresses according to the announcer and promoter. I heard from some of the company guys she had met who were close by that these had been shown before but the growing crowd suggested she still had the poise and body to attract visitors. As Ron did not come back out I just knew that he was watching and helping her dress and undress. This also turned me on immensely.

The last item she modeled for the crowd was a bathing suit and you could have heard a pin drop when she first came out. Wow, was she ever stunning. As she turned to go back the crowd went wild and did not stop until she came back for a bow. She came out maybe a half hour later when the large crowd had dispersed. She came over to me and asked how she had done. I told her that I was not alone in finding her fantastic. I took her in my arms and we kissed. I knew she has been active as I tasted semen in her mouth. When we finally stopped she looked down and said that she had been naughty. In her ear I whispered that I knew she had been naughty as I tasted semen but still loved her very much and as she could feel, I was turned on.

Ron came out said "Just like the old days, huh" which was certainly open for interpretation. Marie blushed, which told me how she interpreted his comment. To shorten a long story we ended back in his room in the hotel having a cocktail when he asked me if Marie had told me anything about her old job with him. I told him that she had indeed and that we had no secrets. He seemed pleased with that. I do not remember what he said but he walked over to my wife, pulled her willingly out of her chair and led her over to the bed saying to me, "Then I know you will excuse us as it has been a long time."

Then to my wife he said, "Lets get these cloths off and catch up". As he was hugging her he started undressing her while I watched. When she was down to her bra and panties he started undressing until he was naked. I was taken back be the length of his cock as he picked up my wife and laid her on the bed. For the next two or more hours I was able to see first hand what Marie had told me about what they did those many years before. I was very turned on watching them have sex in many positions and the fact that she seemed to be in a constant state of orgasmic bliss.

We did not leave his room until 1:00 o'clock in the morning and I had to practically carry my wife out to the car and up to our apartment, as she was so exhausted. We slept in and she awoke me with a blowjob. Heck of a way to start a new day. We talked about Ron and what had happened for several hours reassuring each other of our undying love for each other despite her submissive compulsion.

CHAPTER V

Even My Boss gets Action

The next incident hit closer to home for me. My company has an annual Christmas party and wives are very welcome. I was a little anxious as our President, Kurt, is known as a ladies man and there was the odd rumor, which I didn't pay much attention to because I was not married, that he delighted in having affairs with wives of his company executives. I had gone with a girlfriend in previous years but none of them could hold a candle to Marie.

Anyway after talking this over with Marie and her wanting to do whatever I wanted. She though we should go for appearances and besides, she did not think she would even meet him and if she did there would be too many people around.

So, we dressed for a Christmas party and got a room at the event hotel as alcohol would be involved. It was really fun as the food was good and Marie and I danced many sets. I saw Kurt working the crowd and meeting everyone as he usually does so became more and more relaxed.

At one point we were sitting alone at our table as the other 10 had either left or were dancing. Kurt came by and I introduced him to Marie as my wife to which he asked why I had hidden such beauty. He sat down and started talking about things in general and answering his many questions about when and how we met and how long we had been married. He sort of teased me about marrying someone so young and appeared astounded when I told him that she was in her 40's. He was good as Marie had a pleased look on her face.

At one point he asked if he could have the honor of a dance with my very beautiful wife. What could I say as he was our President and he had behaved as a perfect gentleman so off they went. Marie looked back at me with a willful and questioning look. After a couple of numbers the set was over so they headed back. I noticed he had his arm around her waist and she was smiling.

We talked normally for a bit and when the next set started Kurt just got up and took Maries hand and led her to the floor. He did not even ask this time. I was watching them closely and it seemed that he was dancing much closer this time. The lights were down and the floor was crowded but from where I was sitting I could see them fairly well.

During the second slow number I saw Kurt's hand slide down to Marie's bottom. Immediately I saw her hand on his about to try to move his hand back up. He stopped dancing without moving his hand and leaned in as if were saying something in her ear. She then put both of her arms around his neck leaving him free to rub and play with her bottom. I got instantly hard as I knew she had succumbed to his demands and it was a matter of time before he would be screwing my wife. She later told me that he had said to her, "Put your arms around my neck, now. This bottom is mine."

I caught glimpses of them dancing the next two numbers and then I lost sight of them and did not see them even as I got up and looked around. Maybe a half hour later I saw them coming back to the table Kurt had a big smile and Marie seemed to be excited. Kurt thanked me for the honor of dancing with my wife and as he was walking away he said "See you later" looking at Marie.

I wanted to find out where they had been but the only private place was the dance floor so I led my wife to the fringe and took her in my arms. She was breathing a bit rapidly so I told her I loved her and to relax. I gave her a big kiss and then I knew what had happened and I could taste and smell the typical aroma of semen. I looked her in the eyes and she said "Please forgive me, I couldn't help myself as he is very demanding. I told her that it was OK and I loved her and did she feel my excitement?

She then told me what happened. He had been fondling her sensitive bottom and occasionally brushing her breasts all the while telling her that she was built to please a man. At one point, she told me, he put my hand between us and a moan escaped my lips as he was large and very hard – almost as you are now. He then told, not asked, her to follow him after a delay so as not to arise suspicion. I did and he quickly ushered me into the men's room around the corner and out of sight and into a stall. After closing the door he gave me a deep and wet soul kiss leaving me tingling in my sex.

He sat me down on the toilet and said "My cock needs attention" "You know what to do". As if in a trance, I unzipped his pants and fished out his very large cock and started sucking it earnestly. For some reason, because he was your boss, I wanted him to get the best blowjob I could for you so I mouthed and tongued and sucked until I felt him cumming. I was surprised at the amount of cum but was determined to get it all, which I did.

I then asked her what he meant that he would see us later. She averted my eyes and in a soft voice she said that he asked her for our room number and told her – not asked her - that he would bring up some champagne for a nightcap and to allow him to pleasure her as she had pleasured him. He did not seem to care that you would be there, she told me. "Honey, I think I want him to come and do that". "Does this make me a bad person?" I assured her that it did not but I would always spank her if she felt guilty after. Her response was "Oh, please do" and we had a good laugh. I remember telling her that also, I would always love her.

We talked to many of my colleagues and I introduced Marie to far more than she could remember. I asked her what time Kurt would be coming to our room so when she told me I said that it was time to leave. We said our goodbyes and left the party room and made our way to our room. I had splurged a bit getting a larger room with an alcove bedroom which I now knew was going to get double duty.

We were hugging and kissing and professing our love when at the time he said, there was a knock on the door. I thought it best for Marie to answer the door so I nodded and she went to let him in. Kurt came in with two bottles of champagne and three glasses.

He put them down and literally swopped Marie into his arms and gave her a big and long kiss. That done he shook my hand and told me that I was one lucky guy to have such a sexy wife.

We all, initially, sat down on the three stuffed chairs, which were in front of the coffee table and in view of the television. Kurt opened the champagne, filled the glasses, and we toasted to a great year. He then asked me to go down the hall and get some ice to keep the champagne cold. I went out and quickly found the ice machine and filled the bucket with my heart beating very fast not knowing what I would find when I returned.

I came in and Kurt was standing with his arms around my wife and feeling up and down her body. What turned me on the most was her soft moans when he fondled her bottom. He and they did not stop when I came in and filled the container with ice around the champagne bottle. He stopped what he was doing long enough to finish his champagne and refill all of our glasses. I knew my state but it was obvious that there were two men with erections in the room.

Kurt then took off his jacket, loosened his tie and took off his shoes stating that he wanted to get more comfortable. Kurt sat down in one of the chairs and I was in the further chair. He motioned to Marie to come closer but as she got even with the arm rest he first put his arm out to stop her progress and then it was clear that he was putting his hand under her dress and was feeling her legs as the front of her dress was jiggling. I could not see exactly where his hand was but from the look on my wife's face and the occasional closing of her eyes and the biting of her lower lip, I knew she was feeling something that was turning her on.

It was clear that he was reaching higher and higher and when she opened her stance wider and softly moaned, I knew he was rubbing her pussy lips. No one said a word as he reached higher and then I could see that he was lowering her panties as I could see his hands moving when he was lowering the front side. My wife looked at me with a guilty look on her face so I smiled as I was resigned to what was happening and with my cock hard and pulsing who was I to complain. No pornography film could have been better than what I was witnessing.

I saw that she now moved legs closer together and raised first one knee and then the other. I suspected that this meant that her panties were off. This was confirmed as he brought his arm out from under her skirt and brought her panties to his nose and then he deposited them on the coffee table between us. He sure knew how to tell me that he was in control.

He put his arm back under my wife's skirt and shortly she moved her legs apart and now he could and obviously was rubbing her pussy lips. She now started to moan and move her pelvis. When her eyes shot open I knew he had at least one finger in her vagina. Kurt, my boss, looked over at me and smiled as he moved his hand up and down. When he did that she moaned audibly and then had her first climax of the night. All this was making me very horny and hard and I wasn't sure how long I wanted to watch. Not sure I would have moved but had to get to the bathroom.

When I look back I saw that he had pulled my wife around to kneel between his legs. He said something to her and just before I went in the bathroom, I saw her take his large cock in her mouth. When I came out she was bobbing up and down while he was saying "Suck it good, girl" Yes, that's a good girl" and finally, "Get it all, I'm cumming."

As I sat in the background he told my wife to bend over the back of the chair while he took off his pants and shirt. He got behind her, raised her skirt to above her waist and entered her slowly. Then he started to fuck her like he was possessed. After her third screaming orgasm he pulled out and went around to feed his cock in her hungry mouth until he shot another load of cum in her mouth.

After he pulled out he told her to "strip and get in the bed". On her way to the bed we made eye contact and she mouthed that she loved me. She reached the bed naked ahead of Kurt. He stopped and asked her what she wanted. She knew what he wanted to hear and said, "Please fuck me again". He got on top of her and did she ever get a fucking. She repeatedly cried out "fuck me, God, fuck me good" and "Oh, it is so good, you feel so good, don't stop."

I watched them while masturbating while he was on top in the missionary position, then when he did her from the rear doggie fashion, then when she was on top riding him, then when they were in the 69 position, and then when he fucked her to orgasm in her ass. Then I fell asleep only to awaken sometime in the night to a screaming orgasm and then again in the morning they awoke me by the noise of her orgasms.

Kurt got up took a shower, dressed and on his way out looked at me and said "Your wife is something else and for sharing her you have gone up in my books." Then he left. I finished undressing and got in bed with my exhausted wife. We slept, waking up in each others arms. Reliving the night before I awoke hard with Marie sucking me until I shot my load to join that of my boss in her mouth. After that we made passionate love and reconnected. Yes, I spanked her at her request for being such a bad girl but this was hardly 'punishment' as it was clear that we both liked this a lot.

CHAPTER VI

The Promotion

The next week I was promoted to a Vice Presidency, which did two things. The first was more responsibility and a larger paycheck and the second was monthly Staff meetings with our wives at Kurt's mansion. The second made me a bit anxious as I felt that he could and maybe would have his way with Marie each time we were there. Marie was excited about my promotion but was not sure about the monthly meetings as she knew that he had a staying power that was unbelievable and she did not know if she wanted more of him – at least today this was her position.

The first meeting of the Vice Presidents at Kurt's mansion was very interesting. As I was a new VP there was congratulations and introductions all around. While the men met at a round table and talked business the women got to know each other better. After the meeting there was a fabulous dinner with after dinner drinks in his 'library'. The evening was smooth and at around 10:00 PM couples started to leave one by one. At one point I signaled to Marie and we got up and we slowly made our departure saying good-by till next time to the couples remaining and to our host, Kurt, who was a model gentleman.

On the way home Marie told me that I would not believe what she learned in talking to this wife or another or sometimes in groups and sometimes singly. She said every one was nice and some had the courage to ask privately if I had had an affair with Kurt as I was so beautiful. She told anyone who asked that she was not having an affair with Kurt. She told me that they seemed relieved and 3 of the ladies admitted that they had had affairs with him but their husbands did not know about it. One told her in confidence that she had been seeing Kurt weekly for almost 5 years and had managed to keep it from her husband. One learns something every day.

CHAPTER VII

The Picnic

M arie's and my life goes on. She still works for Carl and for a while I had to wait until the next day to learn what happened at the now monthly card parties. Some weeks ago, Carl asked me if I would like to come as he knew first hand that I accepted my wife's sexual activities. I go there not as Marie's husband but as a friend of Carl's. Now, I see first hand what she does at Carl's bidding and when we get home now, I give to her the wanted playful spanking and we make love like newlyweds. It is great.

Carl's "Card Parties" have now become monthly instead of weekly as he has seemed to be slowing down a bit. This is a good thing because, now my boss, Kurt, somehow arranges to see her least once a week or occasionally two weeks. Marie always has an interesting and very stimulating story to tell me and occasionally I am present when Kurt does to my wife what most people see only in pornography films. In any case, I am turned on to the limit and when we are home we cannot get enough of each other.

One new adventure that happened a few years ago now still excites me. My company has a yearly picnic at a local picnic ground, which can be reserved for large groups. The way it is set up, the company brass and workers in all departments are sort of randomly assigned tables of 10 so that everyone gets to know everyone so to speak. The second year I took my wife, Marie, to this event we were seated or assigned to a table with a very heterogeneous group including Ray who was a foreman in the heavy equipment construction division.

Ray is an impressive black man at 6 ft 4 inches and 220 pounds of all muscle. He was, at the time, 62 years old and one or two years from retirement. He looked and acted much younger as the story was that he could bench press more that anyone in his division and probably the entire company. His arm and chest muscled literally rippled as he moved. I sensed that he knew this and used it to his advantage. He may not have a long formal education background but he ran a solid department and was well respected by all who knew him.

Anyway, he sat down next to Marie with me on the other side of her. He was a charmer and kept her and me interested through most of the dinner. As the wine and beer flowed we all got looser with and more familiar with everyone at the table. I could see the obvious that he was a dominant male and my wife, Marie, was enthralled. That he was a touchy feely type I also saw. Quick touches of my wife's arm or leg as he was making a point all looking very innocent.

I began noticing that the contact was longer and longer as the night went on. I am sure he did not think that I was noticing but I know Marie noticed. When he went to the bathroom I asked her about it and she said that even his hands were powerful and that his touch was having an effect. She looked me in the eye and holding my hand said, "please don't be upset with me but he is sexy and I have never known a black man". I knew what she meant and where this might lead to and as Marie's other hand was on my upper leg, she knew I was turned on.

He returned to the table with a fresh round of drinks for everyone and commenced with his fascinating stories and making points by touching my wife's upper leg or arm. His touching became bolder and I am sure I saw him actually stroke my wife's leg a couple of times. Then it was my time to find the facilities. I asked Marie and others at the table if there was anything they wanted. Hearing nothing I excused my self and went to the bathroom area.

I came back a slightly different way and noticed that our table had thinned out and Ray was holding forth with only a few people. I saw that his arm was below the table and I could see him actually stroking my wife's upper leg and then I saw his hand disappear beneath her skirt to stroke her leg. This got me hard as could be, as

I knew something would follow. It always did.

I backed up and went around the usual way to come back to our table. Ray told me that he kept an eye out for my wife and she was safe. I thanked him and sat down to join the group. I noticed that his hand was still under the table and my wife was smiling. She put her hand on his biceps and asked him what he had to do to get his muscles so big. He smiled and said that one day he would show her. She laughed at that and lowered her arm to her lap. I sensed movement and she quickly looked over at me and her eyes widened with a look of surprise.

She later told me that he had taken his hand off her leg and placed hers on his stiffening cock and left it there while he went back to her upper legs and even rubbed her pussy through her panties.

He then asked Marie if she wanted to see some of the heavy equipment, on display near the parking lot, for which the company was famous. She quickly said "Oh Yes" then looked at me and asked if it was OK if she went with Ray for a bit to look at the big stuff. I said "Of course", "I'll be around here when you get back". While they were gone, I made the rounds seeing my staff and meeting their families but certainly was anxious at what I was sure was going to happen.

She came back alone about an hour later and the first thing I noticed was that her eyes were quite red. She had a guilty look on her face so I knew I was in for a new story. She gave me a big hug and kiss and once again I tasted semen on her lips. She hugged me tightly and said, "I'm sorry but I just did not expect Ray to be so aggressive", then, "Let's go home so I can tell you what happened, but please don't spank me tonight".

On the way home she told me that I may not believe it but she got the longest and hardest spanking of her life. When I asked her to tell me the story she told me that after a tour of the big equipment he took her hand and led her to the main parking lot. He unlocked and opened the door of one of those very large touring campers.

When she asked him if it was his, he said that it was as he intended to travel once retired in maybe less than 2 years. Inside it was huge and looked almost like a home.

Once inside, he became serious and told me that I was a very naughty girl for letting him play with her back at the table and especially naughty for letting him bring her to his camper. She told me that she blushed and averted his eyes until he raised her chin so she had to look at him. He then said that she deserved a hard spanking and he was going to give it to her. Marie then snuggled close to me while I was driving and said that she was actually frightened and excited at the same time.

She then went on to say that he sat down, pulled her over his knees, raised her skirt to her mid back and pulled her panties down to her knees. She then told me "God, honey, I felt so vulnerable but excited". She said that she was flooded with old memories of being spanked by her uncle as a child. He then commented as to how he was going to enjoy spanking her and reminded her how naughty she was. "Honey, I have never had such a hard spanking in my life". She went on, "At first, I almost liked it but he went on and on and got harder and harder until I was pleading with him to stop. Of course, he didn't stop and I was soon crying from both the shame and stinging pain". I then knew why I had seen that her eyes were red. I was hard as a rock.

When he stopped he pushed me off his lap and said only "Undress". As I removed my clothes I saw him doing the same. When he removed his Jockey short I almost fainted as he had the largest cock I had ever seen. It was at least 10 inches long and very thick. He then came over to where I was and said "Suck it, my naughty girl". Well, I got on my knees and did the best I could, as it was so large I could only get the head in so I used my tongue the best I knew how.

I used both hands to pump his cock and after a bit he flooded my mouth with squirt after squirt of semen. When I had cleaned him up he picked me up as if I weighed nothing and carried me to his bed. "God, is he strong" she said to me. Then, "On your knees" he ordered so I dutifully assumed that position. He licked me from my clitoris to my anus until I had a thundering orgasm and squirted my lubricating fluid. He then said, "get ready to receive the fuck of your life". It took maybe a half hour but he did get it in and he was right. I came so many times I lost count.

When he climaxed again he pulled out and told me to clean it up. Then he got dressed and told me to do the same and "get back to your husband". We walked out of his camper and he pointed the direction and said "Scoot, your husband will miss you". Then patting and fondling my bottom gave me a piece of paper which he said had his phone number on it and told me to call him in a week or sooner.

We were now home and parked but Marie saw that I was uncomfortable hard so she unzipped my pants and sucked me to a wild orgasm. We went upstairs and quickly undressed and jumped into our bed to snuggle and relive the adventure. The first thing my Marie did was tell me how sorry she was that she was just not able to control her emotions and that she let Ray fondle her at the table and then let him lead her to his camper. She then said, that she still felt her bottom tingling and painful but somehow this made her hornier.

She pulled me over her and we made love again and again until I could get hard no more. Then we talked again about what happened. Marie wanted to be sure that I was OK with her "slips" of "desire". I assured her that as long as I knew about all instances of interest and as long as she wanted me to watch when I could that not only was I OK with it but nothing made me hornier and more in love with her than being included.

After a thought pause, she asked me how I felt about Ray as she was sure that he would do nothing in my presence and she found him almost irresistible as she had never before had sex with a black man or anyone with such a large cock. His sheer strength and dominant demeanor was just too much for her to resist. She asked me hesitatingly if she could call him as he requested. I told her that she had to do what she had to do and it was up to her. I only wanted to be in on the before and after and with that I would love her forever.

It was then that I had an idea and I proposed to her to see if she could get him to come to our house, as you would tell him that I had told you that I had a very full day and would not be home for dinner. I told her that this way I could watch her being pleasured by his cock. "OK", she said, "I will call him next Wednesday as I have no plans that day". "Thanks, honey, I love you more and more each day"

To be followed....

My Wife's First Affair - But Not Her Last

By **Chris Dawson**

Forward

This is the story of a man who falls in love with a woman who he finds out is very submissive, actually compulsively submissive, to strong dominant men. He loves her and marries her knowing that she has been and will remain a true sexually active lady. When one falls in love, one accepts ones wife's weaknesses as well as her strengths. In this story, she succumbs to sexual advances of not only her bosses but also her husband's bosses and others. The hardest part of writing this story was to come to some conclusion and not make it go on forever.

CHAPTER I

The Beginning

M y wife and I have been married for 17 years, and had been talking about and I fantasizing about adding a third person to our sex life for the last 5 years or so. My wife, Jen, is 5' 3" and 130 pounds She is in her forties but really looks much younger as she has kept her body well toned.

I am in my fifties but also have not let myself go. I am 5' 9" tall and weigh 170 pounds. I am probably a bit larger than normal at 7". Our sex life is quite acceptable except I am not usually able to last long enough for my wife to orgasm or orgasm more than once with intercourse. She always tells me that she is satisfied but I have noticed that when we have spoken about a past lover or a potential new one, her orgasms are much longer and more fulfilling to her. At least this has been my perception but I get very excited when this happens.

I have been asking myself questions like; What would she think if she was in the arms of another man and what would I think of her if she was in the arms of another man? What would it feel like for me to see him on top of her, pounding his cock in and out of her? Indeed, what would we both feel if he made her moan and scream with pleasure more than she does with me? Would she like him better than me? These emotionally draining questions come to my mind often.

We had been talking about this rather openly. Jen, my wife, has admitted a curiosity but at first she was sure it could never happen. She would explain that she did not think that she could actually do it as she would tell me that she loves me very much and does not want to do anything to alter our marriage and, besides, nice women do not have affairs or cheat on their husbands.

I would tell her that with the husbands knowledge and permission it would not be "cheating' and could hardly be called an "affair". She would always seem 'reflective' after one of these conversations. The sex we would have after this was discussed was always the best as she was sure to orgasm at least once. The main question I would ask myself is how I would feel if she would like sex with him more than she likes sex with me?

We did not know how it would feel, but we knew that we were both very aroused anytime the subject came up. Usually when it came up we ended up in bed with a round of very hot sex. It was on these occasions that she had the biggest orgasms and was the wildest. This was not lost on me but how to take the next step was a puzzle.

When a potential opportunity finally arose, I don't remember how it started, it just seemed to gradually come up now and then what we had talked about, in theory, seem to becoming a reality. Our discussions had been more a "what if" scenario. We had never even talked about how we would actually do it, or even whether or not we would or could actually do it.

We only talked about her with another man. We never talked about me and another woman, and that seemed completely natural to me. Finally a possible opportunity presented itself. It was in the summer at one of those networking affairs where businessmen gather to have drinks and network. Wives usually stand around pretending to be interested but usually bored, or some dance a little, and that is how the evening goes.

I was always aware of my wife at these functions, and hated for her to have to stand around bored so I always introduced her to my fellow professionals out of politeness. She seemed to enjoyed a bit of light chatter with them. Sometimes we would dance, and sometimes she would dance with other men. I always enjoyed that. Even before we started talking about possibilities.

It was a bit sexy and just enjoyable to see her having a good time in someone else's arms. It was also fun to see her smile, and to watch her charm someone. I must have been born without the jealousy gene but certainly with the voyeur gene. As much as I love her, I have never felt possessive toward her. I want her to be happy. If that means she dance's with someone else, or even if she has sex with someone else, then so be it. In the back of my mind, I had hoped for this eventuality but did not think she would go that far. She never really showed a lot of interest in any of them other than just light chatter or perhaps a bit of dancing.

Then there was that special evening in July. It was hot and muggy. The band was not very good and no one was dancing. Even the men were bored. There was a new face in the crowd. It was a gentleman I had met the week before. He was new in town and had just joined a company we competed with. He seemed nice and was rather goodlooking.

My wife and I were having a snack and some wine when he happened to walk by. He said hello, and we nodded. Then I stopped him and told him I would like to introduce him to my wife. I laughed and admitted I had forgotten his name. "Roger, Roger Johnston," he said, as he gently took my wife's hand and smiled at her. She responded, "Jennifer, but call me Jen," and I saw immediately her special smile and she gave him her firm handshake that always surprises men.

Roger's first response was, "Paul you have a very lovely wife, thanks for introducing us." He then turned to me and shook my hand. Then I looked at my wife, and saw something I had not seen in many years. There was a twinkle in her eyes. She seemed flushed, even embarrassed. It appeared to be the sameway she looked at me the night we had met nearly 20 years before.

I saw immediately that she was attracted to him. I had not seen her attracted to anyone like that in a long time. She looked at me, quickly regained her composure and smiled at me. There was a look in her eyes that told me she may have found something that interested her. Roger started to walk away as we had suddenly become silent. I quickly invited him back to join us, which he did.

We started talking about this and that mostly the weather until

I had an idea. I excused myself for a trip to the men's room. I didn't go to the men's room. I just had a feeling about this so I walked around the corner and hid myself so I could watch them. I saw Lisa flash that smile that melts people. She was touching her hair, the way women do when they want to be noticed. She also licked her lips. He also seemed almost uncomfortable. Perhaps a bit shy, as if he did not want to offend her or me.

After about 10 minutes I came back to the table and joined them. Jen hardly looked up at me and continued to chatter away with Roger. He was very polite to her and showed no outward or obvious signs of attraction. He was probably keeping his distance because I was present. Lisa from this point on seemed to hardly notice me as she kept talking with him. She had found a mutual interest, which was gardening, and was having a great time. Deep down, I knew that was not the only interest she had in common with him.

At one point in their conversation, he looked at me, I suppose to see if I was getting jealous or objected to this conversation. My response was to smile as if everything was 'A OK.' I was a bit surprised myself as I felt my penis making a bulge in my pants. I was getting very aroused just watching them talk. Soon it was time for us to go, and we all said goodbye. Jen gave Roger a little hug, and he seemed taken aback, but smiled and returned the hug as he only saw a smile on my face.

When we got home Lisa almost attacked me. She was very amorous and wanted sex almost immediately. We got undressed in the living room and had sex on the couch. I asked her if she thought that maybe she was excited because of meeting Roger. She looked at me with a new look in that I could not read her thoughts and said, "Of course not, silly I love you and just felt like having sex". I smiled and said OK as I have always enjoyed making love to her but knew very well that Roger had ignited her sexiness and I loved it.

I sensed that something had gotten her hot and she did not want to talk about Roger or what had happened at the event. She kept asking why I was grinning. I said I didn't know except that I loved her and when she is hot, I am hot. At the same time I was starting to hatch out a plan in my own mind based on what I had observed and wanted to happen.

It may have been a week later before I saw Roger again. It was in one of those fast food restaurants, and we sat together for a quick lunch. I asked him if he had enjoyed meeting my wife, Jen. He said he had, and asked me if I was bothered about anything. I told him I wasn't and said I had no idea why I should be. He laughed and told me he thought I had a very pretty wife. I then said, "Yes, she is that and also very sexy." His face got a bit flushed so I knew he felt the same. Thinking of the two of them got me hard again.

Roger had just joined his current employer and had moved from out of state. His family was more than 800 miles away, so he was living in a hotel in town. Roger and I hit it off very well. He wanted to be around people but didn't know many people in town. He was happy that I seemed to be befriending him. We met a few more times. Another lunch, a drink after work.

I would occasionally mention something about Jen. I could tell he liked her, but he was a bit careful to not say too much. I assured him that I was not the jealous type, and asked him if he thought she was attractive. He said she was, and before long we even joked around sometimes about her. After several of these meetings, I decided it was time to put things in motion.

We were joking around some, talking about the women in the bar. I asked him how he would like to have the blonde that was tending bar. "Oh yeah," he said with a laugh, "She is very nice." Then I looked directly at him, staring him in the eye, and asked the fateful question, "Roger would you like to have Jen in the same way you would like that blonde?". He nearly spilled his drink and looked at me shocked. "What did you say?" he asked. "You know what I said," I responded. "Would you like to have my wife, Jen, in the sameway you would like that blonde bartender?"

He looked at me for what seemed like minutes, but was only

seconds, trying to take in what had been asked, and no doubt trying to think of what to say. I smiled and tried to look relaxed. "I ... I.. I don't know how to answer that", Roger stammered. I told him it was OK, and that he could tell me the truth. I told him again that I was not the jealous type. He thought for a moment, and then said, "Yes Paul, I would like to have Jen that way very much as she is very nice looking, has a great body, and is very fun to talk to, but I know she is your wife."

He shrugged as though that were the end of it. I was not sure what he was thinking. Later, I told him how Jen and I had talked about the possibility of inviting another man into our bedroom. How the idea had turned her on so much, and how I thought she was attracted to him. I told him I thought he would be a good candidate. "Are you serious Paul," he asked me and he looked hard at me. I told him I was very serious and that this turned me on also.

We both sat in silence for awhile. We finished our drinks and ordered another round. Finally he broke the silence. "Are you inviting me to have sex with your wife," Roger finally asked me, saying the words as if he couldn't believe it himself. "Yes Roger, I am," I responded, "I have had this desire to watch my wife being pleasured by another man for some time but, until now, had not met a man that I thought Jen would like and who I also like." "In your case, I see things that tell me she likes you already", I added.

The Plan

Roger looked at me and smiled. He shook his head a few times, still trying to figure out if I was serious. I had befriended Roger because he was new in town, and now had invited him to have sex with my wife. My wife, Jen, and I had been talking around and about this for awhile, and we had recently met Roger at a business networking gathering. She knew nothing about me asking Roger if he would like to have sex with her. Roger looked at me across the table and asked the obvious question. "So how … when can we do this. How does this work," he asked.

I really didn't know for sure since we had never done this before. I told him the entire story. About how Jen and I had talked about her having sex with someone. I told him I would want to watch of course, but not participate. I also told him that even though Jen wanted to do this, and she was attracted to him, I had not told her that I intended to invite him to have sex with her.

Roger looked at me quizzically and said, "Well when are you going to tell her?" Then Roger said, "I guess this isn't a done deal yet." I then suggested to Roger that I thought it would be a good idea if he seduced her. I could arrange some meetings and would not be in his way. I wanted him to convince or seduce her, and for her to tell me as though it were her idea. "So I'm going to have to work for it," Roger said with a laugh. To that I told him that, "She is certainly worth a little work and I assure you that I will not interfere."

"It will be an adventure," I responded, trying to encourage him. "It's pretty much set up, you just have to close the deal. He laughed and said, "OK". I explained that watching him seduce her would be a huge turn-on for me, and I thought Jen would enjoy the sex even more that way as well. He agreed that he would pursue her as long as I made some meetings possible.

That weekend I took Jen to another business networking gathering where I knew Roger would also be present. In advance I told her I thought Roger would be there, and she smiled slightly. I asked her if she was interested in him. She laughed and said "No' but I saw her eyes widen and she smiled again. It didn't take us long to find Roger at the event. He was standing alone at the bar. He almost ran over to us and said hello. "You remember Jen, don't you Roger," I asked? "I most certainly do," Roger responded with a smile and took her hand.

He held her hand just a little longer than one usually would while shaking hands, Jen smiled and I could tell she was interested in him as a person. There was a band playing. Roger looked at me and nodded toward my wife, Jen. I smiled and nodded. He asked her to dance. She looked at me for approval, and, again, I smiled and motioned for her to go.

They both headed for the dance floor. There was fairly lively music at first and it was fun watching them move around together. I began to get hard watching them, imagining them laying together instead of dancing. They came back to the table where I was sitting and we all had a drink and talked for a bit. I told them I didn't feel like dancing tonight, and said they should go ahead if they wanted. I winked at Jen and she flashed me a mischievous grin.

She bent down to kiss me and whispered "thank you – I love you" in my ear. They continued dancing. There were some slow dances and he held her in his arms. Jen pressed herself against him. At one point he put his hand on her sexy butt and I noticed that she did not move his hand away. Then I saw her rest her head on his shoulder and saw a look of contentment in her eyes before she closed them as they continued dancing. I wasn't totally sure, but I thought at one point they kissed. Regardless, it was obvious Jen was greatly enjoying being swept around the room by a tall handsome guy.

I was enjoying too. I was so hard that I was almost uncomfortable. Finally we said goodnight and headed home. Jen was again very horny and wanted to have sex as soon as we got home. We had a good round of sex. She even had a big orgasm before I came inside her and we then held each other for quite awhile. I fingered her to a second orgasm. Try as I might, I could never make her cum with intercourse more than once, and even then not always with my dick.

Still I could give her an orgasm other ways and she never complained. We lay in silence for awhile. "Paul," she said as though that were a question. "Yes my love," I answered and looked in her eyes. "Umm. You know that talk we have been having about sex with other people. I, ummmm just wondered how serious you were about that. If you aren't its fine, just forget it", she said with a laugh.

A fake laugh at that. My sweet wife was nervous, which was very rare. I told her I was serious. I asked her if she was interested in Roger? Again she said, "no" and laughed. She said she was just curious because I had not mentioned it in a week or two. I tried to talk with her more about sex with him, but she said that she didn't want to talk about such a subject at this time. I could tell, however, that she was deep in thought.

The next weekend we went to another business gathering. It was almost exactly like the previous one. She danced with him for a long time. They both were very aroused. Again when we got home, she was so horny, we had sex almost immediately. This time I asked the question. I asked her if she still wanted another man. "Oh my goodness," she said, and buried her face in a pillow. She didn't say anything else, but I swear she was blushing. Well, I had my answer and now only time would tell when it happened.

The next Monday she told me Roger had called and had invited her to lunch. She asked me if I was OK with that. She said it wasn't any big deal, and if I didn't want her to, that would be fine. I told her I thought it was perfectly OK, in fact, I encouraged her to go. I reminded her that he is alone and kind of lonely and that she would be welcome company to him.

The next morning she put on one of the new Panty and Bra sets

I had gotten for her and one of her more sexy dresses. She seemed to have more make up on and she also spent an extra 20 minutes on her hair and was almost late for work. I knew then, for certain, that she was vey interested in Roger and I would soon get my wish.

I asked her what the special occasion was. "Nothing", she said. "I just felt like dressing up." I asked if she was having lunch with Roger. She shrugged and said yes, trying to sound nonchalant. That evening I asked how the lunch had gone. She seemed a bit nervous but said it went fine, and she finally admitted she liked him. She told me that he was very handsome and polite at all times. There were two more lunches that week, and I noticed that she was dressing much more sexily for work on those days.

On the weekend she asked me if there were any business gatherings to go to. She seemed disappointed when I said no there weren't. The next week there were two more lunches with Roger, and she came home a couple hours late two evenings. She told me that she had to work late but I sensed in her voice and eyes that there was more to it than that. I decided to not question her and let time take its course. On Friday she came home just a little late. She usually gets off early on Friday's but I supposed she didn't this week.

When she came home, I was already there and when she came in, I noticed that her makeup was smeared, almost wiped off her face. Her hair was a little unsettled. Her dress also looked funny, like she had dressed quickly or something. We hugged and kissed hello. I was sure that I tasted a new taste in her mouth and immediately got very hard thinking that it might be from Roger. Then she looked at me with a serious look on her face and said, "Paul, we need to talk."

CHAPTER III
The Confession

"We need to talk." She said those words to me with a serious tone. She seemed nervous. It was obvious she had been with him, so I was pretty sure what it was she wanted to talk about. I felt an adrenalin rush, and sexual arousal all at the same time as I awaited expectantly for what I hoped she would be telling me. I gave her a big hug knowing she would feel my hard-on and told her that I loved her and that she could tell me anything.

We had been talking for a long time about my watching her being intimate with another man. It was something I thought I wanted and that she was curious about but we had not yet acted upon. I had set her up with a friend. His job was to seduce her. Over the past few weeks they had been talking and even meeting for lunch. Now she was coming home from work late. Her hair messed up, her makeup smeared and her clothes ruffled. I smiled at her and asked what she would like to talk about.

"Well, uhhh," she stammered. "You know you have said you want to watch me with another man. Do you really want that baby?", she asked. I nodded and asked her if she was with Roger today. "Ummm yes, yes I was," she said, as though she was not sure what to say or how to say it. Her face turned a bit red. I asked her what she and Roger had done today. She stammered and looked down as if embarrassed. Again she asked me if I was absolutely sure that I wanted her to have sex with another man. I told her I was and that I loved her no matter what she had done with Roger. She looked as if she was about to cry, and said. "I'm so sorry baby, I'm so sorry. I hope you wont be mad at me," she said as she ran toward me. We hugged and I kissed her. "I wont be mad love," I told her. Then, knowing what she was about to relate and with a smile I asked her why she thought I might be.

She told me they had been making out in the car and it went too far. She told me they had been necking and fooling around and it sort of got out of hand. "Honey", she said, "He put his very large penis in me in the back seat of his car while we were parked just before he dropped me off." She looked up at me and asked if I was really OK with that. I kissed her deeply and could taste something salty on her mouth, which I knew in a moment must be his cum. I felt an amazing surge of arousal as I realized it was his cum. Without a word I started taking her clothes off and we started making out frenetically and passionately on the couch. I told her again and again that I loved her and was OK with her having sex with Roger.

Soon I was licking her pussy, and tasted that same thing I had tasted on her lips moments before. I looked up and asked her if he had cum inside her. She moaned and said, "Oh God I am so sorry but, yes he did". "Was he good," I asked? "Yes it was wonderful," she replied. and began squirming and moaning louder as I licked her pussy. I was so hot I started fucking her immediately. I shouldn't have been concerned though. She was very wet. She was slick, as there was a load of cum already inside her to add lubrication.

I was so aroused I came pretty fast. She came again with my fingers inside her. I asked her to tell me about it. "Oh Paul, it was amazing," she said. "He is huge. I've never had sex like that before." I asked her if today was the only time he had fucked her. She told me, with a look of guilt and fear in her eyes, "No it was not, after our first lunch date we had, he took me to a hotel room and fucked me several times. It seemed like we were there for hours. I just could not stop and neither could he. Honey, I was so turned on but felt very guilty – so guilty that I just did not have the courage to tell you."

Well I was so turned on I didn't know what to say. I had really not intended or wanted him to fuck her before we all three got together, but I couldn't help but smile and get very hard again. I swallowed my pride and asked her if she was going to see him again.

She responded by first saying, "I swear I've never done anything like this before, but yes, I would like to see him again if this is OK with you". I said, "Yes" and then I told her about my desire which became my plan and about my asking him to seduce her. She laughed and said, "He sure did a very good job seducing me and I just love it when he is fucking me". She went on to say, "I really love you even more with this new freedom you have given me but now I want him again and sure hope this is OK with you".

CHAPTER IV

And Then...

J en then asked me with almost pleading look in her eyes if I was sure I wanted to watch them have sex. I told her I was very sure and loved her more then she could know. "Good," she said. "I thought this would be your response so I asked him to come over tomorrow afternoon." With that, we made love again and I was able to bring her to a climax well before I came again.

"The next day could not arrive fast enough. But he did finally arrive. When he entered the house he gave me a sheepish smile. "Did you enjoy Jen," I asked. "Very much so," he responded. He then looked at Jen, embraced her and they shared a long kiss. Neither of them seemed to act, at this point, as if I was there or not. They didn't waste a lot of time on small talk as they kissed and fondled each other's body like they were long time lovers.

Within 10 minutes they were in the bedroom and completely ignoring me. Which I did not expect but I was OK with it as, after all, I had set this up. I sat in a chair by the bed and watched. He did indeed have a large cock. A good two inches longer than mine and bigger around. She sucked his cock for a long time until he finally came in her mouth and I saw her swallowing his load. This was new as she rarely sucked my cock. Seeing this turned me on greatly and she seemed to love it. She moaned as she sucked it. She had never moaned while sucking mine before, but that just turned me on more.

He ministered her pussy with his tongue and slowly and sexily kissed her all over. After about half an hour of foreplay, he laid her down on her back and mounted her. I watched as he pushed his dick inside her pussy. She let out a gasp as it filled her up, stretching her. "Hey aren't you gonna use a condom," I asked. He looked at me as if he were amused, and just said "no." Lisa was looking up at him totally engrossed and not only a big smile but a look in her eyes that told me she loved what he was doing to her and did not care whether or not he used a condom. This told me that he had fucked her bareback on the times he had been with her before today. Yes a feeling of jealousy and anxiety swept through me but what could I do, I had asked for this and now I had to live with it as I knew my wife would see Roger again and again in the future.

He started fucking her slowly and soon was pushing in and pulling out faster and faster with long deep strokes. And my lovely wife started moaning and then screaming. He must have fucked her 20 minutes without stopping. She came several times. Her body convulsing under him. She almost never screamed, or at lest that enthusiastically when I fucked her. And she never had repeated orgasms with me either. I knew then, that my wife would be fucking him and maybe others from then on. This made me very anxious but at the same time, very excited,

I had to admit that I did feel jealous, and very anxious as this man was pleasuring my wife in ways I never had or could. I felt arousal that was amazing but could not get out of my mind what this meant for the future. Would my wife still love me? I couldn't help but stroke my own cock. I finally could stand no more and came myself.

They then switched to doggy, and she came again saying again and again, "Oh, you give my such pleasure", and "You're so deep, I love it, please don't stop". He came inside her and I could see cum dripping from her pussy. He didn't skip a beat. Just kept fucking, pounding her harder and harder. Then they went to her riding him from on top and then back to the missionary position where she had her legs either around his back urging him on or over his shoulders.

His cock finally went down. She started sucking him immediately and got him hard again. I had never seen her this wild before. She had become a fucking machine. She had never been shy about having sex with me, but I had never seen her fuck with such reckless abandon.

As Roger continuously plunged his cock in an out of my wife's pussy she had several orgasms or at least it seemed that she was as she kept moaning louder and louder. While being so pleasured she became very vocal moaning and saying over and over that she just loved his big cock and the pleasure he was giving her. I admit to feeling pangs of anxiety and jealousy as it was clear that another man could give her what I could not. That said, I also had the good feelings of happiness that the woman I loved dearly was receiving pleasure that I could not give her. Talk about mixed emotions.

Roger fucked her for almost three hours before they finally stopped. She was breathing hard and holding on to him very contentedly. She looked at me and smiled and mouthed 'I love you'. Roger asked me to get them some drinks. After I brought us all some water we talked openly about his and her desire to continue seeing each other.

Thus began my wife's first affair, and my time in the roller coaster life as a cuckold. Nothing would ever be the same again. My wife has now been with Roger several times, mostly at our house. Sometimes I have been present and sometimes not. She has admitted, with some misgivings and guilt, to spending some time with him at the same hotel and she has discussed her concern that in the next few months his family will be coming and she selfishly hopes that this will not be the end of their affair.

Through this, our relationship has seemed to have gotten closer than ever as she almost daily thanks me from her heart for the opportunity to be pleasured by a man who is not her husband and not feel guilty of 'cheating'. Life goes on but certainly the old adage of "Be careful what you wish for" comes to mind when I either watch or hear about her times with Roger.

CHAPTER V

Once started...

O
h, and Roger has done well in his job and his family has now moved to this city. As a gesture of friendship we have had he and his wife over for dinner several times. This has only slightly decreased the number of times he either comes over to be with my wife alone, telling his wife that he is meeting me for business reasons, or meets my wife after her work for an afternoon of pure unbridled sex in one of our hotels.

When they meet in a hotel she now tells me about it in advance, and when she comes home now we have the great sex. She always excitedly tells me that she loves having the "affair" with Roger and wonders how long it will last. I told her recently that Roger is not the only man in this world who would find her attractive and sexy. I love the look she gets when I mention this.

My wife cannot be happier with the way our life has gone. She gets hopefully, all the sex she needs and She still comes to me often enough so I have no complaints. I have noticed that she dresses more sexily at work and has been telling me that one of the guy's at the gym has been coming on to her. When she asks me if this is OK with me I tell her that her happiness is my happiness and pleasure, and that as long as she tells me everything our life can only get better.

Well, as I write this she has told me that Carl, one of the trainers at the Gym has been flirting with her and occasionally patting her bottom, has asked her to go out with him one evening. She tells me excitedly that he would be the first black man she had ever been with but she had always had a quiet fantasy of making it with a black man.

She has voiced her concerns about taking this step but with my assurance she has now told me that she recently told him 'yes', she would when "my husband" is out of town. She told me that this way, I could be hidden and watch. In addition this would be not only safer for her but more discreet. Believe me she attacked me when she told me of this coming adventure and was assured of my acceptance of her being with Carl.

As I say this, I must admit that I had not wished for what is happening as in my gut, I am often anxious about her some day meeting a single man who pleases her more than I can and she might leave me. When I bring this up she assures me that I am her one true love and that as much as she enjoys the extra sex, she is mine forever. I now know that being a "Cuck" is an almost always-anxious state but so far, her pleasure is mine and I am happy and always horny. That I get all the sex that I can handle is an understatement.

Unexpectedly Entering a Cuckold Life

By **Chris Dawson**

This is a story about how a "normal" young man came to accept that the woman he fell in love with and wanted to marry had, and would continue to have, lovers. It is basically mixture of events in his life from college on that led him to know that he accepted that his dates and then his wife would have sex with others and somehow this excited him rather than angered him. Once married, his main desire was to actually be present and watch his wife have sex with others. This desire was experienced in spades on a vacation in the Caribbean.

CHAPTER I

In the beginning

Not sure where to start but what I am experiencing and living now, 12 years after I married my college sweetheart, has roots that go back to my late High School and early College days. At that time I seemed to be attracted to women who dated many men or who had the reputation of being loose party-girl types. I was a bit naïve about sex but somehow I was attracted to women who were sexually active and especially if I knew the guy, or his reputation, that they were dating.

Oh, I dated virgins like everyone else but the greatest attraction was to those with experience sexually, at least by reputation. I had absolutely no idea why I was attracted to, and wanted to date, women who I knew or believed that they had been having sex frequently and currently.

I had no idea where this came from as in college I certainly was not a wallflower or submissive, or at least I thought I was 'normal'. I was on both my High School and College Swim teams and was not only active in student affairs like being on the All University Congress. In addition, I was President of my Fraternity my senior year. I dated normally but, as I said, tended to be most turned on by girls who I knew were loose or had the reputation of being an "easy lay". I did not know why I felt this way.

A bit about me: I am 5' 10" and am now in my 40's. In college I weighed around 180 pounds and was fit from playing sports including Freshman football and swimming and always squash. I was also an accomplished water skier including bare-foot skiing and jumping. I now weigh 170 pounds and still play squash but certainly not as fit as I once was. My endowment is average at 7" with a slight upward curve.

In College, I knew some of the guys who dated the girls I was most interested in. They were fraternity brothers or on the swim team and I knew that they were "ass men" who usually scored with the women they dated. At least this is what they bragged about around the fraternity house or in the locker room, where I learned that many of these "studs" had much larger cocks than I did. Actually, I did not doubt them as occasionally they would sneak one into their room at the Frat house and sometimes, if his room was close to mine, I heard the unmistakable sounds of sex and moaning orgasms.

I had the occasional great pleasure when I was able to sneak a peak through a partly open door at the rapture of the young lady as she was being fucked. If I knew who she was or saw her later, I would always approach her in a friendly and respectful nature. Occasionally this would pay off in a date.

So, once I knew about a girl they had had sex with, I would try, often successfully, to meet them and ask them out. I guess I was a sympathetic ear as many of these girls would tell me how much they liked this person or that one and occasionally they would tell me what they did with them. This always excited me a lot and when I got home I would masturbate to the memory of what they told me.

Occasionally I would date them long enough to have sex with them, but knew or at least believed that they had to be comparing me with at least a couple of the "studs" who I knew from the swim team or my Fraternity who were very well hung indeed. All of these girls saw more than one guy and none wanted to go out with me alone. Somehow this always excited me. My accepting them for who they were benefited me as I almost never sat home or went to movies alone.

As I was in college for longer than one degree, this type of dating went on for about six years until I met my present wife, Jennifer, who was a very attractive sexually active girl more than 5 years younger then I was. She was 5'6", about 135 pounds and had a body that was not difficult to see why she attracted men like crazy. She was full breasted and had an amazingly round and firm butt and legs that did not seem to end. I knew that she was like a magnet to many guys who I knew dated only those that "put-out" for them. This fact increased her attraction to me but she was one attractive lady who I would have dated under any circumstances.

We hit it off on many fronts but she insisted that she did not want to commit to one person even me, who she seemed to like very much. When Jen asked me if I was OK with her dating others I then knew that my answer would be "Yes" but I did not have the courage to tell her that her having sex with others excited me in an unexplained manner. I explained it that not only was I OK but she did not have to hide anything she did - that her dating was OK with me as I cared for her that much.

One of the things I loved was that her orgasms were very vocal. Sometimes the build up of audible moans ended in almost screams as she had her orgasm and this never ceased to bring me off at the same time. Another factor in her bringing me to climax was that she had super vaginal muscle control, which at orgasm would spasmodically contract. No one could remain in control when this happened, I thought.

So I continued to date her when we were both free, which with my Graduate School workload and her schedule was about once week. For many reasons I knew that I was falling in love with her and I knew she cared for me. We began to talk about the future at which time she asked me straight out if the fact that she had been and was sexually active would affect our relationship negatively. I assured her the "the past is the past" and as long as she was not secretive that I was OK with whatever she did. I still did not yet have the courage to tell her that her sexual activity turned me on greatly or that I hoped she would continue to be taken and used by others.

We dated like this for almost three years until after my graduation and while in my first job got an offer in another part of the state, I could not refuse. I talked about this opportunity with her and as she had a year left for her degree we agreed to try a long distance romance and after her graduation, if we both still felt the same we would get married. I did not bring it up but knew very well that she would go on being sexually active as no woman I had ever met loved sex as much as my Jen did. Strangely, this excited me.

Jen did agree to be honest with me about who she was dating and I told her that she was free to choose not to marry me if after time and our separation she came to feel differently about me. Jen's assurance that she wanted to be my wife as among all the men she had dated, I was the most loving and honest and she really did and would love me. In addition, our sex life was the best I had experienced and as she was on birth control pills we did not worry about getting pregnant unexpectedly. We left it at our agreeing to see what happened.

That last week before I left for this new job we made love every night and sometimes more often. She kept saying that among all her lovers, I was the most gentle and tender and she felt safe in my arms like nothing she had experienced with others. She was able to tell me this knowing that, to her, my response was that I was OK with her being active sexually and she trusted me enough to be able to be honest with me.

She even started to feel free to tell me about some of her dates and even about those she had been seduced by. That sex after she would tell me of an adventure was the greatest may have been missed by her but certainly not by me even as I did not understand why at the time. After some dates her orgasm was so loud that I worried that my neighbors would complain.

Well, we made it for the year and made plans to get married. When it became known, some of my old friends from the swim team and fraternity brothers tried to tell me to think twice about this decision as she had the reputation of being a wild one. A few went as far as asking me if I trusted her, and things like "did you know I heard that she fucked the whole basketball team at one party". I had not known many of the things they told me but told them that I loved her and the past was the past. Of course what I heard turned me on frightfully whether it was true or not.

After we were married and moved to the big city life went on almost idealistically. Jen was able to get a job within weeks of our moving and or love/sex life was the best. Nothing was said but I suspected and later had affirmed that Jen was having affairs, meaning she was getting some sex outside of our marriage. This made me jealous and excited at the same time. I did not want to confront her as, for some reason, I wanted her to have pleasure when she wanted it but what I really wanted was to watch her being taken by a lover.

There were hints like her getting home late or having to be out of town for a few days supposedly for business and then I would find her panties in the bottom of the dirty clothes basket that were thick with dried goo (cum) and the unmistakable smell of cum. That there was always a packet of condoms in her purse was another give-away.

One evening when I had gotten home from a trip a day early, she came home and had obviously been partying. I pretended not to notice and because I was glad to see her I gave her a big hug and a bigger kiss. The smell and unmistakable taste of semen in her mouth got me hard as a rock. She noticed my hard-on and must have put two and two together as she asked me directly if knowing that she had been unfaithful was the cause of my excited state.

I told her that it definitely was and that even knowing that she had been with someone else was somehow and unexplainable to me a real turn-on because I loved her so much that her pleasure was what I wanted the most. That my greatest pleasure was in knowing that she was enjoying who she was with. I also told her that knowing she was having sex with someone somehow made me love her more. That I could not explain why I felt this way did not bother me.

What followed was a watershed of two people who love each other crying from happiness that secrets would become a thing of the past. She told me of some recent trysts and how they made her feel. At one point she told me again that I was her true sole mate and that she now knew that I loved her and would love her even when she was unfaithful, which she admitted was likely to be often as she had an almost uncontrollable urge to have sex with a man if he came on to her with 'desire" and 'lust' in his voice and actions.

She was happy that I would still be there if she got home late and full of cum. At this point I still did not have the courage to tell her that I wanted, in the worst way, to watch her being taken and that I desired to see her being satisfied by another man.

In the months that followed I often brought home gifts of fancy and sexy bra and panty sets that I knew she enjoyed wearing when she was stepping out with one lover or another. All along my desire to see her being fucked by a well-endowed man remained a fantasy. Actually, it almost drove me nuts with sexual excitement when I would find her panties thick with dried cum or she would tell me a bit about a date she had.

Jen would tell me in advance about a coming date and when she would come home I would get a summary of what she had done but always had the feeling that there was so much more that she did not tell me. With time, my wife became bolder and even had some of the men come to the house to pick her up. Before she left she would always give me a big kiss and tell me she loved me and to not wait up.

The First Time Watching

A t one point I was doing well enough for us to get a timeshare apartment in the Caribbean hoping that we would have most of our time together swimming, sailing and fishing. We made friends mostly of older people who, I guess, had more leisure time. One year we brought some gifts to a friend of my wife's sister and her husband. His name was George and he was a retired executive. His wife was Alleen and she still ran a small shop in town. They were great showing us all around the island in our rented car but I couldn't help but notice that despite George's age, which I gathered was in his mid sixties, he was particularly attentive to Jen. That he was black intrigued me even more.

When George's wife was not around his hands were nearly always touching Jen's shoulder or her waist or arms. Once when I came in I saw his hand on her butt. When he saw me he instantly reverted to normal behavior. As we were on an island far from home it occurred to me that maybe this was the chance to get Jen to let me watch.

One day I had the opportunity to talk to George alone while we were out and we started talking about how I noticed that he liked Jen. He pretended innocence so I just came out with telling him that if he wanted to get closer to Jen, he had my permission and approval as long as I was nearby and it was not done in secret. He seemed surprised and questioned me further so I told him that I have always had the strong desire to see my loving wife being "satisfied by another man". Also that she was quite free to be with another man for her enjoyment and pleasure if that is what she wanted.

Well, from then on he did not stop touching her when I was around (and his wife wasn't). At night when we were in bed I told Jen that I was sure that George was attracted to her and what did she think. She then told me that she knew that he wanted her as when they were alone he always found a reason to hug her, fondle her bottom, and one time kissed her. She then told me that she saw that he got hard sometimes when around her.

I told her that I loved her and hoped that she did whatever she wanted to do. We made very passionate love that night. Jen's louder than usual orgasm attested to her being turned on by the possibility of being taken by George at some point in this vacation.

The next day we were to pick George and his wife up to go to an event that was to take place on the island. When we arrived at their house and went to the door George told us that his wife Alleen had to go into town to her sisters and would not be going with us. So, he said that before we went we had time for a drink or two. I noticed that he was more open with his touching of Jen's body and even sat next to her on the davenport with his arm casually around her shoulders. As I did not object, he had his approval to continue and he did.

After a couple of drinks, I had to go to the bathroom so I excused myself to go and relieve myself. Before I flushed I quietly peered into the living room and sure enough they were kissing and he was already playing with my wife's breasts. As I stood there watching, I saw him place my wife's hand on his lap and him loosen the top of her sundress and slide his hands down to her bare breasts and then I heard her moan.

He looked up at a point and looked me square in the eyes as he unbuttoned my wife's top and bared her breasts for his hands to play with. He then opened his fly to expose his cock. I then saw Jen take his cock in her hand and then I knew my dream was about to come true. I was surprised at how long and large George's cock was but did not get to see it for long as he guided my wife's head down until she opened her mouth to take what she could in. Then all I could see was her head bobbing up and down and George moaning and telling her in a normal voice to "suck it like a good little girl".

This went on for several minutes with George saying loud enough for me to hear such things as "suck it good girl" and "you love black cock don't you" and what really got to me and almost made me cum was, "After I cum in your throat we'll see how your pussy feels."

It didn't take to long before I knew he was cumming in my wife's throat as his moans grew louder and my wife was clearly swallowing a mouthful. George than told my wife to take off the rest of her clothes. While she was stripping George stood up and also undressed. For 65+ year-old man he had an absolutely fantastic muscular body looking much more fit than any 65 year old man I had ever seen.

His cock was longer by an inch or two but much thicker around than mine. I knew that my wife was in for some pleasurable fucking. He told her to stand before him when she was down to her panties. He then slowly lowered them while playing with her bottom saying, "My god, you have a beautiful ass, I am going to love fucking it".

As we had not done that, I had a twang of jealousy as I wondered if she would let him but hoping that she would so I could see it being done on the woman I loved. Once she stepped out of her panties he pulled her to his mouth and began licking her pussy to her great pleasure as indicated by audible gasps and moans. She looked over at me and our gaze met. I saw pleasure, lust and love in her eyes as she mouthed "I love you."

He then turned her around and looking back at me he said to her, "Bend over so I can get you ready for my cock". He then proceeded to lick her pussy and anus alternately to her great pleasure. As he was licking her she kept saying, "God that feels good" and "Don't stop". Then she had her first climax marked by audible moaning and almost screaming in pleasure, in ways I have not experienced with her.

George then asked her what she wanted to do next. She responded "put it in" to which he said "That was not very enthusiastic, put what in? My wife then said "Put your cock in me". His response was "Is that all? Tell me what you really want". "Beg for it". Guess she really wanted to get fucked as this started a torrent of "Please fuck me with your big cock, please" followed by "Please fuck me with your big black cock now, Please" and "I want you to fuck me now" as she lay on the couch and spread her legs.

George then asked her if this was OK with her husband to which she replied, "Oh yes but even if it is not I want to be fucked by you now". George literally pounced on her and with only a few stokes was buried in my wife's pussy to his balls. This triggered a second large orgasm and pleas of "More.. Faster.. Fuck me good" and that is what he did. I had never dreamed my wife could take such a pounding as she screamed to at least a couple of orgasms.

As he had just cum in her mouth he was able to pound her for what seemed an hour but was probably more like 20 minutes. I had pulled my cock out and had cum twice watching, the first with out even touching myself. He finally grunted and released his cum. The second time I was able to see his contractions and cum oozing out of my wife's vagina. God, what a sight, which I will never forget as it was the first time I actually saw my wife making love or rather fucking someone else and I was able to witness how vastly different his lovemaking was from mine as he used my wife for his carnal pleasure. To hear her moan through orgasms was the highlight but more was to come.

Once he pulled his cock out of her pussy, he pushed my wife's head to his groin and ordered her to "Clean it up good girl, there is more to come". My wife took as much of his momentarily flaccid cock in her mouth as she could and while she was cleaning his cock and bringing it back to life George turned to me and said, "I really enjoyed fucking your wife and looking forward to many more times" then, "That is OK with you isn't it", to which I said in a rather quiet voice, chocking back the emotion of jealousy and envy, "yes, of course, anything Jen wants".

After he was hard again he got up and lifted my wife into his arms and carried her down the hall to his bedroom. As they passed me Jen's and my eyes met and whereas nothing was said, the smile she had on her lips and the look in her eye said that she loved me but wanted to be fucked again by our host, George.

I followed them down the hall and got a glimpse of the room with the bed but George closed the door with his foot telling me that he wanted privacy. So there I was out in the hall listening to the moans and groans and utterances of pleasure from my wife and the bedsprings creaking and headboard hitting the wall at a very fast rate indeed. After my wife's second orgasm the noise stopped and I heard George tell my wife to "turn over and get up on your knees". After some almost screams of delight, my wife yelled, "god I love it this way, don't stop" – "please don't' stop."

I knew he was fucking her from behind doggie fashion and I knew that this was her most favorite position but I did not know that she would have so many orgasms doing it this way. It was hard just to listen and not see what was going on but I did not want to spoil my wife's enjoyment and I really was hearing her enjoy the fucking she was getting.

After what seemed like forever the bouncing stopped and George said, "I want that ass" to which my wife said, "I don't think I can take you in there as you are so big". What I heard next got me instantly hard as George said, "Just relax it will be OK" then "I want your ass to be mine". "I just love fucking white girls asses."

I couldn't take it any longer so I very quietly opened the door a crack and saw that he already had the bulbous head of his cock past her anal sphincter and as she moaned he kept inching his monster into her anus. Seemed to take forever until be was all the way in and now the utterances from my wife were oohhs and aahhs. I just couldn't believe what I was seeing with my own eyes as he went in and out of her well-lubricated ass. Wow, some site. I couldn't help myself, as the scene was so exciting, as I masturbated to a record, for me, third climax.

As they were nearing the end of their session, I ducked out to go back to the living room to relive what I had witnessed. I loved my wife more than ever as she trusted me enough to let herself go, in front of me.

Soon they came out of the bedroom and went in to the bathroom for what I thought was a shower. Yes, it was for a shower but when I heard more moans I peeked in the bathroom and George was fucking my wife for the third time; this time against the shower wall. She had her legs wrapped around him and was bouncing up and down moaning pleasurably with each bounce. I had to admit that his stamina and power amazed me and I knew that we would be seeing him again this trip and in future years.

When she finally came out of the bathroom she picked up her clothes that were on the floor and dressed while I watched. Even that was exciting as it reminded me as to why she was naked in the first place. She then came over to where I was sitting and sat on my lap, hugged me, and told me that she loved me and hoped I really enjoyed, "Watching, for the first time, my getting fucked by someone". I assured her that I loved her more than ever and very much enjoyed watching her receive such pleasure.

When George came out he sat down and we began anew our previous conversation about the islands history as if nothing unusual had been happening. At one point he asked me if I liked "Cricket" which I told him that I knew so little about it that I was not sure if I liked it or not. I admitted that I was curious as we had been coming to the island for a few years and had not yet seen a Cricket game.

CHAPTER III

More Then One

He then invited us back in two nights as the Caribbean team was playing the Indian team in India and it was to be televised. He said that 'they' were having some friends over and would love to teach me and us what Cricket was all about. At the time I thought that it was he and his wife and some of their friends but I was to learn, women rarely come to watch Cricket.

I guess I should not have been surprised when we arrived at his home two nights later that his wife was gone and two of his buddies were already drinking beers as the pre-match festivities were on. George gave my wife a long hug and an equally long kiss, which I saw as showing off to his friends. Soon after we arrived two more of his friends arrived. After introductions were made all around, Jen and I got a lesson about Cricket so we would know what was happening.

George sat on the couch next to my wife with me on the other side as the match started. As we watched he and his friends told us what was happening and how they expected the present batter to get a "Century". Heck I did not even know what a "Century" meant. I was a little anxious as he rather soon had his hands on my wife's legs going up and down under her skirt and it had to be obvious to his 4 friends what he was doing. He then put his arm around her and started almost casually feeling her breasts and I could feel her getting excited as I knew well how sensitive her breasts were.

I heard and I am sure the others heard George ask my wife how she enjoyed her last visit. I could see where this was going and felt my heart racing with this rather unexpected turn of events. Here was a room with 6 men (me included) and my wife and I sensed that 5 of them were going to pleasure themselves with my wife.

Nothing was said but I saw 4 pair of eyes watching more what was happening on the couch than what was on the television screen. When Jen was hesitant to answer, George asked her if she wanted him again. Her response was warm smile and a nod but I also saw smiles around the room.

George's hands had been under my wife's dress as had to be obvious to all in the room. He then said aloud to me "Chris, your wife is a very horny lady as she is wet already", followed by, "Help me remove her panties". I had not expected this to happen but slowly reached under my wife's skirt and lowered them first to her knees and then off while searching for a signal from her eyes. I couldn't help myself at this point as I put them to my nose and inhaled the aphrodisiac I had come to know of the scent of my wife's pre-cum lubrication. I was uncomfortably hard. While George was making out with my wife next to me and I was inhaling the evidence of my wife's readiness from her very moist panties, one of the guys came over and said, "Let me smell your wife's pussy" at which I reluctantly passed him her panties. Soon they were being passed around to all of the guys who were all smiles as they inhaled her smell.

George then got up and pulled my wife to him and while they were hugging, he raised her skirt baring her bottom to the room while he played with it. He then turned with her and walked down the short hall to his bedroom all the while fondling my wife's bare bottom for all to see. They went into the bedroom and I fought the urge to go watch as the 4 guys were too close by and I felt I had to be brave especially as they were all looking at me as often as they were the spectacle of my wife's bare bottom.

They started talking among themselves about what a great find George had made and they could hardly wait to get into her and have her suck them off. They seemed to be bragging about what, in fact, was likely to happen. They talked about my beautiful wife as if I was not there and what they were going to do. At one point one of them asked me "Is it true that this is your wife?" My nod was met with "Is she always this sexy?". Again I only nodded as I was too embarrassed to speak.

It had been quiet in the bedroom but now the room was filled with loud moans ending in a long scream, which told me that she was being pleasured indeed. At that point the guys all started to undress and talk among themselves as to who goes first. I had expected that they would want to fuck my wife but now I knew that it was going to happen. What I saw in the room was four guys and all had different size and shaped cocks just like in the locker rooms back in college.

One was my size or a bit smaller in the 7-inch range with a very large bulbous head. A couple were larger and about the size of George's at an estimated 9 to 10 inches but they were sure different. One had a gigantic head as large as a large plum and the other was thick at the base and almost tapered and the crown was the smallest diameter. The last was a monster in terms of both length (10 to 11 inches estimate) and diameter. Knowing that my wife was going to feel and maybe suck all of these had my juices flowing and my cock aching.

After what seemed like an eternity George came out and almost immediately one of the guys with his cock at full mast sauntered down the hall and into the bedroom. He must have started fucking her almost immediately as the sounds the bed squeaking and of a new orgasm filled the room. There were 'high-fives' around the room. George sat next to me and told me "Thanks for coming over and the offer of sex with your wife" and that "Your Jen is some woman who just cannot seem to get enough sex" "How do you keep up with her". I am not sure he really wanted an answer but asked the question just to be sure his friends knew the situation.

When the first guy came out he told his buddies that "George's girl is one hot fuck". Who's up for round three". The next was one of those with a cock the size of Georges but with the large head and he started down the hall commenting as he went so we could all hear, "Girl, are you ready for more lov'in" "Here I come get your mouth ready."

For a while it was quiet, which told me that he had her sucking him. I really wanted to watch but it seemed that this was not going to happen. After a rather long period of no sounds, once again the bed was squeaking and hitting the wall followed by the very sexy and familiar moans and wails of an intense orgasm. Then it was quiet, out he struts saying for all to hear, "Showed her what a good fuck was like" and amid snickers from his buddies he sat down to watch the match.

Jen later told me that he first put his cock to her lips and said "Suck it babe". She told me that she loved the large velvety soft 'helmet'. She also told me that after he came in her mouth he remained hard and simple impaled her when she was on her back. "he was good and I had a couple of great orgasms.

The next to go down the hall was the guy with a cock my size or maybe a bit smaller but he was what looked like very hard and sticking out as he went into the room. Again it was silent for a while and then the bed started squeaking and Jen was heard moaning with what must have been each stroke. This went on for a long time and finally we heard what must have been an orgasm but it was not as loud as the others.

Jen later told me that he made her lie on her stomach and then get up on her knees. He first licked everything from her clitoris to and including her anus. Than he told her that he wanted her ass, which is what he did. When he was done, he told her that she had the best ass he had known and said that the next time he wanted her to suck him off.

When he came out with an ear-to-ear smile he said to the group that "that girl has the best ass I have ever had" "I can hardly wait to do her again" as he again smiled broadly and sat down to watch the match. Then the last guy, the one with the gigantic cock got up and said to the group, "Now she will see what a real cock can do" as he sauntered cockily down the hall.

When he entered the room Jen was heard to say, "Wow, I'm going to love that one". Then all we heard was he saying, "Yes, suck it good babe". As he was speaking loud enough for all of us to hear in the living room, it was clear that he was a show-off. Well, he may have been but in a bit we heard the bed hitting the wall and I counted three orgasms as well as oohhs and aahhs and her saying, "Please don't stop" as she had multiple orgasms.

Jen later told me that when he came in the room he first asked her to get him harder with her mouth. She said to me, "Hon. He was so big that I could hardly get past a couple of inches but he did get hard". Then she said, "He was so big that I had my first orgasm as he was entering me. He had great staying power and as you must have heard, I had several orgasms"

It was almost an hour before he came out of the room with a cocky grin and a flaccid penis. George was about to go back to the bedroom when his phone rang. From what he was saying it was clear that it was his wife as he rather frantically motioned for the guys to get dressed. When he hung up he told them that his wife and some girl friends were on their way so they better get dressed and cleaned up quickly. He told them that they could stay but they all thought it better if the leave. "India was too far ahead anyway".

I went down the hall to the bedroom to get this message to the love of my life and she sure looked satisfied and well fucked. Giving her a kiss, I tasted the distinctive taste of semen, which got me hard instantly. I told her that I loved her but Alleen was on her way home so the "party" had to stop for now. She jumped out of bed telling me to grab her clothes and headed for the bathroom. I rounded up her clothes and brought them to her in the bathroom just as she was getting into the shower.

When I went back into the living room the guys who had all just fucked my wife were saying good bye to George and then to me they all shook my hand and said in one way or another that "Your wife is the sexiest woman I have been with in a long time and I really enjoyed the sex" One of them said, "Sure wish I could turn my wife into a "Hot-Wife"". I told him that I had nothing to do with her love of sex, which started in college before I met her. A couple of them thanked me and asked if we might do this again. I told them that it is always up to my wife but anything is possible.

After they left, I turned around to see George going into the bathroom so I quietly followed him. What I saw startled me as Jen was sitting on the commode naked and sucking George's cock. He kept saying, "suck it good, babe and I will give you what you want". As this continued, I got worried that Alleen might come home and this was not what I wanted to happen.

After George loudly erupted in my wife's throat, he grabbed her hand and led her to the bedroom. When I saw what was going to happen I asked him if he wasn't worried about his wife coming home while he was in bed with Jen. He then said, "Heck, she will not be home for a few hours as she never comes back until the Cricket match is over for the day" then he added, "These horny guys would have continued to fuck your wife all day and I wanted some more of her, uninterrupted, for myself."

The smile on my wife's face said it all and she then said, "Hon, come watch, I love it when you are around to see me being made love to", "I get even more excited when you are near", so I followed them to the bedroom as I was determined to not miss a thing.

Well, for the next 2 hours I watched as George fucked all of my wife's holes. His first cum was in her throat and after she sucked him to hardness, which did not take long at all. He then proceeded to fuck her in every position I could imagine. Her largest screaming orgasm was when he did her from behind doggie fashion, which I know is her favorite.

He had amazing staying power and stamina for a 65+ year old. He kept up a chatter of "You are the best fuck I have had in years", and "That's it, girl, contract those muscles, take my entire load", and, "Ride 'em cowboy" (when she was straddling him and supplying the action).

For her part she was having almost continuous orgasms and kept saying, "You feel so good, don't stop", and "Honey, he fills me so well", and "More, more, more, I want more". Most of her orgasms were of the 'screaming' type, which I do not hear that often when we make love.

After his second load it took a bit longer for him to get hard but when he was he lubed up my wife's ass and slipped it in her hole as if they had done this forever. My Jen was moaning like crazy and said, "Oh, his big cock fills me so good, I do not want it to stop". It took awhile but he finally deposited his load in my wife's bowels. I thought that this would be the end for this visit but I was wrong. George got up to go to the bathroom and take a quick shower and came back with a hard-on. My wife welcomed him back with legs spread apart and open arms.

This last one was, to me, almost the best as George slowly and deeply brought my Jen to orgasm after orgasm with her legs hooked over her shoulders. This was the first time that I could actually see a cock going in and out of her vagina. A real turn-on and my feelings of love were never higher. Yes, I had pangs of jealousy and thoughts about where this would all end but the feeling of joy that my Jen was being pleasured won out. When he finally came he rolled over and said, "Not sure I could do that again as good a fuck as she is". Made me very proud of my Jen.

They went to take a shower and I went back to the living room to relive what I had seen. Loved every minute of it. They came out all dressed as if nothing happened and Jen came to sit beside me on the couch. We kissed and hugged and she thanked me saying, "your being present was the best and got me so hot, I couldn't believe it". She then told me, again, that she wanted me present if we ever do this again. I remember thinking that now I would get my lifelong fantasies fulfilled.

We talked about a number of things for an hour more and when Alleen came home. I guess she assumed that we had been like this all day watching the Cricket match. Soon after we left as we were leaving the next day and we needed to pack. We said our goodbyes and George walked us to our car.

While walking out to the car he mentioned that he now has time to travel especially to see the US crazy sports such as American type 'football'. When he asked if he would be welcome if he were to come to our area of the US, we both said "definitely, "we have a room for you as well as a bed for all of us". We all laughed at that but I felt that if just might happen. As we pulled away he said "see you next year if I do not see you before."

CHAPTER IV

Reminiscing on The Trip Home

The sex we had that night was one of the best to that time. Each time I would think about George and his friends and Jen, I would get hard again. Jen kept commenting on my long 'staying' power. We did not talk much about what had happened except I did tell her that I really loved to see her enjoying sex as much as she did and hoped she had as good a time as it seemed. We spent the night in each others arms and I then knew that not only was our love strong but that this was not a one time thing.

We left the island by plane the next morning and both of us slept for a couple of hours as we were both that tired. We had even missed the beverage service as we slept. When we finally awoke and were snuggling, I asked Jen to tell me about some of her best lovers of the past. She looked at me and said, OK, I will. As you have guessed, I have had many lovers but, honestly only one Love. That is you, honey and I really mean it.

She then started, "I guess the one I remember about the most is my first lover". "I was in High School and my older brother had a friend who was over to the house almost as much as he was at his own home". "His parents were very rich and often out of the country and when they were gone, he stayed with our family." "He and my brother were inseparable friends in High school and still are good friends." My brother never knew about this story I am telling you about my developing relationship with my brothers best friend, Doug".

My love paused as if reflecting and then went on, "His name was Doug and I think I was in 10th grade when I first met him." " One night I had trouble sleeping and was walking down the hall and through their partially open door I saw him with his cock in his hand". "I didn't even know the word at the time but he was masturbating". "I may have seen my brothers cock but this was the first time I saw one that I remember". "I remember being frozen to where I was standing and watched with great interest as he brought himself off."

When he finished I ever so quietly went back to my room and all I could think of was Doug's cock squirting in his hands". "I was fascinated and hooked". Another reflective thinking pause and Jen continued, "For the rest of the year, I made a point to sneak down the hall and hope to see him playing with his cock". "Actually, I was able to watch him only a few times but the more I watched the more excited I became". "I even started doing the same thing to myself.

She went on, "Well, I guess it had to happen". "One evening he saw me watching". "He waved me in but I was so afraid that I ran back to my room and locked my door". I was so embarrassed that I avoided both he and my brother for almost a week. Then one evening, he came in while I was watching TV and just sat down beside me. I just did not know what to do but continued to stare at the TV. Finally he said, "Hey, Jen, You know what you saw was natural for guys and anytime you want to watch, just come on in".

"I really did not have a response but managed to say "Thanks" but do not know what I was thanking him for". Well, a few nights later I dared go down the hall to his room and sure enough he had his cock in his hand and this time when he waved me in, I came in and sat down at the end of the bed. He took his cock out and right before my eyes he masturbated till he came. This was the most I had ever seen of a cock and it sure got me excited. He told me that he liked it when I watched as it made him especially horny. It made me very excited and horny also."

"This went on where once or twice a week I would go to his room when everyone else was asleep and watch him masturbate. I guess, I was sitting closer and closer to him when one time he took my hand and placed it on his cock and the feeling was so pleasurable that I did not pull away. He then asked if I would help him to cum like he had done. I was so excited that I moved my hand up and down his cock like he had done until he shot his cum all over my hand and the bedclothes. My heart was racing as I ran back to my room and masturbated myself."

"Well, this went on for a number of months and I was now in my Senior year of High School. By that I mean that a couple of times a week or so, I would go to his room and masturbate him. At no time did he push me to go further but I was so fascinated by what we were doing and so curious as to what cum tasted like that one time I was masturbating him I leaned over to get a closer look and he shot it in my mouth. I was hooked, and he knew it. It was not long before I regularly put the tip of his cock in my mouth while I masturbated him. It was then that he started to touch and fondle me, innocently at first, until I knew I wanted more".

"All in all up to this point it had been almost 2 years since I first saw Doug masturbating and now I was sucking him and loving it. We still had not gone further and as I was a Senior and heard some of my girl friends talk about their sexual adventures, I decided it was my time. When I asked questions of my mom, who you have met, she had me start birth control pills so in case I went too far with a boyfriend, I would not get pregnant."

"I started to get more aggressive with Doug as I wanted him to take my 'virginity' in the worst way. Finally after almost two years and some time after my 18th Birthday, I got the nerve after I had sucked him to an orgasm to ask, and then almost beg him to show me how to "make Love" (as I put it)". I wanted to feel him inside me to give me pleasure like the pleasure that I was getting having his cock in my mouth." Little did I know that the pleasure of penetrative sex far out did anything I had experienced to date."

"Well, it finally happened and the experience and feeling just blew my mind. I had not conceived what the pleasurable sensation of an orgasm would be like. I was hooked for sure. Hooked on orgasms, not love. I knew that with Doug, who was my first, that I wanted to do this again and soon." As she concluded this story about her first time she noticed that my cock was very hard and said, "Gosh honey, you really do like when I tell you about an experience. Now I know how to get you hard."

CHAPTER V

Be Careful what you Wish for...

B y the time she finished with this story we started our decent as we were home. We weren't home for an hour when we made love again. I knew my life would not be what it was but had no idea what the future had in store for Jen and I except that I did know she would be having dates openly and that I would get my fondest wish of watching my love being fucked to orgasm again and again. I did not know what to expect more than that. I only hoped that her love for me, and my love for her, would not change.

Copyright © August 2011 - Chris Dawson

- - Epilogue - -

The Many Reasons Wives Have Affairs?

By **Chris Dawson**

Forward

This article goes over a number of the many unexpected and expected reasons a wife may have an affair. The woman marries for love and may still love her husband but for a variety of reasons she finds herself seduced or otherwise seeks sexual gratification or stimulation from other than the man she married. The reasons a wife enters into this adventurous life and chooses or is seduced into an affair are many. The results of the affair will surprise many, as there are men who can handle it and men who love and crave these activities and these outnumber those who are destroyed by the activity of a cheating wife. It turns out that most of our societal beliefs about females are grossly distorted and many are completely erroneous.

This is an article of opinion. This work is intended for adult readers 18 years or older. The story contains acts of adultery, sexually explicit language and sexual scenes that may be considered offensive to some readers.

Introduction

The following is a survey of what I know from what I have been told and what I have surmised from reading about this subject of "Why Wives have Affairs". This is based on not only personal discussions but from what I have been told through dialogs and confessions and what I have read on this subject over the years. I place no pejorative judgment on any lady who goes down this path of this type of adventure and has her needs fulfilled by someone other than the man she married if he does not or cannot fulfill her needs. I accept that her needs are real and it is in the husband's best interests to know his wife's needs as well as her interests and fantasies as early in the courting or marriage as possible and to accept her as who she is and becomes with love.

Setting the Stage

Who would have thought that the subject of wives who have sexual relations with men other than their husbands would be of interest to anyone but the sexually depraved and amoral among us? It is true that society, in general, has not viewed women who step out of their marriage and break their marriage vows in a favorable light yet have almost seemed to accept that males are free to do this same thing. At least this is the case in the past. The marriage vows state that the wife is to remain true to her man till death does them part and, as well the husband vows to do the same. To do otherwise is less than ideal and in some eyes, evil. At least this was the case and belief in the past. This said, there would be a look of surprise and shock if married couples, especially husbands, as a whole knew how may wives do just that i.e. adventure out of their marriage at least one time and usually more for one or more times for a myriad of reasons. The purpose of this article is to give you, the interested reader some of the reasoning behind why this phenomena (women being the sexually adventurists as much or more than men) is far more common that we all think we know.

The term for a woman being intimate with more than one man

is Polyandry (Poly- meaning "many" or "multiple". "Andras" is a Greek term for "man"). What with the changes we see in a society being more accepting of whatever is not the "Norm" this is not as surprising as it seems at first glance. In addition it is very well known that women can have far more orgasms at one time or over a period of time than men can in that same period of time.

Some even go so far as to say the monogamy is not how evolution intended us to be and is more rooted in male selfishness and ego than it is in the intention of evolution. Some say that Polygamy as generally practiced has it wrong as a woman can handle sexually far more men than a man can handle women.

There appears to be three general responses from Husbands who think, believe or have found out that their wife is having sexual relations with another man. These are:

1. Anger and Hurt, which may lead to a separation and possibly a divorce or at least harsh words. If the relationship survives, as most do, the relationship is different for sure as he may never know what is in her head.

2. Upset but accepting the reality possibly because he also has had affairs and doesn't want to open that door. The husband may just accept because he has no other choice, he believes. To him their love is greater than an affair can break up.

3. Accepting, excited, and possible pleased that his wife has a lover or lovers as this makes him sexually excited or it has been and is his fantasy and desire. This is how many Cuckold relationships start i.e. from the wife's actions and fantasies and not just the husbands idea.

Let us look at some of the common scenarios or stories that I have heard about or have been related to me by women who have gone outside of their marriage for whatever it is that they need or miss from their marriage. In all of these examples the main source of anxiety for the woman is what would happen if her husband found out that she had been "unfaithful" and had a sexual relationship with another man. For some the "excitement" of the affair trumps all other feelings such as guilt, remorse, or whatever else is her motivation.

The main reasons a wife will "stray" or have an "affair", at least initially, behind her husbands back are the following:

The Blosson wilts:

It is fair to say and with some general agreement that marriages start out at a high level of love and sexual activity. Depending on many factors this stays loving, affectionate, and sexual for either months or years depending upon many factors.

The passage of time familiarity, outside commitments (school and work mainly), and kids leads to marriages settling into a routine. This is not to say that the deeper feelings of love and affection go by the wayside but certainly we have all lived what happens when the excitement and 'Wow" stage of any activity passes and things become 'routine'.

The blossom of the rose of a marriage may start to wilt at any time depending on the needs, and I am talking about deep psychological needs, of either the husband or the wife. When in this stage of a marriage a wife meets a man (age not important) who reminds her of her past freedom it should not be surprising that some old feelings return. Feelings engendered by feeling wanted and desirable again. She may still love her husband but the excitement of a 'new' man may be overwhelming.

Women who are having adventurous relationships or affairs in this genre experience feelings unlike anything they have experienced since before they married. They feel "alive" and, in a way, "in love" again. Some do "fall-in-love" with the man they have an affair with and end their marriage but this is by far the exception.

Husband Unable to Satisfy:

One of the most common reasons for a wife to seek extramarital sexual gratification is that the wife finds that she cannot often achieve sexually exciting sex or orgasms because her husbands sexual equipment is either not large enough, he is not able to remain hard for long enough for her to orgasm, meaning her husband orgasms too quickly for her to achieve her own sexual gratification or orgasm.

She may love her husband very much but with time her needs are bound to surface and how better than to find and get satisfactory sex elsewhere as long as this can be done discreetly.

This should not surprise anyone, as it is known that 54% of guys have cocks between 5.50" (14 cm) and 6.25" (17 cm) long and the average penis length is 5.75 inches meaning there are as many smaller ones as there are larger ones. In addition to length they come in many different thicknesses (diameter) and hardness. Also, the size and texture of the crown as well as the taste of the pre-cum and cum differ among men just like breast and clitoris sizes differ in women.

Keep in mind that with time and especially after the birth of a child or two, an average or below average length and girth cock may just not be enough to bring the wife sexual fulfillment she has come to expect, wants, and needs even if she cannot see this as the reason for her restlessness. Some husbands know this and are accepting of their wife being satisfied by another man as long as the love relationship continues and flourishes.

Past Sexual History:

An increasingly common reason why a wife will seek sex outside of her marriage is that she has always had many and various sexual partners before the marriage and maybe subconsciously wishes or may be compelled for reasons unknown to her to continue that practice even though she is now married to a man she loves and cares for very much. To her, this outside 'sex' is pleasure ("It's just sex") and not "love". She may be guilty at first but rationalizes this activity as OK as long as she can keep it from her husband.

In todays society far more women start having sex in high school or early in college (at least) and may, by the time they find a man they think is the one to marry, have been with many men sexually. That this becomes a habit and their personal 'norm' should not be surprising.

So after marriage and once the romance and novelty has worn thin, or even if it hasn't, what is a logical next step? To these wives, getting laid by others is not a sign that they love their husband less but it is that old habits are hard to break. These wives usually crave the excitement of different men like what they knew before they married. Not only the pleasure but the excitement of a different cock or even technic is in their history. Possibly an attitude of "why not, it's just sex" may play a role.

I believe that this cause for a wife to go down this path of adventurous affairs is quite common in todays society where few women marry as virgins.

A Previous Boyfriend:

A woman who has dated a man who pleasures and satisfies her sexually in spades while they are 'dating', but with time she realizes that he is not the marrying kind so they part often with difficulty as the sex is, in her mind, the best. The parting is difficult but easiest if he moves on for job reasons. She then starts dating and, in time, meets a man who she falls in love with who is, in her eyes, worth marrying. They court and marry and all is going well except she finds that the sexual satisfaction is not quite what she was used to with the old boyfriend.

All is well as she is generally happy being monogamous until she gets a call from the old boyfriend who is in town and invites her for lunch. We can guess what happens after that lunch and after 2-3 thundering orgasms the likelihood of her seeing him again whenever she can is great.

The only challenge is keeping this from her husband unless she is aware of his fantasy of her being with another man as she may have told him about her past and perceptively noted he was turned on by this information. That, or she and her husband have shared fantasies in a moment of intimacy and honesty and she learns that he has an interest in watching her pleased by another man.

The fantasy is not as rare as generally thought and the new husband may learn for the first time that he gets excited and hard when his wife shares stories of her past experiences with the stud who wasn't good enough for her to marry. Usually it just does not occur to him that it would actually happen unless this new knowledge becomes his fantasy.

Desired to try a Black lover:

A woman who has a hidden or almost subconscious desire or wonderment as to what sex might be like with a person of a different race or ethnic background is more common that we would all expect. Very few, indeed, have not heard the saying of "once you try black you never go back". So along comes an attractive and sexy black man who puts the moves on a happily married monogamous woman and her curiosity wins her over for the adventure. Once she has tasted this illicit sex, the likelihood that she will want it again – and again is far higher than any of us believe.

The other aspect that has her curiosity is the myth that black cocks are quite a bit larger than white cocks. This may actually be true and once she has been filled to beyond her previous experiences and has been stimulated in places she has never felt before it may be difficult, if not impossible for her to stop. On top of that, she has now had the pleasure of far more thundering orgasms with this new lover than she ever had with her husband.

Would anyone wager as to whether or not it may be impossible for her to stop seeing this and other black lovers. The excitement of this taboo and illicit sex may be too much for her to stop. The wife may actually live what is said and 'never go back' except to her husband to keep her marriage on track.

At Work Away from Home:

In todays economy plus the increase in not only expectations but also opportunity for women to also have a career, the exposure to men in the workforce who would like nothing better than to take an attractive lady to bed whether or not she is married to someone else. That she is married means little or nothing except for the positive aspect that she is most likely to be disease free and would, for her reputation and marriage be discreet. This later is especially true if he is also married.

If at work a married woman is continuously propositioned or being exposed to desirable and maybe dominant men is it any wonder when at a company function or some time when her husband is away, she succumbs to his advances and gets seduced into starting an affair.

The excitement alone from forbidden sex with a new male could very well bring back the exciting and fond memories of when her husband was wooing her. That was a magical time in her psyche and here it is again. This is a very hard temptation to resist. She may love her husband but the temptation of new, exciting, and forbidden sex adventure may be overwhelming.

Keep in mind that sexual variety is not just a male craving. More and more women are finding that they have the same wants. What with the increasing number of married women in the workforce, is it any wonder that even more affairs do not start in the 'work' environment.

Succumbing to Power:

Another example out of the increasing number of married women working is when someone in power, like her boss, sets his sights on seducing her. He is in the position of arranging her travel and it may start out almost innocent but it is not difficult to envision a man smart enough and dominant enough to be top management echelon or owner of the company knowing the art of seduction. Once plied with compliments, gifts, wine, and flattery in addition to 'opportunity', what woman would not want to please her boss further?

She may love her husband very much and feel guilty about being 'unfaithful' but once done, the likelihood of this being done again and again is rather high. She may find that sex with her mate has improved as she learns to love new tricks and passes these off to her surprised but pleased husband. For this newfound sexuality she will, at least subconsciously, thank her lover boss.

As the lover boss is not married to his new bed partner, the possibility of his introducing her to his friends for the purpose of extending her sexual activity is quite likely. If she likes very much her boss or co-worker this extended sex may, at first, be to please him but once started may become almost like an addiction.

To help her Husband:

A woman is in a good marriage and gets wind of the possibility of her husband's possible advancement or there is a change of management and the new CEO is assessing the candidates for higher management positions. She meets or has known the (new) boss and he finds some reason to see her alone under one circumstance or another. He implies or even states directly that he is considering her husband for a major promotion but needs to know how committed the wife is to her husband's success.

Unless she is dim of wit she will see what is going on and might very likely tell him that she will do anything to help her husbands future but because she loves him anything she does outside of their marriage must be very confidential.

Her husband's boss now has his answer and the rest is history. He will see that the husband is out of town or otherwise occupied and then under the excuse of a dinner discussion, he will wine and dine her then take her to bed. Once done the likelihood of this being repeated is very high. The wife may feel very guilty about this activity but will rationalize that if no one knows about this activity and this has furthered her husband's career, what is the downside. She now knows that the upside is exciting orgasmic sex.

The benefits to her and her husband of the promotion will be her justification to continue the affair at her husband's boss' will. Should her husband be chosen for the promotion she will be grateful to the 'boss' and what better way to show her gratitude but to continue the sexual liaison.

She should not be surprised if his "will" is to share her with select friends. Once this formerly faithful wife has tasted and experienced orgasmic sex, including acts she would never have contemplated with her husband, with strangers as well as her husbands boss she would find it very difficult to stop.

A Submissive Needs Dominance:

A woman who is a bit or a definite submissive marries a man who is also on the submissive side or at least is not at all a 'take charge' or dominant personality. If her main deep down and maybe subconscious fantasy is being under the sexual control of a Strong Dominant Male (or Female), and thus be that Dominant's sexual submissive and her husband, who she may love, is not a strong dominant it is not difficult to see how easily she could fall prey to a dominant man on the prowl.

She may meet this overwhelming and dominant man in a variety of situations but be sure you know that a man with a dominant personality can spot a submissive woman quite easily. Once he spots her it is a matter of time before he has her doing his will, whatever that may be. Once she falls under his dominant personality she will very easily do his bidding even to the point of sexually pleasing him and doing his bidding, even with his friends. All of this is to succumb to whatever his dominance brings out in her.

It is not easy for people who do not have a submissive trait to understand the power of the subconscious feelings or desire to be controlled in any of several scenarios. To these individuals the desire to be tied up, restrained, controlled, or spanked is at least weird if not "sick". In fact the submissive may not even know that they are submissive until they are in the presence of a dominant.

The exposure to a very dominant man could come out of the blue. At any function where there might be dancing the wife may be asked to dance with a handsome well built man and early in the dance he might say, "I think you should let me fuck you", and then as she was recovering from such a direct line he might say, "Yes, I want to fuck you and I know you want it to happen." The woman will probable say, "But, I am married and my husband is right over there." She will know something will happen when his only response is to say, "Find the time and he can even watch." At this point she knows that it will happen and may even want it to happen.

Husband Sexual Dysfunction:

A normal woman who marries either an older man or a younger man who for several reasons (including health reasons) develops Erectile Dysfunction (ED) and she finds herself in a loving but an almost sexless marriage is an almost compelling reason for a previously monagaminous wife to seek or succumb to the advances of a man on the lookout for a new 'piece-of-tail'. Actually, she may be the one on the prowl even if she does not know it.

There is even an online service where the enticement to males states: "The #1 rule if you're having an affair is never to do it with a single woman. Instead, date a "married woman who has just as much reason to keep your affair a secret as you do."

This site goes on to say that a man will meet MILLIONS of married women trapped in sexless marriages and looking to have a discreet affair. The site implies that many of the women who list themselves are in "need" of sex for whatever reason. It is thought that the most common reason is that the husband cannot perform.

A woman who finds she is living with, and loving, a man who just cannot satisfy her sexually because of his age or a medical condition is bound to turn first to the printed word or devices to bring her sexual satisfaction either with or without her husband's knowledge. This only works for so long until the urges to be satisfied overcomes her monogamous beliefs and she either somehow meets or actually seeks satisfaction with a real man and not a story or a dildo.

Relief From a Sexless Marriage:

The woman may indeed be 'trapped' in a sexless or almost sexless marriage where her husband, who may not have sexual dysfunction, has seemed to have lost interest in sex due to his large increase in weight or at the expense of hunting, fishing, card playing, golfing, or a number of activities with his buddies leaving his wife to fend for herself.

Ignoring ones wife is a sure ticket and an open door, which can and most likely will be entered by one of the many men who normally come into the life of all housewives whether they are a 'stay-at-home' mom or are out in the workplace.

A woman of normal libido finding she is in a marriage where the only sex she is able to get is when she initiates it is a setup for any man on the lookout for a new conquest. It could be a neighbor, a delivery guy, or anyone who pays her attention. Being horny, whether the wife knows it or not, and wanting relief is a guarantee that an affair is right around the corner. A woman in a marriage where she perceives her husband has lost interest, whether this be the case or not, is very vulnerable to the desires of a man on the lookout for his next 'piece-of-ass'. It is believed by some that this is a very common way "Affairs" get started.

Cougar'sville:

How many women wake up one morning after they hit 40 years or 50 years old and wonder, "How in the hell did I get to be this old." They will think or say that it seemed like yesterday that they were in college and partying every weekend and having sex often. Then marrying and enjoying sex almost nightly. All that did not seem that far away but here they are "an old lady".

Almost the worst is turning 50, which she dreads and maybe she just recently has become a "grandmother" to top it off. She feels like an old lady but does not look like an old lady at least if she believes her husband, her friends and her kids.

Yes, part of dreading turning 50 has led her to take off a bit of weight so now when she goes to the gym or looks in the mirror she becomes less depressed. It has seemed to her that some of the young men (and even older men) are looking her up and down. Oh, and there are other happenings. She finds the children of her friends and younger co-workers seem to come on to her. All this embarrasses and surprises her as she has been monagaminous and faithful to her husband and having an affair has not (yet) entered her mind.

She takes comments she hears as compliments but does not think they mean anything. Well what happens should her husband throw a 50 year birthday party at a downtown hotel and she gets talked into dressing more sexily than she has ever dressed in the past. As the evening progresses and the alcohol flows she will hear what she was not supposed to hear like; "Wow, she looks far younger that 50", or "She has been my favorite MILF since high school", or Wow, I would sure love to get into that Cougar."

Even her girlfriends, neighbors and co-workers get on this "Cougar" bandwagon. As this gets into her head she finds she is dancing almost every dance with guys as old as her son. If her husband drinks too much and goes home early what is the bet that one of her friend's sons dances away her inhibitions and takes her to bed. Once started, we all know, this will continue.

When the Cats Away:

The husband who spends far too much time in school, on the

road, or at building his business and less attention to the woman he marries may as well give her a "hall pass' to seek others as this is what most bored women do. It is not that they do not love their husband but when needs are not met – even if the 'need' is not readily known to the woman. This is similar to the woman who is in a sexless or almost sexless marriage.

When "the cat's away, the mouse will play" is the ageless saying but think about how this fits in a real life situation. This is especially true early in a marriage when the wife is in the peak of her sexual activity and misses the excitement of regular sex.

Take this away from her and a loving and faithful wife may be swayed to try something new. Ah, the excitement of a new adventure or, in a time of weakness, she might fall for a seduction ploy from an acquaintance, a friend, or neighbor. What better to do but slip under the sheets with a neighbor or friend who, by observation, became aware to the wife's needs and steps in to be her 'friend' when her husband is absent? To keep this adventure secret is the wife's biggest concern.

Revenge:

When a woman suspects and/or later learns that her husband is having an affair she might just get angry or create such a fuss that the marriage crumbles. If the marriage is to the wife's advantage, she might use the approach of "What is good for the Gander is good for the goose" and start saying "yes" or "maybe" to the men she meets where she has been saying "no" to since she got married.

Knowing her husband is 'fooling around' lessens considerably the guilt she would have felt if she had been the initiator of the extra-marital activity. Now she can get laid and get new and maybe more stimulating sex and not be guilty. It is believed that some women actually use the excuse of they "think" their husband is cheating so why can't they get in on the fun. They have no proof and it may not be true but if this reason lessens their guilt at being unfaithful why not use it.

In a similar vein, a wife may be upset following an argument with her husband and in a moment of anger she is a set-up to be seduced by the nearest male. Once she has tasted this new and exciting sexual experience she may find it hard to stop or may not want to stop even as she may initially be consumed with guilt.

Tired of Control

A husband whose personality or insecurity demands that he have total control over his wife can expect the same result as if he gives his wife a "hall Pass" to be free and do what she wants at least once in a while. This 'control' by the husband will get frustratingly boring and she will think about and may plan an escape. What better escape than to be in the arms of a man who she thinks will not be controlling.

The control may be because he is very jealous of any and all of her friends. He will question her at length if he sees or suspects that she has even talked to a contact who is a man even if this man is a friend or neighbor. He will get angry should she dance with another man at some function where there is dancing like a wedding even if he does not like dancing. If she dares to seem to be having fun and liking the attention, she will learn to expect the third degree of questions.

The term "Possessiveness" may describe the jealous controlling husband. Initially the wife may interpret this as his undying love for her but with time she will yearn to be free and her thoughts will then be that her husband does not trust her. There is no doubt that a woman in this type of relationship will crave some time to herself free from the oppressive yolk her husband has covered her with. Many an affair has started with a wife wanting to have some control of her life.

Because she can:

Marriage in the 21st century is very different from marriage in the last two centuries if one knows history. Far more women are now in the workforce and in some case have achieved a status equal to that of the male. Some evidence of this change is the increase in the divorce rate in the last 50 years. What was once 'rare' is now, sadly, almost common.

There is a steady increase in the number of women, for example, in Politics, as University professors, as doctors, as lawyers, or even as engineers, which has given women throughout the world far more confidence and 'macho' than their sisters did even 50 years ago. Women now are more in control of their lives than ever before. With that control they now have the confidence and aggressiveness to call the shots at work and at home.

In that position of authority, which in the past was only the domain of men they now can and do call the shots in their lives and this includes whom they take into their bed. They may be the initiator of an affair "because they can".

A Medical condition:

There is a medical condition known as "Manic-Depressive" psychoses or any of the subsets of this condition where psychological hyperactivity is a part of the process.

Not all, but many women in the manic phase of this illness become hyper-sexual and actually seek sexual activity to satisfy sexual needs quite different from the needs when this same lady revolves back into a more normal phase.

Genetic booster:

This reason is perhaps the most unbelievable and certainly the least common. The wife finds that she has married (for love) into a family of less than successful people and discovers that her husband, who she may truly love for his good traits, is not very bright or not as dominant as she think he should be.

This woman will actively seek intelligent men, even nerds, and seduce them for the sole purpose of having bright kids who might make something of themselves when they grow up. She will frequent libraries, go to symphonies and attend lectures at the university while being dressed sexily but not slutty. She will make herself available and accept invitations for "coffee" and more. Her husband will almost never attend these functions, as they are not his 'thing'.

As odd as this sounds, it is very real. There are both men and women who have minor inferiority complexes who actually look for a mate who has the markings of intelligence. In college it may be the "Cum Laude" graduate or the Phi Beta Kappa or the person with multiple degrees. For whatever the perceived reason, the wife sees an opportunity to have smart kids and finds a way to get the person between her legs again and again hoping to get pregnant and then to convince her husband that it is his child.

None of the Above:

Then there is the group of women who after 3-4 years of marriage just turns off on sex with her husband. The reasons are many but many do not know why themselves. The reason may not, initially, be a boyfriend or another lover but with time these are sure to follow.

When this happens and the wife gives as a reason that she needs to 'find herself', the marriage is most likely to end in a divorce. When the first boyfriend emerges this only expands the confusion going on in these women. The 'unfaithful' woman is also typically in pain, the pain of choosing between their husbands and their new love interests. The "high" from the later often wins out. They typically believe that what they are doing is wrong and unfair to their husbands, but yet are unable to end their affairs due to the emotional "high".

Those who elect to stay married and continued their affairs state that marital sex was improved by maintaining the extramarital relationship with or without the knowledge of their husband.

Conclusion

There are many reasons why a woman in a seemingly loving and happy marriage, at least on the surface, would find herself contemplating stepping outside of the marriage and having a sexual adventure by sexual relations with another man without the knowledge of her husband. There are also many more women than most men think who would take this step. Female infidelity will not only continue to be extremely common but it will also continue to be on the rise according to Michelle Langley the author of "Women's Infidelity: Living in Limbo."

The major conflict these women face is how, when, or what to tell their husbands that they have been 'unfaithful', if ever. This comes up when either their guilt becomes overwhelming or their love for their husband is such that by the admission they are sure that everything will be OK and they will be forgiven. If "communication" is part of the couple's marriage, this has a greater chance of the affair 'ending well'.

In all of the scenarios above when the wife has an outside affair she is quite likely to do acts she had never or would never do with her husband such as interracial sex, oral sex, anal sex, or even group sex. Once she experiences these acts from beyond her marriage, the husband may be the beneficiary of her new sexiness, learned technics, and acts.

In the end it is invariably the husbands love for his wife and his understanding about how this came about that determines what happens to the relationship next. Many husbands, for many and varied reasons, accept that their wife has had 'sex' with another man and if their ego is not damaged they accept what has happened and move on. In some cases they realize that the wife did what he had done and the marriage takes on a new and renewed vigor.

Keep in mind that not all affairs end well. There are wives who literally fall in love with their new lover and think that by divorcing their husband and marrying the new man that all of their previous problems will be solved. As she met her new "love" during a hidden relationship from her husband she does not think that this could happen again or that her new husband might always wonder if his new wife could ever be faithful. Not the best way to start a marriage.

Some husbands find that they are turned on by their wife's activities and in many cases, the husband and wife realize pleasure from her sexual adventure as a "Hot Wife" while the husband remains in a normal monogamous sexual relationship with the wife. This defines the classical Cuckold relationship, which is more common today than many would expect or admit.

In the end, the relationship between a husband and wife is only as good as the energy and love both parties add to the mix. A good marriage should be able to withstand upheavals and trauma if the foundation is good communication. It is true that "communication" is the glue that keeps many marriages together for a lifetime.

One marries for love and companionship and the path a relationship takes, whether to an early separation and divorce or to old age, depends on the level of communication and 'trust' that is present from day one or has developed over time.

The ~~End~~ Beginning.

ADENDUM; A dating site for Married women (and men)

Comments by "Noel Biderman" from the Ashley Madison site.

"If you are "stuck" in a sexless marriage and want to discreetly find likeminded individuals in your same situation Ashley Madison is the world's most famous dating website for married people looking to meet new married people looking to have fun on the side, no strings attached."

"Ashley Madison (2001) is the most famous name in infidelity and married dating. Ashley Madison is the most recognized and reputable married dating company. The site states, "Our Married Dating Services for Married individuals Work". Ashley Madison is also the most successful website for finding an affair and cheating partners."

"Thousands of cheating wives and cheating husbands signup everyday looking for an affair. Married Dating has never been easier." "If you are married you probably have felt lonely, and sometimes you have felt like your life needed a change. We understand that many cheating wives and cheating husbands do not want to lose the stability of the marriage. **Cheating wives come on Ashley Madison looking to discreetly meet new people and live a brand new adventure without having to worry about getting caught or in any way jeopardizing their marriage."**

"Ashley Madison is an online place where cheating wives and cheating husbands can meet and find that lost spark from their relationships and refresh their love life. On Ashley Madison, it does not matter if you are married or not, **cheating wives are all looking for one thing: to feel desired**. Think of this website as a safe place where you cheating wives can find great married men or single men that will make you feel sexy and wanted again."

There is nothing wrong if you are married and feel the need to try something new with another men or another woman. Just because you find yourself in a committed relationship does not mean that you are not human and you have to stop feeling wanted and desired. Cheating wives come on Ashley Madison looking to make that change happen, and you have the freedom to initiate contact with who you want and when you want."

"If you are married and are looking to discreetly find people in your same situation we know it can be difficult and that is why **Ashley Madison** is designed to offer maximum privacy and discretion while allowing you to connect with other married men and married women in your area."

"Registration is simple, in 30 seconds you will be able to browse thousands of profiles of people that just like you are looking to have an affair and meet people outside of their marriage. Pick a nickname and answer a few simple questions on what you are looking for, and you are all done!" Take advantage of the affair guarantee package, we are the only ones that can guarantee you will have an affair, or your money back. **Life is Short. Have an Affair.**

Guide to a Cuckold Relationship

By **Chris Dawson**

Forward

The Author of this guide has based his recommendations on some years living the lifestyle and gleaning from others involved in this fetish. The first edition of this Guide first appeared on FetLife and garnered many favorable comments and the request to make the Guide more available.

This Guide is primarily written for men who have the desire or wish or fantasy of seeing their wives in the arms and being taken sexually by another man. This activity is "Cuckolding" and the man whose wife has sex with another man is a "Cuck". Being a "Cuck" is exciting and desired by many men..

Introduction

Cuckolding takes what is perceived as the largest threat to a marriage and turns it into something that binds a couple closer together. This lifestyle will bring a couple even closer emotionally than ever before – even for couples who already have a good relationship. The key to make this relationship work is 'communication". Cuckolding is not "Cheating". ***Cheating is a violation of trust; cuckolding is an expansion and exploration of trust and love.***

At an instinctive level, polyandry or polyamory (sexual variety) is actually more natural than what we practice today. There are many who say that genetically, humans were never designed/intended to be monogamous beings. Keep in mind that in the animal world females most often have many mates. It is also well known that females can have far more orgasms and have sex with far more partners than can a male. Cuckolding allows a female to get more sex and a couple to experience greater sexual satisfaction while still enjoying the other aspects of their relationship.

This should surprise no-one as it is well known (but not readily admitted by many men) that women can have many orgasms at one sitting or period of time. Yes, a woman can have sex for hours on end whereas a man can only have a limited number of orgasms. Yes, there is the rare man who can have 3 or 4 orgasms at a given period of time but most of us admit (sadly) to maybe having a couple of orgasms unless we are quite stimulated (such as watching our wives being pleasured by a cock other than ours).

Many wife who goes down the path of having affairs – mostly behind her husbands back – state that they love him dearly but he can not keep up with their sexual appetite. Some further state that have an insatiable sexual appetite and need to relieve the tension before it ruins their marriages or that they are a very sexual being and just love sex in all forms.

Cuckold marriages can evolve into a great variety of preferences. I have seen cuckold marriages that range from those in which cuckolding wives enjoy subjecting their husband's to humiliation and punishment, to those in which wives will have sex with other men in front of her husband as a form of entertaining them, to just about everything in between. Most couples, however, have very loving marriages with playful arousal and denial that seem conventional in every way except that the wife dates and beds other men while her husband remains faithfully hers.

Cuckold Definition:

A cuckold couple is normally a couple wherein the female seeks on her own or is encouraged by her husband / partner to seek sexual stimulation/gratification from other males. This may be because of any of the following or a combination of this list where the husband:

- Perceives or knows that he has an average or smaller cock and thus believes that he can never fulfill all of the wants, needs, and desires of his wife and, because he loves her very much, really wants her to know this pleasure.

- May be bisexual, whether he knows it or not, and wishes to have his partner under the sexual control of other men, and, perhaps subconsciously, also wishes for himself to be under the same sexual control even to the point of fantasizing some male-male sexual contact. May also desire or feel the need to suck the ejaculate from his wife's/partners various holes (as a bisexual submissive humiliation act) and also may desire to suck clean any males penis that have penetrated his wife's/ partner's vagina or anus. This later is for sure a bisexual act that may be wanted if only out of curiosity.

- May also wish to feel humiliation/embarrassed in knowing or seeing that his partner is intimate with other males for sexual satisfaction, and that the feeling of humiliation, anxiety, and jealousy is a total sexual turn-on to that male.

- Through medication for various medical conditions or

unknown reasons, has found that he no longer can get a hard-enough erection to pleasure his wife by penetration and thus wishes her to find sexual pleasure/gratification elsewhere. Do not discount ED as a stimulus for a male desiring his wife to be sexually active beyond the marriage.

- Simply feels that seeing or knowing about other males fucking his wife/partner is a tremendous sexual turn-on for him for reasons totally unknown to him. Ladies, you have no idea how many men have this desire, fantasy, or dream.

- Is Dominant in the relationship and wants to control his wife in all aspects including who she spreads her legs for. His main pleasure is 'control' and that he is a better lover than anyone he has acquired for his pleasure. This is one type of "Alpha-Cuck".

Whereas this guide was written for males who want a cuckold relationship, the other side of the coin should be respected and known. There are couples where the initiation of the relationship begins with the wife's desires, need, or wants. It may be that the wife:

- Finds that she cannot often achieve orgasm because her husbands sexual equipment is either not large enough, is not able to remain hard for long enough for her to orgasm, and/or her husband orgasms too quickly for her to achieve her own sexual gratification or orgasm. She may love you, her husband, dearly but knows that you cannot keep up with her sexual needs. A vibrator might help but, to her, there are sexier ways.

- Who always has had various sexual partners before the marriage and wishes or may be compelled to continue that practice even though she is now married to you. She may love you with all her heart but isn't it better that she sees others with your knowledge than behind your back.

- Fantasizes being under the sexual control of a Strong Dominant Male or Female, and thus be that Dominant's sexual submissive and her husband, who she may love very

371

much, is not a strong dominant personality. She fell in love with you for important reasons that did not include her deep down submissiveness. May have a strong Dominant personality and may wish to control, embarrass, or humiliate her husband as she knows it is something that may or does excite him and thus will submit to an outside Dominant's sexual demands and control.

Getting Started:

In the beginning, Wives, when first approached about the idea of being enjoyed by someone else, often first assume that you, the husband, have lost interest in her for this idea to interest you or that you, the husband, are looking for a reason to do the same thing. This later must be clearly disavowed from the start. The idea that you have lost interest in your wife is quite untrue and quite opposite of the truth. In fact, it is the wife's appeal to you and other reasons (see above) that fuels the erotic appeal you have of sharing her with another man for her pleasure.

All the cuckolds I've known have stated that this arrangement felt 'strangely natural' once they became comfortable that the marriage is solid and rather than being replaced, the boyfriend or lover is simply part of an expanding 'family'.

Regarding the new "boyfriend/lover", many of the qualities that make an alpha male/Dom/Bull appealing to women romantically and sexually also make them very much less suitable as a life-time marital partner, which leads back to why young women tend to be attracted to and date males doomed to disappoint them from a relationship standpoint. My best advice is to marry for love and companionship and cuckold for pleasure – hers and yours!

Making of a "Hotwife":

Simply put, a Hotwife is a married woman who, more or less openly engages in sexual activities with other men. This ideally from your point of view is in addition to sexual activities with you and not in place of them. There are some "Hotwife's" who will minimize the sexual contact with their cuck husband especially when they are on the prowl. The look (dress etc.) and feel of the Hotwife lifestyle is simply the tools used by a Hotwife when attracting other men for sexual encounters. That you assisted in this transformation is lost in time except by you.

Step one for the husband: Go slow, you will not arrive at your destination overnight. It is only the effect of many and persistent small steps that will bring this lifestyle into your life unless it is your wife who initiates the action. Forget everything that **you want** your wife to be as a Hotwife. It is not applicable here. This is **not** about **you**. It is about your wife and the cultivation of her needs and desires.

The key to understanding how this change takes place is to realize that you can have what you want when your wife gets what **she** wants. She will, however, usually need reassurance that her seeing and sleeping / fucking others will not mean you love her less or that you want to see other women. I cannot stress enough that an open communication based on real love is the key to success.

There is no way that you could ask your wife today to switch her lifestyle around and be a "Hotwife" tomorrow. First she would most likely not do it and chances are she would both not like it and would think less of you for suggesting it. But by being lovingly persistent, but not sneaky, over time she will not be opposed to the changes. She will discover in herself that she likes it and it has not adversely affected your love for her – conversely she will see that is has enhanced your relationship and, in addition, she will now know that you are committed and faithful to her alone.

Feelings:

The toughest part of considering a Cuckold relationship is the feeling of inadequacy and jealousy you will feel with your wife being with any other man sexually especially if you suspect or know that he has a larger cock or is a better lover. This is especially true if your time to orgasm is regularly short. You have to realize that, yes; size may play a role in your wife's decisions. The size, shape, and thickness play a role in any woman's thinking. All of these characteristics of the male organ are a visual and physical turn-on for women. Know that the characteristics of a cock play an important role in his psychological effectiveness in dating/mating.

The husband must know that all cocks are different in addition to length and circumference. The head/crown/glans is the most different. She will find that the size and texture as well as the taste of the pre-cum is very different among her male lovers. In some men the head is up to twice the diameter of the shaft and in others it is the smallest diameter. It can also be safely said that no two heads / crowns / glans have the same texture or 'feel'. This alone is an attraction to some wives and plays a role in their becoming a "Hotwife".

In my view, cuckolding is most effective and enjoyable when practiced as a threesome. This means that for wives who are primarily having random hook-ups with different men or primarily meet their boyfriend away from the home are missing out on some of the best experiences in cuckolding and you are also missing out on what you need and want. The reality is that a steady guy or a small stable of reliable companions for your wife is not only less risky in terms of physical and health safety, but is much more rewarding in terms of an experience. In fact, there are fewer risks for a happy couple with a steady boyfriend than there are for the wife who is hooking up with random males you or her know very little about.

This said, to be sure a "new conquest" to your Hotwife is as pleasurable as any new conquest was to you when you were single. If you want her pleased, you will not discourage this. This does not negate what I said in the previous paragraph. Keep in mind that no two cuckold relationships are the same. Oh, I said that before?

With time and after the outside dating has started, the advice I would give to the wife is the hope that she, of course, gives you a kiss goodbye in front of the 'date' before she leaves and immediately reinforce this with a kiss to her boyfriend and let it be known how sexy it was to kiss him in front of you. This turned me on but may not be for you but, as I have said, no two cuckold relationships are the same.

Next, I would suggest to the wife that she invite the lover/boyfriend in for a few minutes before she leaves on her "date" if this is the arrangement. She should let him know beforehand this is what she wants and let the boyfriend know how much it turns you on to kiss him in front of you (her husband). Hopefully, she will think about calling you during her date and let her boyfriend listen as she teases her cuckold (you) with at least a partial description of what's going on and then tells you everything when she comes home.

How to get started:

Dress is everything and you must tell her repeatedly how good and sexy certain clothes make her look, you will notice that she wears those particular clothes more often not because you like them but because she likes the reaction and attention she gets from you. The best-kept secret in using words of reassurance is what I call third party verification. It is really all about perception. If she believes someone is checking her out then she will like it. No one would argue that compliments are good for ones ego and self-assurance. Possibly, make up something about someone else looking at her or a comment that someone else made about her. Do not overdo this or be phony as if you wife perceives that you are less than honest all bets are off.

Unless your wife is an absolute prude it is OK to ask to wear something just for you on occasions when you go out. Ask her to wear a nice lacy bra, a sheer bra, or some article of clothes that you like. Maybe, on special occasions a thong, no panties or something like that which you have purchased for her. Even just asking her to wear something around the house or just in the bedroom will let her know that she is desirable. Of course, heartfelt compliments about what she has on is always helpful. Whatever you say, be honest and genuine.

Treat your wife with respect and compliment her often on her clothes especially the sexy ones. Pretty soon She will be dressing better so that she can keep getting the comments. The real goal here is to get her desiring the compliments about being sexy even from other men. Please be genuine in your compliments.

The types of clothes that she should want to wear on a regular basis, which will attract attention and bring compliments are real stockings, sheer bras, decorative stockings and shorter skirts. As the husband, you should carefully and very slowly make less available her old bras and bad clothes. Sexy, lacy underwear will make her feel sexy even if her outer-garment clothes don't. Be respectful about her clothes but remember how one looks on the outside often mirrors how they feel inside.

At one point consider buying her an ankle bracelet and have her wear it on her right ankle. It doesn't matter what kind at first. After she gets used to wearing it (with frequent compliments from you) then get her a new one with the little slave bells on it or a heart. This will tell males in the know and on the lookout that your wife is approachable. She may be quite surprised if she is approached but she will also be flattered and who knows what else she will be feeling.

Never miss an opportunity to tell your wife that some guy was checking her out - her shirt / skirt or whatever. I hope you realize at this point that it is completely irrelevant if another person actually says anything or not but do not overdo this or be phony. She will pick this up. Tell her more often how good she looks in a specific outfit. Use words like; sexy, hot and frisky. Tell her how you like that one blouse that is cut low because it shows her cleavage when she bends over.

Tell her how that skirt really accents the shape of her sexy bottom/

ass. Tell her that you were thinking about her all day wearing the clothes she had on and that they made you really horny. The reason for telling her these things is not only because they are true but also to keep in the front of her mind that she is sexy and desirable to you (and others).

The Black Experience:

An added element of excitement or thrill is to encourage her looking into a man of a different race. The contrast alone between a dark lover and a white wife can be an immense thrill for both the wife and you, her cuckold. Many, many white women have the secret fantasy and wonderment about what sex with a black man would be like. Foster and encourage this as the rewards may be great for both of you.

Guys, you would be astounded or very surprised at how many women have an internal and often quite hidden desire to be with a man of another nationality especially a black man. The contrast in their mind is very stimulating and they all have heard at one point in their life that "If you try Black you will never go back". Then there is the urban legend that all black men have much larger cocks than white men. This may be only partially true but your wife's curiosity about what it would feel like to be fucked by a large black cock is real.

If your wife is white, believe me she looks at handsome black men with a special eye. To open her eyes and mind is your task and will be your pleasure if and when you succeed.

Black doms love white married women for myriad of reasons including:

- They like telling a white married woman what a good girl she is, or how good it feels to be "inside" her, filling her with their cum.
- They like cumming in a white married woman's mouth, knowing that her husband will kiss her later, and when

he does she'll get a little moist just thinking of what he is tasting.

- They love hearing a white married woman beg them to fuck her, because they know she deserves the attention and pleasure not to mention her hidden desire to be with a black man.

- They love fucking in the bed she sleeps in with her husband, her white nakedness pressed against his black skin.

- They like hearing a married woman thank them after she has been well fucked as an "adulterous" lady.

- They like knowing her husband might fuck her later (after they did) and wonder why she is so moist and loose.

- They enjoy feeling-up a married woman in a public place, where others might see her. Gives her so much excitement and her erect nipples betray her naughty pleasure.

- They like a white married women's sense of time. Get right to it and don't need a lot of priming. But always ready for a slower re-do.

- They like it when her husband goes down on her. Knowing that he is getting more than her cum and secretions!

In addition, a Black Dom will heighten your anxiety and humiliation as he takes charge of your wife's sexual needs. There are Dom's who get off on breeding, so before you go down this path, make sure you can live with the consequences. Again, *marry for love and companionship and cuckold for pleasure – hers and yours!*

Denial:

Adding "denial" to the equation is often employed. Even among cuckold couples where intercourse is mutually satisfying, forms of denial can help make good sex great sex when structure is provided around when and how such couplings can take place. When a couple offers this authority to their Dom, it not only relieves the wife of the guilt that can come with her husband's denial, but increase the bond between the couple and their Dom or boyfriend.

Most wives involved in a relationship with a lover take comfort in having him play a role in establishing her husband's denial. This is a natural extension of the dynamics of cuckolding.

Communication:

This is a touchy subject but if you can get your wife to talk about one of her past sexual experiences before she met you then it is really good foreplay. The advantage to this is that after you and her talk about it then she can see how much you are really turned on by it.

Once in a while tell your wife that she must have been having a good sex dream because you woke in the night and she was moaning pleasurably and moving around in the bed just like when "We make love".

Make sure she knows and feels comfortable with your love and desire to see her happy and your disdain for seeing others yourself.

Public Exposure:

With time, one of your "dates" with you, your wife and a "boyfriend" could be for shopping for sexy clothes. As much as men don't enjoy shopping, they do when it's for sexy outerwear and underwear/lingerie, which she would usually try on while shopping. Yes, it would be humbling for you, the cuckold, to be present with the "boyfriend", but also very erotic for you when you reflect on it and very empowering for her "boyfriend". Imagine the stares, the giggles, the jealousy as other women watch your wife with two men – one obviously you, the husband, and the one she is most obviously more flirtatious with than you.

Then, If you can arrange for a good friend to dance with her and touch her seductively and she sees that you are not angry but, later, turned on by it. This gets her used to having other men touch her, she now knows it's OK with you as she sees first-hand how horny it makes you. But mainly it creates a desire in her that she will need to have recurring attention for.

Up until this point it has been all about getting her in the right frame of mind and to help and encourage her to want the attention. After that first touch from another man though, it is time to move forward. It is no longer a question of "if" or "what" it is only a question of "when" and "how".

Before you try to meet someone who may be a potential lover for your wife, go back and reinforce wearing the right clothes and the ankle bracelet.

The next most important thing is to often and sincerely let her know how much you love her and how turned on you are when she plays around with another man. You are her husband and she will naturally want reassurance from you. The goal is to make her want your reassurance that she is sexy, hot and desirable when she is even thinking of having sex with another man and this makes you love her all the more.

First Time:

After the first time she has sex with another man she will be unsure about how she feels. As important as "good and honest communication" is, the first thing you would ask should probably not be if she was OK with it because it may create doubt in her mind. In my view, you should focus on how hot she is and how you know how much the other man liked being with her. Also tell her again and again how much you love her. I do not think it wise to mention the words trust, guilt or jealousy. It must be assumed that she should be having sex with other people and that both of you approve and like it.

It has been proven that routine events in a person's life that is repeated for three or four weeks will become habit. Just make it common and routine for her to have sex with other men. Remember at the beginning of this guide where we were talking about her wearing a different blouse or skirt or you telling her that some guy was checking her out? It all works over time if you are patient.

Sexy is, is sexy does. She needs to show off her best assets. Tell her to let the skirts and dresses ride high enough so that other people can see that she is wearing stockings and garters. A woman wearing stockings and garters along with the ankle bracelet is very likely to be taken as a sign by many dominant men that she needs and wants sex. That you approve will be obvious.

No matter whether true or not, NEVER, Never miss an opportunity to tell her how much attention she is attracting. Also do not miss an opportunity to tell her how sexy she is, and how much you love her. If she is comfortable in her own skin and knows your love is strong and real, you have a far better chance of getting her to turn the corner and take on some of her own fantasies let alone yours. Hopefully you have **Married for love and Companionship and now can enjoy the Cuckold life for pleasure – yours and hers.**

Lightning Source UK Ltd.
Milton Keynes UK
UKHW020702180121
377244UK00012B/1265